ANODIC

KRISTIN TRAVIS

THE ROGUE QUILL

Cover by Kristin Travis and Red Thread Co.

ISBN 979-8-9883211-0-1 (Paperback)

ISBN979-8-9883211-1-8 (Ebook)

Published by The Rogue Quill

To my relentless anxiety,
thank you for pushing me to create a safe
and magical place beyond you

Dear Reader, please be advised this book contains scenes involving: depression, violence, abuse, and sexual situations (both consensual and nonconsensual).

Synodic: relating to or involving the conjunction of stars, planets, or other celestial objects

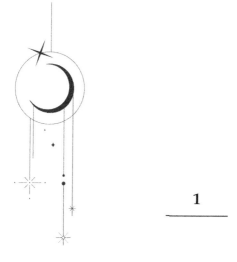

1

"This isn't real," I pleaded, even as the gripping hand of darkness tightened around my throat. Shadowed limbs robbed me of my senses and clutched at my mind, leaving me in a pitch-black cloud that swarmed my every step.

The dense mist clung to me with the dragging weight of shackles around my wrists and ankles. Some small part of me knew I needed to keep walking, keep resisting, for fear that if I stopped, even for a moment, I might never move again.

I pressed on blindly, my fingers sliding through the fog like the bow of a ship through inky waters, but with no sense of direction, I was a mariner left without a compass or even the stars to guide me.

The only thing that gave me the slightest bit of comfort was the feeling that somewhere just beyond my outstretched hands, someone was reaching back for me.

"Hello," I choked out to that twinging illusion. "Is anyone out there?"

No one ever responded, not even a whisper.

Aside from my desperate pleas, all was static silence—that is until faceless growls and vicious hissing began stalking the ripple of my wake. I couldn't see a thing, but I knew my presence in these opaque shadows had garnered the attention of the monsters that lived here. Whatever they were, they remained at a distance, as if waiting for the spring of a hatch to release me into their eager clutches. But something was venturing close. Too close.

Undecipherable noises whirred and clicked around me as a creature slithered inside my cage of darkness. A pungent, sticky-sweet breath panted at my neck, and invisible tentacle-like limbs crept along my arms and chest. I was entirely locked in place by the beast who poked and prodded at me like a giant insect.

A cold terror attacked my body, and I couldn't help thinking how horrible it would be to die in this hostile wasteland where no one would ever find me. A thousand wiggling legs skirted my hair off my shoulder, revealing the thudding pulse at my neck. The creature breathed in my scent and thrummed in excitement as it coiled back to strike me.

I braced myself for what I hoped would be a swift ending when a revolting screech erupted in my ear and nearly split my head in two. The spindly beast instantly released its hold on me, but didn't go far.

Too dark to make out more than fighting shadows, I knew a vicious battle was unfolding just beyond my line of sight. It appeared my hunter had become the hunted.

Grateful for the arrival of the second predator, and that it had no desire or interest in me whatsoever, I sprinted with a determination I reserved for the lanes of a track field.

"This isn't real," I repeated over and over though it was hardly enough to drown out the deadly duel raging behind my back. I ran as if my life depended on it—or at least I tried to—my feet refused to move as fast as I willed them as if I were knee-deep in mud.

Eventually, the horrific noises faded, and my senses wavered as I barreled through a small copse of trees. I stumbled to a stop, blinking away one darkness only to be greeted by another. Terror stuck to the base of my spine as I realized I was sleep-walking—or more like sleep running. I braced my hands on my knees, out of breath and sore, standing in the road in the dead of night barefoot, cut up and bruised.

I let out a sob of relief. My near-death experience had only been a dream, yet my body still shook uncontrollably. The icy echoes that followed me from my nightmare chilled me so deeply, they may as well have traveled across the frigid expanse of space before settling into my bones.

I couldn't remember the last time I dreamt or slept anything less than perfectly sound. Though recently, my nights were fitful and endless, devoid of any light, heat, or sanctuary, and now here I stood, stranded in the middle of nowhere.

Gathering my bearings, I picked up a slow jog home, hoping to warm my body from its violent trembling, though I doubted it would help. This cold ache from a dissipating presence was more than skin deep, and it was, unfortunately, becoming my new normal.

Over the past few weeks, I'd wake from the same nightmare that left me grasping at what was real and what wasn't. Each night grew subsequently worse as the darkness bore heavier, and something got...closer.

Though I knew running in the street at night wasn't safe, the impression I'd escaped the greater threat lingered with me like a trailing phantom.

Beyond exhausted and wearing next to nothing, I ran home, intending to take this secret to my grave.

⸺ ·⟨ ☾ ● ☽ ⟩· ⸺

I quietly entered the historic row house I rented with my roommate, Natalie. I gently tiptoed up the stairs, trying my best not to alert her that I was just getting in from a late-night run.

I'd wandered farther than I thought; it had taken me over an hour to get home. And as I padded through the low-lit halls, I knew Natalie was already up and ready to start the day, most likely taking tiny sips from her blended smoothie. I never understood how she could be so routined and disciplined all the time; it was maddening and, quite frankly, too early to deal with right now.

"Keira?" Natalie yelled up to me from the downstairs kitchen. The home may be restored, but the old planks still creaked beneath my weight, and I cursed the traitorous floorboards that gave me away. "You're up early."

I was not a morning person by the farthest stretches of the imagination, and it was a near-impossible fact for me to hide. "Must be a chilly day in Hell," I called back to her before slipping into the bathroom, relieved she hadn't heard me sneak in through the front door.

I made a point not to look in the vanity mirror. I didn't need to see my tired features and tangled hair to know that I looked like someone who'd just run miles in their t-shirt and underwear. Getting a decent night's rest was becoming harder and harder to achieve; I just hoped no one noticed.

Suddenly, a horrified gasp over my shoulder startled me— Natalie had crept up on me out of nowhere. "What?" I screeched, searching for the bug that was most assuredly crawling all over me.

"Don't take this the wrong way, but you look like shit," she stated with a matter-of-fact air that people either loved or hated about her. I usually appreciated it, but not today. It all but confirmed my restless nights were bubbling to the surface, plain for all to see, and I wilted at her observation.

She glistened in the hallway like a polished ivory stone while I stood an exhausted, cut-up mess. Maybe I could convince her I was coming down with something or that I'd been overwhelmed with work, but she beat me to the punch. "I suppose you can't help that you don't get much sleep with all your tossing and turning and mumbling incoherently. It's amazing how anyone around here gets any sleep, especially when I hear you pacing the halls. Sometimes you scream, Keira. It's actually kind of scary."

I jolted in shock, nearly knocking an assortment of beauty products off the counter. *No. Not again.*

Natalie's candid statement completely caught me off guard. I had no idea she could hear me through the walls of our home or that I'd fallen back into the old habit of screaming in my sleep.

I shivered as I recalled the hidden creatures that lurked, hunted, and warred in my dreams. It was very possible I had screamed.

A lot.

I involuntarily wrapped my arms around myself, warding off the cold coursing through my veins when I realized Natalie was waiting for my reply. "Sorry," I muttered, shame and embarrassment flushing my cheeks. "I...didn't realize."

She'd touched a sore spot. My parents used to say the same thing to me when I was younger; that my cries kept them up at night.

"You worry me sometimes, you know," Natalie said, a perfectly manicured hand sweeping her blonde bangs back into place.

I cringed. I couldn't stand people worrying over me, it brought up memories I'd rather avoid, but I faked a smile anyway. "It's just a few bad dreams, nothing to worry about."

My excuse seemed to appease her, and she shrugged. "Anyway, I came in here to tell you I have meetings all day, so I won't be back until late."

"I'm starting to think this new job is stealing you from me."

"Trust me, I would much rather spend time with you than work as an unpaid intern at a stuffy mid-size law firm, but this place will look great on my resume."

"I know, now go be amazing," I said, proud of how hard she'd worked for this opportunity.

We'd both graduated almost a year ago, and Natalie beamed with pride while collecting her hard-earned undergrad in preparation for law school, whereas my degree had just been a formality. I couldn't think of a single thing I wanted to do, much less do it for the rest of my life, and I almost didn't attend college, but when I received a full-ride track scholarship, I couldn't refuse. Running was my only escape.

I wasn't sure if I truly loved the sport or if the quicker I moved, the better I felt—the more I knew I wasn't slowly crystallizing like a dragonfly in amber.

I know it's said you can't run from your problems, but for the whole twelve-plus seconds of a race, I felt like I could.

My parents always said I enjoyed running because of the link between aerobic exercise and cognitive clarity—they are both psychopharmacologists who manage their own practice, and between the two of them, there was never a moment I wasn't being analyzed. But whatever the reason I ran, it had me skewing just on the right side of sanity and kept my body lean. Healthy.

However, it soon became habitual, in more ways than one. I was so terrified of waking up stuck in a life I couldn't escape that not only did I run for sport, I ran from everything else as well: jobs, boyfriends, relationships, and now my bed.

Natalie was my only constant.

"And try some concealer for those under eyes; they're pretty bad. Oh, and don't forget I made you some breakfast. It's sitting on the counter. I'll see you tomorrow, okay? Don't wait up." She flashed me a quick reassuring smile before pivoting on her heel and disappearing around the corner.

I was alone, alone with my thoughts, which at times was very dangerous because I could think my way straight to the bottom of a deep, dark oubliette. Plus, this was all starting to feel vaguely familiar: dreams that felt too real, restless nights, concerned roommates or parents kept awake by my screams. I'd been able to manage the night terrors for years, but I was slipping again, and I needed to regain control before I lost my footing completely.

I finally decided to brave my reflection in the mirror, hoping to find answers locked somewhere within my pewter irises. My mother once told me my grey eyes looked like twin moons caught in a lunar storm. With their faded glow and dark, scattered shadows, they mimicked the mountainous peaks and imprinted craters of the moon. But just like the orb in the sky, my eyes appeared as smooth and round as glass marbles.

Usually muted and dull, I noticed they were a bit more alert, and it gave me hope that my appearance could be salvaged today.

Twenty minutes later, I managed to mask my restlessness with dabs of makeup, highlighting my high cheekbones, slender lips, and winged lashes. Knowing my brown hair would be an ordeal to brush through, I left it down in long, unruly waves; but still, I looked infinitely better than I did this morning.

Natalie would be proud.

Feeling somewhat accomplished, I walked into the kitchen, and sure enough, the lumpy beige concoction Natalie called breakfast was waiting for me on the counter.

Over the years, preparing healthy breakfasts had become Natalie's *thing*. She took an interest shortly after we moved in together, and kept the tradition alive ever since. I told her count-less times she didn't have to cook for me, but Natalie always emphatically insisted, going on and on about the importance of breakfast, or something like that.

It did seem to make her happy, plus I got sustaining meals out of it, so I'd stopped objecting. And while we used to eat breakfast together every morning, her busy schedule of late prevented it.

Recently she'd been on a chunky smoothie kick, and I had to admit, I was not a fan. But because breakfast was so oddly important to her, I couldn't bear telling her they were inedible. So instead of facing her and admitting the truth, I would quickly throw it down the sink without her noticing.

And today would be no different.

I picked up the unappetizing brew, shaken by how quickly I was losing control. Not only was I sneaking around my own home, unable to get a good night's rest, but now my nightmares were creeping up and bleeding into my waking life.

Somehow I had broken through the thin firmament that separated consciousness from unconsciousness, and it was beginning to distort my perception of reality, trapping me in a perpetual dream.

Tired, hungry, and on edge, I didn't even give the murky goo a second glance before I dumped it down the drain, wishing my qualms were as easily disposable.

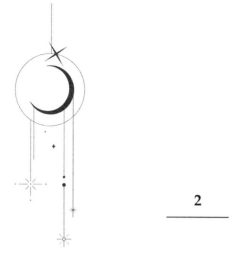

2

I walked to a nearby coffee shop in hopes of clearing my head, to make sense of where I had derailed and how I could get back on track as soon as possible. Maybe I'd even get some work done.

For the time being, I kept busy with freelance data entry. It was far from glamorous, but the positions were short-term and ever-changing, and for someone terrified of solidifying in place, the constant variation was definitely a plus.

I preferred to remain self-employed, working from the convenience of my own home or varying cafés with decent wifi. I set my schedule and hours, which was proving useful at the moment, especially considering my new sporadic sleep schedule.

Being my own boss had its perks as well. After being constantly interrogated my entire childhood, I had grown an aversion to answering to anyone. I would rather maintain my distance, turn in my work, and keep to myself; it prevented people from asking too many questions, questions that invariably led me to empty answers.

Closing the gate of my row house, I went to take in a deep breath of February air. I could almost taste the silver winter thawing into a watercolor spring, but something stopped me short, leaving me craving a sensation I swore was just on the tip of my tongue.

I let the lacking breeze fill my lungs anyway, holding it for a few beats before slowly letting it trickle out my nose. It was a trick I'd taught myself to keep my parents from shoving pills down my throat to curb my "overactive imagination," as they so delicately liked to phrase it. Growing up, I would tell them stories about my day or the dreams I had, only to find them exchanging worried glances.

Concerned teachers and alarmed parents approached my mother and father, reciting to them what I said or did in school. I believed my experiences to be common, and that everyone lived life the way I did, but it didn't take long to realize how wrong I was. I began to tell people less and less for fear of what they would say...or do. I was punished for being myself, accused of lying and fabricating disturbing stories.

Afraid of backlash or ridicule, my parents began diagnosing my symptoms, trying various medications and therapies to help with my night terrors, maladaptive daydreaming, and misbehaving. My parents were determined and relentless in their plight to "fix me." Word couldn't get out that the renowned couple of Copeland Psychiatry had a daughter with unmanageable behavioral issues.

Nothing ever worked—until one day, it did.

The newest little pill my mother brought home helped with the vivid dreams almost instantly, but it did something the others hadn't: it made me so lethargic I could barely see straight. Even from a young age, I'd loved to run, but it became impossible with the way my limbs lagged.

At first, I was relieved the dreams were gone, that I was rid of the thing that made me so different, but then I began to miss them. Though some were so frightening they made adults quiver, I knew some were beautiful too. But no one ever seemed to remember that part, and eventually, I grew to forget my dreams altogether.

Before high school, I told my parents I would like to try life again without the powder-packed capsules. Promising and swearing left and right I would never act out again, that I would stay in line.

It took weeks of begging and bargaining for them to tentatively agree on a trial basis. I honestly thought they would put up more of a fight, but I wasn't going to argue a case I'd already won.

Having stopped taking the pills, I began to manage my condition on my own. The dreams never returned, so I was quick to think I'd outgrown my childhood ailments, and I prided myself on my mental capabilities.

I also discovered that when I ran, I was fast, and was quickly recruited to the varsity track team as a sprinter.

Flying down the straightaway of the track was the only time I didn't feel I was a puddle of water slowly hardening into sludge. Some part of me always felt stifled, suppressed, and running was the only device that gave me some semblance of control.

After all these years, I managed to block out most of what happened to me, the things I saw, or the stories I told. And while I wished I could recall what I had said to shake everyone so entirely, I never mentioned it, and neither did my parents.

But now, after years of silence, the dreams had returned.

I tried to keep the building panic at bay, but it did little to stop my stomach from twisting into heavy knots.

Grounding myself, I clung to the strap of my bag, focusing on something tangible and within my grasp. The satchel was draped comfortably over my shoulder, carrying my laptop, wallet, phone, and the new book I happened to be reading, though it was hardly holding my interest.

Bells tinkled as I entered the cozy local café, and once I settled into an open seat, I dove into work.

The day passed in a quick blur of lined computer documents and caffeine. The coffee lost all flavor within the first few hours, which was just as well; I wasn't drinking it for the taste. Drowning myself in work and caffeinated drinks was a paltry method for delaying the inevitable; my dreams would find me sooner or later.

I dreaded sleep, fought it as much as I could, but being awake came with its own set of difficulties as well. Figuring myself out lately had been like trying to tell time on a clock with rapidly spinning hands. I could feel shifting currents of space moving and stirring within me, wanting more, needing more, demanding more. The newfound sensation had me realizing I was a glass half full, a cup wanting to brim and spill over like the waters of an infinity pool.

I'd always been content living life and going through the motions, but suddenly, for the first time, it didn't feel like enough.

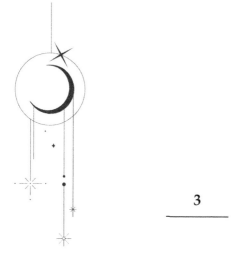

3

If darkness were a thief, it was stripping me for all I was worth, creeping in and stealing whatever precious fibers held my sanity intact.

I wished I could remember how I'd gotten here, then maybe I could get the hell out. The last thing I remembered was working at the coffee shop, but now I was encased in shadows, my vision going black and my body wracking with tremors.

The darkness I'd not-so-silently been living with was compounding on me by the second. Normally, I could still walk, move, and cry out into the night. Not this time. The impossible weight pressed down on me with the force of a pitch-black centrifuge, causing my body to fight in on itself.

Every second was an agonizing eternity.

Night after night I endured this hell, but it had never been this bad. I knew something was bound to break, I just couldn't let it be me.

I pushed back on the nameless and faceless enemy that threatened to destroy me, fighting back with the faintest embers that existed in the small in-between spaces of myself. I was battling with everything I had, however meager, and it wasn't going to be enough. I was about to shatter all over the floor of my mind.

Resisting to the bitter end, I gave one last pathetic yet defiant push with my whole body and soul.

The compressed atmosphere popped with a releasing hiss, and I gasped in a breath that pierced my lungs. My whole body arched skyward as if I were coming up for air, as if I had been submerged my entire life and this was the first true breath I'd ever fully taken.

The inhale was full and unstinting, and it immediately welcomed in the spiraling scents of wild evergreens, rain-soaked earth, burly wooded bark...and something else, something *more*.

The breath rocked me so thoroughly that I collapsed to my hands and knees, panting as inky whorls dispersed around me.

The fissure of relief was just enough that I was able to lift my gaze to a lush forest teeming with emerald life. But what should have been a resplendent view was distorted and warped by the fumes of my broken darkness. Strands of midnight billowed unnaturally between the towering trees and lofty canopies while shadows twisted at the splayed ferns, gnarled roots, and large, mossy stones. Even the ground shifted with a lazy fog.

My skin prickled under the weight of a commanding gaze, and my eyes snapped to the tall, unmoving shadow in the distance. Fear spasmed up my spine as the faint silhouette of a man appeared through the sweeping coils of mist.

Petrified to move from my plush nest of greenery, it was all I could do to squint to see him more clearly. Despite the murky brume, and the shadows that pooled in the hollows of his face, I could still tell, or more accurately *feel* when our gazes locked. He seemed to peer closer, as if shocked to discover my own stare intently fastened upon him. I thought I detected the slightest twitch in his expression, but it may have been a trick of the fog.

I let my sights wander to the rest of him, only able to make out prominent attributes like the tanned hue of his skin and the loose waves of dark hair tousled around the nape of his neck. Rugged stubble shaded the lower half of his face and outlined the hard, unflinching line of his mouth. His powerful frame implied a raw strength of body and movement, and his stature belied a height sure to tower over my own five-foot-seven.

He could easily overpower me, if it came to that. But he came no closer than the tree line; only the smoke daring to move between us.

His rigid body suggested he was waiting for me to make the first move. But why? Who was he?

Unsure if he would let me by unscathed or if he only enjoyed pursuing what ran, I rose to my feet, not a thought beyond what I would do after that.

Standing before the mysterious figure in the trees, I was suddenly very aware of my vulnerability. I wore nothing but a thin shirt that barely covered me and a pair of panties that left my legs visible like two slips of moonlight. I was nowhere near adequately dressed for a midnight hunt through the woods.

I shivered uncontrollably from the dark wind drifting through the leaves, but it was the hidden gaze I sensed trailing all over my body that had my skin erupting into goosebumps. Every instinct blared within me that this was still a nightmare and he was just as dangerous as he looked.

"Keira." I heard someone yell my name from behind me in warning, and the stranger seemed to glance over my shoulder in irritation.

I knew the voice from somewhere...it was close and pulled at me to turn around, but I hesitated, caught between the familiar and the unknown.

"Copeland," they said more firmly, a demand to take a step back when my foot itched to move forward. I scrunched my nose at the use of my surname and ignored their call.

The last thing I should want to do is investigate this shadowed man and forest any further, but my mind desperately wanted to fill in the details still hidden by the eclipsing fog.

"Keira!" the voice shouted in my ear as a firm hand grabbed me by the shoulder and yanked me around. My vision fluttered as I spun, and with each blink of my eyes, the forest faded from view, and a man's face slowly shifted into focus: light, smooth, and blonde.

"Harlan," I said, waking up in a grog, remembering now that I had invited him over last night in hopes he would keep my mind from the haunted illusions of sleep. A decision I firmly regretted now that I was waking up next to him in my bed.

"You okay?" Harlan's brown gaze skirted over me standing at the side of the bed. He pulled me back into his embrace, clutching me as if to secure me by his side. "What were you dreaming about? I wasn't sure if I should wake you, but you were shaking pretty hard."

Harlan was someone I was occasionally intimate with, but recently I'd been trying to distance myself from him. Despite my wanting to keep things strictly physical and casual, he'd been pressuring me to take our relationship to the next level. I knew he desperately wanted more from me, but it was something I just couldn't give. Not to him, or anyone else for that matter. That part of me seemed to be broken.

There were a few others before Harlan. I had enjoyed them and our carefree time together, but no matter how clear I was with my intentions, they inevitably wanted more; they always did, so I would have to let them go.

"I'm fine," I said, still shivering from the effects of the chilling dream. "It was probably from all the coffee I drank yesterday."

"Or from all the fun we had last night," he said, flashing me his flawless smile. His hand on my shoulder loosened only to run along the indented curve of my side. "You've never invited me to stay over. You always kick me out before the sun rises, but this is nice. I could get used to it."

Oh shit.

I realized too late the repercussions of my decision to let him stay the night. I'd given him hope; I'd further opened a door to his emotions that was firmly closed for me. It was a bad call, but I was a woman, not a saint.

I wouldn't have even called last night fun. It was more of a distraction, not just from nightmares but from waking life as well, from the hole the size of another life sitting inside me.

"Harlan, nothing's changed. I meant it when I said I didn't—"

"Let me ask you a question," he said, cutting me off. "Is there someone else?"

"No, but—"

"Then that's good enough for me. I'll make you mine eventually," he said before kissing me on the lips. "Which reminds me," he added, stretching a long, shirtless torso over me to reach for his satchel by the bedside. The accentuated indents of his ribs and lateral muscles rippled as he rummaged through his bag one-handed. "I meant to give it to you last night, but you didn't seem to be in the mood for talking."

He hovered above me on one elbow and passed me a sturdy white box about the size of my hand. I reached for it tentatively, knowing his gifts were barbed tokens that pricked with insult no matter how well-intentioned. They were usually things he wanted for me and not things I actually wanted for myself.

I drew back, realizing it was the newest, most expensive phone in production; and it wasn't even supposed to be released until next month.

I didn't need to ask how he got it. He was one of those Silicon Valley types, highly invested in major software, internet, and technology companies. There must be tons of these just lying around his office.

"You know I can't accept this."

"Why not?"

"Because I don't want it."

"You need to replace that old phone, Copeland. It's practically a relic. It still has buttons on it for Christ's sake. I've got this one all set up, even downloaded a few apps for you. It's weird that you have zero social presence, plus I'd like to see what you do when I'm not around."

Harlan had been harping on me to update this or trade-in that, always accompanying his remarks with offhanded jabs. Each time I politely declined, but now he was practically shoving pre-programmed devices in my hand, and I didn't appreciate it.

"I happen to like the buttons on my app-less phone, thank you very much," I said, crawling out from under him.

It wasn't that I hated technology, it was that technology hated me. The newer the device, the more likely it would crash and glitch in my very hands. Screens would freeze, and batteries would drain in an instant.

Either I had the worst luck in the world, or I was technologically inept. Only the most basic phones and computers lasted; they seemed to be made of stronger stuff. And I honestly didn't mind. I found the more that became available at my fingertips, the more my apathy grew.

I scrambled to put on the nearest clothes, sparing a glance at Harlan's tall, lean body ornately wrapped in my white sheets. I briefly wondered how his hair was still so perfectly coiffed three inches above his head, but I shook off the distraction. I needed to get out of here. "I have work to do. You can let yourself out."

"I'll get you to change your mind," he said with all the confidence in the world, leaning back on my headboard.

"With the phone?"

"With us."

"I have to go. I'll see you later," I said, not shutting the door fast enough.

I fled down the stairs, my pulse thudding and my breath quickening at the nerve of Harlan's brazen attitude. Although, as I rifled through my heightened emotions, I realized they weren't because of the blonde Adonis in my bed but because of the dark figure in my dream. His presence knocked me off my center and slammed me against cold iron bars. I'd learned to live in the cage that surrounded me, could almost convince myself it wasn't there if I didn't fight it too much, but moments like these were a frigid reminder of my prison, and the broken illusion of freedom hurt more than anything else.

I knew it was impractical to blame the misted man for the gaping wound of my half-life, but I held him personally responsible all the same.

Thankfully he wasn't real, none of it was, and I would never see him again.

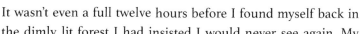

It wasn't even a full twelve hours before I found myself back in the dimly lit forest I had insisted I would never see again. My dark cloud still oscillated thick in the air, and I shivered as I remembered how it once ensnared me.

Knowing what might find me if I stayed in one place for too long, I took my first unencumbered step through the cascading foliage and fog.

As I wandered, a wild canniness prickled along my senses in tiny bursts of cooling mint, and the branches seemed to brush by me with welcoming arms. Even the breeze sang to me in a vaguely familiar melody that eased the flow of my breathing.

I had no idea where I was, where I was headed, or what I was hoping to find when a shadow flashed in my periphery, stealing a breath from my lungs.

It was *him,* wavering in the distance like a cloak of shadows.

His dark presence in these familiar woods sent a jolt against my ribcage—a painful reminder that my constant state of numbness had parameters.

I knew I should run far from these delusions that were sure only to bruise and scar me later, but I ignored my own advice and moved towards him. I had no thought beyond one foot in front of the other, no plan of discerning who he was or why he was here. Just pure unbridled curiosity driving me forward—but after a few determined strides, it became apparent I couldn't get closer to him no matter how hard I tried. He may have been moving towards me too, but the mist was too thick and cunning and kept us apart until my alarm went off, jarring me with a gasp back to reality.

I frantically searched for my phone, lost within the sea of sheets, scrambling to shut off the incessant alarm that grated on my frayed nerves. Lately, I'd been setting my clock earlier and earlier as a failsafe to escape my never-ending nightmares, but now I was practically waking before dawn.

Beyond exhausted, I kicked my way out of the sheets. I was never one to eagerly jump out of bed, but after another long and fretful night, I needed to keep busy, stay distracted—anything to keep my mind grounded in reality.

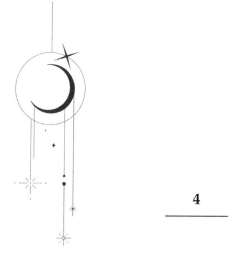

4

Night after night, I dreamt of the mysterious stranger, and as my darkness retreated in trailing ribbons, his blurry image sharpened into hard lines, rugged edges, and cut muscle. I hated that he was turning out to be beautiful. It only made him more dangerous.

His shadowed eyes were watchful and attentive, always warily taking in our surroundings, as if at any moment something would emerge from the black recesses of the forest. However, if he was overly concerned, he didn't show it. In fact, his veneer of calm assurance never broke, and I guessed not much went undetected past his steely gaze.

Occasionally he would try to talk, call out to me from the distance that stretched between us. His lips moved with an undaunted grace, but the sounds were swallowed and swept away on the warped drafts of the night. Nothing could be heard but a warbled echo.

Even when I tried to respond, words that held no meaning fell from my lips like ancient coins drifting lost at sea.

After a while, we realized the futility of communicating in any way and relegated ourselves to slowly circling one another.

Our movements, however guarded and apprehensive, were smooth and measured like an old-English Regency dance that swept up the fog around us.

A part of me was grateful he couldn't get to me, I still had no idea what his intentions were, but I had to admit the curiosity about what he was trying to tell me drove me insane. So much so that throughout the day, I would bite my nails down to the quick, wondering, worrying, speculating as to why he visited me. Was he the catalyst for my dreams returning? The one who summoned the darkness upon me, or the one who released it and left it lingering like the smoke from a candle?

Thankfully the darkness cleared, and as the terrain slowly awakened into a pale-glowing phosphorescent wilderness, I knew I was nowhere within the observable universe. The vegetation peaked and stretched as buds opened into glowing blossoms and vines unfurled into shimmering cords. Silver-white veins ignited inside paper-thin leaves, and currents of light traveled up the trees like synapses firing in the brain.

The myrtle forest became alight, creating and reflecting pools of petaled moonlight. And even through the lingering film, it was the most beautiful place I'd ever seen.

Seeds of dusted light swirled around me in a twisting helix, blowing the strands of my wayward hair about my face and the light hem of my camisole across my abdomen. My skin pebbled under the weight of a familiar gaze, and I twisted around to see the man of the woods nearby. He watched with questioning interest as if I were the mysterious puzzle to be solved.

His audience roused my lethargic blood in ways I wanted to revolt, and I wished he'd leave me in peace. I wanted solitude in the luminescent forest that sparked my own tired tendrils.

Two weeks passed this way, with the same disorienting dream that consumed me while I slept and preoccupied my every waking thought—each moment the taste of another life teasing at my tongue.

Though I knew these blurry interactions were just deceptively real dreams, I woke feeling warm, flushed, and heavy. The line between reality and reverie was blurring, dangerously so. To the point where when I opened my eyes, it was my own room and the life beyond its four walls that felt like the dream. Not the other way around.

Lying in my bed, I tried to rationalize my feelings, put my thoughts into neat, organized piles that made them easier to comprehend, but I found myself buried in more questions than answers.

My fixation over this handsome hallucination, and the glowing forest that encompassed him, was absolutely absurd. I was a fool for letting it hold any power over me whatsoever.

Feeling too big and too small for my body all at once, I decided I was well overdue for a proper run. I quickly dressed in my black practice gear, grabbed my drawstring bag, and did a slow mile warmup to my old track field. The sun had yet to rise, and the gates were locked, but I jumped the fence anyway. If I were caught, I would be arrested for trespassing, but seeing the red rubber laneways, I knew how badly I needed this.

I only meant to do a few light practice drills, but stumbling upon a stray starting block, I opted for a different approach. I changed into my spikes, adjusted the block, set myself up at the hundred-meter line, and ran myself ragged.

Race after race, I timed my sprints. I even beat my personal best, but there was no victory, no celebratory dance, just another race to follow it, and another, and another. I ignored the sweat dripping from my body and the painful stitch in my side and ran until the sun rose over the cement horizon.

All this brutal labor was in hopes I would finally get a good night's rest, a full eight hours of uninterrupted sleep. A part of me desperately wanted that, but a louder, more prominent desire whispered through me. Perhaps tonight would be the night my strange visitor explained his presence and released me from this spell.

But an unnerving question shot through my mind like a reverberating shockwave—would his words be a good omen or a dark prophecy?

———— ·((●) ·) ————

During my cool down, I completely bypassed my house. I wasn't ready to go back there. Not yet. I still hadn't told anyone about my recurring dreams—would barely even admit them to myself. I couldn't go home, not until I dealt with this. Who knew what kind of an irreparable psychotic break I was having, and there was only one place I knew I could go to make it all stop.

"Darling? What's wrong? You look like you've been running from a ghost," my mother said, opening the wood and wrought iron door of the Tuscan-style villa she and my father had built several years ago.

"Well, I did run here, and..." I trailed off, unsure how to continue.

"You ran here? That's miles, and you don't have water on you. You engaging in these acts of self-neglect is troubling," she said in her even alto, already seeking to apply psychological theories onto me before I stepped through the front door.

She ushered me inside and offered me ice-cold water, pouring herself a glass of her favorite red wine. It was a little early, but I bit my tongue as we sat at the high-top kitchen counter

"How's work going?" my mother asked, taking a sip of Cabernet, holding the stem of the glass with an effortless curve of her wrist and fingers. Her strawberry-blonde hair was styled in impeccable finger waves, and her slight features were carefully arranged, as always, so that nobody could see anything other than what she allowed them to. She was absolutely beautiful, dangerously clever, and had achieved great success with my father and their practice.

"Good," I said, nervously thumbing the stacked pages of psychology journals on the marble counter. My parents kept their fingers on the pulse of evolving research and stayed up to date on exciting new developments in their field. They had even been featured in a few issues, but that was years ago, and I knew they were itching for another breakthrough study that would launch their practice back into the limelight.

I'm sure they would have a few questions if I told them about the hazy figure who visited me in my sleep. But I had questions of my own, and since the mist-shrouded man was incapable of providing me any answers, I would have to seek them elsewhere. Maybe these current dreams were somehow connected to my old night terrors. If I could just remember them, I was sure they would help connect a few missing dots.

"Do you remember the dreams I used to have?" I asked, finally spitting it out.

My mother's perfect posture flinched, almost spilling a drop of rare vintage red. Recomposing herself and straightening the journal I had turned askew, she said, "I can't say I recall exactly, but you used to scream and scream, and no amount of shaking would wake you."

"There must be records. Maybe I could look through my old files?" I inquired hopefully. "Do you know where they are?"

"Why are you asking about this, darling?" Her azure eyes regarded me with a panicked interest. "Are they bothering you again?"

Since the dreams returned, I'd seen my parents multiple times and had plenty of opportunities to tell them, but I could never work up the nerve. Although, being asked point-blank was another matter. This was my chance, my opportunity to rid myself of the antagonizing dreams, of *him*.

I knew if I admitted everything to her right now, my parents would waste no time treating me. They would immediately resort to prescription meds, antipsychotics, judgmental looks, the works. It would be embarrassing and painful, but was it finally time to come clean?

"No." It was a bald-faced lie. "I was just curious," I said, attempting to sound as nonchalant as possible. My parents had a knack for unearthing one's secrets; they did it for a living and were paid quite handsomely to do so. But in that moment, I knew I wasn't ready to go back to that life. Not yet.

I remembered when this all started, those horrible pitch-black nights I thought would break my mind, and the unseen creatures I was sure would devour me. All the nights before *he* appeared had been absolutely unbearable. I couldn't deny that.

I needed to see him again.

I tried to convince myself it was strictly to hear what he had to say and nothing more. But the spike in my pulse professed another reason, one I'd never admit to myself.

It seemed my subconscious was trying to tell me something, the least I could do was listen. Whatever the reason for these strange dreams, I was only closer to discovering it in my sleep, and every moment I was awake, the further I drifted from the truth.

I would give myself one more night, and if nothing useful turned up, I would confess everything to my mother.

She set her wine glass down and turned to me, her elfin features scrutinizing. "Keira Copeland, if something is going on, you need to tell me."

"Nothing is going on," I said, cringing at the tone of my full name as if I were a child being scolded all over again. "Everything's fine. In fact, me and Natalie—"

"Natalie?" My mom perked up. She'd developed a fond attachment to my roommate and loved asking after her. "What has she been up to?"

I filled her in on how busy Natalie was with school and her serious but unpaid internship.

Seeming pleased with the update, my mom changed the subject and asked, "How's your boyfriend?"

"His name is Harlan, and he's not my boyfriend."

"That's what you say about all of them, darling," she said, analyzing me again.

I couldn't begin to unpack what my mother was inferring with this new topic of conversation, but I guessed it wasn't good.

I knew she was trying to help me in her own way, offering unsolicited advice about how my lack of commitment towards anything was unsettling. She theorized that I ran away from everything good in my life because I was afraid it would eventually end.

But how was that possible? How could I be afraid of endings when I found myself searching for the rays of a new dawn?

Lost in an endless eclipse, I suffered through another long day of unwanted psychological assessments. Whatever the secrets of my past, it was clear they were so disturbing my mother was protecting me from remembering them.

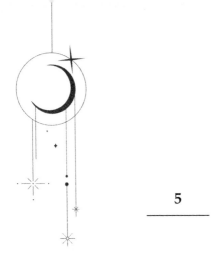

5

I'd made it home safely from my mother's, or at least I thought I had. I now found myself in a forest that felt...*wrong*. Nothing like the glowing woods that reinvigorated the push and pull of my breathing.

How had I gotten here?

The empty air and lack of life whispered grave warnings against my skin. The heavy branches bowed over me like the wings of a fallen angel, hovering and closing in on its innocent victim. What little light leaked through illuminated the small clearing in shades of coal, ash, and iron.

It was as though all life had hardened into a glass-like state, locking the entire glen in a frozen winter. Except it didn't feel like winter at all, there wasn't even the barest hint of a chill in the air. But still, a bitter shiver ran down my spine.

Looking at the barren scenery, I may as well have been staring in a mirror—my dormant existence reflecting the image of a lifeless forest—and a choked sob caught in my throat.

"I've had a hard time reaching you," a voice like black velvet caressed my spine. "Then again, nothing about you seems easy. And now you show up here of all places." His accent was unfamiliar, but the way he spoke raised the hairs on the back of my neck.

"Who are you?" I asked, whipping around so fast that my foot caught, and I tumbled to the ground.

Something firm grabbed my upper arm, just over my sleeve, and kept me from falling forward. I peered up, only to see the face of the man who'd been haunting me for weeks.

But he had never been this close—never touched me.

What little fog remained cleared in trailing wisps, and my mind rushed as I saw him completely unobstructed for the first time. The enigmatic man's face was all pleasing lines and angles that caught the best of both shadow and light. He regarded me keenly, like a falcon mid-flight, with his piercing green eyes, strong brow, and high cheekbones.

Wavy dark brown hair haloed his face and neck in an effortless messy array, his prominent square jaw was covered in a rough stubble that framed his crescent-shaped lips, and his nose sloped down in an impossibly straight line. The hollows at his temples were accentuated by the clenching and unclenching of his jaw as he no doubt fully took me in for the first time as well.

I was suddenly very conscious that I was only wearing an oversized t-shirt and panties, and I made a mental note that what I wore to bed hardly felt like enough around him.

I tore my eyes away from his massive body, searching for what caught my foot. The culprit was a giant tree root twisting out of the ground in an ankle-breaking arch.

How had I not seen that gigantic thing?

I scolded myself for letting this man distract me so fully from my surroundings. Normally I was much more coordinated than this. I jumped hurdles for goodness' sake!

"You're going to need to be more careful if you plan on surviving out here, Copeland," he urged crossly as he pulled me upright, his free hand gesturing to the looming black and grey forest.

I chose not to address his underestimating comment; instead, I looked up his towering figure. His once-obscure face was now so distinct, as if a lens were slightly adjusted, sharpening his features into crisp focus. Even when I had seen him from a blurry distance, I knew he was beautiful, but that was definitely an understatement. "It's Keira, wha—wait. How do you know my name?" I asked warily.

"I make it a point to know the happenings in these woods, and lately, that very much includes you." He practically purred the last word.

"Then I suppose you know what happened here?" I said with a slight tilt of my chin, showing him I wasn't afraid despite the shaking of my knees. It broke my heart to see all the life, greenery, and beauty snuffed out, frozen. Destroyed.

"Its life was stolen," he replied through tight lips.

"Were you the one who stole it?" I asked, fearing he might be the one responsible for all this...death.

His brow darkened and his strong hand squeezed tighter on my arm, doing things to my body that should not feel so real in a dream. "You think I did this?" he growled deep from the back of his throat.

Terrified that I'd provoked him, I shrugged imperceptibly in his grasp. How stupid could I be?

"I may be no stranger to death, but this is not my doing."

To my relief yet disappointment, he let go of my arm, and where I first felt his warm hand through my shirt, I now felt a cool draft prickling along my skin.

It was taking nearly every ounce of my control to keep it together. I refused to make even the slightest noise or gesture that indicated he could faze me, even though his eyes on me shook me to my very core.

His beauty was shadowed and haunted, just like this forest, and I desperately wanted to tilt a light to cast away whatever darkness preyed upon them both.

"You know my name," I said, finally finding my breath. "It's only fair I know yours."

"Such a demanding little thing," he replied, his voice like water to a dry, dehydrated throat, so soothing and needed. "But I suppose you're right. My name is Rowen."

Satisfied, I ripped my gaze from his face to explore the rest of him. He wore a fitted, charcoal-grey shirt; the sleeves rolled to reveal his powerful forearms, and the open neckline was deep enough that I could make out the etched moldings of his chest. His rough-spun but perfectly tailored pants emphasized a tapered waist and muscular thighs that could snap me in half.

Everything he wore appeared earthy, frayed, and purely raw as if carefully woven from natural materials. By his posture, physique, and subtle yet decisive movements, he exuded a strength and assurance that told me he was dangerous. Very dangerous, if he needed to be.

Slung low around his narrow hips was a weathered holster I doubted was just for show. And sure enough, resting against his hip like a trusted companion was a single-handed ax, glinting with a deadly sheen.

My whole body tensed.

I should run, but I couldn't bring myself to move. It was as if the dead roots had gnarled around my feet and anchored me like a tree in soil.

Noticing where my gaze lingered, he looked down at his weapon, then back to me with dark amusement. "You should be afraid. Do you even know the creatures that hunt you in these woods?"

I gave him a good once-over, up and down. "I think I have a pretty good idea."

A wicked grin pulled at his lips, flashing his white teeth. His smile was genuine enough to reveal the sharp peaks of his canines. "Oh no, sweet girl. No, you don't."

He was trying to scare me, and he was most definitely succeeding. But we'd gone weeks without being able to speak to one another, and now that he was here and practically within my grasp, I wanted answers.

"Rowen," I said after a while, trying out his name on my lips. His gaze quickly darted to my mouth, then back to my eyes, as if shocked by my saying it. I met his stare equally and asked, "Why have you been dream-stalking me?"

"As I said, it's more of a hunt." He crossed his arms over his broad chest and ground his teeth. "I would suggest you start running." His eyes slowly raked up my body, tracing over my bare feet and exposed skin like a forbidden whisper. "Though I doubt you'll get far."

Fighting the instinct to take his advice was a physical effort. It seemed he wanted me to flee from him, but I wouldn't give him the satisfaction. I'd stayed this long, and I was determined for more of an explanation from him.

"You have something you've been wanting to tell me. Before I go anywhere, I demand to know what it is," I declared with more bravado than I felt.

He laughed at my pathetic attempt to intimidate him, but the amusement didn't last long. His face grew dark and harsh as if he remembered he wasn't supposed to laugh, not even for a second, and I took a step back, shaken by the abrupt change in his demeanor.

He looked painfully validated as I retreated, almost satisfied that I was smart enough to withdraw from him.

"And what makes you think you are in any position to make demands?"

"I deserve to know why I'm being followed."

His eyes rippled the color of a gold-green forest, not the hue of the wildwood itself but more its reflection upon the water of a loch. Striking in and of themselves with his tan skin and dark hair, but even more so against the colorless grey woods.

His voice lowered to a menacing whisper, "Did you really expect to scream out into the night and not attract the notice of the monsters that live in its darkness?"

The question alone was enough to knock me off balance—it seemed my screams could be heard from all sides of my consciousness. Was nowhere safe?

He darted forward and reached out to steady me, grabbing me lower on my arm just above my elbow. This time, however, there was no fabric between us, just skin on skin.

His touch on my bare flesh shocked me in a brilliant silver-white flash, and I sucked in a sharp breath. Electricity traveled through me, tracing a pattern that branched across my body like the limbs of a tree. The ignited current followed the path of my veins and marked me as if I'd been struck by lightning, creating a fern-like embossment on my body. It seared me like stardust, then absorbed into my skin in a glimmering blaze.

I felt forever marked by that touch, whether for good or evil, I had no way of knowing.

I glanced up to see if he had felt it too, that lightning bolt, that collision of worlds. Surely something that powerful couldn't have only traveled through one body, but his face showed no change whatsoever.

He carefully released me, and I studied his tapered fingers that looked smudged in black graphite as he flexed his hand by his side.

"The truth is, I'd like to help you," he carried on as if nothing happened. "Unless you'd prefer to take your chances with whomever, or whatever, comes along next. And believe me when

I say something will come along. Although I can't promise they will be as charming as me," he said with a positively sinful grin.

I let out a scoff. Did he consider this charming? "I don't need your help."

His cryptic smile widened, mocking me as if I was blissfully unaware of something so obvious. It unnerved me that he could see into my blind spots, and my fists curled in frustration.

"I've been doing just fine on my own," I thought I would add for good measure, trying to regain some semblance of control in this conversation. Even though we both knew I had none, not even a little.

"Is that so, Copeland?" he asked casually, taking a small step towards me.

On reflex, I took a step back, suddenly missing the protection of the fog. "It's Keira, and yes, it is," I said, not all too convincingly, ignoring the trembling in my bones that came from equal parts fear and raw, pulsing energy.

He took another step in my direction, backing me up against a tree before placing his hands on either side of me, caging me in against the trunk. His height surged over me as the bark bit into my back and my blood rushed through my veins. We were almost chest to chest, nearly touching, but not quite.

"If I were to leave you right now, I'd wager you wouldn't make it ten steps before your pretty little mouth started screaming my name."

Half of me wanted to run and never give him a second glance, I'd get farther than he thought, but the other, slightly more prominent half wanted him to put his hands on me. To touch me again and see if that lightning bolt from earlier had been a fluke—a strange, singular moment never to happen again, or if we were two electrical fields charging for another blast.

But it appeared he had no intention of laying another finger on me whatsoever. The small yet infinite distance between us taunted me. He was just close enough that I could feel his breath wash over me like the breeze of the ocean, bombarding me with scents of rosewood, brine, and charcoal.

"Why are you here?" I asked in a desperate whisper, my chest heaving from his all-encompassing proximity.

He paused for the briefest of seconds, his eyes dancing across my face.

This was it, the moment I'd been waiting for. I would finally know why I had been dreaming of this man night after night for weeks. My pulse was erratic, pounding at my throat, wrists, and inner thighs, and I felt I was about to explode.

Rowen's emerald gaze flared with my reflection. "You're asking the wrong questions, Copeland. It's not why I'm here, but why are you?"

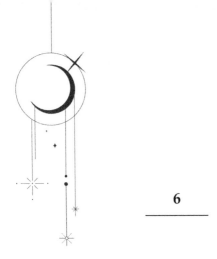

6

Within the blink of an eye, I was lying back in my bed, the white sheets kicked to the floor. My heart battered against my ribcage, and I fought to catch my next breath. I lifted my hand and pressed it to the side of my face. I was flushed and trembling.

I sat up bolt straight in my bed, taking in my surroundings. How was I in my room? How was I within the four walls of this small, insignificant room when I had just been with him? That couldn't have been a dream. It felt so real; *he* felt so real.

It was the first time he had spoken to me, had told me his name.

Rowen.

He said he wanted to help me, but for the life of me, I couldn't imagine with what. If it was for a better night's rest, disappearing altogether would be greatly appreciated.

This mesmerizing being had to be more than just a figment of my imagination. He had a purpose, a reason for appearing to me. Even the memory of the desolate forest pushed against me like a vine growing through concrete.

I'd needed answers, not more questions.

I slammed my body back down onto my bed and squeezed my eyes shut. "Take me back, take me back," I kept repeating to myself, waiting for my body to obey. It either ignored my request or it wasn't listening, because Rowen was nowhere in sight.

Unable to fall back asleep, I swung my legs off the bed and started pacing. My mind was racing; images both remembered and long forgotten flashed before my eyes. Then it hit me like a brick wall. A memory of a dream, or a dream of a memory, I couldn't be sure, but talking with Rowen had unlocked some part of my brain, and I found myself clinging to the awareness.

I didn't want to forget, not again. I sprinted towards Natalie's room, needing to tell someone before the memories slipped back behind the veil, only a thin swathe away but still just as hidden.

Without thinking, I whacked her door open with a loud thud and stood at the entrance of her bedroom. She woke with a jolt and shot up from her pillow.

"Whaa, what's going on?" she screeched.

I felt guilty for waking her, but it was too late to take it back now, so in the most polite voice I could muster, I said, "Oh. I'm sorry, did I wake you?"

"Well yes," she said, heaving in gasps of air, "as well as scare me to death."

"I..." She looked at me expectantly. Why were words failing me now? When I didn't respond, she sighed and patted the edge of her bed. I filled the distance between us and lowered myself onto her coral sheets. "You're going to think I'm crazy."

"Going to?" she questioned jokingly.

I ignored the slight because if I didn't tell her now, I never would. "Well, I had this dream, or more like I've been having this dream, but then again, I wouldn't exactly call it a dream." I was rambling and waving my arms theatrically in front of myself. Where words failed, I hoped hand gestures made up for it.

"Alright, just slow down," she advised. "So what's happening in these dreams?"

Suddenly I very much wanted to get up and leave, but Natalie seemed sincere in her curiosity, and I did just wake her up in the dead of night.

"My dreams have never really felt like dreams. There's always been something more, something real, something I can't explain." The words were now flowing from my mouth with ease. "When I was little, my mom bought me the most beautiful pair of white slippers. I loved them and put them on immediately. When she came to tuck me in, she noticed I was still wearing them and asked if I was going to take them off for bed. I shook my head no, refusing to ever remove them from my feet. Later that night, I found myself walking through a glen filled with silver flowers as far as the eye could see, like a field of stars."

I remembered walking carefully through the glowing night-blossoms, my fingertips gliding over their velvet-soft petals. The sweet scent of dew, florals, and pollen wafted through the air, and I opened my mouth to it, catching the fragrance on my tongue like a delicate snowflake. The wind stirred the leaves in a peaceful melody that composed the notes of my own Moonlight Sonata.

Each one of my senses was so receptive and alert, I knew it couldn't be anything but real.

"After what felt like being in my own personal heaven, I found myself back in my room. I laid there in disappointment before realizing I held a silver petal in the palm of my hand, still wafting an extraordinary scent. I was about to get out of bed when I realized my white slippers were caked in mud."

I had tossed the petal aside in absolute horror, freeing my hands to fuss over my destroyed shoes. I remembered how much trouble I got in for wandering out that night. My parents couldn't figure out how I'd done it, and quite frankly, neither could I. They doubled down on their efforts to subdue me, and I never saw the field again. With that, the petal was out of sight, out of mind, and forgotten...until today.

Natalie looked at me as if I had just grown a third eye. "So what you're saying is you sleepwalk?"

"I was holding a petal that was shining like the moon. How many of those do you see just lying around?"

Her face contorted in disbelief. "Let me get this straight. You think your dreams are actually happening then, like you're transported somewhere?"

I nodded. "I can't come up with any other explanation."

"Have you ever considered that you might be delusional?"

"Actually, yes," I acknowledged miserably as my shoulders slumped and I looked down at my hands folded feebly in my lap. Where was all that strength and determination from minutes ago with Rowen?

"Listen, it's late and you're tired. Why don't you go back to bed? I'm sure once you get some rest, you'll be able to think clearly again."

I didn't want to accept what she was telling me, but I knew she was right. Plus, she was eyeing me with a look reserved for those about to be committed.

I got up off her bed in a trance and began walking away. I'd just confided a secret so deep and tender, and Natalie had dismissed it as mere exhaustion or lunacy.

I desperately needed an ally to keep me tethered to earth, to my sanity, but it felt like a losing battle, one that I was waging all on my own. The implication of what was really going on in my mind was too much to think about. I was scared I was losing myself. That I was going too far down the rabbit hole to ever find my way back.

I barely remembered the walk to my room or putting myself in bed, and as soon as my head hit the pillow, I knew no more.

———— · (C · ● · Ɔ ·) · ————

For a split second, I felt rested and refreshed as my eyelids opened to the harsh light of the afternoon sun. Then, the memories of last night came flooding back: the resurfaced dreams, the sea of silver roses, my confession to Natalie.

All of these things should have sent me into a state of panic, but it was my interaction with *him* that I couldn't shake.

For the first time, he had been close enough to touch me. And he had.

I felt it, could still feel it.

Unease pitted in my stomach as the memory of his touch rippled through me like a stone dropped into a stagnant pond.

After returning to bed, I'd had a dreamless sleep. I was upset I didn't see Rowen again, to ask him more questions, but I was relieved to have finally gotten some rest, though it didn't disguise the fact that my mind was getting out of hand. I needed to drop these dreams and forget about them as easily as I dropped that shining petal years ago. I couldn't explain what happened that night, and I might never be able to.

For my own sanity, I needed to get a grip. Focus on reality. Not some crazy, beautiful, fictitious man spouting tales of me being hunted in a dying forest.

Two swift knocks on my door startled me out of my inner battle. "Come in," I said, calming myself. There was no reason to be jumpy. No one was really after me.

The door slowly opened and Natalie peeked her head through, "Wow, you're finally up! It's past one, you know. You've been sleeping all day." She stepped inside, and opened the curtains. "I wanted to let you know I got you some herbal sleep tea for tonight."

"Thank you," I whispered. It was a thoughtful gesture from a friend, but I knew now that she would never understand. Falling asleep wasn't the problem. It's what happened once I got there.

"I thought it might help with, you know," she said, gesturing to my entire body.

It stung, her implying all of me was tainted with the smudge of madness, but I supposed I was the sum of my parts. The nightmares in my head were affecting my whole body. Nothing felt right.

"Alright," she said awkwardly, "I'm going to make some lunch. Come join me once you're up." She left my room, quietly closing the door behind her.

I let out a loud sigh, relieved she hadn't questioned me further about last night, but before I could fully exhale, Natalie darted her blonde head back inside, and I almost choked. "Oh, and we're going out tonight."

"Wait, what?" How had she thought slipping that in at the last second would keep me from objecting? "I'm not really in the mood to go out."

"If anything, you need to get out and let loose. Especially after last night." She looked uncomfortable as she recalled my midnight bombardment of her room, spouting mad declarations of dreams come to life and mysterious roses. I couldn't blame her. It *was* madness.

"Harlan sent me a text. He got us into the grand opening of Prism!" She nearly screamed the last word in elation. "Said to do whatever it takes to get you to come."

"When did you two start talking?" I asked in surprise, more curious about that than the actual event.

"He got my number somehow." She shrugged her shoulders as if such a thing was a regular occurrence, and with Harlan, it was. He knew how to get what he wanted; the new phone on my nightstand was proof enough. "He gets worried and asks after you. He's got it bad for you, Keira. It's really kind of cute!"

Cute wasn't the first word that came to my mind, it felt more intrusive, and now he was using Natalie to snoop on me.

Suddenly I felt very exposed, stranded on an island without even the barest of palms to shield me from the sun. What else had they talked about? Would she tell him about last night?

"So you two are conspiring with each other now? To get me to go to one of the biggest events of the year? Subtle. Really subtle." The gall of these two had me questioning my alliances.

Natalie spoke her next words like a patron saint committing an act of great service and self-sacrifice. "He said he's been having trouble getting ahold of you lately and asked for my help."

It was true. I had been avoiding him. He didn't move me in the way I expected love would. No one did. No one even came close.

The touch from Rowen immediately jumped to mind. *That* definitely felt like something.

I couldn't believe I was referring to the fictional man within my head. It was horrible and embarrassing, and I would never admit it to anyone. Even though I'm sure my parents would have some uncomfortable diagnosis for why that is.

She could barely contain her excitement. "Keira, please can we go? Please. Please. Please. Do you know how hard it is to get admittance into an event like this, much less be on the VIP list? Harlan has some friends in high places. We have to go! It would be rude not to accept."

I had every intention of saying no, of not giving in to their scheming, but sitting at home fixating on Rowen wouldn't help me get over him. I could use some distance from my thoughts, and what better way to do that than by going out and getting lost in the lights of the night?

"Fine. We'll go," I said as I punted my pillow at her playfully.

She caught it easily and squealed so loud it was enough to wake me as if I'd just shot back a double espresso.

My phone buzzed on my nightstand. "That's probably him now," she said mischievously, smiling as she ducked out of my room for the second and final time.

I looked down at the name on my screen. Wow. Natalie was an evil genius.

I was tempted to ignore Harlan's call, but I'd been dodging him for weeks now. Plus, if I went out with him tonight, I should at least get some more details.

I took the call, already knowing where it was headed. "Hi."

"Did you hear about tonight? Exciting, huh?" His baritone voice was casual. Playing it cool.

"Yeah, Natalie filled me in. I'm still trying to wrap my head around it actually," I said, not even trying to hide the aggravated tone in my voice. I was less than enthused with his round-about methods of seeing me and I wanted him to know it.

"What part of VIP experience do you have to wrap your head around? It's going to be great. Unless there's a reason you've been avoiding me," he said, insinuating his biggest nightmare. "Is there someone else?"

"No. Of course not." No one real, at least.

"Good. If I saw you with someone else it would destroy me. Tell me you'll come and won't leave my side the whole night? I want you to be the beautiful girl on my arm."

I rolled my eyes, he should have majored in theatre with these dramatics. He had the face for it. "I'll be there, but you'll have to share me with Natalie," I said, knowing I was past the point of no return. I wouldn't disappoint Natalie by backing out now, and maybe she was right. Maybe a night out would help get my mind off the things I couldn't control or fully comprehend.

I heard Harlan's smile through the phone. "A beautiful girl on each arm? Even better. I'll pick you up at ten."

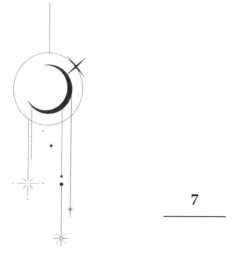

7

It wasn't hard to spot where we were headed. Massive floodlights surrounded a building that glinted obnoxiously like broken shards of manufactured light and crystal. I stared out the car window, more interested in the moon hanging like a sliver of fine bone china in the near starless sky than I was by the thousands of flashing bulbs and hordes of people on their way to Prism.

After an hour, we were still half a block away, stuck in the narrow streets more crowded than usual. This event had garnered quite the attention for its opening night, and I could already tell it was going to be a madhouse.

How Harlan managed to get us all on the guest list was beyond me.

"This is insane! How did you get us in?" Natalie asked, mirroring my thoughts. Her ecstatic voice chimed through the spacious SUV Harlan had picked us up in. Undoubtedly, he ordered the monstrous car through whatever ride-hailing taxi app he deemed best, but he had gone way overboard for just the three of us.

"I know some guys inside," he replied arrogantly as he

squeezed my hand. I had the sudden urge to rip away from his hold and ruffle his hair, just to slightly dishevel his maddeningly flawless veneer. "In fact, I might have to step away for a bit to make a few appearances, nothing I would want to bore you with. It shouldn't be too long."

"Sounds important." Natalie shot me a wicked stare and winked.

So much for staying by each other's sides. This night hadn't even begun and I was already feeling on edge, especially from sitting in this infuriating traffic for so long. We would have been there by now if we had just gotten out and walked, but Harlan insisted on rolling right up to the front doors in style.

Claustrophobia and anxiety crept up on me like an invisible snake, slowly coiling tighter and tighter around my chest, and I tugged at my dress uncomfortably. I'd opted to wear a blush corseted number that draped loosely across my thighs. The thin straps, wired bustier, and sweetheart neckline accentuated my collarbones and décolletage while revealing almost all of my bare back and arms. The near flesh-toned piece clung to me like a second skin and emphasized my wavy brown hair and natural rose-toasted makeup.

It was a far cry from the tangled hair and holey shirts Rowen saw me in every night, and some part of me wished he could see me like this, but I immediately shut down the thought. I refused to let my mind wander any farther down that road.

Rowen's words and touch were already written all over me as though I were made of paper. It was dangerous, and for the sake of my sanity, I had to scorch him from the pages of my mind. From this moment on, I would never think of him again. He was as good as gone, no more than burnt letters by the bedside.

Simple as that. Mind over matter.

"Here you go," our driver spoke for the first time, bringing me back to the congested streets of the entertainment district.

After the agonizingly slow crawl, we had finally arrived at the illuminated entrance of Prism. "Heard it's nearly impossible to get in there tonight."

"That won't be a problem," Harlan answered with a smile, following Natalie out of the car.

"Thank you," I said to the man behind the wheel as I plunged into the smothering atmosphere of the night. The air was thick and smoky and had my lungs straining against my ribcage. It was all too much—the city, the smog, the people. Thankfully Harlan offered me his arm before extending his other to Natalie, linking the three of us together as we walked towards the club.

The long entry line wrapped around the building and disappeared out of sight. I was fully prepared to walk to the end of the queue and wait our turn, but Harlan guided us right past it, bypassing people who looked like they'd been waiting hours. The envying looks and agitated scoffs didn't go unnoticed as we headed to a second entrance surrounded by photographers and flashing bulbs so bright they nearly blinded me.

Harlan gave his name to the burly bouncer who checked his clipboard and waved us through the doors noncommittally.

"That was amazing!" Natalie practically squealed, breaking apart our chain and rushing forward. She looked the definition of elegance in her tight emerald slip dress that cascaded in silky waves over her curves. Her honey-butter hair was parted down the middle and pulled into a tight chignon at the base of her neck, highlighting her creamy-soft features.

"It pays to know people," Harlan said, flashing his ultra-white teeth. He wrapped his thumb and middle finger around my wrist like a leash and pulled me into the misty nightclub that smelled of fog, alcohol, and zested citrus. Saturated beams of pink and purple light strobed across the chic nightclub, piercing the smoke in hazy spheres that hypnotized the senses.

True to its name, it looked as though we had stepped into a black prism. The mercury-mirrored walls infinitely reflected streaks of light within each other's planes, creating the illusion of a never-ending rave trapped within a jewel. Massive wrought-iron chandeliers and gilded birdcages hung from the ceiling like ornate teardrops. Curtains of dark sand crystals hung from the rafters, enclosing off private suites and alcoves on both this floor and the curved balcony above. Squared nicely in the center of it all was a pulsing dance floor that beckoned me to get lost within its carousel of light and limbs.

"I'll get us drinks," Harlan said, leaning in close enough that we could hear him over the ear-splitting music.

"Just a water for me, please," I said out of habit.

He gently released my wrist and headed to the bar, expertly weaving through the crowd in his black slacks, white buttoned shirt, and name-brand everything. He looked so at ease and comfortable within the psychedelic circus that pulsed around us.

Natalie whipped towards me, and shouted in my ear, "Remind me of why you've been avoiding him again? He's gone through a lot of trouble to impress you tonight."

I rolled my eyes. I couldn't think of a single topic I would rather discuss less. "If you're so impressed, you can have him."

"What? Seriously, Keira. He's asking me if you're seeing someone else."

Okay, so there was a topic I would rather talk about less than Harlan, especially since I'd just sworn to never think of said subject ever again.

I was, in fact, seeing someone else, but not in a good way. More of a losing-your-mind type of way, but I couldn't ignore the fact that my heart rate spiked at the mere thought of him.

Forgetting him was going to be easier said than done.

In that moment, I decided I wanted to be anything but sober

tonight. I would make it my sole mission to drown out the dark-haired man from my thoughts, and with the plethora of alcohols and spirits around me, I knew it shouldn't be too hard of a goal to achieve.

I had never really indulged in drinking before, just small sips here and little toasts there, never enough to impair me in any way. Track kept me from liberally imbibing any sort of alcohol; there was always the next big race or meet to train for, and retaining that competitive edge was paramount.

But my stringent track days were over, and for the first time, I had every intention of fully letting loose. I was more than ready to go wherever this night would lead me, as long as it was far away from green eyes, dying forests, and forgotten memories.

Natalie eyed me suspiciously. She knew I was hiding something and had expertly backed me into a corner with her line of questioning. She was going to make a ruthless lawyer someday. There was no question about it. "Well?"

"Everything just feels like a bit of a show with Harlan, don't you think?"

She sighed and brushed a piece of my loosely waved hair behind my shoulder. "You are way too picky. I'll never understand it."

Harlan returned, skillfully carrying three drinks within his grasp. "Did I miss anything interesting?" he asked, handing a glass to Natalie.

"Not unless you find Keira's finicky tastes interesting."

"Oh? Tastes in what exactly?" His brown eyes glinted at me, and a crooked smile lifted his mouth as he handed me my usual water.

"Nothing," I cut in quickly, grabbing Harlan's drink instead and downing it in one long gulp. The deluge of alcohol scorched my throat and warmed my belly, and I slammed the empty glass on a nearby table. "Let's dance."

Both Harlan and Natalie eyed me in shock; they had no idea the mission I was on tonight.

I ignored their stunned faces and headed straight for the mass of dancing bodies. I could feel them follow after me as I led the three of us to the center of the dance floor, directly under the largest of the exquisite chandeliers. I didn't even turn around before I began lightly swaying my hips to the music.

The repetitive beat thrummed in my chest, goading me to move more freely within its resounding wavelengths, and I willingly obliged. I traced my fingertips down my accentuated silhouette, warming to the dance floor in a way that was foreign to my body.

I found I enjoyed embracing the power of my sensuality as I matched my movements to the highs and lows of the song. I whipped my hair all around me, twisting and turning with abandon, determined to give in to this night and let go of everything if it was the last thing I did.

Harlan's hands were suddenly on me, outlining my every curve before latching onto my waist and dragging my backside closer to him. He moved and guided me from behind as Natalie pressed to my front.

Already feeling the effects of the drink coursing through my veins, I saw something willowy and earthy flash in my periphery. When I darted my eyes to see what it was, there was nothing, only the dizzying haze of smoke and light.

I shook it off, trying to bring my focus back to the here and now, to the bodies firmly bracketed around me.

Harlan spun me to face him and pulled me tight to his chest, grinding against me as we tangled in breath and body.

The song ended, segueing into the next, and he leaned into my ear. "I have to go talk business for a minute with the boys. Keep having fun with Natalie until I come find you," he said with a possessive squeeze of my hips and a kiss to my mouth.

Without skipping a beat, I spun to Natalie and we continued dancing, losing ourselves in the sea of music and people.

After a few more songs, our parched throats begged for another drink, and Natalie braved her way to the bar. She returned a few minutes later with two sunset-ombre drinks that tasted of the tropics.

With only a few sips left of our colorful cocktails, Natalie gestured to one of the balconies. "Hey, I know that guy, I think his name is Damon," she said excitedly, and I followed her line of sight up to the second floor.

Observing the crowd from the wrought-iron railings was a handsome Black man with a drink in hand. His textured curls were longer on top and faded down in a tapered style that was as sharp and stylish as his patterned suit. He made eye contact with Natalie, his face brightening in recognition.

"We intern at the same firm. Would you mind if I went and talked to him?" she asked with not-so-subtle yearning.

All night she had been such a trooper as the third wheel. She deserved to have a little fun herself. "Oh my gosh, yes. Go!" I urged in support.

"You can join us if you'd like," she said halfheartedly, extending the offer to be polite, but I could tell she wanted to be alone with her fellow lawyer-to-be.

"No, I'll wait here for Harlan. He should be back soon."

"Are you sure you will be alright?" she asked, seeming to battle her inner conscience for leaving me.

"Go!" I nudged her shoulder playfully. "I'll be fine."

"I won't be long. Promise," she said before whirling around with the grace of a trained ballerina and headed up the winding staircase. Her worry for me was clearly outweighed by the allure of the beautiful like-minded man waiting for her on a balcony. I honestly couldn't blame her.

Once I knew she was safe in the company of her friend, I

glanced around for Harlan, but I didn't see him anywhere. He could be in any one of the several private rooms lining this place. I hadn't even paid attention to which direction he'd gone when he left to meet whomever it was he needed to rub elbows with.

I didn't mind; I was content to be on my own as I slowly finished my second drink, the buzz around me intensifying. The effects of the alcohol were hitting me harder now, but I welcomed the relaxed edges.

Noticing my empty glass, a stunning woman in a black bodycon dress approached me with a silver tray of fluted drinks. I gladly accepted one of the bubbly elixirs and charged it to Harlan's tab.

If he was going to up and leave me, the least he could do was keep a steady supply of tasty beverages coming my way.

I was about to take a sip from my newly replenished drink when my head spun like a top and I thought I was going to be sick all over the club floor. The music began pounding in my skull like a sledgehammer and my legs turned to jelly beneath me.

That was fast. Surely two drinks couldn't have affected me in such a way. Even though I had nothing to compare it to, this felt way too extreme for the amount of alcohol I'd actually consumed. Now was not the time to learn that my body didn't metabolize alcohol very well.

Needing to sit for a moment and get some space, I set my full drink down on the counter and began woozily making my way to one of the lounge areas. The brightly patterned lights burned through my eyelids, and I blinked repeatedly, trying to focus on a clear path out of here.

Abruptly, between one strobe flare and the next, my entire surroundings changed. The massive chandeliers flashed into treetop canopies and the long strands of crystal beads blinked away into lush hanging vines, then it instantly morphed back to the opulent space of the club.

Was Prism experimenting with some new projection mapping technology I'd never heard of? If so, it was extremely disorienting and hauntingly realistic.

I glanced around to see if anyone else noticed the sudden shift in environment, but everyone continued to drink and dance with their half-glazed expressions.

I shook my head, fighting the feeling of passing out right here in front of all the people, press, and cameras, but I was getting worse by the second.

Had the bartenders been heavy-handed with their pours? How was I already feeling this inebriated? I knew I was going to be a lightweight but there was no way only two drinks could have done this to me.

The club closed in around me, and I nearly stumbled with every step as if I were a lush. Walking in heels was hard enough, but with the added layer of distortion, it would be a miracle if I made it to one of the seating areas before collapsing.

My world flashed again, from extravagant nightclub to...to darkly veiled forest.

Oh no. Not here.

This couldn't be happening. I only came here in my sleep, while I was dreaming, not while I was wide awake, albeit considerably impaired.

Fear crept up my throat like a toxin. Had someone drugged me?

It wasn't possible. The only people to get me drinks had been Harlan and Natalie. Where were those two anyway? At least one of them should be back by now.

It took a bit longer for the world to right itself before I was back in Prism, and not having been fully able to see where I was going, I knocked into a group of men, nearly spilling their drinks all over the place.

"Hey, watch it, you idiot!" one of them bellowed angrily before circling to face me, rearing for a fight.

"I...I'm so sorry," I apologized earnestly to the man with too much gel in his hair.

"Oh," he said, changing his tone as he looked me up and down thoroughly. "It's not a problem."

Repulsion swarmed my senses. Everywhere his pitch-black stare roamed left streaks of grease on my skin, and I immediately wanted a shower.

"Looks like you've had one too many, doll," he said, nudging his buddies to take in his find. They didn't even try to hide their greedy gazes as they clearly undressed me with their eyes. It made me want to vomit.

"You're a pretty little thing. Are you here all alone?"

"Yeah, do you need some company?" asked another one of them with yellow teeth. He lassoed his hand around my elbow and pulled on me, attempting to corral me into their company.

I didn't have time for this. Who knew how long I had before I was plunged back into the forest, blind to the world in front of me. And I was certain these were the last men on earth I wanted to be with if that happened again.

"No. I'm heading to my friends now," I said, wrenching my arm from his grasp, nearly falling over in the process.

"You sure?" came the voice of a third man.

I didn't even bother responding as I pushed my way past them. I could hear them laughing and calling after me as I desperately sought a quiet place to sit.

After an unsteady journey, I finally found an unoccupied lounge in the far back corner of the club. I pushed beyond the sheet of crystal drapery and plopped down onto one of the plush rose settees, hoping this dizzying two-world Russian roulette would end. And soon.

I pulled out the phone from my small clutch and fumbled for Harlan's number. It rang and rang until it went to voicemail.

Irritated, I hung up and quickly tried Natalie, but same thing, no answer. It was too damned loud in this place to hear your phone ring or even feel it vibrate against you. I would just have to hunker down here and wait.

Suddenly, I was back in the shrouded forest sitting on a wide, moss-covered tree stump. For a moment, I was worried my dress wouldn't be much protection against the elements, but then I remembered that no matter how real this felt, I was still only sitting in a secluded room of a nightclub.

The deafening din of the bar completely vanished, leaving only the calming sound of the wind whistling through the branches and wooden hollows. Grateful for the relaxing hum of nature, I closed my eyes and focused on my breathing.

Now there was nothing to distract me while I fought for control over my mind and body.

"I wasn't expecting to see you here, Copeland," came the deep lulling voice of the man I had been trying to avoid all night.

My eyes shot open.

Rowen's large, muscular frame peeled from out of the forest shadows. He holstered his drawn blade and moved until he was completely within my view.

"What are you doing here?" I demanded angrily, waving my arm as if I owned this stump and everything around it. Losing my balance, I nearly rolled off the tree in an unbecoming flail of limbs, but miraculously caught myself at the last second.

"Are you drunk?" Rowen asked, almost amused.

My blood seethed. How dare he!

His mere appearance seemed to mock me as if my will to keep him away was only paper-thin and not the stronghold I'd envisioned. Not to mention the added slight of his near spot-on observation. Whether or not getting drunk had been my intention all along was privileged information, he didn't need to know that.

"I don't see how that's any of your business, but no, not entirely," I said indignantly, holding onto the sides of the stump like my life depended on it. There was no way I was letting Rowen see me fall.

Unconvinced by my performance, he stalked towards me with a primal confidence that had my insides twisting. His steely green gaze pinned me in place, and I clutched the edged bark even harder as my breath quickened. I expected him to step right up to me, tilt my chin to his face and inspect me at close range, but he deliberately stopped a few feet away, keeping a calculated distance.

Wearing his usual trousers, dark linen shirt, and holstered weapon, he looked exactly as I remembered him. Beautiful yet dangerous, just like hemlock—the philosopher's bane, and now mine as well.

Rowen was lovely to look at and admire from a distance, but get too close, inhale him once, or stare too deeply into his eyes, and he could be deadly. How fitting that he and his eyes should match such a plant both in color and character.

"That's where you're wrong. As I've told you before, I make it a point to know the happenings in these woods. So? What. Happened?" he pressed with the annunciation of every word.

"I'm not sure..." I said, wishing I knew the answer myself. My mind and body felt out of control like a Tilt-A-Whirl, and my feet were killing me.

Determined to fix at least one thing about my horrible situation, I attempted to break open the clasps at my ankles. Rowen made no move to assist me as I struggled and cursed the tiny buckles that ensnared my feet. I wouldn't have accepted his help even if he offered, but still!

Sensing my frustration, the slightest smirk lifted his lips. He was enjoying watching me flounder spectacularly. "You don't know?" he asked, folding his arms across his chest in a languid movement that suggested he had all night.

I finally managed to release my feet from their stilettoed hells with a relieved groan. The victory, however, was short-lived. "That's right. I don't know!" I said, exasperated. He was angering me with how calm and collected he was, whereas my whole world was slipping from my grasp, and it felt like I was losing my mind. "Any other helpful questions?"

"Do you intentionally wander about clueless and half-naked with such little regard for your safety, or does it just come naturally?" he asked pointedly.

Not appreciating his tone in the slightest, I did the only thing within my control. I chucked my high heel right at his arrogant head. It landed somewhere with a thud, about three trees away from where he stood.

His green eyes widened in surprise and a full smile broke out across his face. "Were you aiming for me? I should hope you are drunk with how off your aim is. Really, Copeland, it didn't even come close."

How infuriating! I knew my shot was better than that, but right now I had about as much aim as someone who'd downed an entire bottle of scotch.

"I only had a couple of drinks," I confessed crossly. "But it seems that I'm having some sort of negative reaction." I couldn't think of any other reason why my body would react this way.

"So it would seem," Rowen said, pulling his dark eyebrows together, forming a crease on his flawless face. He still made no attempt to come closer to me but the muscles in his jaw hammered in contemplation. "Has this ever happened before?"

"If it had, do you think I would be repeating the experience?" I asked as the strap of my dress slipped past my shoulder. I tried righting it, but the thin piece of fabric didn't seem to want to stay up. "The worst part is I'm not even sleeping. I'm awake, or at least I think I am. I'm hallucinating in a very public place with hundreds of people around, yet you're the only one I'm actively trying to avoid."

Rowen's face flashed with shock and he opened his mouth, but before I could hear his reply, I was back in Prism with its flickering lights and pounding music.

Barefoot and probably looking blackout drunk or drugged, I knew I wasn't safe.

I wondered if Harlan or Natalie were looking for me yet. I checked my phone but there wasn't a single missed call or text.

Where were they?

I attempted to stand and find them but a dizzy spell took over and pressed me back down with a firm hand. I fumbled for Harlan's number again, but still no answer. When I went to try Natalie, my phone disastrously powered down in my hand.

This night couldn't get any worse.

I closed my eyes in frustration and opened them to Rowen's face. He was no longer amused or calm and his nostrils flared angrily. "You just disappeared for a moment. That isn't normal. Where are you?"

"I...I'm out...at a...party."

"Are you alone?"

"No, but my date left me, and he—"

"He left you?" he growled in disbelief. "In this state?"

"He didn't know this would happen!" I clamored back, not sure why I was defending Harlan. He should have at least checked his phone by now and seen my missed calls, but I wasn't about to admit I was completely helpless just yet. "And besides, he can go where he pleases, I'm perfectly capable of taking care of myself. I managed to make it to a room where I can wait this out. So you are free to go back to whatever scary ax-wielding thing you were doing."

I barely got the drunken words out before another wave of nausea hit me like a swirling undercurrent, and this time I was sure I was going to be sick. I dropped my head between my knees and rocked back and forth, hoping it would neutralize the spinning.

"I'm not leaving you. Not like this. I know someone who can help." He motioned to help lift me, almost landing a palm on me, but stopped short. "Can you walk?" he asked, lowering his hand to his side.

It was taking everything within me just to hold myself upright, but somehow I managed an unbecoming snort at his ridiculous proposal. Where was he going to take me? He and this other imaginary friend he mentioned couldn't help. Not really. They were only in my head and nothing more. "Definitely not. But really, I'll be okay. You can go."

He crouched down in front of me, holding my gaze. "We're waiting this out. Together." His command was final, but something about the way he said it made me think he knew what it was to suffer alone and would never wish that on anyone. And I had to admit, no matter how strange this was, it was comforting having him here with me while I experienced this waking nightmare.

"Tell me about where you're from," he said, and I tried to focus my spinning world on his full lips.

"You're trying to distract me."

"Is it working?"

My speech was slurring more and more by the minute, but he had a point; anything to keep me from passing out was sure to help. "It's noisy, crowded, all cement, mortar, and media, and...and nothing feels real anymore."

"What do you do to keep from going mad?" he asked, seeming genuinely curious.

I scoffed, nearly losing my balance again. "That ship has long sailed, my friend, but running, running helps. But lately I've been...busy."

"Busy with what?"

"Tripping through darkness."

Rowen's nostrils flared on an exhale and he placed his hand on the tree that was tethering me to earth, his graphite-smudged fingers resting an inch from my own hand. He still made it a deliberate point not to touch me, even though it seemed like he wanted to, to reach out and comfort me, but didn't dare push himself beyond a very specific point of control.

He'd touched me once before and it had been electrifying. For me, at least. I wondered if he had felt it too.

I contemplated just reaching out to touch him, to hold onto the wide birth of corded shoulders. He looked more steadying than anything else I was experiencing at the moment, but within another blink of an eye, I was back in the low-lit lounge of Prism.

I scanned the room in a haze, my eyes snagging on three large silhouettes lurking on the other side of the crystal curtain. Their boisterous laughter and stocky frames pinned them as the men I had run into earlier.

I hoped they weren't looking for me, but the chances of them coincidently lingering outside the very alcove I was utterly indisposed in were slim. Either way, if they found me in my current state it wouldn't be a good thing. I could barely keep my eyes open and head up.

"I think she's in here," said the man with overly gelled hair, confirming my fears.

I accidentally let my head lull, and when I snapped it back

up, I was staring into murderous green eyes. "What?" Rowen demanded, reading the change in my demeanor.

"It's some men I bumped into earlier. I…I think they are about to bother me," I said, unable to hide the tremor in my voice.

Rowen's eyes widened in sick realization before darting all over my body, clearly adding up all the ways this did not look good. "Keira, listen to me. You need to get out of there. Now."

He tried to grab me but I was already gone, and his voice trailed away, swallowed by a dark, endless hallway.

It would be so easy to close my eyes and sleep through this, but my mind jolted in self-preserving panic.

Stay awake. Stay awake. Stay awake.

Stout fingers ran across the beaded doorway in taunting strokes before finally latching on to open the curtain. All three men stepped through the threshold, smiling as if they'd just won the lottery, and I cursed myself for having picked such an isolated area.

"There you are, doll. We've come to check on you," said Gel Hair, apparently the ringleader of the group.

"Yeah, you don't seem so good," said Yellow Teeth as they all sauntered towards me. "Would you like to come with us to a more comfortable place? Or we could stay in here and have some fun."

"No. You need to leave. Before my boyfriend comes back. He…he won't like it that you're in here." I tried to sound strong and alert, but I was fading fast and I knew they could tell.

They were right in front of me now, blocking my only exit. "I don't think there is a boyfriend, doll, but don't worry, we'll take good care of you," the ringleader said, petting my hair as if to console me. "Make sure we aren't disturbed," he ordered to the third man, whose excited expression quickly turned sour. He looked irate to be the one to stand guard while the others had all the fun. "Don't worry. You'll get your turn with her."

My eyes pleaded with him for help, but like the obedient dog he was, he bowed down to the ringleader's command and left the room.

"Don't touch me," I snarled weakly, trying everything within me to stay present, but I was merely a pair of eyes watching through a worthless body that couldn't move, couldn't fight, and couldn't run. Even if I screamed, no one would hear me over the relentless booming of the music.

"Shhh, it's okay, doll. Just relax. Everything's alright," Gel Hair said, crowding me from the front with his stocky frame while Yellow Teeth circled behind me, slithering his finger under the fallen strap of my dress. Their movements were too synchronized, too well-rehearsed for this to be their first rodeo, and the sickening thought filled me with a raging fury I'd never felt before.

I wanted them to hurt.

"Ow!" Yellow Teeth cried, pulling his hand away. "She shocked me!"

"I'll do it again," I said, speaking madness. I had no idea what he was talking about but I would say anything if it kept their hands off me.

"Just some static electricity. Hold her still, would you."

Yellow Teeth sucked at his discolored overbite before reluctantly reaching for me again. I tried to jerk away, but once he realized he wasn't going to be shocked, his fingertips dug into me like grappling hooks.

Bolder now, he leaned down, pressed his nose to my irregular pulse, and licked the length of my neck, burying his face, mouth, and tongue in my hair.

"Stop! Now!" I begged. If I wasn't having some sort of debilitating allergic reaction, these men would be doubled over on the floor, clutching themselves between the legs. Begging *me* to stop as I trampled them into dust, into nothing.

Gel Hair pulled up on his pant legs and squatted down in front of me, almost in the exact same position Rowen had been in moments ago. He gripped my chin and angled my face before him like a precious diamond in the light. "Is it just me, or is she glowing?"

I kicked at him but it was a feeble attempt, and he only smiled as he grabbed my leg roughly and held it still. His broad face regarded me with a hungry fascination, and his thumb began rubbing the sensitive flesh of my inner knee. "So soft. You even feel like porcelain, doll."

I futilely tried to wrench away but his accomplice held me still, trapping my arms by my sides like a straitjacket. Their hands, eyes, and breath were suffocating, holding me down as if I were a small creature caught in their sickening oil spill.

Gel Hair's sweaty grip crept higher up my leg, and bile burned at the back of my throat. He continued to invade his way up my thigh, bunching my skirt at his wrist as he pushed his revolting touch past my dress. "Now I just wonder what you taste like."

I opened my mouth to scream bloody murder, but before a sound left my lips, their hands flew from my body amidst cursing howls.

"What the hell? Did you feel that?" one of them barked out.

"I told you," the other yelled back.

"No, I told *you*," I said, completely delirious. I had no idea what was shocking them, but maybe I could use the situation to my advantage. "It's a new phone app, you idiots. It acts as a taser. Every girl I know has it downloaded, frying the dicks off every one of you perverts."

"You're a crazy bitch and a liar."

"Am I?" I said, slurring like a madwoman with my dead

phone in my hand. I would fight until my last conscious breath, which was nearing closer and closer by the second. "Care to test that theory again?"

Their faces blanched. "Check her phone!" Gel Hair barked.

They were about to find out my lie, but soon it wouldn't matter. I wouldn't be awake much longer, and a part of me almost wondered if that would be better.

"Keira, there you are!" Harlan's voice bugled through the air with all the relief of day-late cavalry.

The two men jolted upright and slithered from the room like two snakes in the grass. So much for their trusty watchdog, who I was sure would have to face Gel Hair's wrath sooner or later.

I just wished I could have been the one to scare them away like that, but they had been no more afraid of me than if I was a baby bird, so weak and easily crushed within their grasp. It sent my blood boiling. I hated them. Hated how they made me feel. And Harlan had barely spared the creeps a glance before they disappeared through the beaded curtain. He seemed entirely oblivious as to what almost happened to me.

I hoped I at least got into their heads, made them think twice before they ever touched anyone ever again.

It was only after the men completely vanished from my sight that I gave in, and finally let my body black out.

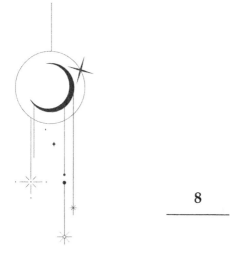

8

Soft cotton rustled against my bare skin. I was lying in bed. My bed. Somehow I had made it home, even though I had absolutely no recollection of how.

Tangled and wrapped in my white sheets like a towel, I noticed I wasn't wearing much, only the thong I'd put on before going out.

There was a quick moment of panic before I remembered I was in my room. Alone. Safe.

I breathed a sigh of relief, realizing Natalie must have slipped off my dress and put me to bed. But why couldn't I remember anything?

"You must remain calm," said a male voice I'd never heard before.

Startled, I sat up, clutching the sheets around my naked body like a shield.

I glanced around my room, bracing myself. But there was no one. Only pale rays of morning light greeted me as they slanted through the wooden shutters and fell upon the ground like lined soldiers.

"You must breathe and steady your mind," the stranger said,

and even I couldn't stay panicked with the way he spoke. It was the most soothing voice I had ever heard: resounding, smooth, and true. It reminded me of leaves stirring in the wind or a gentle stream trickling through the forest. I was immediately put at ease.

Then, I heard wood burst and splinter as if someone had crashed into a hard surface, maybe a wall, and I jumped again. Someone else was fuming and breathing heavily next to the composed man.

So much for remaining calm.

"For her sake and your own, you must take control of yourself. Putting your fist through my wall isn't going to help anyone. Here, let me look at your hand."

It dawned on me that I wasn't the one this tranquil voice was speaking to. I was merely eavesdropping on a conversation with people who seemed entirely unaware of my presence.

Was I having some sort of auditory dream? I'd never had one before, but I didn't much like the feeling of it. It was never a good sign to be hearing voices out of nowhere.

"What kind of a pathetic man would leave her alone for the wolves to descend?" Now *that* was a voice I'd know anywhere, but I had never heard it so strained, so furious. "I'm going mad with not knowing, wondering if she's hurt. Hating myself that I could do nothing as she needed me. She could be The Marked."

"Have you seen such a marking upon her?"

Silence.

"We still have no idea who she is and must tread carefully. You know the Summit is weary, especially with the whisperings of Erovos' return. If she is harmed, which we don't know that she is, it won't do anyone any good if you are wounded as well."

I realized with a start they were talking about me, and the night came back in fragmented flashes. The clunky memories reeled through my mind like an old movie projector: getting ready in the bathroom with Natalie, Harlan picking us up in that monstrous SUV, drinking, dancing, and Rowen—he had been there. And something had made him angry. Very angry.

Suddenly, my whole body recoiled as I remembered the men from the club. I recalled the look in their eyes as their hands pressed on me and invaded my space. Almost invaded me. Their faces were a muddied blur, but their intentions were clear. Both Harlan and Natalie had left me, which normally wouldn't have been a big deal, except for last night, it was.

I had been abandoned and left vulnerable in a dangerous situation.

The men would have succeeded in their malicious motives had Harlan not entered at the last possible moment, scaring them off. My knuckles were bone-white as I fisted the sheet at my chest. The narrow window in which I evaded being defiled was too minuscule to fathom.

"I saw her face. She knew what those men were about to do to her, and I couldn't do a damned thing to stop it," Rowen said in a seething fury.

How odd for a delusion to worry about the happenings of a past dream. Not only did it seem like some sort of waking hallucination for me, but an actual memory for him.

"You chose this, Rowen. You must be prepared to be there for her. However she returns to you."

I didn't want Rowen to worry needlessly about me. I'd made it home safely. There was no reason for him to torment himself any further for not being able to help someone in need.

Rowen. I'm fine. I tried to tell him, reach out to him.

The air stilled with a pregnant pause.

"What is it, Rowen?"

"I...she...I think she's alright."

Had he actually heard me?

I wished I could tell him more, but my eyes succumbed to the pull of darkness once again.

——— ·((· ● ·))· ———

That afternoon I sat rolled up on the couch in the baggiest sweater set I owned, wrapped in the comfiest blanket I could find. In my hands, I cradled a steaming cup of lemon ginger tea, steeped and kindly prepared for me by Natalie. The rich aroma wafted towards me, and I deeply inhaled the warm notes of spice and citrus.

Apparently, this drink was a hangover cure, and while I didn't think that's what I was suffering from, I was willing to try anything that would calm my stomach and pounding headache.

"So you think you had an allergic reaction? You're sure no one slipped something in your drink?" Natalie asked from the opposite side of the couch, looking ill herself. Was she suffering unintended reactions from last night as well?

"I'm positive," I said before taking a tiny sip of tea that tingled down my throat. "I didn't accept a single drink from anyone except you and Harlan. There's no way someone could have slipped me something. Those men never had a chance, though they definitely cashed in on the situation."

She bit down on her lower lip and looked at me regretfully with her hazel stare. The apparent guilt for leaving me alone dulled the usual sparkle in her eyes. "I just got off the phone with the club. Apparently several of the security cameras were faulty. Any footage of you is too bright and hazy to make anything out. There is no evidence to corroborate your accusations of the three men."

I gripped the cup, trying to keep it together. "Can you...can you at least tell me what happened after? I don't remember much."

"Harlan found Damon and me on the upper level and said something was seriously wrong with you and to come help."

My jaw almost dropped in my lap. Harlan had left me not once but twice!

I fumed at the thought of him knowingly leaving me alone in that room completely unconscious. So unaware of his surroundings, he hadn't even stopped to consider mine. He'd barely given those men a second glance before they disappeared off into the shadows, not even sparing a moment's thought that they might come back and finish what they started.

Harlan had avoided the whole conflict altogether, probably worried he would scuff his loafers or mess up his hair.

"You were pretty out of it. You could barely stand, let alone walk, and you were barefoot. I didn't have much time, but I couldn't find your shoes anywhere. Damon carried you out of the club. We ordered a cab and came straight here. Harlan wanted to stay with you, but I made him leave. I got you as comfortable as I could for bed and left you to sleep it off."

My cheeks flushed with mortification. I had been unconsciously carried out of the club by a man I didn't even know. A man that Natalie was clearly interested in, but still, why hadn't Harlan done it?

I didn't think I'd ever been this embarrassed in my whole life. I squeezed the mug tighter. "Natalie, I'm so sorry. He sounds like an amazing guy, and I completely ruined your night."

"Don't worry about it. We all wanted to help," she said, shifting uncomfortably and quickly looking to the kitchen to check the kettle.

"What was...what was Harlan doing?" I choked out. I already knew, but I had to hear it from her.

"He was losing his mind. He was so worried about you, he didn't know what to do. Damon and I pretty much had to take charge of the whole situation."

If Harlan thought he was losing his mind, he should really try walking a mile in my shoes, wherever they were. I remembered darting back and forth between the club and the forest I only saw in my dreams. I'd been so out of it that I slipped between worlds as if they were merely the turn of a page apart.

I thought back to Rowen. He was seething, but he would never have let the situation get the better of him the way Harlan had. Too bad he wasn't real. But that was a whole other problem for another day. I wasn't ready to face that just yet. One thing at a time. "I can't believe he left me again."

"Don't blame him, Keira. You were pretty bad. It was...hard to see you like that."

Hard to see, yet harder to experience. And they didn't even know the half of it.

"Are you going to be alright?" She placed her polished hand on my knee and gave me a pat through the thick blanket.

"Now that I know not to pick up another drink of alcohol ever again!" I answered as if all was well and I wasn't facing a mental breakdown. Or that I had no control over my mind as it slowly tore in two.

Pretending I wasn't on the precipice of losing my mind was getting harder and harder to fake. I didn't know how much longer I could keep it up.

My phone buzzed obnoxiously by my side. It had been going off all morning with texts and calls from Harlan, but I wasn't ready to talk to him yet. Especially after learning about how poorly he handled the whole situation.

It had been bad enough that Harlan left me for so long, but worse to find out my own date couldn't even discreetly carry me out of the building.

I ignored my phone as it buzzed and stared blankly forward, while Natalie's fingers flew across her phone. As she furiously typed away to whomever, I realized just how garishly she decorated our living room. Bold colors, obnoxious prints, and flashy decorations covered every inch of our living space. Not even a breath that I lived here.

How had I not noticed this before?

I'd never expressed any interest in decorating, what with my room barely containing a picture on the wall and a few track plaques, but Natalie had completely taken it upon herself to become our interior decorator. She must have assumed I was okay with it because I never said a word, and now here I sat in a gaudy room I didn't even recognize.

What was happening to me? How had all of this escaped my knowledge for so long? How had I never cared?

I was merely a ghost living in a shell, my life on autopilot, never really seeing or hearing anything at all.

Something was awakening within me, a dormant phoenix itching to rise and spread her wings of pale white fire from the confines of her cage. A cage I never even knew existed until recently. Something was calling to me, waiting beyond the bars of the prison I was finally expelling. I just didn't know what.

My phone went off again several times in a row, and I spared it a glance.

Natalie told me everything.

I can't believe you had an allergic reaction.

I should have never left you.

Forgive me.

Please, let me make it up to you.

My eyes shot to Natalie. "You informed him of all this just now?"

"I had to tell him, he's worried sick. And if you weren't going to tell him, I was," she said defiantly, placing her phone down on the awful purple couch.

The reins on my composure were slipping. Everyone was acting as if this was something that happened to *them*. "I planned on it. I just needed some time. Last night wasn't easy for me either in case you missed it."

"What's gotten into you lately? Just promise me you'll never drink again," she begged, her eyes pleading. "I hated seeing you like that. You can't know how sorry I am."

"I'm sorry too, for how the night turned out," I said, reeling back my temper. "You know I appreciate all your help in getting me home. Be sure to thank Damon for me as well."

"He's so sweet and smart. I can't wait for you to meet him." Her worry seemed to lighten as she regaled me with stories of their conversations and flirtatious touches before they'd had to race downstairs to help me.

A silence lulled between us, and I contemplated what I should say to Harlan as I finished my drink. He knew he was in the wrong, and I wasn't above wanting to see him grovel.

I set the cup between my legs and texted him back.

I am available for acts of the forgiving type.

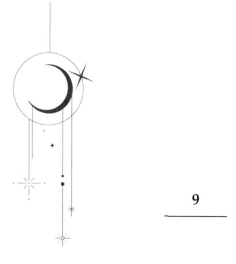

9

Days passed without a single word or appearance from Rowen. I should have been relieved and overcome with joy, but I secretly worried he was gone forever or that something horrible had happened to him.

It came as quite a shock at how invested I was in his well-being. He wasn't even real, yet I worried about his whereabouts and safety. More so than my own at this point because I was entirely lost.

I must've taken a walk, though I couldn't remember consciously deciding to do so. Somewhere along the way, I'd taken a wrong turn because I found myself walking through a strange red forest, which was most assuredly nowhere near where I lived.

I searched for a path or trailhead to lead me back home, but none were in sight. How had I gotten so far off track out in the middle of nowhere?

I itched at my throat uncomfortably. I didn't like it here.

I passed under the red-clouded treetops that, against the white sky, looked like pools of blood splattered on linoleum flooring. The trunks themselves seemed to be made of bone dust, covered in burls that jutted out like thorns, thirsting for the slightest prick of my skin. The woods pulsed like the inside of a body, a body somehow surviving without flesh, sinew, and muscle holding it all together.

But still, it breathed.

The leaves exhaled stale air that left my skin scratchy, dry, and cracked open like the barren salt flats.

Somehow it was even eerier here than in the dead, glass-like forest. Instead of a frozen death, everything here felt half alive, as though nothing truly lived so it could never fully die.

A dryness was beginning to coat my throat as if I'd drunk a mug of talcum powder. I tried to swallow to ease the irritation, but I was depleted of all moisture.

I clawed at my throat. The thirst was growing more and more unbearable by the second.

I desperately searched around me, hoping to find some sort of fresh water source. I no longer cared about getting home. I needed to wet my parched throat. *Now.*

My very wish was answered as the sound of water trickled to my ears from beyond, carried along by the craggy cliff-front to my left. My throat burned and ached, and I placed a trailing hand on the rock surface, following the water beckoning me in the distance.

Rounding the bluff, I was greeted with a clear, wide waterfall that flowed into a pool of iridescent blue. The water pulled me as naturally as the moon compels the tides, and I had no objections whatsoever. I wanted nothing more in my life than to taste the crystal liquid of the lakelet.

Each step closer drew in the focal point of the pond, blurring and warping everything else out of focus.

I was almost there. My mission singular.

I knelt at the edge of the spring and ran my fingers along the mirrored cerulean surface. It was cold and biting, but surprisingly I didn't mind. I normally hated anything below room temperature, but I was too fascinated by the spectrum of light trailing within my tiny currents to care. Diamond bursts of light refracted and glistened off the ripples I created with my lazy strokes, and I laughed as the water begged to be tasted.

My heartbeat was in my throat now, and I smacked my dry lips together.

I lowered my cupped hands into the pond and watched as the sparkling water filled my makeshift chalice. I brought my wrists to my mouth and took one glorious gulp, then another and another. It was delicious and filled me with an overflowing sense of euphoria.

I replenished my chaliced hands, greedy for more.

I was about halfway through my second helping, when out of the corner of my eye, two tall humanoid figures emerged from the thick of the trees. Still some distance away, they hadn't noticed me yet.

I ignored them and returned to my drink when a force pummeled into me and knocked me off my feet.

My entire body was thrown to the side by a large, dark battering ram that came out of nowhere. The water fell from my hands, and I was more furious about losing the precious liquid than I was by getting tackled to the ground.

I toppled sideways as something wrapped tightly around my waist, pulling me in until my cheek was firmly pressed against a rock-hard chest.

A man?

An arm scooped up to cradle and protect my head as we rolled together down a slope of shrubs. Up and down lost all meaning as the sky and forest floor tumbled around me.

Suddenly I was jerked around, our spinning at an end, but the impossible weight of the man still pressed down upon me.

Crouched with one knee out from under him, he sat me between his massive thighs and pushed me smaller and smaller as he hunched his head and torso over me, completely cocooning me within his body.

His arm wrapped further around my waist, and his fingers dug into my hip. The hand that was once cradling my head was now firmly clasped over my mouth and nose. I tried to squirm away, but the locked embrace tightened around me.

I couldn't move or breathe with his iron bar of an arm crushing into my stomach and his hand covering my airways. Whoever this was, they were going to suffocate me right here in the silence of the red forest. I thought nothing could die here, but I was wrong. *I* would die here, and for some reason, I didn't seem to care. I was swept with such a sense of lightheadedness that I was perfectly content to die here at the hands of this unknown man.

Despite not being able to breathe, I had never felt this light, this free. And a million tiny electro-bursts erupted all over my skin, setting me off like a chain of firecrackers.

Was it due to the lack of oxygen? If so, it didn't seem like the worst way to go. I welcomed the spots that closed in around my vision, wishing I could have taken one more sip of that clear spring water.

Floating in my euphoria, I jerked involuntarily from the loss of oxygen. My captor, or savior, I couldn't tell which, must have realized I couldn't breathe because he shifted his hand, allowing for the slightest trickle of air to seep into my lungs.

I thought dying had felt wonderful, but it was nothing compared to breathing. Had I ever felt this high?

The man pressed me even tighter and deeper into his body

and I slackened into him, welcoming the hard rigidity of his marble stature. He bowed over me, his cheek resting on the side of my head, and his broad chest expanded with an inhale behind me.

The breath he carefully loosened skirted along the curve of my ear and swept down the nape of my neck, gently blowing the wayward strands of my hair across my exposed skin. My entire body ignited into shivering goosebumps, tightening every inch of me to the point of painful sensitivity. A shiver radiated down every one of my vertebrae until it landed at the base of my spine, and I arched my back involuntarily.

I hadn't meant for it to, but my reaction had me pressing the slope of my ass even closer to the body that held me. The intimate proximity let loose a mindless need that grew more unbearable by the second. I needed more of this man's body and breath on me. I needed it as badly as I'd needed the water minutes ago, only now I craved something else entirely. The broad hands that restrained me dug into my skin, and an unbidden moan escaped my lips, captured in the palm of my stranger.

What was wrong with me? My body had completely turned against me. She was calling all the shots and I was merely along for the ride.

The growing ache between my legs overrode all sense, and I bowed into him even further, rolling against him in eager waves. I was waiting for him to slide into me and fill this desperate need consuming me by the second, but to my irritation, he didn't move at all, didn't even seem aware that I was enticing him.

Was he an idiot?

It agitated me immensely that my desires weren't being met. How obvious did I need to be? I began rolling my body more fervently beneath him like a depraved feline, and against his stronghold, I twisted my face towards him, searching for his mouth to claim.

It took the stranger a moment, but once he realized what I was attempting, a low growl rumbled in my ear and he jerked me to stop, prying my face forward.

I was briefly reawakened to my senses. What in the hell was happening?

We were hidden behind a slight slope of earth, but I could still make out the flowing waterfall and lapping pond. The two figures from earlier now stood exactly where I'd been when I drank from the falls.

Were they the reason I was so rudely torn away from the ambrosian water?

All I wanted was for them to leave so I could drink and drink until I couldn't consume a drop more. But just as I was growing impatient with their prolonged presence, I shrank back in horror, realizing they were anything but human.

The creatures looked like flat-faced deer walking straight on their hind limbs with hoofed feet and taloned hands. Their fur was completely white and giant bleached-bone antlers sprouted from their skulls, curling pointedly towards the sky. Mossy green hair cascaded down in long ferns and vines around their anthropomorphic bodies, and the little mushrooms that budded around the crowns of their heads matched perfectly with the blood-red color of their eyes.

They sniffed at the air savagely, their crimson-stained mouths curling back over jagged teeth.

If it weren't for the hand still tightly clamped over my mouth, they would have surely heard my screams, but instead, the noises choked down my throat in lacerating hacks.

My fear was all-consuming, stinging at my skin like a swarm of murderous hornets. I wanted to run fast and far away from here, but the man's arms held me securely in place, crushing my squirming body against his.

After what seemed like forever, the two buck-like creatures retreated into the forest, scouring the path I'd come from like a pack of jackals on the scent of a wounded gazelle.

Once they were fully out of sight, the man whipped me around by my shoulders and looked me square in the eyes.

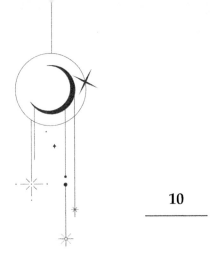

10

"Rowen?" I asked, trying to grasp a single thought.

The beauty of his face shocked me all over again but had it always been this severe, this bracketed with panic and fear? His strong sculpted jaw clenched to the point of breaking, and his usually straight eyebrows were mounted harshly over unflinching hemlock eyes.

I briefly wondered how he always knew where to find me, knew exactly where to be at just the right moment, but then his finger moved to my bottom lip and all thought beyond the tip of his touch vanished. I lifted my chin into his caress, breathing him in, wanting more. Needing more.

Something was seriously wrong. I knew I had just seen something frightening, but for the life of me, I couldn't recall what.

A blood-red memory gnawed at the back of my mind, pleading to be remembered, but I swatted it away. Rowen was touching me now; that was all that mattered. My skin itched and burned and begged for relief. Relief I knew he was capable of giving me.

I could tell I was looking at him through half-lidded eyes, a clear invitation that he could do whatever he pleased with me right here on the forest floor and I wouldn't object. His finger pushed beyond my lower lip. The earthy taste of his skin was intoxicating, and I opened my mouth wider for him, inviting him in.

I was reveling at his touch, his taste, his scent, and a whimper escaped my lips in anticipation. But before I knew what was happening he plunged his fingers down my throat, choking me. My eyes shot open and I bucked at him savagely, gagging as his fingers descended deeper and deeper into my throat.

"Stop fighting me, Copeland. We have to get that water out of your system."

This was definitely not where I thought this was going, and for a moment, my ego was severely bruised.

"You drank poison, you are not yourself. Hold still." He struggled with me as I fought against him like a wild animal.

I managed to land a punch or two on that sharp jaw of his, eliciting curses from that beautiful mouth, but in the end, he was bigger than me, and I was helpless as he easily overpowered me with his massive strength.

"Always drinking things you shouldn't," he seemed to mutter to himself as he battled to hold me still, his fingers fixed firmly down my throat.

Then I began to heave.

Rowen lurched me forward, pulling his fingers from my mouth, and coming up right behind him was the water I had swallowed from the pond. It tore its way up my esophagus and retched out of my mouth in violent coughing spasms.

But it wasn't the water I remembered at all.

What came back up from my stomach was black and inky and tasted like death. Rowen gathered my hair in his hands and held it away from my face as I expelled and spat out every last drop of the acrid liquid. My throat was on fire, and a taste of rotten decay coated my mouth.

"What? How?" I managed to croak as I wiped my mouth with the back of my hand.

"Look again," he said with exasperation, rubbing his jaw where I'd rammed my fist into his face.

I looked up, but where I once saw a beautiful oasis, I now saw black sludge tumbling into an even darker pit of syrupy water. Opaque charcoal bubbles formed and popped along the waterline, and broken bones of all sizes littered the shore as if they'd been carelessly tossed aside after being picked dry.

I gagged again at the sight of the filth, but my stomach was empty and my body wracked with painful dry heaves. Rowen's broad hand gently rubbed my back, recirculating my blood and bringing air back into my lungs. "Good girl. I think you got it all."

I collapsed onto the ground in front of him. I had so many questions but my thoughts were reeling. Was I still in Prism reacting to the alcohol? No, that was nights ago. This was something new.

Did he say poison?

If it wasn't so frightening, I'd be annoyed that Rowen was always finding me in inebriated states of consciousness. Things like this never happened to me; my life always folded and unfolded along the same creased lines, nothing new, beautiful, or interesting ever being created. Until recently.

Before I could pull myself together enough to voice a single thought, Rowen beat me to it. "I haven't seen you in days. What happened to you that night?" he growled through a tight throat, sounding as if he was trying but barely succeeding to tamp down his fury. "Did they touch you?" he asked, his eyes clinically searching my body, assessing for any signs of trauma.

"Nothing happened." I gasped, still sucking in air. "My boyfr

—I mean, Harlan finally came and got me home safely." More or less.

His tight jaw loosened, and his eyes hooded over. I'd never seen anyone look so relieved and so enraged all at the same time. "So he's not as worthless as he appears."

I was too busy spitting to answer.

"Why are you wandering around Weir Falls? This place is dangerous. Crawling with beasts that would skin the flesh off your bones while you still breathed. Are you even aware of the danger your presence draws? Here and apparently everywhere else you go."

"I never had any problems until you came around. Maybe you're my unlucky charm," I said in annoyance, only my eyes peering up at him.

He didn't seem amused as he offered his hand down to me. "We need to leave."

I took his wrist, wanting to get out of this gruesome place as soon as possible, but as Rowen pulled me up, the frightening creatures flashed across my memory, and the fear rushed through me like a rogue wave. I jolted unexpectedly, plowing right into Rowen with all my weight, and he hissed between his teeth as if he'd just been electrocuted.

He stumbled back, trying to right us, but his heel caught over a fallen log, and we both toppled to the ground like dominos.

He fell on his back with a grunt, breaking my fall as I landed on top of him with my hands splayed on the hard crests of his pecs. We were chest to chest and nose to nose, his hands finding purchase on my hips. My hair fell in golden-brown waves that haloed and grazed the sides of Rowen's shocked face. He was flush against me, matching us up perfectly like the sides of a fault line brought back together.

His pupils dilated into vast chasms that threatened to

swallow me whole if I didn't look away. But I couldn't. I was too intrigued with the contracting rings of his emerald irises.

Instead of heeding the prickled warning of my instincts to flee, I peered deeper into the dense forest of his eyes. I felt like prey that was already ensnared, it just didn't know it yet.

I was only rested atop him for one startling moment, a thickness growing in his pants that pressed against me. I tried to stifle my moan, I really did, but Rowen's furious expression told me I'd failed miserably. He turned swiftly, rolling me beneath him, and I inhaled a sharp breath as our eyes locked again—green above grey—a stormed forest turned upside down.

Despite Rowen's large frame, he was careful not to smother me, bearing most of his weight on his vascular arms. But not all of it. I was painfully aware of all the places his powerful body met mine.

His touch was utterly visceral, shaking me to my core, and I ached with an unfulfilled need between my legs. All I'd have to do was lift my hips to find release.

Sensing my contemplations, Rowen brought his mouth to my ear. "You just escaped two monsters, Copeland. Are you sure you want to provoke another?" he asked, his voice low and guttural, and a pained whimper that I wasn't sure was a yes or no escaped my mouth. He pushed himself off me, and my body arched reflexively to fill the space between us. I immediately felt torn, our fault line ripped apart once again, causing tremors to shake throughout my existence.

He'd felt so solid under my touch that it twisted my sense of what was real and what wasn't. I had no idea anymore.

He grabbed my hand and lifted me carefully, making sure not to overbalance me again. Without letting go or uttering a single word, he quickly led me away from the red forest and all its dark horrors.

Still in disbelief, I stole one last glance behind me, but I wished I hadn't because the red leaves were now dripping with blood.

We walked, sometimes ran, and even darted behind a tree or bush if Rowen thought he heard someone...or *something*. He put a finger to his lips, gesturing for me to remain silent.

In the past, he'd made it very clear he would prefer not to touch me, but as he guided our way through the forest, his calloused grip never left me. And even though Rowen's guiding etiquette was brusque and abrasive, his steady grasp was reassuring and had me coming back to my senses.

I'd been so out of control, my mind fleeing from one base instinct to the next. Now that I could think clearly again, I was mortified by my actions. How I'd pressed and moved myself against Rowen, my eyes practically begging him to take me. And how for a moment I thought he wanted me back. Even for a dream, it was so embarrassing, and just as bad as those nightmares where you show up to school naked.

My eyes widened in panic. *Please don't be naked. Please don't be naked.*

I looked down at myself and breathed a sigh of immense relief. I remembered now, I'd made it home after work and dressed for bed. It had been a chilly night, so I opted to wear a silky sleep top and shorts with a pair of grey thigh-high socks.

At the time, the ensemble seemed cozy and warm, but here it just felt vastly inadequate. Thankfully, the ground was soft beneath my socked feet, blanketed in shrubby layers of moss.

Once we made it a far enough distance away and the trees resumed their natural emerald color, Rowen stopped us by a flowing creek. "We should be safe here. This water is safe to drink from as well," he said, motioning to the stream.

I emphatically shook my head no and took a step back. "I'm not drinking anything else. Not after *that.*"

"I promise this water is safe. It would be good for you to rinse your mouth in case the blight still lingers on your tongue." He scooped some water into his hand and gulped it down, the strong column of his throat contracting as he swallowed. "See?"

He looked at me expectantly.

He had a point; my mouth did taste curdled and chalky. If he just drank the water, it had to be safe. I trusted Rowen. Didn't I?

I knelt beside him and gargled the crisp water. "What happened back there?" I finally asked after I was sure I had sufficiently washed out my mouth and cooled my fevered skin.

"You drank from Weir Falls." Rowen's jaw clenched through his shaded stubble. "Its purpose is to lure in prey under the guise of a false paradise. Unable to help themselves, the victims drink the poisonous water believing it to be some sort of delicacy to quench their thirst. The more they drink, the more they want, lessening any control they have over their senses. The blighted liquid lowers their inhibitions until they have almost none. Nothing to warn them that danger is coming for them. Stalking them. Hunting them."

A sickening dread flooded my limbs. I drank a poisonous substance that stripped me of my sensibilities, robbed me of logical thinking, and drew my deepest desires to the surface. That would explain my actions, why I'd had absolutely no self-control. Why one moment I was happy to die, the next lusting after a man I barely knew.

I tried not to cringe when I thought of what I had done back there; my hints hadn't been subtle. I'd made it painfully obvious that I wanted Rowen's body, but if he felt uncomfortable, he wasn't letting it show.

"Rowen, we should talk about what happened—"

"You weren't yourself, Copeland" he said, saving me from

having to elaborate. "And do you really want to discuss all the things I could have done to you in that state?"

Looking at him sitting beside me, in all his grand-muscle glory, I realized he could have easily taken advantage of me. To be honest, many a man would have, and I shuddered at the memory of Prism.

Steering the topic away from my body, I asked, "What were those...creatures?"

"They are the forest laiths of the Weir, and they live on the blood of their game. One scratch from them is poisonous, inciting hallucinations until your heart gives out. Sight isn't their strongest sense during the day, so you were lucky. They mainly rely on their sense of smell. I—I tried to mask you with my body. They picked up your scent. If I hadn't been there..." He stopped himself from continuing, but his hardened gaze held the stories I most likely never wanted to hear.

"Even though this is just a dream, or more likely a nightmare, I'm glad you were there. So thank you for what you did. You always seem to appear out of nowhere, literally crashing into me and disrupting my life." I hadn't meant to say that last part, it just sort of rushed out before I could stop it.

Oh well, he should know the havoc he was wreaking on my life. Nothing out of the ordinary ever happened to me until he started showing up, and I viewed him as the common denominator. Maybe if I held the mirror of truth up to his face, he would disappear back into the mist from where he came.

But my slip-up only seemed to amuse him, and a wry smile played at his mouth. "What if I told you it was you appearing to me, disrupting my life?"

I couldn't help myself. I threw my head back in waves of laughter. A hallucination was actually trying to convince me that *I* was complicating *his* life!

Rowen watched me with a sparkling expression as if I were the entertaining one.

My belly ached as my laughter finally subsided, and I wiped a tear from the corner of my eye. I hadn't laughed that hard in ages.

"I hate to break it to you, but it's definitely you. I'm too much of a delight," I said, batting my eyelashes at him over my bare shoulder.

His carefully adorned mask of rigidity slipped just a little, and the slight laugh that escaped his lips twisted my belly. Yes, he was most assuredly the problem here. Not me. Feeling such emotions in a dream was one thing, but having the thoughts linger with me long after waking was another entirely. It wasn't natural.

"Your right hook to my jaw would say otherwise," he said with a crooked smile that exposed one of his peaked canines. He leaned forward, resting his elbows on his knees, and the deep cut of his linen shirt billowed forward, allowing me to see even more of his etched chest lightly dappled with dark hair.

I noticed he wore two necklaces, one beaded with crystal dowels, the other worn and silver, with a medallion hanging like a flattened stone against the hollow of his sternum.

His gaze shot up to mine, serious again. The mask firmly back in place.

"Do you know how you came to be in Weir Falls?" he asked for the second time.

"No idea. I was just there. Which seems to be happening more frequently—me winding up in places, having no memory of how I got there." I had yet to speak these words aloud, and it was cathartic in a way, letting loose the secret I clutched so close to my chest, especially to someone who already felt like such a part of me. "It takes me a while to figure out whether it's only in my mind, whether it's real or not, but it's...it's getting harder to tell the difference."

He seemed to consider how to respond, choosing his next words carefully. "Even if it were all only taking place in your mind, that doesn't make it any less real."

I let his statement settle in my reasoning. Could it really be that simple?

"I have this memory," he said as a dark shadow settled over his features, and his gaze went where I couldn't follow. Even if I could, I didn't think I'd want to. It looked like it hurt too much. Maybe there were things my hallucination needed to get off his chest as well. "When I think of it or when it bombards my thoughts without provocation, I relive it over and over again. And it's real, Keira. It's real every time."

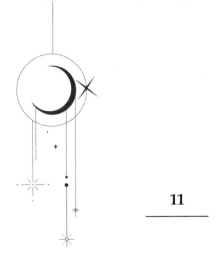

11

A plate shattered to the ground, the clang of the impact making me jump as Rowen's words reverberated through me like a cymbal. *It's real, Keira. It's real every time.*

I sat at a table across from Natalie, who looked the epitome of poise and perfection. Not a single hair out of place with her manicured brows and blonde hair pulled up into a tight top knot.

We were at one of our favorite restaurants. Though, I had absolutely no memory of coming here.

I suddenly realized my roommate, along with a slightly perturbed server with browline glasses and a handlebar mustache, were waiting for me to order.

Snapping out of my stupor, I quickly asked for my usual and placed the menu in the server's already outstretched hand. He flashed a quick, agitated smile and sped off toward the kitchen.

"Anyway, as I was saying, I'm so happy you let me take you out today. Even though every time we come here this place gets busier and busier," Natalie said, side-eyeing the crowd.

"I guess the secret's out," I tried to respond casually as if my mind wasn't falling apart and that chunks of my days weren't going missing.

But if Natalie noticed me acting strangely, she didn't mention it. My lapse in time had gone completely unnoticed by her. She seemed preoccupied, nervously twisting at a piece of torn napkin. "I have to let you know I still feel terrible about pressuring you to go to Prism. I feel like I should have known that would happen."

"Don't be ridiculous. There is no way you could have known," I said yet again. I'd been trying to assuage her guilt for days, but she was hellbent on reliving and apologizing for it every chance she got.

I knew she still felt terrible about leaving me alone at the club, but no one could have predicted how my body would react to alcohol, and I was sick of talking about it. I just wanted to move on.

"How are things at the firm?" I asked, changing the subject.

"They have me doing nothing but cease and desist letters all day. I can't believe I'm not getting paid for it. It's literally so mind-numbing and boring...nothing like the sounds I heard coming from your room last night," she said with a devilish smirk. "How did you sleep last night? Any dreams?"

"Don't people hate hearing about other people's dreams?"

"Typically yes, but it seemed like you were enjoying yourself, more so than when you actually have someone in there with you."

"We really need thicker walls."

"So who was the dream about," she pressed. "Those noises! Really, I was beginning to feel a bit lonely and envious. Please spare no detail! Who was it? The cute guy from the coffee shop, your track coach, or..." She gasped, putting her hand to her mouth. "Did you sneak someone in? I know it couldn't have been Harlan."

"I didn't sneak anyone in, but even if I had, Harlan and I aren't exclusive. I'm free to do what I want. But if you must know, I'm meeting with him tonight. He wants to make things up to me."

"So you were dreaming of Harlan then," she said confidently as if she'd cracked the code.

It would have been so easy for me to agree and go along with her assumptions, but somehow denying Rowen in any capacity felt like too large of a lie.

"No," I told Natalie. "It was someone not from around here. You've never met him." It wasn't technically untrue.

"Keira! Who?" she practically screeched. Natalie was like a hound tracking the scent of blood. She wasn't going to let me off that easily. I knew she wanted a juicy story, and she wouldn't drop it until she got one.

"A sprinter from a competing college," I said, thinking on my feet, hoping she wouldn't sniff out the lie. I would have to be careful with how much she heard through our paper-thin walls. I'd already divulged too much with the story of the silver rose, and look how that turned out.

She'd tried to be compassionate, but there was that underlying look of uncomfortable pity, and I couldn't have anyone look at me like that. Not ever.

To my relief, my response seemed to appease her. "Oh, a sprinter huh? You know I love watching them run," she said as our server returned with plates full of fresh food.

My quinoa burger with greens spilling out the sides smelled delicious and my stomach growled in response. "I'm so hungry. I haven't eaten all day!" I exclaimed, eyeing my burger, determining the best angle of approach.

As soon as the words left my mouth, I realized my mistake. "What about the smoothie?" she asked, her voice rising with alarm.

"That sludge is far from filling," I said through a mouthful of food.

It was a lie by omission, but I was *so* not ready to have this conversation with her. I had way bigger problems to deal with.

"Those are so incredibly good for you. You better be drinking them."

"You don't have to keep cooking for me. You're way too busy as it is," I said for the millionth time.

"I know, but I enjoy doing it for you, okay? Growing up, I never had anyone to cook for or eat with. It was always just me." Natalie was very open about her childhood. With neglectful parents, she'd practically had to raise herself. For as long as she could remember, she'd done everything on her own, and I admired her for it. "Being there for each other seems like something families do. And I have that with you. I really miss our breakfasts together. I'm sorry I haven't been around much lately, and when I am, only terrible things happen."

"Hey, we're together now, and having a great time. Even if our server is scowling at me as we speak." We both burst out laughing when we confirmed that he was indeed looking at me not all too pleasantly.

We finished the rest of our meals, exchanging easy conversation before parting ways at the sidewalk.

I window-shopped the streets of the new art and shopping district, thinking about what a consistent figure Natalie had been in my life these past few years. I found comfort in our friendship, and though there were parts of me she would never understand, I was glad I had her. But I still found myself longing for something I couldn't quite put my finger on.

I continued to walk down the busy sidewalk, a sea of unfamiliar strangers surging by. I found myself scanning each face in hopes I'd see Rowen making his way toward me through the crowd.

I knew it was impossible and foolish, but I couldn't seem to get him out of my mind. Quite literally. Any man that looked vaguely like him had me turning my head.

He was in so much more than just my dreams. He was in the beating pulse of my veins, the unheard whisper across my ear, and the flicker of shadows in my periphery.

I'd been dreaming about him for a month now, each encounter more real than the last. Especially last night. I had felt every inch of him pressed up against me as he shielded me from the forest laiths. Looking back, I should have been more terrified, doing everything I could to claw myself away and run.

Rowen said my lowered inhibitions were from the poisoned water, but there was no water, was there? Just my mind creating these scenarios I had no idea it was even capable of making.

Still, I had been too oblivious, too distracted by his breath and hands on me. Even now, just thinking about it had my palms sweating and heart racing. The mere thought of him made my body react physically. It seemed I could never escape him.

An alert on my phone suddenly knocked me back to reality. A reality where Rowen didn't exist. Not my favorite place to be, but the real world was a bitch that way.

Excited to see me tonight?

Annoyed, I left Harlan's text on "read." I was going to see him in a few hours anyway.

With time to kill, I moseyed around the colorful shops and art exhibits, knowing full well I should work instead. I'd let the emails pile up in my inbox, and for the most part, I'd been doing an outstanding job of avoiding them. The thought of inputting even one more number had me wanting to rip my hair out. I couldn't believe how long I'd been doing work I absolutely hated.

As much as I'd tried to avoid it, my dreams had officially started to hinder my day-to-day, but I feared the worst was yet to come. Because as much as I fought to deny Rowen, I wanted to know him—in every way.

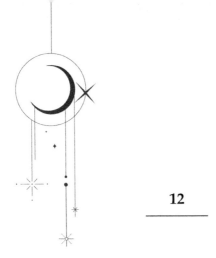

12

I headed to Harlan's after forcing myself into a somewhat productive day, miraculously managing to get some work done. It had taken nearly every ounce of willpower to concentrate on the menial tasks at hand, but a girl still had bills to pay.

I'd come straight here, wearing my high-waisted jeans, crop top, and chunky heeled boots from my lunch date with Natalie. There was no reason to get dolled up. This was Harlan's last chance, not mine.

I rapped my knuckles against the door, secretly hoping he wouldn't answer, but when he threw open the door and gathered me into a hug, I was taken aback. Not because he looked so good framed in the doorway, barefoot in his fitted jeans and t-shirt, or because of the overly fragranced aftershave wafting off his skin, not even for the way his lean body molded around me. But because standing before me, I could see, smell, and feel him just as easily as I could Rowen.

"Is everything alright?" Harlan asked, catching my head in his hands and staring at me with wide brown eyes.

It was disorienting how Rowen was just as real to me as Harlan. Even though Harlan was about the same height as

Rowen, he packed nowhere near the raw muscle and strength the man from my dreams did.

"No. I mean, yes," I said quickly and awkwardly. "I'm alright."

With a full-fledged smile, he led me into his sleek, modern apartment, all chrome, straight lines, and skylights. "Let me get you a drink," he said as he stalked off toward the kitchen.

Harlan's home was installed with all the latest technologies and smart devices on the market, not a single out-of-date item in sight. His materialistic tendencies hadn't bothered me in the past, so long as he didn't force them on me, but looking around now, it just seemed excessive and exhausting.

I let my thoughts wander to what Rowen's home might look like but I stopped myself short.

Why was I thinking about Rowen right now? He was just a beautiful delusion my imagination invented to either delight or torment me, and to be honest—it was beginning to feel more like the latter.

Whereas Harlan was real, made of flesh and bone, not shadows and mist.

A notion struck me. Was that what my dreams were trying to tell me? That I shouldn't keep entertaining the idea of a fabricated life, but focus on the real one right in front of me? Had I been clinging to this false hope for so long that it sabotaged everything in my path, even my relationships?

People often told me I was too picky and that my standards were too high. Were they right?

Was this feeling I sensed stretched out over space and time not real, this telescopic inkling that somehow I was meant for more? Or was it just a mirage I could see glinting on the horizon, and no matter how long or hard I ran toward it, it would always remain an unattainable bit of light in the distance?

What if all along, what I ached for was right under my nose? An oasis overlooked by a leaky pipe dream.

If that was what my subconscious was trying to say, could I have been overlooking Harlan all this time?

If he managed to make up for his debacle at Prism, this could turn into something more. Wasn't that what I'd been searching for all this time? Something real.

Considering this new perspective, I would try with Harlan tonight. Attempt to give in to him and see how it felt. How *he* felt —to search for any sign of life somewhere between us.

It could be amazing if I let it.

"You've been avoiding me," he said as he handed me a drink. "Don't worry. It's alcohol-free."

"I've had a lot of work," I said between sips. It wasn't technically a lie. Besides, I was used to living my life on the precarious line of omissions and half-truths. It was how I got by.

"You've changed up your look. I like it."

My brows pulled together. I hadn't changed anything since the last time I saw him.

Seeing the confused look on my face, he clarified. "The colored contacts. Your eyes are glowing like bits of stars. I couldn't see it before at the club but..." he slowly trailed off, remembering the sensitive topic.

"Oh." I hadn't noticed. "It's probably just your lighting," I replied. Lord knew he had the fanciest uplighting rigged in this place.

"I had some food ordered," he said, shrugging off the comment. "You good with the udon noodles?"

My interest piqued at the mention of food. "Veggie?"

"Sorry, no. I forgot," he winced. "But it should be here soon."

Despite being disappointed he hadn't remembered my eating preferences, I let him lead me to his grey mid-century couch. We hadn't had time to catch up the night at Prism, so he filled me in on his friends, family, and current tech job.

I did the same for him, minus the vivid dreams featuring a

very large, hatchet-wielding man. I especially didn't tell him about the gaps in my memory or ending up in places having no recollection of how I got there. He would no doubt tell Natalie, and they would find some intrusive way to confront me.

Our food arrived with an abrupt knock, and Harlan strode to the door, returning with a bag of inviting scents. We stayed on the couch and ate straight from the takeout containers.

"What are you thinking about?" he probed after a while, eyeing me in earnest.

I elected to ask him something I'd never thought about until now. "What's the full story on how you got my number? I mean, I know you got it from one of my teammates, but I don't know any of the details."

"Ah, I was wondering when you would ask me that," he chuckled without shame. "I got roped into going to one of your track meets. I didn't want to be there, but I was at the mercy of a buddy who said he only needed to make a quick appearance for his sister. It felt like we'd been there forever, and I was extremely bored—no offense—but then I saw you walking onto the field, and I'll be honest, you caught my eye right away. Suddenly, I became very interested in track." His brown eyes glinted mischievously.

"You were wearing those little bikini shorts and that sports bra," he said like he was conjuring the very image in his head, and I rolled my eyes. I wore what I wore to create the least amount of drag possible, not to be ogled at. "I watched you until it was your time to race. I was curious to see if you were any good."

Good? Of course I was good. I was racing at a collegiate level, but I let the comment slide.

"You were so in the zone before the race started, but as soon as the gun went off, your face changed. It didn't look like you were merely racing like everyone else, it...it looked like you were running from something, something that was going to devour you whole."

I almost flinched. Harlan was more perceptive than I thought. Then again, he didn't get to where he was in life by not being able to read people.

In all the moments leading up to a race and even the seconds in the block, I was always eerily docile and unfeeling. It wasn't until the starter pistol went off that the fear really set in, and I remembered that every time I ran, I escaped.

I fled like a wild, desperate beast from a hungry cage that chomped at my heels. If I wasn't fast enough, it would catch and utterly consume me, trapping me in its empty, colorless belly.

I hadn't raced in months since graduating, but I could never forget that feeling. Lately, the cage was less hungry, less relentless. It only hovered threateningly above me like a Venus flytrap silently biding its time.

"Anyway," Harlan said, bringing me back to his modern apartment. "That's when I knew I needed to talk to you. After I first saw you run. I asked my buddy if he could get your number from his sister. I knew it was a long shot," he said, nudging my knee.

I knew Harlan had gotten my number from one of the long-distance girls, but I had no idea it passed through her brother first. At the time, she stated he was some sort of tech mogul and that I would be stupid not to agree to meet up with him. She'd even tried several times herself to catch his eye. I reluctantly gave in, and now here we were.

I had to admit, Harlan had gone through quite the trouble.

He took the picked-at food from my hands and walked back to the kitchen, returning with two pink mochi ice cream balls on a small plate. "And for dessert," he said, giving me a lopsided grin as he sat and offered me one of the strawberry rice cakes.

At least he got one thing right.

Harlan devoured his mochi, then watched me intently as I savored every last refreshing bite of mine. His glinting eyes never left my face as I licked my fingers clean.

I had initially come here with completely different intentions than the one written all over Harlan's face. But I decided I would try.

Still on his couch with our knees slightly grazing, he asked, "How did you manage to get powder on your cheek?"

"I never know," I replied with a guilty laugh as I brought my hand to my face.

Harlan readjusted his lean body more comfortably beside mine, dipping me further into the couch.

Eyes burning, he brought his hand up to my face, and I felt the smooth edge of his thumb wipe at the powder on my cheek. His Adam's apple bobbed as he slowly transferred the stray bit of dessert onto my lower lip.

My breath hitched in my throat. Not because of Harlan's caress, but because the ghost of another's touch flashed before my memory. Heat rose to my cheeks when I thought of Rowen's hand at my mouth before inducing me to purge the poison from Weir Falls. He'd saved me from enduring the horrifying effects of the corrupt water, turning what could have been a full-blown night terror into simply a strange and unforgettable dream. But Harlan took my flushed reaction as a sign to take his touch further, snaking his hand around the side of my head and pulling me towards him until our lips pressed together.

The kiss started slow and gentle, and he licked at the strawberry powder on my lips like a man who'd been denied sweet delicacies for years.

Not wanting to overthink this, I pushed Rowen to the dark recesses of my mind just as Harlan's tongue dove past my teeth. His lips picked up speed and urgency against mine, forcing my mouth to move to his rhythm.

His other palm traveled up the length of my leg until he grabbed me by the hip and pulled me down onto the cushions with a swift tug. He came up over me with the weight of an anvil, and I let out a small grunt as he sank me deeper into the couch.

The memory of when Rowen had rolled himself on top of me shivered through my being. I couldn't help but think how conscientious he'd been with my body beneath his, how his welcoming pressure made it easier to breathe, not harder.

It was Rowen's weight my body craved as Harlan smothered me with hot, breathy kisses. I begged myself to forget the phantom of my dreams. At least for now. There was no point in torturing myself, and I realized I'd desperately needed release since last night.

I tried to focus on Harlan's hand tracing the taut skin of my belly. His touch was smooth and soft, not a single callous. You don't get many of those from being a tech mogul.

He slinked his way up and under my shirt and palmed one of my bare breasts. At some point, he'd pressed a knee between my legs, rubbing at the seam of my jeans, and my body arched slightly at the contact.

I could feel him growing impatient, though I didn't know what the hurry was. His free hand toyed with the waistband of my pants, working open the top button.

We had been intimate before, but this time it felt different, suffocating.

"There's a hidden light about you," he groaned at my throat. "I see it, and I don't want anyone else to have it. Ever. No more of this open-relationship bullshit. Move in with me."

I didn't make a sound or even flinch. I was still somewhat pliant beneath his touch, imagining the life I could lead with him. And for a few moments, I contemplated it.

It wasn't until Harlan's eyes found mine that I stiffened completely.

Brown irises met mine. Not green.

My spine went as rigid as the line I was about to cross. Rowen may have only just appeared to me, but the feeling of him and this other life waiting to emerge from the dark side of the moon had always been here. There was nowhere I could push it, nowhere I could hide it where it wouldn't be felt.

Something that inherently deep within me couldn't be wrong or imagined. It was too much a part of me. Too intrinsic and ancient to be ignored.

I couldn't go through with this. With any of it. No matter how much I tried to talk myself into it or how much Harlan wanted it. It wasn't happening.

"Harlan," I said, my voice completely flat. "I can't do this."

He lowered the zipper of my jeans and dipped his hand inside. "Come on, baby?"

Broadening the divide between my clothes, he pushed my shirt past my breasts as if searching for that light he swore he saw in me, as if he could reach in and take it, bottle it up, and put it on display for all to admire as his.

He hadn't even realized I had stopped responding to his touch, just as oblivious as ever. "Stop," I said, making sure to enunciate the word.

"Come on, Keira. Really?" His hands stayed on me, one lightly tracing circles over my panties in entirely the wrong area, waiting for me to cave.

Had this type of behavior worked on me in the past? Had I always been this shallow? Had he? And why, all of a sudden had it started to bother me?

Whatever the reason, I cared now, and I wanted him off me.

"Really," I said with dead-serious conviction. It didn't matter how far along we were, I could say no at any point, and he needed to respect that.

His hands flew off me with an unbelieving scoff as I slid out from under him, refastening my jeans and adjusting my top.

Why had I not trusted my instincts? I knew I wanted to end things with Harlan, especially after Prism. Why had I talked myself out of it? I had always been a shiny accessory to him, just like everything else in his life. "We're done."

"I knew it," he said, looking as if I just dumped an ice-cold bucket of water on him, equal parts annoyed, shocked, and offended. "I knew there was someone else. Someone else you are doing this for."

"Yes," I said, finally agreeing with him. "Me."

— ·((· ● ·))· —

This was it. The moment I finally lost it—the moment I chose the world beyond my closed eyelids over the life Harlan offered me.

I wanted to see Rowen again, learn the secrets that haunted him, and discover more about the dying parts of the forest.

I would be committed soon enough, wrapped in a strait-jacket, drugs shoved down my throat. Even electroshock therapy wouldn't be too out of the question.

I might as well lean in and enjoy every moment before it was all taken away from me. I couldn't hide this forever. Eventually, people would notice. I had been fighting it for so long, what would be the harm in going along with it for a little while, giving in and surrendering to the madness?

The bellowing rational voice within me screamed and thrashed, refusing to accept that I had just lost my mind. But a smaller tentative voice told me I had just found it.

I went to sleep that night, determined to find Rowen and demand answers.

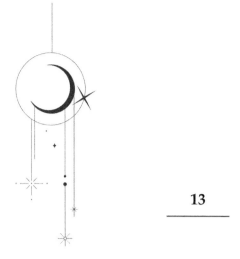

13

I opened my eyes, instantly hit with the panic of not knowing where I was.

This constant state of disorientation had come to be expected, though I doubted I'd ever get used to it. But I wondered: would it inevitably lead me down a shiny gold road to insanity, or did this all stem from a mind long planted with seeds of madness?

I guess it's impossible to draw such a line through circles of infinite regress. Either way, I had already accepted the web of my own making last night when I ended things with Harlan. I remembered the indignant look on his face as I walked out the door. But now was not the time to dwell on the past.

As my senses expanded to my new surroundings, I noticed I was lying on a cushioned bed stacked with light-knitted blankets and pillows. A sheer white net canopied the mattress, enveloping me like petals around a pistil.

I looked beyond the netting to the wall in front of me, only to realize it wasn't a typical wall at all but a wooden framework curving up and around me in a dome-shaped interior.

I was in some sort of earthy sphere.

My next startling realization was that I wasn't alone. A man sat crouched in front of the bed, staring at me. Even though I had never seen him before, he looked relieved to see me awake.

I sat up with a gasp, frantically searching for anything that could be used as a weapon.

"My apologies, star-touched. I didn't mean to frighten you," he said, tranquil as running water over smooth brook stones.

Something about him was familiar, but my mind struggled to pinpoint what. He was striking with his silken white hair and cool gypsum skin gleaming with sapphire undertones; I was sure that if I'd seen him before, I would have remembered.

What did he call me? And were his ears slightly pointed?

I'd have to unravel that later. Right now I needed to figure out what the hell was going on.

I was projecting the body language of a woman who would do whatever it takes to get out of here alive, but the quiet kindness emanating from the man's dark eyes calmed and relaxed me.

"My name is Takoda. You are safe here with the Wyn. I am a healer. I watched over you as the sun rose."

I wasn't sure whether or not to thank him. Aside from Rowen, I'd never seen anyone in my dreams. This was uncharted territory.

Takoda offered up his empty arms in a gesture of goodwill and asked, "May I see something? No harm shall befall you by my hand."

I was beyond skeptical, but maybe this healer could help figure out what was wrong with me, so I agreed with a terse nod.

Acknowledging my permission, the healer slowly reached inside the netted drapery and hovered his palm a few inches above my chest. He looked much younger than the typical person with entirely white hair; there wasn't a single wrinkle or crease on his beautiful face.

His eyes closed and his head cocked slightly to the side. "Hmm," he sounded displeased as his eyebrows pulled together, and he retracted his hand. "You sing of a struggled awakening. Rest here, while I let him know you have roused."

He turned to leave, but I grabbed his forearm, which was tight, lean, and corded in my hand. I hoped he got the gist that I wanted answers, and I wanted them now. He stopped and turned back at me, his high cheekbones prominent on his long, slender face.

Secretly wondering if this mystery person could be Rowen, I asked, "Let who know?"

"The one who searches for you each night," he said as if that was answer enough.

"Why is he looking for me?" I asked, hoping I might finally learn something useful.

Rowen mentioned others would come for me and, in so many words, said they would be dangerous, but he had yet to say who or why.

"To make sure another doesn't find you first," Takoda said gravely, heaving a sigh deep from his chest.

I swallowed at the lump in my throat. That did not sound good.

Was I in danger? It didn't feel like it, but it was best to be on my guard anyway.

Without another word, Takoda exited the room through a circular wooden door that rotated around a central shaft. He was so swift and light on his feet that I barely registered the movement, and I sat there for a few startling moments waiting for him to return.

Shaking out of my stupor, I hauled myself out of the bed, refusing to sit idly by and wait for answers to be given to me. I walked determinedly toward the revolving door and followed suit of the healer.

Once outside, I blinked at the dim yellow sun in the sky and marveled at the sight before me: dozens of teardrop-shaped villas surrounded me, sprouting from the ground like a garden of wooden flower buds. Connecting each forest bungalow were stepping stones and spiraling pathways that begged to be walked upon barefoot. Other structures made from fluid branches sat upon stilts or high up in the trees with natural open-air balconies and elevated walkways that dripped with leaves and greenery.

The architecture blended seamlessly with the environment, winding and bending along the natural curves of the earth. It was as if the land hadn't been disturbed in the slightest as the village melted into the scenery. From the wooden buildings to the evergreen vines crawling up every surface, it all flowed together seamlessly. Even the moss cushioned everything in place, settling the village in a deep comforting sigh.

Tumbled glass sun-catchers and tapestries hung from leafy-covered pergolas, and wind chimes tinkled and swayed with every gust of wind. Tightly woven baskets of all shapes and sizes were stored at the base of every home and seemed to glint with shimmering iridescent thread. Some were haphazardly stacked tall, while others appeared filled with herbs, grains, and vegetables.

Surrounding one side of the village were massive mountains and forest canopies that caressed the top of the sky. On the other, a dark sparkling ocean scalloped the shore, scattered with rock monoliths and vertical sea stacks.

Even though the sun was out, it was subdued and cast the sky in a pale purple glow. But what shocked me most was that the stars were still visible in the daylight. Thousands of celestial lights twinkled like the brightest diamonds against the golden-purple hue. And in the light of day, the glowing plants billowed like translucent fabrics dyed in hues of sea glass.

I had stepped into paradise.

Walking through the village, I passed its inhabitants going about their day, and by now, I'd attracted quite the crowd. I noticed they all had the same beautiful milk-white hair, varying shades of cool under-toned skin, and pointed ears as Takoda.

The villagers were all clad in neutral and earth-toned articles of clothing that blended simple designs for freedom, comfort, and practicality. The attire ranged from fringed and knotted dresses, wrap-around skirts, harem pants, and singlet tops to laced vests, trousers, and scarves with hoods. Almost everyone donned crystal beads around their necks, braided into their hair, or slung around their waists. Many had feathers, flowers, leaves, and shells dangling from various parts of their hair or attire as well.

The Wyn people were free, ethereal, and inherently part of the wild nature in which they lived, but something akin to despair glinted in their eyes.

I didn't see Takoda anywhere as more and more villagers emerged and gathered around me. Men, women, and children pointed and whispered, and I could feel their dark umber eyes assessing me, questioning me. They all seemed curious of my presence, but they remained at an inquisitive distance.

Embarrassment flushed through me as I became painfully aware of my appearance. My brown hair was pulled into a messy bun, and I was barefoot, wearing essentially only my favorite sweater and a pair of black running shorts.

I continued to search the area, hoping to see someone I knew because this was getting awkward.

Finally, I spotted Takoda. He was much taller than I would have guessed as his long statuesque frame walked towards me with gazelle-like grace, and by his side was an older woman with an ornate walking stick. Despite her cane and age-withered body, she walked with regal authority. The crowd hushed upon her arrival, and I could immediately tell she was highly revered amongst the village.

She wore a plain ankle-length frock that flowed from her thin limbs, but that's where the simplicity ended. Circling her brow was an exquisite smoky quartz headdress adorned with strands of precious stones. They dangled from one side of her crown to the other, covering her neck and chest in varying lengths of shimmering necklaces. And the sleek obsidian cane by her side stood tall, tipped with an upturned crescent moon.

Magnificent, commanding, and implicitly authoritative, the woman walked right up to me; her intense stare making me stand straighter.

By the way she navigated the world with her walking stick, I could tell she was blind or nearly there. But the power emanating from her every pore was palpable; strength a part of her very essence.

She was fierce to behold.

"So you're the disturbance lingering at my doorstep," she said, shocking me with her blunt address. She spoke as if she already knew me. "Welcome to the Wyn, child, though I can't say for how long. It is up to the Summit to decide how the fate of your stars aligns with ours." Her voice was sure and resounding, with only a hint of the many years lived.

I shot a glance to Takoda, waiting for an explanation or introduction. "Nepta is the heart, voice, and eyes of our village," he said, gesturing to the formidable woman standing before me. "Born under the Astrellan black moon, master of energy, and speaker of the night, she is the Elven-head of the Wyn people."

The etiquette for how to respond to such an introduction was beyond me. Do I curtsy? Do I bow? Somehow, nothing felt adequate. "Thank you for allowing me into your home," I said, hoping that was a safe place to start.

"Indeed, outsiders are rare to our village," she responded,

and I sensed something deep behind her opaque eyes dissecting my very essence, peeling away at the shadows I used to protect myself. "Your presence demands explanation. Why are you here? Have you come to spread the sickness that devours these lands?"

My blood ran cold. "No, I—"

"Do you possess markings of any kind upon your flesh?"

"Um...I don't think so."

"Who sent you?"

"No one—"

"Are you aware of the Synodic Prophecy?"

"The what?"

"The star-cast prophecy that speaks of a returning light?"

"No, but—"

One by one, she bombarded me with similarly brusque questions, barely registering my answers before demanding yet another reply to something I knew absolutely nothing about.

"This is one of the last thriving lands in the territory, and I refuse to watch it succumb to the sickness closing in around us. You will not be the cause of that fall."

I was stunned silent, grasping at how to respond like a stage actor struggling for their next line, leaving an enthralled audience waiting on the edge of their seats. Everyone was watching and waiting as if I knew what to say or understood any of this. "I have no desire to harm you or your people in any way."

"I'm supposed to trust the word of a half-faded creature such as yourself? Even now, you wane like the fading moon."

My body flinched; Nepta saw me with much more than her eyes, and it unnerved me that the masks I hid behind didn't stand a chance against her. She could into the deepest parts of my soul, could read me as plainly as an open book. I'd always felt half alive, and here she was outright confirming it.

"She could be who the Synodic Prophecy spoke of," Takoda said.

"The prophecy spoke of a son, not a daughter." Nepta motioned at me with exhausted regret. "And she said it herself. There are no such markings upon her body. Our hope must be found elsewhere. I have more at stake than the life of one girl, however strange her sudden appearance to this land may be."

Takoda looked at me with a sigh. "Whatever she is, she is stirring the forest. Never have we heard of so many summoning-demons on our borders."

"There is only one capable of such conjurings, and what Erovos could want with this young creature is still a mystery, but it cannot bode well. She must remain here until the Summit decides what's to be done with her," Nepta commanded with finality, each wrinkle on her face a hard battle fought and won.

Being publicly exposed, embarrassed, and put on the spot like this was a nightmare all of its own, and I pulled at the hem of my sleeve, wishing I could disappear.

Everyone around me seemed uneasy as well, shifting like disturbed seafoam upon the water. I didn't blame them, I'd just been accused of bringing demons to their sanctuary. But I quickly realized they weren't moving from ill-ease at all. They were parting for someone making their way to the front of the crowd.

A dark presence I'd recognize anywhere maneuvered through the white-haired strangers, and my breath caught in my throat.

Rowen had been here the entire time? Witnessing my verbal and very public trial without so much as saying a word? It couldn't be true what they were saying. Surely he would set the record straight.

But his intentions were unreadable, and he didn't even spare me a glance as he walked into the circle of spectators. His brown hair fell in thick tendrils around his stern face, and his tan skin was brushed with the slightest of sun-kissed glows.

The contrast of Rowen standing amongst the Wyn people was glaringly evident, the only thing they had in common was the type of clothing they wore.

He clearly wasn't born into this village, but the Wyn seemed to accept him all the same, and I couldn't help but wonder about the series of events that led him to live here.

Rowen finally met my surprised stare, and my skin surged with a heat that shot to my belly, but he barely acknowledged my existence before turning to Nepta. "For reasons unknown, summoning-demons are drawn to her. She still goes undetected since each summoning has been destroyed, but more will surely come," he said, and my knees almost buckled. "Erovos' ignorance of her could be all the advantage we need over him. She could prove...useful."

"If Erovos truly is the one behind these demons, it's a miracle he hasn't found her yet," Takoda chimed in again.

"I'd say a little more than a miracle," Rowen pointed out wryly.

Hearing these two men speak so freely jogged my memory of where I'd heard Takoda's voice before. The night of Prism, after I made it to bed. Rowen had punched a hole in a wall as Takoda tried to calm him, all the while I had been an invisible spectator. Mute. Unheard. And unseen.

I hadn't been able to speak my mind then, and I'd be damned if I was going to let that happen again now.

"I would like everyone to stop talking about me as if I weren't here," I demanded, glaring at all three culprits. This may not be real, but I refused to be regarded as air, as if I couldn't speak for myself. "Can someone please tell me what's going on?"

"Take her and prepare her. She must be brought before the

Summit tonight," Nepta commanded, waving her arm in dismissal.

Complying with her orders, the crowd broke apart slowly, whispering and glancing back before returning to their daily lives. A younger boy passed in front of me with eager curiosity. His messy hair framed a wide, blinking face that was open and bright, receptive to the world and all its yet-to-be-found treasures. He flashed me a deep-dimpled grin before darting away.

"Sleep well, princess?" Rowen asked, seeming to suddenly remember my presence. He remained several feet away, his clear green eyes taking me in from a distance.

After our experience together at Weir Falls, I thought his cold exterior would have thawed somewhat, but he was as distant as ever, looking at me as though his fingers hadn't been down my throat. Or that we hadn't felt every inch of each other on the ground of the red forest.

"What was that all about?" I asked, shaking off his cavalier demeanor.

"You have much to hear and understand, star-touched," Takoda answered. "It will take time to fully comprehend."

"Comprehend what?" I asked, my voice on the verge of agitation. "Could someone just spit it out already?"

"Perhaps we should go somewhere more private." Takoda nodded to the groups of people lingering and watching intently.

I nodded, eager not to have an audience. I already felt like a fish out of water. Everyone seemed to know what was going on except me.

Rowen and Takoda guided me away from the prying eyes of the village, leading me to a nearby clearing surrounded by imposing trees. The air buzzed with the energy of what they were about to tell me. I braced myself, but somehow I knew I could never fully prepare for what they were about to say.

"You are not from Luneth, are you?" Takoda asked gently.

"Luneth?" I asked, the name rolling off my tongue like a trea-sured pebble from a lost and ancient world. "So the place from my dreams does have a name."

"Star-touched, you are not dreaming. I believe you possess the gift of walking between worlds. An astral traveler," Takoda said plain as day. "Living in your world but tied intrinsically here, to Luneth."

Yup. Definitely wasn't ready for that.

"Oh," I said brilliantly.

Takoda, sympathetic to my stunned processing, nodded. "Yes. Do you have any idea as to why? The Summit will want an explanation for your presence to this land."

Rowen's tactics of explaining were not as delicate as Tako-da's. "You were making quite a scene in the forest," he said harshly, his eyes tracing over my bare skin as if it offended him. Takoda flashed him a silencing glance, but he continued on, unfazed. "You'll be lucky if others don't come looking for you."

I had wanted, craved, and sensed there was more to my life, but this? This was too much.

What they were telling me was too crazy, too absurd to be real, yet it explained so much of what I'd been going through. I'd even suspected it for a moment myself: the dreams that felt so real they had me guessing which life was the imposter, the moments it took me longer to realize where I was, or where I felt too big for my own skin. How my whole life I felt like a sleepwalker.

Was this me truly waking up?

The logical part of my brain wanted to deny it. All of it. This grandiose delusion that I could walk between worlds was clearly my mind's way of coping with the mental break that cracked down my psyche like a serrated glacier.

It just wasn't possible.

And while I knew I shouldn't acknowledge or encourage

these fantasies in any way, I still found myself saying, "If I'm a danger to you all, I shouldn't come back here."

Tension ridged throughout Rowen's wide shoulders and his eyes flared with fleeting panic. "A darkness greater than you can imagine is descending upon us all, there is nowhere for you to hide anymore. We have no idea what you are. You could be a deadly tool in the wrong hands or a useful one in ours. Better we discover what you are before anyone else."

"You said you had to find me first, that others will come looking for me. Who are they?" I asked, glancing between the two men expectantly. But before either of them could respond, a crash of wood erupted from the wall of trees, and the ground began to tremble beneath our feet.

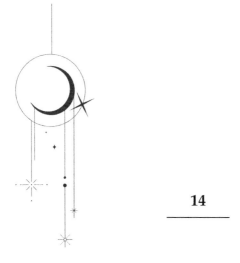

14

A large figure barreled from forest, rattling the earth with each pounding footfall. The hulking creature was almost certainly a man, though he was bigger than any human I'd ever seen. He had to be about nine feet tall, and his full, inconceivable mass was charging right towards us like a raging bull.

Hackles raised, my first instinct was to bolt back to the safety of the village. The man's massive body was large and clumsy—there was a chance we could outrun him, but Rowen and Takoda stood firm, refusing to relinquish an inch of ground.

"You are not welcome here," Rowen warned with a growl, holding his footing with unwavering dominance. The man nearly crashed into us as he stumbled to a halt, darkening us within the shadow of his towering form.

The intruder wore filthy pants and a cut-off shirt, torn in places where his bulging frame burst through the meager fabric. His patchy hair was shorn to the scalp, and one side of his face drooped severely down into a frozen scowl, emphasizing his wildly shifting eyes that had yet to land on me.

Rowen's fingers itched over his sheathed weapon but his

voice remained impossibly steady and calm. "Leave now, Graem. We have no wish to harm you."

"I am here for the Synodic Son," the giant's voice blundered as if he was speaking around a mouth full of stones. His eyebrows puckered up in excitement, and a grimace of a smile spread across his misshapen face. "Give him to me. In exchange I will grant you a swift death. Something my Lord will not bestow to those who get in his way."

"You are gravely mistaken. No sign of The Marked has been seen here," Takoda said, somehow even more collected than Rowen. How they both remained so stoic and level-headed was beyond me. I was a shaking ball of nerves that wanted nothing more than to run as fast and far away as possible, but I found I couldn't bring myself to leave the two men beside me. Some part of me trusted they knew what they were doing, even if I didn't.

The man called Graem faltered for the first time, unsure what to believe, and his forehead puckered in confusion. "He is here," he insisted. "He must be." His eyes began to whirl in his head like a crazed animal, and his breathing became erratic. Chaos brewed just underneath his thick skin, threatening to boil over and destroy anything in his path.

The men beside me shot each other tense glances.

I saw now why they were handling this giant with kid's gloves. He was unstable, and worse yet, unpredictable.

I was relieved I hadn't run back to the heart of the village. Who knew the irreparable damage he could inflict on the town and its innocent people had I led him back there.

"The Marked is naught but a failed prophecy," Takoda said, still trying to placate the giant. "He never arrived and never will."

"Erovos sensed his summoning-demons awakening in this forest. Where is he?" the colossal man bellowed in confusion, pushing his vocal cords far past their intended purpose as he tore and pulled at his head.

Both men from the Wyn village slowly stepped together, creating a barrier between the ticking time bomb of a man and myself.

"Go now, and we will let you return to your Lord unharmed," Rowen yelled over the distorted wails. "Be sure to report back your findings, or lack thereof. And never return here again."

My skin prickled in anticipation, and I willed the giant to leave. But Graem's whirring gaze shot through the shoulders of the men between us and landed directly on me. "What is this?" he asked, reaching for me as if I was a glass figurine in a display case.

Fast as a whip of lightning, Rowen and Takoda drew their blades, snapping back the burly arm that grabbed for me.

It was then that the giant lost control, and Graem thrashed his flailing limbs like a tree in a hurricane.

With no way to predict his erratic movements, the back of his massive forearm caught Takoda, flinging him through the air as if he were a mere sack of flour. The healer landed across the field in a graceful roll, and my eyes shot back to Rowen in dread.

Graem swatted again, but Rowen was faster and ducked just in time. The giant's swings were wide and unwieldy, and the force behind his momentum was ferocious.

I watched in terror as he swiped again at Rowen, missing him by a breath. The time it took the giant to recover from his over-swing was just the opening Rowen needed. And in one quick motion that I almost missed, Rowen slashed his small ax down, opening the meaty flesh of the giant's thigh.

Graem's scream cut through the forest like a knife, splitting my eardrums. And in his pain-addled fury, his arms became dual pendulums, careening towards us with no rhyme or reason.

Takoda sprinted to the fight as a mighty blow connected

with Rowen's ribs, knocking the wind out of him. I screamed as Graem lifted Rowen by his neck and waist and hurled him directly into Takoda. The collision was brutal, smacking both men to the ground in a rolling ball of limbs.

Now nothing stood between the imposing giant and me.

Before I had time to think or move, he snatched my arm in a bone-crushing grip that stole a cry from my mouth. He yanked me towards him, and pain roared in my shoulder as he hefted me up to his towering line of sight.

I was close enough to make out every scar and mark on his distorted face. His dull moss-colored eyes bore into mine. "Are you him? Are you The Marked?" he spat at me, and I nearly gagged when his fetid breath washed over me.

"Do I look marked to you?" I said through clenched teeth, kicking my legs beneath me. But the more I struggled, the more my arm twisted in his grasp.

I was sure my shoulder was about to be pulled from its socket, but the threads of my sweater gave way first, and the sound of my collar ripping filled the air.

Graem froze, the smile of an idea creeping across his bunched features. "Only one way to find out," he said, bringing his free hand up to my shirt.

I thrashed against him, ignoring the debilitating pain shooting up my arm like white-hot fire as he grappled for purchase on my sweater. His daft fingers were tearing and bruising, but he eventually managed to get a grip on the neckline of my shirt, and my body jerked as he violently ripped the fabric from my skin, baring the top half of my body in nothing but my black bralette.

Graem's intrusive stare roved over me, lingering at the swells of my breasts, the indent of my waist, and the contours of my hips. His expression turned to confusion, then indignation. "This cannot be The Marked. This is a *woman*," he wailed as he shook me like a rag doll, rattling my brain and clattering my teeth.

He was seconds away from crushing my bones or snapping my arm, if he didn't shake me to death first.

I slammed my eyes closed, waiting for the inevitable break, when a stir of air washed over my cheek, followed by a sickening thud, then an ear-splitting wail.

My eyes squinted open to the arc of Rowen's ax embedded in the beefy wrist of the man who held me to his face—the blade finding its mark mere inches from my nose. Graem didn't release me as he pried the ax from his hand and tossed it to the ground. A surge of terror and adrenaline rippled through my body like a gravitational wave, and the giant shrieked again.

The last thing I remembered was being violently thrown to the ground, Rowen running towards me as the world tilted and darkness closed in.

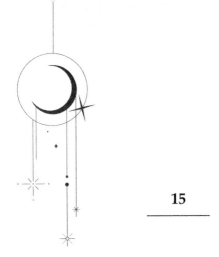

15

I woke up in my room with a jolt, my heart beating out of my chest and my shoulder aching from sleeping on it wrong.

That's it! I needed to see a doctor or finally work up the nerve to talk to my parents, to come clean that the dreams were back and potent as ever. This was bad, very bad. I couldn't go one measly night without having overly vivid dreams, and now I was waking with body aches and heart palpitations.

I pushed myself up from my sheets only to feel a sharp pain in my wrist, and I hissed between my teeth. I gently cradled my tender arm to my chest, noticing my forearm was severely bruised and swollen. I examined the bruise more closely, and to my utter shock, it was in the perfect shape of a hand.

Wincing, I wrapped my own hand around the welt to measure it against the markings. It was much bigger than my own—there was no way I could have done this to myself.

Suddenly, I was hit with the momentum of worlds colliding in a crash of spiraling stars and vines that bloomed into sparks of luminous matter. And I lost my breath.

"It's real. It's all real," I gasped aloud.

My chest felt tight, too tight, and I couldn't breathe. I began running my hands through my hair in building panic. Every conversation, every look, every touch, was *real*.

I kicked off the blankets and started pacing back and forth in my room. In my frantic state, I accidentally hit my knee on my dresser and let out a curse. My parents would be telling me I was having a panic attack right about now, and yeah, no shit I was. I just found out my dreams were really happening and that the forests I visited in my sleep were actual places.

I wanted to fall apart, but I needed to pull it together, especially if I was going to make it back to the Wyn village. Back to Rowen. I found him once on my own, I could find him again.

I slowly pieced together what I could, including what little they were able to tell me before that giant came and nearly mangled me to death. Takoda believed I had the gift of traveling between worlds. An astral traveler.

That would explain the dreams that had always felt too real; the silver petal I woke up with in my hand all those years ago; and the ruined mud-caked shoes. I had probably been slipping in and out of Luneth my entire life.

But it had all come to an end when my parents intervened. Whatever drugs they'd given me must have been powerful enough to suppress my ability to travel. Lord knows, it extinguished more than that; I was a shell of a person while on them —a woman with two worlds yet not a single spark of life.

I hadn't taken a pill in years. Why were the dreams returning nine years later? Had the drugs taken that long to leave my system? Had they caused irreversible damage?

Somehow I was now able to return to Luneth, but Nepta said I was a half-faded creature. Was that a lasting side effect I would have to live with for the rest of my life?

Regardless of why, I couldn't stop marveling at the fact it was all real, it had always been real, and I let out a combination of a sob and a laugh.

With a startled gasp I noticed Natalie in my doorway, watching me with eyes as wide as saucers. Holding my throbbing knee, I froze as she scanned me up and down, no doubt taking in my crazed expression and bruised arm.

Her face twisted in horror. "What happened?"

"I'm fine," I managed to say in a rushed squeak. "I hit my knee on the dresser."

"It's obvious everything is not fine. What happened to you? It looks like you've been mauled." She took a step closer. "You've been screaming."

"I hit my knee," I said again, hoping it would explain the scream.

"Over and over again? Keira, you're scaring me. I think I should call your parents," she said, lifting her phone.

I cursed the day I invited her out for dinner with my family. My parents had taken to Natalie instantly. She learned all about them, what they did, their practice together. She'd been fascinated, asking question after question all night long.

By the time dinner ended, she and my mother had exchanged numbers, acting like long-lost friends. "Call me if you ever need anything," I remembered her telling Natalie. It was always so much easier for her to talk to total strangers than it was to her own daughter. I thought bringing her would be a nice buffer between mine and my parents' skirted conversations, not something she could use against me later.

"No, I'll be alright," I said frantically as I shook off the memory. "Natalie. I'm honestly fine. Actually, I haven't felt this good in a really long time." I hoped she could hear the sincerity in my voice because I wasn't losing Luneth. Not again. "Please don't say anything to them."

She dropped her phone to her side reluctantly. "Fine, but if this happens again, I *will* call them."

Her intrusion into my personal affairs was not her place, and she was beginning to feel like a glorified guard, but if she called my parents, I would be committed. With a press of a button, Natalie could take it all away from me.

"It won't," I said, hoping I convinced her.

"What is going on with you?"

"Please. Can you just trust me?"

"One more scream, Keira, one more and I'm calling them," she said in warning as she retreated from my bedroom, and I knew she meant it. "Make sure you at least wrap that arm."

I'd been holding my breath, and I collapsed to the floor as soon as she was out of sight. Everything was crashing down on me, and I was trying to process whether I felt scared or relieved. Maybe a little bit of both.

I needed to see Rowen again.

The problem was, I wasn't even remotely tired, and there was no way I was going to wait around until I fell asleep, to stand by helplessly and see where my traveling deemed to plop me next.

I would have to force the hand, take control, and choose where I wanted to go. No more waking up lost and confused. I'd had enough of that.

There were instances my body had been active on Earth while some part of me existed on Luneth like an astral projection, which accounted for my blackouts in time. But there were others where I'd been entirely present on Luneth's plane, both in body and soul, hence the muddied slippers and bruised arm.

Perhaps if I was intentional with the crossing, my body would follow suit.

It was an interesting theory, one I planned on testing, but before I went anywhere, I needed a shower—to wash the disgusting feel and smell of Graem off me. His simple mind had struggled to comprehend that I was a woman. He'd been so sure I was the man he'd been expecting. But what did I have in connection with this mysterious male prophecy everyone was talking about? It seemed no one knew.

I quietly tiptoed down the hall, not wanting to draw Natalie's attention. The last thing I needed was her bombarding me with more questions I could scarcely answer myself.

I finally reached the bathroom, closed the door behind me, and turned the lock. Flipping around, I rested my head against the sturdy surface of the door and tried to breathe. I looked down at my hands; they were shaking. I must be in shock.

I couldn't believe how close I'd come to dying: just now with Graem, back at Weir Falls, and who knew how many other countless times when I'd been trapped in the darkness. I'd been blissfully unaware that my body could indeed suffer physical consequences when in my dream-like state, and my stomach turned at the thought. I dashed to the toilet and retched, heaving painfully until there was nothing left in my stomach.

Trembling and exhausted, I stripped out of my shorts, bra, and underwear, and threw them in the trash bin.

I entered the shower and sat under the deluge of scalding water, waiting for my shaking to subside. This was it, my time to reconsider. To turn away from Luneth forever and go back to the life I knew, as empty and hollow as it was. Or, I could return and help fight the impending darkness that closed in around the Wyn people.

The choice was finally mine to make.

But I felt Rowen, the land, and the village all over me, *within* me. I could never deny Luneth. Not again.

I had made my choice long ago.

———— ·(·c·●·)·)· ————

Stepping out of the tub, I left trailing wet footprints along the patterned tile as I grabbed a towel and wrapped it securely around my body.

Standing in front of the foggy mirror, I swiped my hand across the steamy surface, revealing the band of my brow.

My eyes!

Harlan had mentioned something about them looking different, but I hadn't really noticed it until now. They used to be dark and cloudy. My dad would joke that my eyes hid my secrets, and who knew what mysterious creature swam just below the opaque surface.

They were much lighter now, almost glowing with small freckles of light.

My dad had been right. Something was swimming in the grey depths, and I could see that long-dormant creature reaching for the surface. Waiting to be unleashed.

The physical change frightened me, and I shook my hands out absentmindedly as my fingertips sizzled with panicky jitters. I returned to my room and dressed in a pair of black running leggings and an off-the-shoulder sweater that hid my ghastly bruise. I let my hair air-dry, bringing out my natural waves before pulling it back into a messy ponytail. The shorter pieces slipped from my grasp and fell to frame my face.

I sent out a few emails and put my auto-response to *away*. Work was the last thing I wanted to worry about as I dealt with the realization that I'd been traveling to another world. I could definitely take time off for that.

I dimmed the lights in my room, shut the curtains, and sat on my floor with my eyes closed and back straight. Resting my hands comfortably on my knees, I slowed my breathing to a gentle pulse and cleared my mind of everything except for one thing—Rowen.

I was surprised by how arranged my thoughts were.

Normally, they were confused, jumbled balls of yarn, but in this moment I knew exactly what I wanted. Behind my eyes, the tangled mess unraveled, revealing a single strand of silvery starlight. I knew I only had to pull on the string, follow it, and it would take me where I wanted to go.

I gently ran my fingers along the beautiful thread of consciousness, the refracted bits of stardust dancing and sparkling along my skin. My breath was so shallow I was barely breathing at all.

I tugged at the mesmerizing string, and the moment I did, I felt a whisper of hesitation. Would I be able to come back? Would I be stuck in Luneth forever?

But it was too late. I was already falling through stars of dust, light, and shadow.

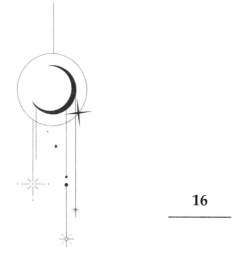

16

A smug grin lifted my cheeks at the success of my first intentional crossing.

I was in Luneth, sitting in the same straight-back position from moments ago in my bedroom. The exact dome, bed, and netting from earlier today surrounded me, but a different gaze greeted me back to this strange new world. Instead of Takoda's kind smile, it was Rowen's worried scowl.

"Thank the Spirits," he exhaled in evident relief as his forest eyes burned with the fire that crackled in the center of the room.

Careful not to put any pressure on my tender wrist, I slid across the blankets, stopping when the slit of the canopy draped down around me. Now face to face with Rowen, his eyes leveled up to mine through the thick of his lashes. He sat on a wooden chair at the foot of the bed, leaning forward with his elbows on his knees. The low neckline of his shirt billowed forward, and the nearby firelight danced across the strong planes of his face, arms, and exposed chest, accentuating the deep cuts of his precise body.

I saw him through new eyes, knowing he was more than just

a figment of my imagination, and I studied him further, attempting to decipher the shadows that leapt across his face.

"What happened? Is Takoda alright?" I asked, snapping out of my trance, knowing I wouldn't solve the puzzle that was Rowen tonight.

"We saw you were appearing, and he left to brew you a healing tea—to help with any injuries you sustained from Graem," he said, his expression twisting with disgust.

"What happened to him?"

"We let him go. He's more useful to us as a messenger than a corpse," Rowen said with a strained edge. "It was one of the hardest things I've ever done—not killing him, watching him scurry back into the forest. After he threw you down, I was frightened by how still you were. When you leave, you are gone in the blink of an eye, as if you were never there. This time you slowly flickered away. And honestly, I don't know what's worse— you vanishing in an instant or slowly slipping through my fingers. I wanted to kill him for what he did to you."

"I'm fine," I said, strangely grateful for the events that led me to know this was all real.

Rowen sighed and slowly took my hand in his large calloused palm. I held my breath. He'd never handled me this lightly before, and I questioned the sudden gentleness. He carefully pushed up the sleeve of my sweater, his fingertips tracing along the translucent skin of my wrist until he revealed the entirety of my marred and swollen arm.

His eyes darkened. "You are not fine."

"It's just one bruise," I said, surprised by his keen attention to my body.

"No, Keira, it's not." He hooked one finger along the neckline of my shirt and gently tugged the material down.

Confused, I followed his gaze. I hadn't noticed before, but all across my chest and down my shoulder were dark sweeping bruises. Most likely from where Graem's clumsy fingers clawed at my neck as he tried to undress me.

"I should have killed him," he said vehemently, and it wasn't just the fire burning in his eyes now but a searing hot hatred.

His fingers lightly brushed against my collarbone, knocking my breath into hyperdrive. Usually he avoided physical contact if he could, but here he was reaching for me, touching me as if he needed to feel that I was just as alive and real as he was.

The walls of Rowen's measured control lowered as he flattened his palm against the bare skin of my chest. He trailed his hand at my neck, gently tracing the purple bruises as if willing to erase them with his touch. My heart hammered through my ribcage, and I wondered if he could feel its rampant beating. Somehow his touch was even more amplified now that I knew he was a man of flesh and blood, not dreams and mist.

With my chest rising and falling beneath his hand, I never took my eyes off his furiously pained expression. He looked to be torturing himself over what happened with Graem.

He was right. It was traumatic and violating, and I cringed at the thought of that giant's eyes and hands on me, tearing at my clothes, but Rowen's soothing touch was more powerful than Graem's, and it overrode the memory of being aggressively strip-searched.

I wanted to keep reveling in his comfort but he dropped his hand from my chest, frowning as if he still wanted blood in exchange for my abrasions. I frowned back, wanting to let him know I was stronger than my easily bruised skin.

"I came here intentionally this time, Rowen. Even after what happened with Graem," I said firmly. "I chose to come back on my own terms. I could have denied whatever it is that I am, fought it, or laid around waiting to see where I appeared next, but I didn't. I set my mind to coming here, and that's exactly what I did."

Rowen's rigid body loosened a fraction, and he raised a dark eyebrow. "You mean you set your intention to coming here, to this exact spot?" he asked with interest, his eyes casually darting from my face to where I sat.

"Well, no, not exactly..." I paused as it dawned on me. "Why? Whose bed is this?"

A dark smile flashed across his stubbled face. "Mine."

The blood drained from my cheeks. I had unconsciously willed myself into Rowen's bed, and not even for the first time today. I'd been here before I truly set my intention on seeing him again. Somewhere deep in my mind, I had always been searching for Rowen. But before I could fully admit it to myself, my body had gone ahead and beat me to it, bringing me right to his sheets.

I felt betrayed and exposed by my conspicuous body. It appeared she had a mind of her own.

"Imagine my surprise when, after all this time, you end up right in my bed," he said, a dark smirk lifting his lips.

I jumped, scrambling awkwardly through the tangled sheets and netted drapery. "Don't flatter yourself," I said, trying to regain my composure after tumbling from his bed as if it had caught aflame.

His molded body didn't move an inch, but he never took his eyes off me; they followed my every move and regarded me with no small amount of amusement. "Wouldn't dream of it."

He seemed awfully relaxed, whereas I felt like a supernova, building in pressure, on the verge of exploding.

Rowen stayed seated, peering up at me intently through his heavy lids. Now that I was up, I scanned the rest of his enchanting spherical room. The earthy space was brimming with living plants that hadn't been disturbed in the slightest, and the timber canopied roof leaked with the light of the stars.

Near his bed was a stack of worn, leather-bound books piled

one on top of the other, and I itched to open the deckled-edge pages. At the back of the dome was a pile of transportable cooking utensils, a waterskin, and a bedroll. He could be ready to flee and live in the woods at a moment's notice.

More bound books lined the shelves, along with heaps of loose parchment; sticks of charcoal, feathers, crystals; and various pointy objects that looked deadly if in the right hands.

My gaze circled back to his canopy-encased bed, where I noticed a talisman of sorts hanging from the middle of the netting. The outer frame came together in an intricate prism of twigs and shimmering twine, spiraling towards a shard of crystal.

It seemed I wasn't the only one who needed help sleeping.

There was a door to an en suite, a large wooden chest, and a small rack with hanging linen shirts and trousers. Beside the front door was a weapon rack housing a myriad of daggers, axes, and long blades.

I gulped at his lethal arsenal but wished I'd had a blade handy when Graem grabbed me.

"So," I said, remembering I came here for answers. "Graem paid a visit to collect me and kindly take me to this Erovos prick I've been hearing so much about?" I'd been able to piece at least that much together. "Who is he, and what does he want?"

Rowen let out a troubled breath. "Erovos is a conqueror of darkness over light and destroyer of balance. Only death and destruction follow in his wake. He must have learned of the prophecy and is searching for The Marked." Rowen stilled, his eyes lost in the flames. "And it appears you are now caught in the crosshairs."

"You think Graem will tell Erovos I'm here?"

"The prophecy speaks of a male, and he is certain it cannot be otherwise. Hopefully, that will hold him off for a while."

Suddenly, exhaustion overcame my body like a weighted

blanket. The realization of everything from the past few days finally caught up with me. First, my dreams were actually happening. Second, the man I'd been obsessing over for weeks was real. Third, I could walk between worlds. And last, perhaps the most frightening of all, someone was after me.

The door of the dome rotated open as Takoda entered, carrying a crystal mug. "It is good to see you again, star-touched. Drink. The pearl root will help with your ailments."

His words immediately reminded me of my pain. My swollen forearm ached, my shoulder throbbed, and my chest looked like someone had a field day with blue finger paint.

The rational part of my brain told me not to drink the tea, that I'd had way too many bad experiences drinking things I shouldn't, but the caring look on Takoda's face outweighed any further trepidation. I raised the cup to my face and inhaled the mixture of herbs, tea, and another scent I couldn't quite place but was natural and comforting.

Slowly I took a sip, then another, immediately feeling the effects as my discomfort cleared and my limbs filled with a warmth that spread to my every aching nerve. Takoda checked me for injuries and applied a cooling textured balm to my bruises.

"Thank you," I said, meaning it. The healing ointment and tea were already soothing my tense and battered body.

Takoda took the mug back from me and checked my pulse. "You need rest."

"You can sleep here," Rowen offered. "I'll sleep outside."

"No," I replied way too fast. "I mean, that's not necessary. I don't want to put you out of your own bed."

"Why?" He set his eyes on me with a hardness that wasn't there a moment ago when his hands were on me. "You already seem quite acquainted with it, Copeland," he said, cold and detached like it was a knee-jerk reaction to fill peaceful moments with unpleasantness.

If my eyes could scorch him where he stood, he'd be a heap of ash. "Well, I was going to suggest you sleep on the floor in here, but the dirt outside seems more fitting."

"As it happens, I quite enjoy sleeping under the stars," he said, side-eyeing me with no emotion while he hefted a rucksack over his shoulder.

I clenched my teeth. Why was he pulling me close one moment only to push me away the next?

Takoda disappeared through the circular door, shaking his head as if he was all too familiar with Rowen's mood swings.

Rowen exited closely behind him but stopped halfway through and turned to look at me. "Please be here in the morning. I'd hate to send a search party out to find you," he said, his forest eyes flashing through the darkness before he vanished.

Too tired to fight these sleeping arrangements with any real conviction, I brought myself back to Rowen's bed. Lying down, I could smell the masculine scent of his sheets wafting around me. It was comforting and robust, and I curled deeper into it.

I was about to let darkness sweep over me when I heard Rowen and Takoda right outside the dome. "How could Erovos have known she was here? All the summoning-demons have been destroyed." Rowen spoke furiously, and I could practically hear his pacing through the walls.

I fought to stay awake, wanting to hear more.

"It seems someone has betrayed us," Takoda answered solemnly. "But if Erovos was absolutely certain The Marked were here, he would not have sent the fool Graem."

"Agreed. Erovos must have sent him ahead as a scout. Whoever revealed this to Erovos had not yet known she is a woman."

"We have saved a bit of time where Erovos is concerned, but

others will become curious as word of her spreads. Secluded as we are, containing this information will not be easy, especially with a betrayer in our midst."

The wind knocked out of me at the revelation of his words. I'd barely had a chance to catch my bearings before a new piece of the puzzle was revealed to me—each more unimaginable than the last. There was someone in this village I couldn't trust. Had I seen their face in the crowd? Had I already met them? Despite how this land lowered my walls, I would have to be on guard.

I couldn't make out Rowen's immediate reply, but the words I heard next were coated in seething rancor. "When I find whoever did this, Takoda. I will kill them."

It sounded like he had just sworn an oath, an oath to the black pits of hell.

———— ·(C ●)·)· ————

The next day I woke to sunlight leaking through the dome and birds chirping in a strange yet beautiful harmony. The embers of the fire had long since extinguished and a cool breeze prickled along my skin, beckoning me out of bed. My aching limbs felt much better and my bruises were now only faint blemishes, but I was still tired. I'd had a deep sleep with absolutely no astral traveling so I'd assumed I would be more rested than this.

Finishing up in the en suite, containing a simple lavatory and sink, I noticed someone had laid clothes out for me on one of the wicker chairs. I changed into the leggings and dark blue vest that laced up the front and came to a point at my navel. I slipped on the waiting pair of boots, surprised by how well everything fit.

I exited Rowen's home, still stunned by the beauty of the village and mantle of day-lit stars. The chatter of everyday life immediately greeted me as men and women busily sorted herbs, prepared food, and stored spices into intricately woven baskets, while others sharpened tools, gathered timber, or carved away at pieces of wood.

Children squealed as they chased each other playfully, and little girls with white-plaited braids ran up to me, placing tiny flowers in my palm before skipping away like woodland sprites.

A child of about twelve bounded up to me and skid to a stop. I immediately recognized him as the boy who smiled at me after meeting Nepta.

His hair was cut short around his pointed ears, and his deep dimples were ever-present like the stars. He wore loose burlap pants bunched around the ankles and a sleeveless juniper tunic. I noticed he had stray twigs in his unruly hair, and his feet were bare and filthy. It looked like he'd just returned from an adventure of epic proportions, filled with hidden trails and secret hideaways.

"I'm Ven," he said, his brown eyes alight. "I saw you yesterday."

"I remember," I replied with a smile, and his grin widened.

"You slept past midday!" he exclaimed as he handed me a honey-drizzled biscuit wrapped in a wax leaf. "Rowen said he had better things to do than wait around all day for you, but he promised me that if I brought you to him when you woke, he'd teach me to throw like him."

I accepted Ven's offering and took a bite, savoring the rich flavors that oozed and melted on my tongue. "That's very sweet of you, Ven. Would it be alright with you if we left him waiting a bit longer?" I asked, annoyed with Rowen's hot-and-cold behavior.

The boy's smile nearly exploded at the prospect of a little mischief. He took hold of my free hand and began pulling me through the village. "How about I show you around?"

Impressed with my partner in crime, I allowed myself to be shepherded along by him. Plus, I was itching to explore this alluring new world, and a guided tour was as good as it could get. He tugged me excitedly behind him, so I quickened my pace, chuckling to myself as I took another bite of biscuit.

Ven spared no expense in describing every single thing within sight as we strolled through the sculptured walkways and open organic paths. It was information overload, but I made sure to file away the important bits about common trails and discernible landmarks.

Entirely mesmerized by the enchanting beauty all around me, I jerked to a stop, noticing soft globes of light floating above the ground. The spherical lanterns bobbed gently in the air as if votives on the ocean.

"What are those?" I asked wide-eyed and disbelieving, waving my hand under one of the levitating devices. I may have accepted the ludicrous idea that my dreams were real, but seeing something defy all gravity and logic still had the ability to shock me.

"These are luminorbs. They soak up the light of the sun during the day to provide us with sight in the darkness. Do you not have these where you're from?" he asked in surprise, as though they were as common as light switches.

"Definitely not," I huffed a laugh, unable to tear my eyes from the soft-lit orbs.

Ven drew my attention to a tucked-away path of white pebbled stones over clear blue water. "That's the way to the Sacred Vale," he said, his eyes squinting from the sun's reflection. "It's where you will meet with the Summit."

Surrounded by lush greenery and the strange translucent plants native to Luneth, the floating path called to me like a siren's song. I desperately wanted to know what lay beyond the bend of the watery walkway.

Nepta mentioned I needed to meet with their Summit and that they would determine my fate here with the Wyn people, but Graem had shown up, causing me to miss the engagement.

"What sort of things do they discuss?" I asked, trying to sound as nonchalant as possible, hoping to get a better picture of what to expect when I inevitably meet them. I had never been great at interviews and could scarcely imagine meeting the Summit of an entire village. It was daunting, to say the least.

"Ever since Rowen found you, you're all they have been talking about," he stated matter-of-factly as he picked up a round grey rock from the ground. He handed it to me, pointing out the hollowed center filled with tiny sparkling nodules that glittered in my hand like a star.

"It's lovely," I said, my fingers lightly tracing over the precious stones. The young boy took delight in my reaction, then removed the geode from my hands and placed it back where he found it. "Do you know what they're saying about me?"

"Nepta says you could be nothing more than a failed prophecy, twenty years too late. The village is on edge and wants to know why you're here." He stood up and scrunched his face, looking at me as if I had all the answers.

My throat constricted. I'd only just got here, but somehow I already cared deeply for the Wyn people. "I wish I knew. But something called me here, and it seems pretty adamant that I stay." It was a feeble answer, but it was all I had.

I was relieved he didn't press me for more as he said, "The look on people's faces when you finally entered our village and happened to be a girl!"

"What's wrong with me being a girl?" I asked defensively. This village couldn't have backward notions; their leader was a woman.

"Oh, nothing! We just heard so much about a Synodic Son that you showing up instead of him wasn't exactly what everyone was expecting," he replied with his big contagious smile.

Talking to Ven felt natural, easy—like the sibling I never had but desperately wanted, and I found I greatly enjoyed this kid's company.

We continued walking through the lush maze of pathways and homes. Heads turned everywhere we went as Ven introduced me to some of the villagers. Most nodded politely, some smiled at our passing, while others seemed worried or apprehensive. I couldn't blame them, they wanted to know why I was here, and honestly, I was just as curious.

The answer itched uncomfortably at the recesses of my mind, hidden deep within the shadows of grey matter, and even though my darkness had cleared, a pall still lingered in my memories. Before I could grasp what lay just beyond my reach, a massive white wolf came bounding around one of the homes, charging right toward us.

Without a second thought, I threw myself over Ven, shielding him from the fanged beast. I slammed my eyes shut, bracing for the stabbing pain of sharp teeth and razor claws. But the attack never came, and Ven laughed as he pushed out of the measly protection of my arms. He knelt before the wolf and scratched the thick hair behind its perked ears.

"It's only Sabra, my she-wolf," he said, pushing his nose deep into her snowflake-white fur that billowed like a field of wheat in the wind. Her eyes were the most piercing shade of amber, and she gazed into my soul as only an utterly wild thing can.

I offered her the back of my hand, making sure not to move a muscle as her shiny wet nostrils inhaled my scent. Her powerful sense of smell deemed me acceptable, and I gave her a good scratch behind the ear just as Ven had.

"I found her...well, she found me when she was just a pup."

I bent down before her and showered her with more pets

and scratches. She preened and panted, loving the attention. "She is absolutely magnificent."

"She is, and she knows it," Ven said adoringly as he stood up next to his majestic white wolf. They were quite a pair; the sweetly seated beast and standing young man. "Let's head over to the warrior's training grounds," he said with a mischievous glint in his eye, "I think you'll like it."

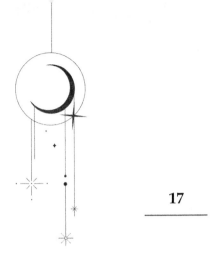

17

The training grounds were off to the far side of the village. The space was long yet ample and allowed for archery as well as spear and dagger throwing.

A few warriors were training in knife combat, honing and sharpening their skills with what looked to be jabbing and feigning exercises.

Suddenly, a gleam slashed through the air and caught my attention.

A woman my age with a long silver ponytail was in the thick of a practice battle against a man slightly larger than herself. I was mesmerized by her strength, litheness, and agility. Her strikes were exact and unforgiving, deadly like a cobra.

Darting, thrusting, and arcing into fierce blow after fierce blow, her partner could do nothing but retreat with each precise attack. Her hair whipped through the air like a second dagger, looking like it could slice just as easily too. There was barely a flush upon her light brown complexion with moonlit undertones.

"That's Dyani," Ven whispered, seeming to know exactly

where my eyes had landed. "She is one of our strongest warriors."

Dyani disarmed her opponent with a vicious swing and kicked him to the ground, leaving him panting in the dirt.

"That's her twin brother, Demil. Also a great fighter but second to his sister. Don't make her mad or you'll be the one on the ground."

My eyes took in her feminine warrior body dressed in traditional Wyn attire, albeit slightly more combat friendly with thicker panels of protective gear. She wore tight but flexible pants and a henna-red jerkin that hugged and moved with her sinewy body. She must have felt the prickle of my gaze watching her because she turned and looked at me with glaring feline eyes.

She made her way towards Ven and me, her pulled-back tresses swaying behind her like an ivory pendulum. Her austere face was all sharp lines and angles as if her features had been pinched from molding clay.

"So you disrupt our borders then decide to grace us with your presence," she said, sarcasm dripping from every word. Her onyx eyes were like double-edged swords, daring me to get within wounding range.

"I didn't know I was on anyone's borders," I said, matching her stare.

Watching her fight had awakened something in me—empowered me. I remembered how Graem grabbed and tore at me, and how the men from Prism held me down and touched me however they pleased without my consent. I shuddered thinking about how completely and utterly defenseless I had been against them, and I vowed never to feel that way again.

"Teach me to fight like you," I said, glancing at her blade and all-around badassery.

"And why would I do that?" she practically huffed.

"I know something is coming, and when it gets here, I don't want to be a burden."

She paused, considering my answer. "Have you ever even held a blade in your life?"

My stalling silence was answer enough.

She scoffed and expertly flipped her weapon through the air, catching it by the blade's tip. "Fine, but only so you aren't a deadly distraction to me and the other warriors."

She offered me the hilt, and I grabbed it in what seemed like the obvious way to grip a knife, but she only rolled her eyes.

Okay...so that was wrong.

Feeling like a fool and clearly exhibiting no finesse for this form of combat, my skin tingled under the weight of watchful eyes. A dark light flashed in my periphery, and I turned to see Rowen leaning casually against a tree, arms crossed over his chest with an amused expression on his face.

Smug, arrogant prick.

He'd made himself scarce all day long, leaving others to fetch me for him, and now here he stood, showing up at exactly the wrong time, looking like he wouldn't be going anywhere anytime soon. He would witness all the humiliation I was sure to endure at the hands of Dyani's teachings, but I wouldn't let his presence affect me. I'd trained in front of all manner of people before, though usually with the advantage of knowing what I was doing. Here, I was clearly and utterly out of my league.

Dyani briskly fixed my hand on the roughly woven hilt and kicked my stance farther apart. "Strike me," she said unexpectedly.

Not wanting to give her the satisfaction of faltering and possibly failing this first test, I lashed out at her as hard as I could.

She easily side-stepped my attack and knocked me down as though I were a minor nuisance. The pebbles on the ground dug into my palms and knees, and my face flamed with embarrassment.

I didn't look at Rowen. I sure as hell wasn't going to let him or anyone else see the humiliation on my face. I turned my self-consciousness into determination and stood before Dyani, expecting some corrections, but "Again," was all she said.

I thrust at her once more, changing my angle of attack, but the outcome was the same. With an easy side-step and a forceful kick to my Achilles tendon, she knocked me to the ground, the trace of a smile pulling on her lips.

It wasn't hard to see where this was going, but I would take as much as she could dish. If it was her plan to get me to quit, she would soon be disappointed.

For what seemed like hours, I lunged at her in every possible way, sometimes feinting and darting, or misdirecting her attention before a swipe. I tried to catch her off guard, but every move I made ended up with me lying beneath her nose.

I was completely drenched in dirt and sweat, at a loss for how many times she'd taken me down, when she finally said, "That's enough for your first lesson, though I can't say I'm impressed. We'll see if you even make it back for a second."

"A second lesson? Does that mean I passed the first?" I asked with a little too much enthusiasm, considering how my ass was just handed to me. Somehow it felt like a win even though her glare cut me just as sharply as any blade ever could.

Leaving me on the ground, she spun away and walked past Rowen as she left.

He hadn't moved the entire time, still leaning against that damned tree with his arms over his chest. "Interesting first lesson, Dyani. I don't usually see that type of tutelage until at least a dozen lessons in," I heard him say as she stalked by him.

She flashed him with what I assumed was the Wyn equivalent of the finger and kept walking, not sparing him a glance as her white ponytail swayed in time with her hips.

Ven approached me with a smile that was actually more of a grimace, "That was... um... hard to watch."

I continued to pant, leaning forward with my elbows on my knees. The sun's descent set the sky aflame in orange and fuchsia swirls, while the perennial plants slowly illuminated with their gentle pastel glow.

"Do you know where I can get cleaned up?" I asked after a moment, standing to my feet.

But it was Rowen who answered, suddenly at my side. "I'll take you to the baths," he said, petting Sabra on the head. "Looks like you three went rogue today."

"It was my idea," I said as I turned to Rowen, momentarily stunned by his sheer size and beauty. His ability to affect me was still an annoying smack to the face.

"I'm sure it was," he replied, eyeing the young boy with a knowing smirk. "Ven is well aware he's not of age to be wandering the adult training grounds without a chaperone."

"What does that make me?" I asked indignantly.

"Uh, I best be getting home now," Ven said sheepishly before darting off with Sabra.

I swatted the dust from my pants. "Did you at least enjoy the front-row show?"

"Not really. It did become pretty predictable after about your third try. I'm not sure you possess the disposition for close combat. Hopefully, you have other skills to fall back on, Copeland," he said with perfect unconcern as he offered me his waterskin. "Especially at the rate you attract danger."

"You'd prefer I use my speed and run from my opponent?" I asked before guzzling down the cool water.

"If it kept you alive," he said, his eyes flashing with a look that was gone before I could decipher it. "You mentioned you enjoyed running, but not that you were fast."

"Fast is one way of putting it," I said, handing him back the waterskin.

"You will have to find a way to incorporate speed into your training. Dyani may be an excellent fighter, but she is far from a good teacher. You learned absolutely nothing today, and it was a complete waste of time."

"I may have learned nothing from her, but she learned something from me."

"And what's that?" he asked, curiosity getting the better of him.

"That I don't give up easily."

"So it would seem," he said, raising an acknowledging eyebrow. "Next time, watch where she twists her hips; it's a dead giveaway where she means to strike."

"Thanks for the tip. I could have really used that an hour ago."

Rowen's unbothered gaze scanned my disheveled appearance. "You need to get cleaned up. The Summit wants to see you. Tonight."

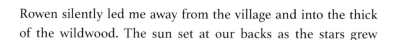

Rowen silently led me away from the village and into the thick of the wildwood. The sun set at our backs as the stars grew bolder, casting the trees in shadow-frosted tips and tinseled fire.

"You're fast," Rowen said, unable to shake our previous conversation. "What is it you run from?"

Caught off guard, I wondered if he really cared, but then again, Rowen didn't seem like the type to start noncommittal conversations. If he asked, he was genuinely interested. "I ran for competition. To be the best and win."

He seemed shocked by my answer. "And did you? Win?" he asked as if he couldn't help himself from wanting to know.

There was no point in being coy or modest. "Most of the time, but..." I stopped myself, sensing all too finitely the cracks in my armor I was exposing.

"Go on," he encouraged.

"Well, it started to feel that no matter how hard or fast I ran, I never got anywhere."

"I know the feeling," he said as his eyes went to that place I could never follow, the dark place where he retreated and punished himself. "But then I came to live here and found all the running I did was a distraction, a lie I told myself to keep from admitting the truth."

"What truth was that?"

"That running from your fear is the surest way straight into its arms. And when it catches you, as it surely will, you are somehow surprised and unprepared, even though—"

"Even though you knew it was chasing you all along," I finished the thought. Rowen pierced me with a gaze of recognition, and I realized we had completely stopped walking. "You haven't always lived here?" I asked, avoiding his intense and dissecting stare. He may dress like the villagers of this land but he didn't speak or look like them in any way, and he had just provided me with an opening to ask.

"The Wyn don't make it a habit of taking in strays, but they welcomed and accepted me all the same, even when I didn't want that for myself."

"Where are you from?" I asked, even though I wouldn't have the slightest clue if he told me. I was still a stranger in a strange land, and apart from glancing at a few strewn-about maps in his room, I really didn't know the layout of Luneth.

"From a place that no longer exists," he said tightly, his pulse ticking at his neck. "Which is just as well, as I can't..." he trailed off.

"What?" I pressed.

"It's a long story, one not meant for wandering ears. And we need to get you looking presentable."

I tried not to let Rowen's comment put me on edge, but the way he eyed the trees as if they were listening had me teetering on a fine line of apprehension. Especially with the threat of a potential mole in our midst.

"Nepta has made this your personal bathing room," he said, leading me to a curtain of emerald vines shimmering in the moonlight. The strands lazily swayed in the very breeze that cooled my flesh as it wafted over my sweat-soaked skin, and the sound of running water had me wanting to shed my dirty clothes.

"I don't need special treatment. I can bathe where everyone else does," I said, finding his dark stare.

"I'll let Nepta know. I'm sure she won't be too offended," he offered as he turned to leave.

I stopped him with a hand to his chest, and he smirked down at me, knowing damn well Nepta was the one person whose bad side you never wanted to be on. "On second thought, I think I'll enjoy the privacy."

"After what you've been through these last few days, I'd say you're deserving of it," he replied softer than usual, lifting his hand to tuck a flyaway lock of hair behind my ear like it was second nature. My breath hitched at the sweep of his touch, and he pulled back quickly as if realizing he hadn't meant to actually touch me.

His face hardened, and I tried to read beyond the shadows that lengthened across his set expression.

For a moment, I longed for the nights when I thought him to be no more than a figment of my imagination, not a living, breathing, temperamental man who could nearly knock me into oblivion with the slightest of touches, all the while him not feeling a thing.

Rowen parted the vines like a thick velvet drape, motioning for me to enter with the tick of his head. I took a step through and hesitated on the threshold, wary of being left alone in the dark. "You won't go anywhere, will you?" I asked, looking back to him.

"I'll be right here when you're done."

Relieved, I walked the rest of the way through the vines being held open for me, and as soon as they closed at my heels, I stopped with a gasp of disbelief. What I saw before me was so beautiful and tranquil, it put any spa back home to shame.

In the center of the flora-enveloped bathing suite was a white stone bath, raised and built into the rock wall of several cascading waterfalls. The basin unfurled beneath the glittering stars like a capsized clam shell and the lush forest walls encircled the room in complete privacy.

A carved vanity and chair sat embedded in the trunk of a tree, further proving the Wyn's sophisticated architecture. The twining and spiraling craftsmanship was as effortless as if Mother Nature had designed the pieces herself.

Resting on the earthy surface were bars of raw soap emitting relaxing berry, eucalyptus, and honeysuckle scents. Wooden hairbrushes, combs, and what looked to be toothpaste tablets also rested on the counter.

I stripped the clothes from my body, grabbed one of the soaps, and padded my way up the floating stone steps. I tentatively dipped my toes into the pool that could easily fit ten people and found the swirling sapphire water to be quite warm.

The baths must be over areas of geothermal heat like a hot spring.

I slowly submerged myself into the liquid heaven, wishing I

could stay here forever as the warm water loosened my tight muscles and opened my breathing. Bathing stark naked in the woods was something I'd never done before, but the freeing sensation was quickly becoming one of my new favorite things.

Well into scrubbing myself clean, a loud howl erupted from the trees, pulling me out of my reverie. I gasped loudly and dropped the soap from my hands.

"It's just the sounds of the forest coming alive at night, Copeland," Rowen called to me coolly through the veil of vines. "Don't worry, I won't let it eat you."

"Oh yes, my big strong protector," I mocked back at him. "I did finally get to see your scary ax-wielding skills in action, though you did cut it a little close to my nose. Should I be worried with your aim?"

"Believe me, you needn't worry when it comes to my aim," he said, clearly unbothered by my insinuation, which only piqued my desire to taunt him further.

"Hmm, 'I'm not sure you possess the disposition for the sport,'" I said, throwing his words back at him, and even though Rowen was bringing out aspects of myself that were burrowed deep, I still managed to shock myself with what I said next. "Does your questionable aim hinder the more...intimate areas of your life?"

He paused for the briefest of moments. "I'm quite proficient when it comes to nailing my targets...in any capacity. Something you'll thankfully never be troubled with."

"Good thing for that," I muttered loud enough for him to hear before I dove beneath the water with a splash. Even though I had goaded him, his words were loud and clear. He had no interest in me whatsoever, and I was better off for it. The way he roused and quelled my blood made me seasick, and the rolling waves of his emotions were a distraction I couldn't afford.

Resurfacing, I laid my body back, letting the liquid hold me as I floated on its gleaming wake. Tilting my chin, I looked to the heavens that could never be dimmed and marveled at their swirling splendor.

The billions of stars sparkled like silver, blue, and purple glitter on a swatch of midnight. It reminded me of the Milky Way—if it had been placed on top of itself several times over. Lavender auras inked the sky, comets arced through the atmosphere, and galaxies spiraled with ethereal grace.

Astronomers and scientists would give their right arm for this view, and it felt like it was all mine. This world devoid of pollution, smog, and city lights made the night sky glimmer like the inside of the crystal geode Ven had shown me earlier today.

It was so gorgeous and freeing here; I found I didn't even miss my phone, computer, or any other conveniences that supposedly made life easier. I was charged here, brought to life by the moon, stars, and plant life.

The feeling appeared mutual as the glowing blossoms pulsed and hummed in my presence.

Where I used to jolt uncomfortably against my cage, I now thrashed against it, pleading for the room my body so desperately needed but had long been deprived of.

I couldn't believe this part of my life had remained hidden from me for so long. I wanted to lie here forever, make up for lost time, forget myself and melt into the everlasting glow of space, but then I remembered the Summit. They wanted to see me tonight, and somehow not showing up for a second time seemed like a bad idea.

I wrung out my hair and stepped out of the flowing pool. I pulled on the woven robe hanging from a tree and wrapped it around my bare, shivering body. Once dry, I changed into the fresh clothes laid out for me and nibbled at the tray of flavorful fruits, breads, and cheeses. I silently thanked whoever had been selecting my wardrobe and supplying me with mouth-watering sustenance. They were lifesavers.

Feeling somewhat replenished, I gazed into the mirror above the vanity. I hoped to see a lively appearance, but the light purple smudges under my eyes spoke to my exhaustion and lethargy dulled my complexion. I was far from an impressive sight for the Summit.

I kept my hair down in damp tendrils, hoping it would mask my fatigue. I popped in a toothpaste tablet before exiting the dreamy bathing area and found Rowen just where he said he'd be. He sat at the base of a tree, his strong hands expertly sharpening his blade with a whetstone. The moment his mindful eyes snapped to mine, he stood and secured his small ax at his hip. "The Summit will be wondering where we are. You certainly stayed in there long enough."

"You said you wanted me clean."

"Clean, not pruned."

Ignoring his gripe, I asked, "Who makes up the Summit? Is there anything I should know about them?"

Rowen led the way back to the village, drawing in a breath. "Nepta, our Elven-head, is the overseer of the Summit. The other members include Takoda, our healer, as you've seen with his mending. And Alvar, the war captain of the Wyn warriors. Then there is Driskell, second in command and reader of the stars. If anything were to happen to Nepta, he would step into the role of Elven-head. It is he who cast the failed prophecy, and between you and me, he holds the stars a little too accountable. He is desperately seeking a way to redeem himself amongst the people. Best to always be on your guard when near him."

"And you, are you on the Summit?"

"I am when it comes to all matters concerning you," he said, not breaking his brisk stride as he turned to look at me, "I am the one who found you after all, and I feel a sense of responsibility towards you." There was something in his voice I couldn't place. Did he regret finding me?

"It sounds like you wish the burden belonged to someone else."

"I would lay down my life for those I've sworn to protect—for you. Make no mistake of that," he said, and seeing the hard look on his face, I knew he meant it.

Rowen rushed a few paces ahead, and despite my questions that still burned to be answered, I knew I would get no more out of him tonight.

We made the rest of the way back to the village without another word, nothing but the crunch of our footsteps to fill the silence. Rowen's broad-shouldered form continued to walk ahead of me without so much as a backward glance. He may have offered to protect me, but it was clear he didn't have to like me.

As he plowed on, the strong planes of his body moved and shifted beneath the fabric of his shirt, and I couldn't help my eyes as they trailed downward. But no matter where my enthralled gaze landed, he was all hard contracting muscle and burgeoning strength—no doubt the result of endless hours spent at the training grounds.

I remembered back to Weir Falls when he'd shielded me with his whole body and I'd felt every rigid line of that power against me. I may have been in a lust-induced state at the time, but some part of me knew his body alone could be wielded as a deadly weapon.

The village came into view, snapping me out of my admiring stare. The domed buildings and flourishing wildlife were lit by the floating luminorbs that lackadaisically ascended and descended like wine-drunk fireflies.

Even though I knew where we were headed, it didn't stop my heart from ratcheting up into my throat. Who was I to meet with the Summit? I was a nobody. At any moment I expected someone to jump out and admit this was all a horrible mistake, that I was free to go. But Rowen led me right to the watery pathway without so much as a slight interruption from anyone.

This was happening.

I held my breath in anticipation as Rowen and I walked across the moon-kissed stepping stones towards the Sacred Vale. We rounded the rippling sapphire walkway and entered a clearing hovering in midair. The ground dropped away around us, creating an island surrounded by sheer rock walls thick with foliage and waterfalls that fell into dark, misty chasms.

I was only vaguely aware of the Summit as my gaze immediately shot skyward. A massive multifaceted crystal hovered above the ground. The smooth surface swirled in milky waves of molten luminescence with veins of orchid matter. The crystalline light spiraled and churned like a galaxy of mist and jewels, and I was utterly captivated.

Almost too bright and beautiful to look at, I blinked, and the celestial light vanished.

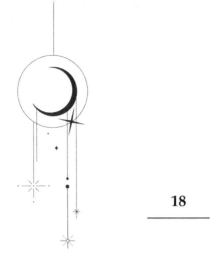

18

My eyes fluttered. I expected a burning imprint to glow just beyond my lids, but there was no sign or remnant whatsoever of the brilliant light that nearly blinded me.

All that remained in its place was a scattering of dull stones, floating in the sky like a shattered asteroid trapped by gravity. An eyesore compared to the otherworldly image that had flashed so quickly and spectacularly before my vision.

"What is it?" Rowen asked, sensing my pause.

"The memory of the stone is potent, is it not?" Nepta interjected, seeming to have glimpsed into my mind. Had she once seen the ethereal light so vibrant it rivaled any star?

My mind, confused and as far away as the heavens, was pulled back to the present as Nepta motioned for us to sit at the glinting white table beneath the levitating stones.

Rowen and I took our seats before Nepta, Takoda, and the other Summit members who had silenced upon our approach. They all sat with taut-string energy, only a pluck away from absolute discord. Even though there was no head of the table, Nepta's chair of woven moonlight sat higher and more beautiful than the rest.

"What happened?" I asked, eyeing the ruin of fractured rocks above our heads, nervous they would tumble down upon us at any moment.

"It is we who will be asking the questions," the most brutal-looking member of the Summit interjected. By the battle marks that lined his arms and the long scar slashed across his lip and chin, I guessed him to be the war captain Alvar. "Why she has been allowed into the Sacred Vale is still a mystery to me."

I agreed with him entirely, but I hadn't realized how nervous I was until Rowen placed his hand on one of my shaking legs. He gave a comforting squeeze, and the pressure of his fingers tightening on my knee tethered me to his strength.

"Rowen, you first told us of her presence weeks ago. Wouldn't that be enough time for her to consort with our enemies?" Alvar asked as if it was the most sensible question in the world.

"When I first found her, she was but a fading image. Here one moment, gone the next. You would no sooner be able to grasp smoke within your hands than speak to her. Not the easiest condition in which to plot with our enemies."

"Rowen has assured us of her innocence when it comes to conspiring with Erovos," Takoda spoke up, shocking me by revealing words Rowen had spoken in my defense. "And I trust him implicitly."

"That doesn't answer who she is. This reeks of a plot we can't begin to understand. This female could be the final ruin of us all," Alvar spat back.

This female?

I seethed on the inside but refused to let Alvar see the effect his comment had on me. I'd been underestimated and unfairly judged by men before, especially when it came to running. They always doubted my speed, and it gave me a sick sense of gratification when I proved to be faster than they thought.

And this was a type of race, wasn't it? Seeing whose mind could keep up.

"I haven't been plotting anything," I said, keeping my chin high and voice firm. "And I'd prefer if you addressed me by my name. Referring to each other by our sexes seems an unnecessary distinction, don't you think?"

Alvar barked out in unexpected laughter. "Ah yes, what a little spitfire you are. We heard all about your antics at the training grounds," he said with a steel sheen in his eye. "However, the distinction is most necessary when the stars speak of a son returning to these lands, not a weakened mare."

"Come now, Alvar. Surely we can give her a chance." I assumed that must be Driskell, the second in command. His long white hair had the occasional braid, woven with twine and crystal beads. The way he eyed me was unnerving, and I recalled Rowen mentioning this man would do or say anything to regain his standing in the village. "Perhaps there is some insight she can provide."

Alvar disagreed with a shake of his head. "She is rousing the evil in the forest, and it won't be long until it rains down upon us all. Tell me, when was the last you heard of a summoning-demon near our borders, and we've had five in the past moon. She brings the darkness we've so long kept at bay, and it is closing in."

"We cannot hide away forever," Takoda countered, his long face looking exhausted for the first time.

"Can you tell us, child, who are you and why are you here?" Driskell asked, his gaze brimming with starved hope.

All eyes at the table turned to me expectantly, but the mysteries compounded. Why had I arrived here around the same time as the demons? Why had it been so hazy and muddled that I could barely see or hear anything? And why was I only now able to travel between worlds?

"I don't know," was all I managed to say. It was the best I could offer, but at least it was the truth. They deserved that much.

"Gah." Alvar slammed his fist on the table, causing me to jump. "I knew we wouldn't get far with this one. Look how pale and weak she is. It appears she barely knows her own name, let alone the weight of the destruction we bear." He turned to stare me dead in the eye. "As of now, you are nigh on worthless, nothing but a pretty face and of no use to anyone."

Irritation flared in my veins, and Rowen squeezed my knee, causing the tendons in his hand to leap.

"Whatever reason her stars crossed with ours, she is here now. And if she is to remain, she will bear the burden of our knowledge and responsibility," Nepta said, gazing toward me with a marble stare that spoke of worlds known through an alternate sight. "The secrets of our village are no small thing; any betrayal will mean a most certain and painful death. Do you accept?"

Her aura rushed over me, compelling me to speak the truth. "I do."

She nodded, then inhaled the breath preluding any tale that holds the weight of a thousand collective memories passed from one generation to the next. "Before our world came to exist as we know it, all was darkness reigned over by six beings known as the Elder Spirits: our first ancestors. What events came to pass to leave the heavens in their care, we will never know. Oceans crash and worlds turn, it is simply the way of things." Nepta's voice was strong and commanding, and I found myself hanging onto her every word.

"Growing tired and weary of the never-ending darkness, where nothing thrived, grew, or even remembered, the Elder Spirits set out to create a repeating pattern of life, for even they had no corporeal form or home to call their own.

"Together, the six Elder Spirits sang a song of life, energy, and balance, of storms, rains, and starseeds; of an interconnectivity in all things no matter how great or small. And above all else, they sang of light.

"From their shared voices, a pure first-light rose in the darkness, casting a glow so mesmerizing the Elder Spirits themselves could barely gaze upon it. Taking great pride, they named their united power the Alcreon Light.

"But a beautiful light does not only shine on that which is pleasing, and the Alcreon Light exposed a great evil—a seventh Elder Spirit growing in the darkness, creating creatures born of ink, and claw, and destruction. Sensing such power, these creatures sought to claim and feed off the Light, slowly eating away at the precious glow that kept the primordial darkness at bay.

"The Elder Spirits, in an attempt to protect the Light's power from the seventh Dark Spirit and his army of demons, coaxed the Alcreon Light into a shard of crystal, thus forging the Alcreon Stone into existence. Now contained within a faceted surface, the Light projected and broadened its reach throughout the heavens, giving birth to the stars, planets, and moons, filled with wildlife, growth, and beauty, the very light of life itself.

"The stone's power secured a sacred balance throughout the cosmos," Nepta said, motioning to the shattered rock, which looked nothing like the stone she described, but more of what I had seen for a split second behind my eyes.

"A people who understood the significance of such a light offered their forces to the Alcreon Stone, guardians who wished to neither own nor possess, but to protect. My ancestors from times long forgotten, to our current tragic plight, have been watching over the stone ever since.

"We are a hidden village, the Alcreon Stone a mere legend. Though that hasn't stopped all manner of creatures from searching for such power. For centuries, our warriors have kept the stone safe from treasure seekers, demons, and other forces of darkness. Until two hundred moons ago, the Dark Spirit took to physical form and entered our territory.

"Erovos, as we came to call him, marched through our borders with an army of demons the likes of which the Wyn had never seen. Many fought bravely that day at the Battle of the Breaking, sacrificing their lives to defend the stone, but to no avail. Erovos made it through our lines, ravaged our village, scarred our war captain, and was seconds away from possessing the Light. I knew if his hands ever touched the stone, the Light would be forever lost. In a moment of despair, I raised my staff and shattered the stone, hoping the Light would seek a benevolent place of refuge. The Alcreon Light sailed through the sky, taking my sight with it, and was never seen again.

"Without the Alcreon Stone, the balance shifts to darkness as Erovos creeps over the world, poisoning people's hearts, minds, and the very land they walk upon," Nepta almost choked, the agony plain as day on her withered face.

Then it hit me all at once. "The dead forest," I said to Rowen, and we shared a look.

He nodded solemnly. "And it is spreading."

"Where are the other six Spirits? Can't they help?" I asked, my heart breaking for all the loss and destruction.

Nepta shook her head. "No one knows their true form, but it is said the Elder Spirits walk the land, taking the shape of water, beasts, or trees. Beings of once-great power have passed on such worries and are merely a watching presence. However, they continue to guide us with messages from heavens. Driskell, our very own star reader scried the Synodic Prophecy."

Driskell shifted slightly in his seat. "It was a failed prophecy, one I can never reclaim and must live with for the rest of my life.

The reading was so clear and crisp. I have no understanding of why it failed."

"Regardless, word of the Synodic Prophecy spread," Takoda said.

"What was the prophecy?" I wondered out loud.

"The lost light of Luneth shall return to its synodic beginning when the first six stars align with the stones of shattered ruin. Through blood, bone, and crystal, the marked son will breathe life anew unto the deadened lands of darkness," Nepta answered with a look that bordered on desperation and hope.

The Marked. I'd heard Rowen say those words before. Could he be the son the prophecy spoke of? But what reason would he have for hiding it?

"This is a test from the Spirits to try our faith," Driskell insisted with vigor. "The alignment occurred nearly twenty years ago, but my star readings are never wrong."

"Perhaps just misinterpreted," Rowen offered unsolicited.

"Impossible," Driskell nearly choked before regaining his composure. "My readings have never failed. He is out there—this son who carries the Light. I have not given up on him or the Spirits. Have you all?"

"Don't be ridiculous, Driskell," Nepta scolded. "Many still believe and seek the truth, as do we all. But with still no sign of the Alcreon Light, knowing what is to become of our fate, we must find a way to live in the precarious balance of a failing world.

"Not a whisper from Erovos since the Battle of the Breaking. That is until his creatures began to resurface on our borders. Not a stirring on our doorstep—until you arrived. It is indeed odd timing that Rowen discovered you when he did, wandering in woods full of demons, barely there, not knowing what you are. Has any of what we've said sparked remembrance?"

Rowen's hand was still on my thigh, it had never left, and I clasped my fingers over his. "I truly have no idea why I'm here, but I want to help. However I can," I said with more conviction than I'd felt for anything in my life.

"She knows too much. With what we know of her, we may as well kill her now to be safe," Alvar said without a shred of remorse, and Rowen's seething form shot up from the table. His chair knocked back behind him with a crash, and the Sacred Vale erupted into all-out verbal warfare.

"You would be so careless with a life, Alvar? After all the death you have seen?" Nepta asked forcefully, reining in the conversation that had quickly snowballed out of control. Rowen righted his chair and sat back down beside me, his breath furious. The Summit members quieted and straightened in their seats, pinpointing their focus on Nepta's small frame, which exuded the authority of a titan.

"Come now, let us also not forget who the true enemy is, or the fact that we may have more than one," Driskell said, eyeing Rowen. "The false queen, Aliphoura, is amassing quite the following. After her land was fully destroyed, she and her people vanished without a trace. More and more go missing every day, whole tribes and villages never to be seen again. We've sent many to discover her whereabouts, but none have succeeded." The star reader never took his eyes off Rowen as he spoke, and I glanced between the two, not understanding their shared look.

"You know I've searched Driskell, every night." Rowen's clipped voice rang with dark regret.

"We must assume Erovos is aware of the weakened mare's presence by now," Alvar said, keeping with the lovely nickname he'd adopted for me.

"He has not returned," Takoda pointed out. "He may still not yet know."

"And let us hope it remains so," Nepta said before turning

her mighty focus to Rowen, his powerful body still tense by my side. "Rowen Damascus, you will continue to keep her in your charge."

Rowen's eyes sharpened into two emerald swords of promise. "I will."

"It grows late. Let us ponder all that we have heard. Perhaps answers will find their way to us in the soft-wind-whispers of the evening," she said in a final benediction, our cue to leave for the night.

Rowen took my hand and ushered me out of the Sacred Vale before anyone could protest. I wasn't prepared for what the Summit had in store for me, and I was more than eager to leave their questioning eyes. I had no real answers for them anyway, and they knew it. But I couldn't tear my mind from the people who had suffered and died for the Alcreon Light. I shivered at the mere thought.

Sensing my chill, Rowen's brow furrowed. "Let's get you in by the fire."

I nodded in a daze, digesting everything I'd learned as we made our way back to his dome. His fingers slowly unfurled from my hand as if his light handle on me was the only thing keeping me upright. I looked down at my hands, then up at the brilliant swarm of stars banding in an ethereal spiral.

How did I play a part in any of this? And what about Rowen? Could he be this marked Alcreon Light-bearer?

"Surely there is somewhere else I can sleep. I can't keep you out of your own home."

"I told you, I don't mind. Sleeping under the stars of late has been a comfort." The silver-forest glow cast shadows on his face like smudged charcoal, matching the dark stains on his finger-tips. "I'll see you tomorrow. Try to get some rest."

I turned from him, weary to the bone. "Oh, and Copeland," he said, pulling my gaze back towards him. He ground his teeth, his eyes severe. "If you truly don't know what you are or why you're here, I suggest you figure it out quickly before someone else decides for you."

And with that, he disappeared, the darkness welcoming him back as if it was his only friend.

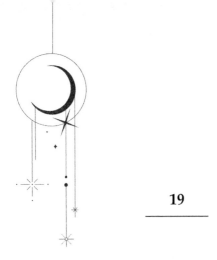

19

Nearly dressed and halfway out the door, my body begged for me to return to bed. Although I'd slept soundly, I still felt exhausted, no doubt from yesterday's training with Dyani. Having used my muscles in ways they'd never been worked before, my limbs were sluggish, which was to be expected, but I found my mind to be tired as well. Apparently, learning the creation and destruction story of an entire world took a lot out of you.

Heading out of the bungalow and finishing up with the lacings of my dove-grey vest, I plowed into Rowen waiting at the front door. As soon as he saw me, he frowned. "You look worse than when I left you last night," he said as if my lackluster appearance was insulting. "Are you ill?"

I dropped my fingertips from the tie at my breasts, Rowen's eyes trailing the movement. "I'm fine. It's probably just from training yesterday," I said, also realizing it might be some form of jet lag, similar to adjusting from one time zone to another, except in this case, from one world to another.

It was just a theory. I didn't have the slightest clue when it came to the intricate mechanics of astral projecting between worlds.

"Did you get any rest or did you...go home, to him?" he asked, a muscle twitching in his jaw.

"Who?" I asked, my eyebrows pulling together in confusion. It took me several moments to figure out what he was asking. "Oh! Harlan? No. No, we aren't together. I...I'm alone," I said, cringing at that last little overshare, and I quickly tried to plow right over it with more words. "I stayed put all night but I should go back soon, at least for a little while. My roommate and parents will get worried."

I hadn't seen Natalie in almost two days, and my last conversation with her hadn't gone pleasantly. She'd seen my bruised skin and might already have a search party out looking for me.

I wasn't sure how time worked here. I had no idea if only a few minutes had passed since then or if I'd really been gone for over twenty-four hours.

"Stay," he said, finding my eyes, and my pulse galloped as something deep inside my core twisted.

He blinked several times, looking like he'd just made a mistake. He ran his hand down his face; his fingertips dipped in faded grey. "I swore an oath to Nepta, and I can't keep you safe in a world where I can't touch you," he said as his eyes darkened with the memories of Prism, where we'd both been helpless.

I would try to go back home eventually. If anyone got too worried, they would see my automatic email response. I couldn't leave. Not yet. I still had so many questions, and the answers seemed to grow closer here like a photosynthesis slowly seeping into my skin.

"I'll take you to eat before your training lesson with Dyani. That is, if training is something you still intend on doing?" Rowen eyed me in challenge as if daring me to admit I was feeling under the weather.

"Oh, I'll be there," I smiled sweetly. "Learning ways to take you down should you continue to annoy me."

"I look forward to you trying, as I'm sure it's inevitable."

"For once, I'd have to agree with you."

Rowen led me to a seaside pavilion made entirely of entwined trees. Small tables were laid upon the sand with only linen floor cushions as seats.

I wasn't very hungry, so I ended up just picking around my tree ring plate filled with an assortment of nuts, berries, nectars, and steaming grains. I could tell it annoyed Rowen, but he wisely kept it to himself. He would occasionally look over at me like he was trying to solve a riddle and scoffed every time I pushed my food around.

"If you don't enjoy spending time with me, why don't you just babysit from a distance. I don't need you hovering." I plopped a berry in my mouth, and even though my stomach wanted to reject it, I forced it down anyway.

Ven appeared at my elbow, smiling wide with Sabra by his side. The majestic white beast proffered her snout towards me, and I let her lick the berry juices from my fingertips with her rough pink tongue.

"Oh look, people who aren't forced to endure my presence," I said pointedly, but Rowen just shot me a seething stare. "Do you have anything in store for us today, Ven?" I asked, hoping it would give me some space from Rowen. My feelings surrounding him were confused and muddied. My body inexplicably burned for him, and at times I swear I could see him burning back. But I saw now it was just part of his oath to Nepta, to watch over me until we knew why I was linked to Luneth.

"I thought I could show you one of my favorite spots?" Ven said with his big toothy grin, so contagious I found myself smiling back.

"I just need to be back in time for Dyani's lesson," I said as I stood to let him lead the way.

We took a few steps along the sugar-sand beach when Ven suddenly stopped and looked back to Rowen. To my utter annoyance, everyone seemed well aware of my ordered chaperon, but he sat still, making no move to follow us.

"It looks like you two are in good hands with Sabra," he said, gesturing to the massive beast at our side, and the white wolf's tail swayed proudly at the mention of her name.

Ven and I shot a glance to the grand beast who panted with a wide-open smile, exposing her massive, flesh-searing teeth, and we laughed as we realized Rowen was right. At present, Sabra was docile and gentle, but I knew the damage she could inflict with her sharp fangs, strong jaw, and razor claws. I imagined watching her attack her prey would be a beautiful yet terrifying sight to behold.

Leaving Rowen, Ven led me to the far inland side of the village, bustling with the morning rush and early chatter. Sabra trotted happily at our sides as we headed up a tall slope that flattened into a lookout about a quarter of the way up.

We sat surrounded by the native plants that gently swayed in the air like coral in shallow currents. Up this high, the fresh wind caressed my face, the breeze like a delicate lace billowing across my skin.

I could see the whole aerial view of the ocean and village from this vantage point. The conical shapes of the lodgings sprouted from the ground as if they'd been planted last spring and were ripe for the picking.

The Wyn elves moved throughout the village with the grace of a choreographed dance. They knew when to go or be still, when to walk or run, never bumping into each other but perfectly weaving their paths together like the strands of a dream catcher.

From up here you would never be able to tell that Luneth and its people were suffering. Suffering because of what the disappearance of the Alcreon Light meant to this land and all that inhabited it.

"You can see everything from up here," Ven said, seeming to sense the quiet that settled over me. "Well, almost everything. Sometimes I sit up here and just observe."

"People watch," I said, knowing the mindless gratification one can get from watching people be people.

His nose scrunched at that, but he laughed anyway. "I've never heard it called that before. I like it."

"It's what we call it back home."

Home. The word caused a swift tug in my chest, and I knew I needed to go back tonight.

Sitting on the plush grass, I contently let the pale sun soak into my skin, but Ven wasn't one for comfortable silences, and he began regaling me with story after story: memories of him climbing, exploring, skinning his knee, or Sabra catching her lunch. The tales were endless, and I found myself only half listening.

Ven absentmindedly stroked Sabra behind her ear, and she happily leaned into his scratches. "People show their true selves when they think no one is watching. You hear a lot too. I remember a girl crying right over there." He pointed his finger down below to two trees wrapped so tightly around one another they looked like lovers locked in a growing embrace.

"Why was she crying?" I asked, having fallen into the rhythm of conversation.

"A few years ago, when Rowen joined our village, it seemed every other girl wanted him. Even some of the boys." At the mention of Rowen's name, I instantly perked up. "Every week someone new was trying to get his attention, making and offering him woven baskets, necklaces, and crowns made of flowers. One even asked him to meet her by the entwined souls' tree. When he never showed, she cried there all day. He denied every single admirer, and never accepted any of their gifts. They all eventually learned to stay away from him. All day long he worked, doing the chores and tasks no one wanted to do, and then he would disappear at night, only to do it all over again the next day."

Attempting to sound as uninterested as possible, I asked, "Do you know why?"

"Takoda said he was a broken man with a broken heart." Ven shrugged, then pulled out a treat from his pocket and fed it to the white beast stretched out beside him. "One day, Takoda found him in the forest covered in blood and near death. He brought him back to the village just in time. Any longer and Rowen would have died.

"Takoda was able to heal all the wounds on his body, but for some reason, he was still dying. Takoda said the wound that plagued him was one we could not see, for it lay on his heart."

I felt a pang in my chest. What could have happened to Rowen to leave him in the middle of nowhere, bloodied and broken?

Something had shattered him, body and soul.

"I remember Takoda telling him: 'the woman you loved is gone forever, and you must learn to live on,' I don't think he ever really did though, but little by little he got stronger and stronger, and once Rowen was finally well enough to leave, he asked if he could stay. Ever since then he has become a full member of our village and one of our best warriors."

That explained some of why Rowen was the way he was; one moment caring and warm, the next, cold and distant. Almost as if he could forget whatever horrible thing happened to him, only for it all to come crashing back in an instant.

I remembered sitting by him at the creek after the incident at

Weir Falls. How a darkness settled over him as he recalled a memory, one he relived over and over again. Could this be that memory?

Someone he loved had died. Someone he loved enough that he didn't want to survive without them. That must be what haunts him.

But then why would he be covered in blood with near-fatal injuries? Had he nearly died trying to save her and failed?

I couldn't imagine the pain and guilt that must come from not being able to save the one you love. Giving your whole body and still failing in the end—a heart so broken it loses the will to live.

I also couldn't help my mind as it strayed to thoughts of her.

What had she looked like? How had she died? How long had they been together? Was she his first love?

The questions kept coming, and I found myself jealous, yet grief-stricken, for the doomed lovers.

It hurt, thinking of them being together.

My thoughts were far away as Ven, Sabra, and I sat silently in the tall swaying grass, the star-strewn sky bright above us. I still marveled at how the stars managed to stay alight throughout the day, even though I recognized none of the constellations.

Back home it always gave me comfort to point out Orion, Cassiopeia, or Scorpius on the rare nights they were visible. To be able to clearly see and name something so far away and unreachable made me feel comforted. Alive. As if stretching myself to that distant point in space made me bigger and braver than I actually was.

Here the sky told me no such stories, and I felt more alone than ever.

———— ·((●))· ————

We finally made our way down the slope and onto the training field. Sure enough, Dyani was there, her ponytail whipping behind her as she sparred a petite woman with a shaved head. Waiting for her to finish, I inspected the knives on a nearby rack. I grabbed one with a medium blade and short hilt and began warming up.

Dyani no doubt had a new way of humiliating me today, but I would at least come armed and prepared with what little I knew.

Finishing their practice, she spoke to her sparring partner with the softest expression I'd ever seen on her face. When she finally turned to face me, that gentle look hardened, and I immediately took the stance from yesterday, knowing there would be no pleasantries with this one.

If she was surprised to see me, she didn't show it. She just dove straight into my lesson.

"When attacking your enemy, you want to use the force from your core, not your arm, and follow through. Like this." Dyani kept her dominant arm close to her torso, then stepped forward and swiped her blade diagonally through the air while unwinding her body. She moved with such fierce swiftness that I could only hope to emulate her one day.

I mimicked her movement, repeating it several times with a few corrections before she barked, "Now attack me."

I swiped as she'd shown me, but as soon as I completed my follow-through, Dyani jabbed at me. I took Rowen's advice and watched as her loaded hip took direct aim at my exposed rib. Using my speed, I jumped back quickly, evading her assault that would have landed me in the dirt.

Shock spread across my face before morphing into a smile. I'd actually missed her attack!

Dyani's already narrow eyes shrank to angry slits, and she charged at me so fast I couldn't tell where she meant to strike. I barely blocked a vicious blow before she kicked my feet out from under me, and I fell on my back with a hollow thud. She couldn't even give me a moment of victory before knocking me on my ass.

Dyani hovered over my supine form and gloated down at me.

I glared back. That was a cheap shot, and she knew it.

I wanted to knock that smug look off her face so badly that, before I could think to stop myself, I swiftly spun and kicked my leg out, hitting her right in the same sensitive area she'd hit me.

Dyani's arms flailed as she fell to the ground and landed beside me with the same painful thud.

She stood so quickly it was as if she never fell, but she and I both knew she had, and that I was the one who caused it.

"I am done training you," she practically spat at me, and I was left speechless on the ground.

"Seriously?" I asked in shock, rising up on my elbows.

"Dead serious. Find someone else to train your sloppy, ungrateful self. I'm done with you." She stalked off furiously without another word.

I continued to sit on the ground, stupefied. I couldn't believe I'd just ruined my opportunity of learning how to fight from someone so skilled.

I hauled myself off the ground, but it took me longer than it should have. My limbs were laden with exhaustion.

What was happening to me? Back home I could sprint for hours without feeling this winded. How long would it take for my body to adjust to being here? Would it ever?

My heart was beating way too fast, and I swayed as a dizzy spell took over me.

Someone was suddenly at my elbow, helping to keep me steady. The hands were foreign yet strong, and I looked up at a face similar to Dyani's but softer and with lighter eyes. It was Demil, Dyani's twin brother.

He was clad in a taupe shirt that hung taut over one shoulder, revealing half of his massive chest. His dark brown pants draped down to his knees, and knives of varying lengths glinted from his waistband. His white hair was half pulled up into a bun atop his head, and circlets wrapped around his thick upper forearms.

He was a warrior, just like his sister.

"Don't worry. She's just embarrassed," he said, his eyes showing love for his sister but no remorse. "She hasn't been taken down like that in a while and has forgotten the feeling. It's about time someone reminded her. I suppose that's what she gets for underestimating you. I'll be sure not to make the same mistake."

My dizzy spell slowly cleared. "Thanks, but I don't think she'll be forgiving me any time soon."

He playfully rubbed his smooth chin. "You're probably right. She'll never forgive you."

At least he was honest, and his candid response elicited a small chuckle from me.

"It seems you're in search of a new teacher. You're quick. I can work with that."

"Oh, and what qualities do you possess that I can work with?" I asked with a wry smile.

He laughed and motioned to where his hands were still on me, "Aside from a steadying grip, you'll have to find out."

A dark shadow pulled my gaze, and my breath caught in my throat as Rowen's penetrating gaze scorched my skin. "What happened?" he asked, and for the first time, I understood the harsh set of his face. *Loss.*

"Keira here just took down Dyani," Demil said with pride.

Rowen's eyes crinkled in skeptical surprise. "Really?"

I scoffed. "Is that so hard to believe?"

"Actually, yes. I would like to have seen it." He sounded impressed, and that appeased me, even though I'd lost my instructor in the process.

Rowen glanced down to see Demil's hands on my arm and the small of my back, and I could have sworn his expression twitched just before returning to indifference. Demil dropped his hands from me and said, "Remember my offer, Keira. I will see you around." His muscled body walked away, leaving me alone with my tempered guardian.

Having decided it was time, I pivoted to Rowen. "You should know I'm going home tonight. I'll think of your award-winning company when I'm ready to come back. Though that might take a while."

"Just imagine my sheets if you start having trouble, Copeland," he suggested arrogantly. "Though I'm sure Demil wouldn't mind if you imagined yourself in his instead."

"I'd sooner try Dyani's," I replied with a saccharine smile, challenging him with my eyes. I reached for my silver tether, ready to leave him alone and speechless on the field of the training grounds. But the bridge between our worlds had vanished.

I explored my inner consciousness for the thread of light, searching again and again.

I searched all day and night, but I was left adrift. Lost in an endless sea of stars. My pathway home nowhere in sight.

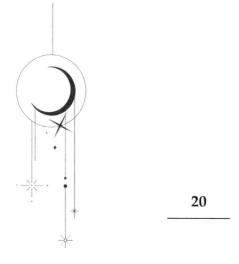

20

Since I was no longer training with Dyani, I attempted to make myself useful throughout the village, taking every spare moment to find my way home. Neither proved very successful: the Wyn people were still wary of my presence, and the beautiful thread of consciousness I'd pulled to get here was gone.

Thankfully two sisters, Quiya and Nyvari, had taken me under their wing. They quickly had me learning the names and uses of local herbs and spices, how to tell time using the stars, and even how to honor and manage our feminine cycles.

I was immensely grateful for them, because aside from Ven, they were the first to truly welcome and integrate me into the village.

Today, the silver-haired women began teaching me the craft of weaving objects from natural grasses. They carefully explained that the night-blooming plants, when respectfully borrowed from the earth, offered decorative threads of reeded moonlight to any creation.

"The moonblooms are rare to light. It is a great luck to have found them this day," Quiya said with a bright smile. "It will be a wonderful addition to your work."

The baskets I'd seen around the village not only served a specific function but were also astounding pieces of art that glinted with starlit ripples. The complex patterns evoked the natural designs of land and sky as they undulated with a touch of swirling energy.

The labyrinthine artistry wasn't only used in creating vessels for harvested food but also for fashioning carriers, mats, furniture, and cooking implements.

"Take only what is needed and nothing more so the growth may continue to protect the land and provide homes for small creatures," Nyvari, the older sister, instructed as we found a thick patch of vines and willows growing from the soil.

"You must imbue your song with the earth as you weave," Quiya said, her wide heart-shaped face kind and similar to that of her older sister. Then she sang with a voice so enchanting it raised goosebumps along my arms as her tone and nimble fingers directed the vines into intricate flowing shapes.

I attempted to mimic her weaving patterns, but it was more complicated than it looked. This craft involved quite a bit of geometry, patience, and finesse, not to mention a beautiful voice.

Wrap, coil, sing, repeat, all while thinking ten steps ahead.

The pliable strands slipped in my hands, and my fingertips were clumsy with the patterns. My teachers insisted singing helped guide the design, but with my tone-deaf self, I found that not to be the case. My reeds still wouldn't cooperate, and I kept losing count of where I was, but both sisters kindly encouraged me as I worked the threads into a somewhat decent shape.

My first attempt at a small basket turned out to be a twisted mess of a thing, but still, I was immensely proud of it.

"The materials are getting scarcer to locate as the land around us dries up and dies," Nyvari said solemnly, taking a break from her melodic singing to cut her creation at the base, thanking the land as she did so. "It is said the false queen Aliphoura did not honor her land. Taking and depleting until there was nothing left. Only death. And such a darkness grows nearer."

The dead forest was spreading closer to their home. This was the despair I had seen in the villagers' eyes on my first day here. I wished there was more I could do, but I needed to get my own body together before I could truly be of help to anyone. Every day I woke weaker than the last.

Holding their stunning pieces of art, the sisters praised me again on my small achievement before we parted ways, and I made my way back to the village feeling tired and defeated.

Suddenly, Rowen appeared out of nowhere like an apparition come to life by the glint of the moon. He had been doing that a lot lately—providing me space during the day, never too far off, only to greet me along with the fire of dusk in the sky.

Startled, I jumped and quickly hid the basket behind my back. I loved it, but I doubted Rowen would be as impartial.

He stood before me, his skin and clothing gleaming with a sheen of exertion, most likely from hours spent at the training grounds. His wide, corrugated shoulders slimmed to a narrow waist, and his freshly worked muscles surged with an energy that had my legs shifting uncomfortably beneath me.

"What's that you're hiding, Copeland?" he asked with humored intrigue.

"Nothing," I quickly chirped, noting his impressive body that demanded my attention.

"Come on, show me," he coaxed smoothly, but I shook my head no.

He chuckled and tried to skirt around me, but I twisted just in time, keeping him from seeing the protruding sticks of my jumbled creation.

"Show me," he said with a devilish grin, and his voice lowered to a velvet threat, "or I'll make you show me."

"Fine," I scoffed, knowing resisting him was useless. "But don't you dare laugh."

He took the basket from behind my back and inspected my handiwork. One dark eyebrow arched up skeptically as he tried to bite back a laugh. "It's not the most elegant thing I've ever seen. I can see why you were hesitant to give it to me."

"You think this is for you?" I asked incredulously, snatching it back from his hands, but then I remembered he was used to being showered with gifts and tokens of affection. "I am way too proud of it to give it away. Especially to someone who doesn't appreciate her unique beauty," I said, giving the basket a gentle pat.

A laugh finally broke from his lips, and the rich sound roused a golden warmth throughout my middle. Him laughing this freely was beautiful to witness, *and* feel, because I knew just how rare it was.

"No, you're right. What is unique deserves to be admired," he said as his deep green eyes captured mine. For a moment it seemed like he meant it for more than just my abysmal creation, but before I could decode his gaze, I stopped in my tracks, unable to catch my breath, and my basket tumbled to the ground as I clutched my pounding chest.

My random bouts of exhaustion were becoming quite the nuisance, even Rowen's playful face slackened into worry. "You grow weaker by the day. Don't think I haven't seen it, Keira. Let me take you to Takoda."

"It'll pass," I breathed, batting away Rowen's suggestion. There was no need to bother Takoda with this.

"Have you been able to return home?"

"No, and I don't know why. I've been trying but it appears I'm stuck here." The mere thought of never seeing my home or family again shot a terrifying jolt down my spine. In all the days that had passed, I failed to make it back even once. Every night I went to sleep with the hope of waking up in my bed, back in my room, yet here I remained.

My heart ferociously beat against my ribcage.

"Tell me something from your life," Rowen said, trying to distract me from my evident and building panic attack. "Maybe recalling a good memory from home will help you find your way back."

If Rowen wanted to know more about me, he would have to give up something as well.

"A memory for a memory," I panted.

"Copeland, just talk to me before you pass out."

"Not unless you tell me something too. It's only fair."

"Fine," he agreed begrudgingly, crossing his arms. "You first."

"Good memories are rare for me but there is one that sticks out," I said, willing the memory to wash over and calm me. "The first time I went to the observatory."

"What is the observatory?" Rowen asked.

"It's a building to help you see the stars."

"Why would you not just step outside?" he asked perplexed, gesturing to the ever-glowing heavens above.

"It's different where I'm from. The sky it's…it's hidden from us," I said, thinking about all the artificial light, smog, and pollution that masks the magic of the sky. And how you have to drive hours from any city to see more than a light smattering of stars.

"For all that is wrong and dying in Luneth, at least we have the sky. To gaze up and know we are not alone, to know we are made of the same cloth as the heavens. I can't imagine not being able to witness that every day."

"Most people couldn't imagine seeing this all day, every day," I said, never tiring of the constant visibility of space. "At the observatory, you can look through a special lens that brings you right to the stars. They are so close you can almost feel the stardust inside you, letting you know that somewhere, something is free. My parents had to drag me out at closing, and I would constantly beg them to take me back, but they were always too busy. Eventually, they bought me a telescope to keep from bothering them, but us being there together was what I really wanted."

"You miss your parents?"

"My parents rarely had time for me. They tend to throw money and pills at their problems instead of time and understanding, but yes, I do miss them," I said as my throat constricted with emotion, and I made the mistake of glancing up. Rowen was watching me intently, too intently, and I cleared my throat. "Anyway, it's your turn. Time to give it up."

He hummed in contemplation, and I swear I could feel his deep vibration through the soles of my feet. "Mine would be the first time I threw this blade," he said, reverently gesturing to the ax at his hip. "When I was brought to the Wyn village, all I had was the clothes on my back, nothing more, not even a life I wanted to live. I desired only to disappear into the forest. Takoda saw I needed a purpose, however small and placed this ax in my hand. He said I could leave once I severed a single leaf from a billowing tree and that I was to present it to him in perfect condition."

My chest tightened. So what Ven had told me was true. Rowen had lost his will to live. I was tempted to ask him about the woman who'd been taken from him, but it wasn't my place to ask such an intrusive question. He would tell me when he was ready.

"Having never trained with a blade such as this, I started with the targets on the training grounds. The first time I ever threw it, it was as if the air from my throw was the breath I'd been missing from my lungs. Takoda knew what he was doing with such a request, though I don't think he expected me to stay this long."

"You haven't been able to retrieve the leaf?"

"It took me nearly three moons, no doubt looking an absolute fool, but I finally succeeded. Though I have yet to present it to Takoda. I find I'm not ready to leave here just yet."

An unexpected laugh escaped my lips, and Rowen's eyes narrowed in suspicion. "What. You mean to tell him?"

"Tell him what?" I asked, stepping towards him, and for once it was his body that shifted uncomfortably. "That it took you so long to do something so simple."

"You think you can do better?"

"Hand me your blade," I said, dipping my chin towards his single-handed ax. "And let's find out."

Too curious to resist, Rowen handed me his weapon with glinting amusement.

Extending up to my tiptoes, I reached overhead, Rowen's eyes tracking my every movement. I clasped onto a branch swaying in the thick canopy above and pulled the lush limb down until it rested in the small space between us. Careful not to lose my concentration, I nicked a single perfect leaf with his blade and handed it to him innocently. "He never specified how to retrieve the leaf now, did he?" I said, releasing the bough back to its rightful place.

He laughed another one of his deep belly laughs. "Well, you're a sly little one, aren't you? Full of surprises."

"I have my moments."

He took his weapon from my hand and replaced it with the leaf that was Takoda's promise of a new beginning. "Keep it," he said, smiling. "You earned it. But can I trust you with my secret?"

"Your secret's safe with me," I said, touching the leaf to the tip of my nose in a sealed promise, confident he wasn't pulling one over on Takoda.

"Are you feeling better?" he asked, his gaze brushing over my skin like a cool cloud.

"A little."

"Good," he said, his chest swelling towards me like he was breathing me in, needing more of my oxygen, and I became hyper-aware of the intimate space we shared on the vast stretch of forest. I instinctively leaned closer towards him, my lips slightly parting for the breath of him as well.

His relaxed body suddenly snapped to attention, as if realizing he'd made a grave mistake in allowing himself to get too comfortable around me. His eyes narrowed, scanning the silent woods as if we were being watched. "I trust you know your way back," he said, his voice suddenly rough and clipped.

He turned from me abruptly and disappeared into the dark shadows of the night, leaving me alone and breathless in the dim glow of the forest, holding nothing but a small leaf of hope.

——— ·(·(· ● ·)·)· ———

I was getting worse.

Each morning I woke more tired and drained than the last. My thoughts and movements grew more sluggish with each passing day. My words and limbs lagged, and my appetite was completely gone.

I was relieved I hadn't been training with Dyani. There was no way I would have been able to keep up with her. Even the smallest act required the utmost attention and effort and left me gasping for breath.

Even though I'd only been here two weeks, I knew I'd lost a dangerous amount of weight. My reflection told me as much when I dared to look at it. My cheeks were hollow, and the light smudges I once had under my eyes were now dark smears of purple. I looked malnourished even though I forced food down my gullet several times a day. My metabolism was burning too fast to keep up. It was as if my body was in hyperdrive, working three times as hard.

I was only too glad to look away from my reflection in the small lavatory of Rowen's dome. I was rapidly wasting away and I wished I knew why.

Was I not meant to be here? Was the environment of Luneth not compatible with my body over a long period of time?

My state affirmed how the Summit viewed me—a weakened mare—and it infuriated me that they were turning out to be right.

I hadn't been called back to meet with the Summit, but the tension in their faces as we all awaited Erovos' next move was evident. So far, we hadn't heard a peep from him since Graem's visit, and the silence weighed on us that much more heavily.

The next morning, I almost couldn't get out of bed. It took every morsel of strength to pry myself from Rowen's plush bedding. I barely made it out the front door before Rowen greeted me as he did every morning since the day Ven and I went off-grid.

I was ready for him to make some snide comment about the way I looked, but with just one glance at my unsteady appearance, his face creased with concern. "You *are* unwell."

"I'm fine," I said, even as my legs threatened to buckle out from underneath me.

The last thing I remembered was thinking what a comical epitaph those two little words would make because I was clearly anything but fine.

And as I fainted right into Rowen's arms, I knew I would never live it down.

"What happened?" I asked through half-lidded eyes, making out Takoda's form hovering above me with his palm over my brow. His suspended hand slowly trailed down the length of my face, chest, and stomach—nothing to be discerned beyond a calm concentration.

"Your body gave out," he said candidly, checking various acupoints along my neck and skull. As Takoda examined me with adept fingers, my eyes scanned around another exquisitely crafted dome. It was similar to Rowen's in many ways, except this was the room of a healer. And gently laid upon the examining bedroll as I was, it was unfortunately clear that I was the patient.

Healing ferns and herbs surrounded me from floor to ceiling. Plants grew in hydroponic glass vials, their roots visible as they overflowed into spiraling green vines while leaves, seeds, and flowers dried from the walls and rafters.

"What's wrong with her?" Rowen demanded with a growl.

"I have never seen this before. She is fading away before my very eyes," Takoda replied, standing from his crouch and turning from me. His glorious white mane was bound at the base of his neck, and I tried to focus on the smooth-shifting muscles of his back as he gathered ingredients from around the room.

Takoda gently plucked and cut various vegetation and ground them into powder using a stone mortar and pestle. "I need to go back," I croaked, "but I...I've been struggling."

"What can be done, Takoda?" Rowen almost pleaded.

Takoda quickly brewed the ingredients into a tea and placed his hand on my shoulder. "Do you remember what happened right before you came here last?" he asked gently, too gently.

"I remember..." My voice didn't sound like my own. It was

muffled, garbled, and far away like I was hearing myself from across the room. "I remember just before I left, I felt a moment of hesitation. I...I was scared I'd be stuck here."

What irony.

"It would seem in that moment of fear, you split yourself in two. Neither fully here nor there. Astrally torn," Takoda said, finishing up with his brew. "You are slipping away from yourself, caught between our worlds. No body can sustain such a divide for long. Drink this, star-touched. It will help you regain a little of your strength, but not much. You will have to find and mend yourself on your own, this is a journey none but you can make. Here, help me lift her."

Rowen's fingers gently swept back my hair before snaking around to cradle the nape of my neck. He lifted me to the mug Takoda held before my lips, and I managed to choke down a few sips of bitter liquid.

Rowen's worried stare darted back and forth between Takoda and me. "There must be something else we can do to help her?" he implored, his eyes going wild. "Perhaps a Hymma ceremony?"

Takoda's brows furrowed. "It will be exceedingly dangerous, although it might grant her the time and space she needs to become whole again. To find her home."

Home? I realized I never really felt at home anywhere, not with my parents growing up, not with Natalie or Harlan—just always alone fighting a silent battle.

Despite those feelings, I still missed them and wanted to see them again. But Luneth was starting to feel like home too, at least for the short time I'd been here.

Not only was my body and soul tearing in two, but my heart and mind as well.

I nodded to Takoda, knowing I had to retrieve whatever

essence of me was left behind. "I'll try it," I said, knowing I had no other choice. "I'll try anything."

"You should know that if this fails, you could be lost to us. Trapped in the void between worlds."

My struggled breath hiccuped, but I understood his meaning —find myself or lose myself forever.

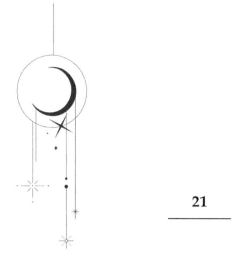

21

Takoda left to prepare the Hymma while I rested. The effects of the tea slowly calmed the rapid pace of my heart, and I closed my eyes.

Rowen sat beside me, his hand in mine, his thumb absent-mindedly stroking the battering pulse at my wrist.

"Hymma ceremonies are considered to be sacred amongst the Wyn people." His voice was low and soothing. "Only those who are well trained use this rite. It is known that one can receive great visions and inner reflections. Some have even claimed to hear echoes from the Elder Spirit's themselves. While others have died trying."

Unexpectedly, Rowen's breath warmed the shell of my ear. "Keira," he whispered, dipping his head ever so slightly to trace his nose along the curve of my jaw. "You have to come back to me."

I felt the scratchy caress of his beard on my skin, then the featherlight press of his lips on my neck, and the simultaneous feeling of soft and rough was exquisite.

Half delirious, I traced my touch along the dark stubble of

his beard. "I like this," I hummed, feeling his scruff with the pad of my finger.

His eyes widened in surprise and he snatched my hand from his face, holding it between us. "Copeland, I—"

"It is time," Takoda said, suddenly appearing through the circular door.

Without a word, Rowen scooped me up and carried me to a small geodesic structure made entirely of reflective crystal. The Hymma mirrored the outside world panel by panel, yet I avoided the sorry sight of myself in Rowen's arms, focusing on the lunar phases adorning the round entrance in flakes of crushed stardust. The full moon hovered at the apex as gradual waxing and waning moons fell down either side of the arch like basins of emptying water.

Rowen carefully set me down, ensuring I was steady on my feet, but I swayed a little, and he grabbed my elbow to keep me stable. I pressed on with shaky legs, but Takoda stopped me short. "You must enter the Hymma same as the day you were born. No earthly possession may enter here."

I hesitated a moment then looked down at my clothing, realizing his meaning, and began to unlace my vest. Both men turned from me as I undressed, but Rowen's hand never left my elbow for support.

I quickly stepped out of my clothes and left them where they fell, trying not to notice all the weight and muscle I'd lost.

Naked as the day I was born, I entered a room of pitch-black nothing. Fear bristled up my spine, and I whirled around to leave, but Takoda's face appeared in the sliver of the doorway. "You can do this," he said as loosened wisps of white hair gently blew across his face. "Set your intention and have it be so."

I nodded, finding strength and determination in his words. "I will."

I turned back to the dark room, but as I inspected the space more closely, I realized it was anything but dark. It was as if I'd pressed the heels of my hands to my eyes and watched as the lights beyond my lids came to life. An ever-changing kaleidoscope of patterns and light thrummed against the darkness like a sentient being aware of my presence.

I sat down cross-legged in the center of the dome, mesmerized as the room came to life around me. The tea Takoda brewed helped significantly, but I still sensed I didn't have much time until my mind completely strayed into the ether.

No longer sure if I was awake or asleep, a wooden flute began playing, and the entrancing melody flowed throughout my limbs. The rhythm harmonized with the beat of my pulse, attuning and grounding me to my body's environment. Takoda's words coursed through me like a river, *set the intention.*

I thought about my parents, along with Natalie and her horrid brown smoothies. I thought about the beautiful silver petal I lost all those years ago, and of all the times I'd been cocooned in my bed daydreaming of Rowen. I sank deeper and deeper into the memories, some happy, some painful, but all from the life I needed to return to.

I focused on emptying my thoughts, imagining them waning like the moons of the archway, mere basins of water slowly pouring out the white noise. I knew I was drifting, quickly now. My thoughts fell away like crystal droplets from the cloth of my mind.

I continued to sink deeper, my mind siphoning between two planes of existence like a thin stream of sand in an hourglass. I could no longer tell up from down, light from dark, corporeal from metaphysical.

I exhaled slowly, and forever happened.

My body jerked so hard and so abruptly it felt like whiplash.

I was in a fluorescent-bright room. The unfamiliar space was sterile, white, and quiet. Quiet except for the metronomic beeps and whirrings of machines.

A hospital. I was in a hospital?

I didn't need to open my eyes to see and sense every square inch of this room, every dull tile and stained ceiling panel. I was covered in wires and tubes that snaked out of my body, coiling to screens that blipped, flashed, and surveyed my every move.

Something had gone horribly wrong if I was in a hospital. If time in Luneth ran along the same timeline as Earth, I'd been unconscious for almost two weeks. I went to rise, but my limbs were anchors, so heavy I couldn't lift them from the stark white sheets of the hospital bed.

I tried not to panic at my inert body, but it was impossible, and my horror only grew as I realized I was completely frozen in place.

My worst nightmare.

I wanted to scream, thrash, and yank out the tubes that penetrated my skin. I wanted to run until nothing mattered anymore, but no matter how hard I tried, I couldn't move a muscle. My mind, however, was hyper-aware of everything around me, almost preternatural. *Body asleep, mind awake.*

The realization helped calm and slow my heart rate, and I reined in my panic. I couldn't outrun my problems. No one could, at least not forever.

I reached out the tendrils of my awareness to see how far I could go, hoping to glean any information about what happened to me. Maybe once I learned a bit more about my situation, I could wake myself up and return to my ordinary life. That sounded pretty appealing right about now.

I kept reaching and reaching until I hit the wall. I didn't so much hit it as I stopped right before it. But maybe I could keep going. Perhaps there were doctors on the other side discussing my condition.

I pushed my astral self on and passed through the wall as if it were merely a shadow cast by a cloud in the sky. The room was nearly identical to the one I was in, with the same stark, sterile walls and rhythmic beeping of medical equipment. Except in this room, connected to all the tubes and wires, was a man lying still as stone. He was so lifeless, not even his eyes fluttered behind his paper-thin eyelids.

Despite his pallid complexion, he was still timelessly handsome. He looked to be carved from glass, so still, fragile, and serene. His black hair swooped back over his strong brow, and his full eyelashes rested against high, sharp cheekbones. He reminded me of a beautiful prince in a fairytale, only in need of a kiss to wake.

His medical chart lay open at the foot of his bed, and I stole a glance: Maddock Mosa, age thirty-four. Comatose for over three years. Nearly ten years older than me, but still much too young to have your life snatched away.

I further inspected his chart—motorcycle accident resulting in massive head trauma. His next of kin refused to take him off life support, hoping and praying he might someday open his eyes. I could only imagine the cost of keeping a lifeless body alive for so long. He must come from a very affluent family.

I extended my consciousness a little further to see if I could reach out to him, speak to him, communicate with someone in the same situation as me. I touched the smooth, waxy skin of his temple and pushed just beyond. But I immediately recoiled, horrified by what I felt.

Nothing.

There was nothing. Not even a hint of a human soul. A complete and utter shell of a body pumped with artificial breath; a heart mechanically forced to beat through an unnatural life.

That hopeful family would wait and wait for a miracle that would never come.

The empty well of a human turned my blood to ice; and if I didn't figure out something soon, Maddock and I might share the same fate.

Footsteps echoed down the hall, and familiar voices pulled me back to my room. Moments later, my parents walked through the hospital door.

I wished I could jump up and hug them, kiss them and tell them how sorry I was for everything. Even though showing such emotion had never been part of our relationship, I was still relieved they were here. My mother with her long strawberry-blonde tresses and my dad with his dark brown hair, greying at the temples.

They stood by my bedside but didn't touch me, not even a reassuring squeeze on the hand or a quick kiss on the cheek, just a cold, stoic presence. My father took my mother's elbow and led her to the small table in the corner of the room.

"Her results are still so puzzling. Even the doctors say they have never seen anything like it," my father said, utterly perplexed. "Keira's epinephrine levels are dangerously high, her heart rate is exceedingly fast, and her brain activity scans are off the charts. She's never in a resting state, on complete overdrive every hour of the day. How can that be, Calliope?"

"It certainly is an anomaly, John," my mother responded in her calculating tone.

"One that if we monitor closely could be groundbreaking work for our next case study."

It hurt hearing the disrepair my body was in, but it cut even deeper hearing my parents discuss my condition like I was a glorified science project.

"Not like the man in the next room over; no brain activity whatsoever. Little more than a cadaver. It's selfish really, for his family to keep him alive, especially after the doctors declared brain death." My mother must mean the man lying comatose just beyond the wall, Maddock Mosa. "Although his case could make for an interesting juxtaposition to Keira's. We could compare the two cases side by side."

"Indeed," my mother ruminated.

They were talking as if they were discussing what was for dinner, not the failing condition of their one and only child. It was so callous and cruel that a tear slid down my cheek. I didn't want to be here at all. I couldn't believe that I'd wanted to return to this life even for a moment.

How much more interesting their study would be if they knew I could hear every word they uttered, even more so knowing that I could project my consciousness somewhere else entirely.

"What could have been the catalyst for our daughter ending up in a coma?" my father questioned. "We'll have to ask her roommate everything she knows. Hell, she was the one who found her when she wouldn't wake."

Natalie found me? I could imagine her checking in my room only to see my unmoving body. Her running to me and shaking my shoulders frantically, begging me to open my eyes. Then calling my mom with tears running down her cheeks, smudging her mascara.

"John, there is something you should know." I could hear the quiver in my mother's voice.

My father sat rigid, sensing my mother's confession would not be good. Whatever she was about to reveal, I knew it would break my heart.

"You remember our experimental drug we gave her up until her freshman year?" she asked, waiting for my dad to say something, anything, but he remained silent. It was as if he already knew where this story was going, but I didn't. My mind simply would not let my thoughts wander to the possibilities.

"When she told me she no longer wanted to take our medication because it made her too sluggish, I knew it was simply out of the question. You remember the things she used to tell us—so disturbing, so ludicrous, not to mention the complaints. I couldn't go through that again, John. I just couldn't, so I made a few adjustments to our drug and slipped it into her food until the day she left the house. She never said anything or suspected, not with the new tweaks, so I kept medicating her. I couldn't stand by while our daughter lost her mind."

I jerked as if a bomb had gone off inside my head. I remembered the bottle she'd come home with had been label-less, a dangerous concoction of her own making. The disorientation had me grasping at where I was and how I got here. A high-pitch ringing ruptured in my skull and it felt like my ears were bleeding.

My father's voice reached me like a targeted beam. "For God's sake, Calliope," he practically yelled before realizing he was in a public space. He lowered his voice, yet it still dripped with rage, "We could lose our practice and licenses if anyone found out about that. We created an extremely dangerous and unethical cognitive suppressant powerful enough to drug an elephant. Even the lowest doses didn't make it past clinical trials. It's a miracle it didn't kill her then, and it's a miracle she's still alive today. What were you thinking? We agreed never to use that again."

"It's not our fault nothing ever worked on her, and I never agreed to stop trying."

My tongue turned thick in my mouth. My mother had drugged me.

The terrible realization that lies and deceit had shaped my life crushed me. How could my mother do such unspeakable things without my consent? And my father barely batting an eyelash, more concerned about losing their professional statuses.

My mother's explanation didn't cover everything. What about the past five years? She must have found a way to continually poison me, and as much as my mind wanted to shut down and drown out the rest of her admission, I knew I needed to hear it to its end.

My father seemed to come to the same conclusion. "And how have you been continuing to give it to her?" he asked, straightening his glasses.

"Well, that was a bit tricky, but I saw how well Keira was doing on the new blend. It wasn't affecting her motor skills in any way. She could still run."

"Calliope. How did you do it?" He accentuated every word through a clenched jaw.

"Her roommate," she finally admitted in a hushed violent whisper. "When I met the girl, I wanted to warn her about Keira's condition, prepare her. She asked if there was anything she could do to help, and I saw my opening. I've been paying her quite handsomely for the past few years, and it seemed like she was competent enough to get the job done. Until recently."

Natalie? It was the final nail in the coffin.

I wished I could destroy everything within arm's reach, break anything I could get my hands on, and scream until my voice went raw, but my body remained frozen. An invisible storm of fury and despair raged in my mind while I was completely inert, dying on the inside.

"Dammit, woman. Witnesses?" Veins bulged out of his forehead and neck. I had never seen him so furious, so out of control. "You better pray they don't find traces of our narcotic in her blood."

"They won't."

"How?" My father asked with clipped yet contained paranoia.

"I'm not an idiot. How do you think she passed all her athlete panel tests? It's untraceable. It's not like it was performance-enhancing anyway. I thought I was doing right by her, John. I really did."

My mother had been drugging me. She'd even gone so far as to create an undetectable narcotic to cover her tracks. The depths in which her treachery reached crippled me. She couldn't even see that what she'd been doing was wrong. Trying to justify herself further, she said, "It was helping her lead a normal life."

Normal? Normal! My normal was always feeling half alive. Numb. Devoid of depth and genuine feeling. It had been hell. Running was the only thing that kept me sane, but only just. My whole life I'd always been half asleep, constantly wandering through an inescapable fog that kept me so drowsed I was merely a shell of a person.

My father ran a hand down his clean-shaven face, looking older than I'd ever seen him. "Hopefully the girl keeps quiet, Calliope. She's just as culpable as you and has no reason to go to the authorities." His drawn expression was tired but completely devoid of shock, as if he always knew the capabilities and deter-minations of his brilliant wife.

I did the math and counted back the months. It confirmed what my mother confessed, and I realized in horror that the dreams had started back up again when I stopped eating Natal-ie's breakfasts. I had gone along and pretended to drink her horrid smoothies, so she assumed everything was going according to plan, still happily accepting a paycheck from my mother to secretly drug me. She had been doing it for years, my mother's perfect partner in crime.

Something fundamental snapped within me, some intrinsic column of belief that held me up all my life was careening, and there was nothing left to brace me as I fell. I was a giant redwood plummeting to the forest floor, but as I broke and roared and crashed to the ground, nobody even noticed.

And if no one could hear me, was I even really crashing?

The life I thought I knew melted and dissolved around me like an oil painting abandoned in the rain, bleeding into something unrecognizable, into something frightening. It was only now that I could see what a static and dull painting it really was. No depth, color, or use of light. Just a flat half-life rendered in monochromatic grey.

I'd like to say I knew I was meant for more. But if it hadn't been for Natalie messing up her one job, who knew how long I would have lived my life in greyscale, blindly accepting the never-ending shades of black and white. I had only started to feel alive a couple of months ago, and now that I had a taste of life, it truly showed me what an empty existence I had been living. An existence forced and tricked upon me by my mother and roommate.

I could barely fathom how fortunate it was that I'd started flushing Natalie's corrupted drinks down the sink. That was also around the time I started dreaming again. Dreaming of a darkness, a dead forest, and of Rowen.

Rowen!

I couldn't stay here another minute. I didn't want to, not any part of me. I had to get out of here. Get back to him, to his dark and emerald presence that always calmed yet challenged me. Excited me.

Back to Takoda and his kind eyes, and Ven who looked at me

like I was his hero. And Nepta, who somehow knew me better than I knew myself. I even missed Dyani.

My father stood abruptly, scraping his chair against the linoleum flooring, making my mother flinch. "I need some air," he said stoically, leaving the room without a backward glance. My mother hesitated a moment, then followed after him, leaving me as alone as I'd always been.

There was nothing left for me here—I'd been betrayed by my parents, my best friend, even by myself for living and accepting such an empty life. I clawed at my mind. I wanted out, but if I weren't careful, I would break and lose myself right here on the hospital bed.

To be whole, I had to be in one place or the other. I couldn't keep straddling both worlds, and now I didn't have a reason to.

With my mind made up, I would consciously gather every cell, every molecule, every inherent part of me, and take it all back to Luneth—no second-guessing, no doubts, no moments of hesitation.

I wanted this.

I closed my eyes to the sterile hospital room, but all was entropy in my fracturing mind—I'd never find my way anywhere. Everything was collapsing all around me, and my foundation cracked at my feet, falling into an endless abyss. I sprinted across my breaking psyche; a single misstep and I'd be lost to the void between worlds.

The faintest glint of a thread appeared on the horizon, but I'd never make it. The ground was falling too fast. I banked to the right and stumbled as my runway shattered beneath me. I barely managed to right myself before another piece of my consciousness dropped away.

My mother was right about one thing. This ending terrified me.

Suddenly, an arm stretched out across the ether; fingers

dipped in faded black moonlight. Rowen's unmistakable hand reached for me, just out of grasp, and I hurled myself forward, barely catching his strong grip.

With his hand firmly clasped around mine, he helped pull me to the life I had chosen. He may have been pulling, but I was running with everything I had as the ground crumbled at my heels.

I was sprinting so fast it felt like wings were sprouting from my ankles, carrying me more swiftly than I could ever imagine. It was the greatest race I'd ever run. One where there was no person or time to beat, just me, my own pounding heart, determined mind, and resolute body, healing itself.

I finally saw the way home; that silver thread now a tunnel of light, and for the first time in my life, I was running towards something.

I took one final step, thrusting my whole body into the waves of undulating particles, leaving everything behind me. I shed my past along with what remained of the inky-black drug in my veins like a second skin. The hospital robe disintegrated off my body, leaving me as naked and free as a falling star.

And I flew, flew through the spiraling helix of worlds, galaxies, and silver light.

———— ·((●))· ————

I woke up with a jolt, my body notching into place like a collapsible baton finally snapping into alignment.

My vision shattered in blinding shards of space and time, and I saw a massive black tree looming before me. The blighted branches twisted and bent at sharp angles like veins stretching across the night sky, spreading their poison.

The base of the tree looked to have been cleaved in half,

creating a tunnel through the giant trunk. You could walk right through it if you wanted to.

Bolted into both sides of the tree's opening were two shackles, swaying lazily in the wind. Their ominous dance was a warning for the hands destined to be captured in their clutches, and my wrists itched uncomfortably at the thought.

Lightning struck, illuminating two figures standing beside me. By sheer size alone, I recognized one of them as Graem. I shielded my naked body from the giant's stare only to realize my skin was shining so bright it was as if I had swallowed the moon.

The other being's presence was dark, frigid, and without end, shrouded in a black cloak of shifting mist.

The lightning dissipated, returning all to shadows, then it struck again violently, clattering my teeth. The hooded figure was facing me now, and we locked gazes. His eyes were like black holes, maelstroms of red and orange matter from which nothing could escape, not even light. The creases around his eyes were deep and prominent because his smile was so frighteningly genuine. His teeth were long and sharp, making his venomous sneer even more sinister.

It was the most horrifying thing I'd ever seen.

"I've been looking for you, my little light," he said, his endless stare unblinking. "It won't be long now until you're mine."

And all turned to black.

———— ·(·(·●·)·)· ————

My eyes flew open, and I gasped for air.

The vision snapped before me so quickly it was as if it had never happened. But I could never forget those eyes for as long as I lived. My bones were still chilled to their very marrow by it.

I was drenched in sweat, lying naked on the ground with splashes of light clouding my sight.

My body swirled, flowing with an energy that had long been suppressed by an insidious drug forced into my veins. But now that I had emerged through space like a phoenix reborn, I was rushing with power, a power that another sought to capture and destroy.

Somehow the Dark Spirit Erovos had found me. And it wouldn't be long until he had me.

My limbs quaked with fear, light, and the weight of a million stars. I sat up and yelled the only thing my mind could conjure.

"ROWEN!"

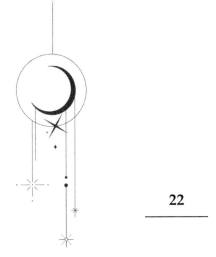

22

I was in shock, lodged in place like a stone as a current rushed all around me. Within me.

Rowen came bounding out of the darkness in a firework of light and dropped to the ground in front of me. But my thoughts were consumed by the betrayal of my parents and Natalie, the malicious stare that could only belong to Erovos, and the dark tree whose chains seemed to call my name.

Rowen shook my shoulders, but still, I looked past him, lost in grief.

My mind had been quelled of feeling for so long that my body didn't know how to handle all the emotions. I felt every-thing, and it hurt more than I could have ever imagined. The pain was physical, and I rubbed the heel of my hand over my chest to stop my heart from breaking.

Rowen's hands grabbed my face, his fingers tangling in my hair. "Keira," he said firmly, and through the fading lights, I saw the blurry outline of his bare body.

Had he joined me in the Hymma?

Suddenly remembering where I was, my eyes snapped to Rowen's, and he sucked in a sharp breath. "By the Spirits, Keira.

Your eyes are glowing like liquid silver...like...like the Alcreon Light."

"He knows."

"Who?"

"Erovos."

Rowen's eyes widened in horror. "Let's get you out of here."

As we exited the dome, Rowen threw a woven blanket around my body before wrapping one around his waist.

We barely made it a foot outside the Hymma before I crashed onto my knees. Here was as good a place as any to tell Rowen and Takoda about my vision of the tree. The rest could wait until later; those emotions were still too raw to touch.

Takoda walked to where I'd collapsed, and I tilted my eyes up to meet him. "By the light of the Spirits," he uttered and lowered to his knees in front of me. "It seems, star-touched, that you have returned with far more than anyone could have bargained for."

"She is the bearer of the Alcreon Light," Rowen nearly choked. "Her...her eyes. She is The Marked."

"The Summit may need more convincing."

"Whether the Summit believes it or not, Erovos has seen my face," I said through a dry throat. "He's...he's looking for me."

Concerned glances passed between the two men as I relayed my vision.

"That was no vision, Keira. You stepped foot upon his land," Takoda said calmly but with a severity that was foreign to his ever-tranquil voice. "Did you maintain the connection? Did he see you open your eyes to the Hymma or any part of this village?" His umber gaze implored mine.

"No," I answered, certain no other eyes had seen through mine.

"Then he can have no way of knowing you are here," Takoda breathed with relief. He reached for my wrist and monitored my pulse. "Your strength has returned. Sure as a river, your pulse beats stronger, clearer, more focused. And while there may be a new light in your eyes, there is also a new sadness."

Rowen shot me a concerned glance as I pulled my hand back to my chest.

Takoda was right on all counts. A cannon blast had pulverized my heart, the barrel aimed and lit by my own family. But I'd also never felt stronger. The truth had set me free, lighting me with flickers of energy that pulsed throughout my veins.

My cage was finally open, but like an eagle held in captivity for too long, I had no idea how to fly.

"You did well, both of you. Even though it was exceedingly dangerous for you to join her, Rowen. You could have both been lost. Only those who have accepted their soul flame have ever dared try a Hymma joining, and with great risk," Takoda said, looking between Rowen and me. His words meant to scold, but they came out more as bewildered shock.

"I knew the risks," Rowen ground out from the back of his throat, a fierce adrenaline rolling off him in waves. "She was breaking in there, and you know it."

Takoda couldn't argue with that. I had been breaking, was still breaking. "I'll summon the Summit and meet you at the Sacred Vale," he said as he stood, then darted away with a speed and grace I could only admire.

"You shouldn't have put yourself in danger like that," I said to Rowen, who vibrated beside me with an energy I couldn't place.

"I couldn't sit idly by," he barely whispered, cupping my cheek and forcing my silver gaze to his. He pulled me closer and tilted my chin until his warm forehead pressed against mine. "I would help pull you out of any darkness. But it was you who did brilliantly, Keira. To come back whole." His thumb gently stroked my cheekbone, and I felt dizzy when his breath hit my face.

I placed my hand over his. "For a moment, I didn't think I would be able to find my way, but you helped pull me back."

"You were screaming. I ran in and you were...clawing at yourself."

"I was frozen, attached to tubes and machines that I tried to rip from my body, but I couldn't move, couldn't speak."

"You're back now. That's all that matters," he said softly, his sensuous mouth so close to mine. His breath skittered along my jaw, and I would only have to slightly tilt my head back for our lips to meet.

Seeming to remember I wore nothing but a blanket, Rowen looked me up and down and cleared his throat. "We need to get you ready for the Summit. They will be waiting," he said, picking up my bundle of clothes and fisting them to me. As I reached for my vest and leggings, my fingers lightly brushed against his, featherlight and unintended, and a spark of ice-white light shot from my fingertips and zapped him on the hand.

He hissed between his teeth.

"Did I hurt you?" I asked, quickly pulling my hand back as memories flooded in—I'd shocked people before: friends, teachers, the men at Prism, even my parents.

Yet another reason I'd been drugged into oblivion.

"No, it was only a slight jolt," he said as a forest swirled in his eyes, but a grave shadow circled his irises like a dreaded forecast. "You've done it before, but now it's more...potent."

Despite the beads of sweat that trickled down my brow, ribcage, and arms, I was covered in goosebumps—hot but chilled all over. And I knew in that infinite second, people would kill for the power coursing through my veins.

<hr>

Dressed and hydrated, we arrived at the Sacred Vale, the symphony of long thin waterfalls echoing in the distance. The Summit members sat under the hovering remnants of the Alcreon Stone.

Alvar pounded his fist on the glittering table, and Driskell's brows furrowed as everyone spoke over one another. Upon my entrance, the valley quieted, and Rowen and I took our seats in front of their expectant gazes.

Nepta, never missing a detail with her unseeing eyes, said, "You are all here now then, child."

It wasn't a question.

"Do you finally have your wits about you enough to inform us of what is going on?" Driskell asked, searching my face as he would the stars. "Why now?"

"As it turns out," I exhaled deeply, "I have been drugged for most of my life." Rowen snapped his head towards me, and a resounding silence settled over the glen. "Growing up I had dreams of you, of Luneth, of walking this land and returning home with things I couldn't explain. It frightened my parents, so much so that they tried to suppress my abilities with experimental medicines from my world. It seems my parents succeeded, to all our detriment."

I barely got the words out as my breath escaped me. There wasn't enough oxygen, it was fraying from my lungs too fast. But stating the facts aloud cemented the truth. There was never anything wrong with me as I'd been led to believe. What I had was a gift so powerful, it frightened those who couldn't understand it.

The Alcreon Light was inside me. I knew that now, without a doubt. And the heavy weight of fear and inadequacy sat in the pit of my stomach. What if I couldn't help? What if I let everyone down?

How could I be The Marked, the bearer of such a celestial

light? It was all too much, too fast. I didn't want to accept it, didn't know if I could, not on top of everything else.

"A potion to suppress power? Takoda, have you ever heard of such a thing?" The feathers and crystals dangling from Alvar's long white hair shook and whipped about his face as he looked back and forth between the members of the Summit.

"I know not of these strange medicines, but for however strong the Alcreon Light may be, it is still hosted within a human body, a human body made of flesh and blood. So I suppose it is possible."

The war chief grunted and flipped his dagger in the air, unappeased by Takoda's explanation. "If that is what she truly is."

Driskell looked from Alvar to me, "One day, out of the blue, your parents decided to stop poisoning you?"

"It was only by chance I stopped taking it," I said, sticking to the main bullet points. Anything more and I would crumble to pieces. I was barely holding it together as it was.

"If this drug is as potent as you say, it would have taken time to fully dissipate from your body," Takoda pointed out.

"As the drug withdrew from Keira's blood, she steadily grew stronger. Revealing herself little by little," Rowen added on, helping add the pieces together.

That made perfect sense. Why when I first met Rowen, I could barely see or hear him, as if *he* were the ghost, not me. How, as it slowly detoxed from my body my dreams became clearer, sharper. Real.

I wondered if my mother could ever have known how successful her drug would be, how perfectly it fulfilled its intended purpose. It kept me safe from Erovos, so I guess I should thank her for that. But it also kept me from Rowen, the Wyn village, and people who needed my help. How could I ever forgive that?

I barely recognized myself. My life. But the truth had always been there, hidden beneath the darkened fog forced into my bloodstream.

My spine snapped as I thought back to Prism. All this time I could never explain what happened that night, how my mind and body had lost all control. With no other excuse, I blamed my symptoms on having an allergy to alcohol, but it hadn't been an allergic reaction at all—it had been a chemical one.

The drug lingering in my system from Natalie's spiked food wasn't meant to combine with alcohol; every pill bottle in the world stated as much. Creating such a concoction could cause the opiates in your blood to turn toxic, leading to serious health consequences, overdoses, even death.

And Natalie had willingly supplied me with both.

No wonder she had looked so guilty the following morning, so apologetic and worried. She knew she had messed up, potentially causing me irreparable harm, not to mention the humiliation and degradation I suffered at the hands of her carelessness.

Now that my body was purged of all suppressive narcotics and I could feel again, would my heart ever stop breaking? I pressed the heel of my hand to my chest to relieve the ache.

"Nepta, her eyes shine with the light of the heavens," Takoda marveled. "She is The Marked, the one the stars spoke of, the one who holds the light of worlds within her grasp."

"We still cannot know," Nepta said. "I will not risk what is not certain."

"How can you deny what she is any longer? Because she's not a man?" Rowen asked furiously. "She has brought back the moonlit glow to the plant life. That is evidence enough."

Alvar scoffed. "The moonblooms have often strangely come back to life."

"Because her presence was near!" Rowen yelled to a crowd of deaf ears.

"After all the lost hope, how can I face my village and dangle yet another questionable prophecy within their grasp? I must provide proof beyond the shadow of a doubt. I will not raise their already fragile spirits for naught," Nepta said.

"Takoda must have told you Erovos has seen her face," Rowen said, raking his hand through his unruly hair.

Nepta's ancient eyes hardened, her mind made up. "Indeed, she now poses a greater threat to this village. But if she is to remain within our protection, there must be just cause. I refuse to put my people at unnecessary risk."

"The risk is already here," Rowen practically shouted in desperation, but him losing his temper wouldn't help either of us. We were both outsiders here.

"Rowen, it's okay," I said, placing my hand on his shoulder, and his muscles jumped beneath my touch. "How can I prove it?" I asked Nepta. "What do I need to do?"

"There is a plant," she answered immediately as if she had already contemplated such a question. Her eyes sparkled with the visions of memory. "It has been long-dead to this land for many moons. Go to the barren meadow of the Sillarial Peaks, and revive a single noxlily bred of light and healing. Then, we will know for certain you possess the Alcreon Light, and your continued protection within our borders will be warranted. Otherwise, we will escort you from this land forever."

"Noxlily?" I asked, my blood buzzing. "What does it look like?"

"Like a petaled and unfurling star," Driskell stated banally, even though what he described was anything but, and I knew firsthand because I'd walked through a field of them.

"I've seen noxlilies before," I said as my childhood projection rushed to the forefront of my mind, and I recalled the plush glowing petal.

"Then you should have no trouble retrieving one," Alvar said in challenge.

"You would have her leave the safety of the village to retrieve a flower?" Rowen asked incredulously. "I felt her power just now, Nepta. It was weak and timid. She needs to be trained, not to go off on some wild goose chase for an extinct weed!"

"It is decided, Rowen Damascus," Nepta said with unquestioning authority. "And she will not be alone. She will have you."

"And me," Takoda replied without hesitation.

"Very well. You will leave at first light."

My head was reeling, but I needed to come to grips with my new reality. The Alcreon Light chose me, for whatever reason. And now I needed to prove it hadn't chosen wrong.

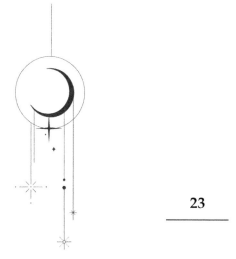

23

The next morning Takoda stood at the edge of sunrise, straight as an arrow, his hair shining like a mane of frost against the dense forest wall. His sleeveless tunic revealed the taut line of a bow draped from one shoulder to opposite hip. He wore sandstone breeches and a calm, reassuring expression that slowed my nerve-wracked heart. "Are you ready, star-touched?"

I nodded, afraid that if I spoke, my voice would reveal just how inadequate and unworthy I was for this responsibility.

"Though the Summit needs proof, the Alcreon Light rests within you. You must learn to harness its power," Takoda said, checking his pack of arrows and supplies for the journey. "Rowen was correct in that."

"Of course I was right," Rowen said, suddenly materializing out of the darkness. "Though it seems I stumbled upon this conversation a little late. Remind me of what again?" The pale golden hue of the sun welcomed and illuminated him, and I was immediately struck by how different he looked.

He was completely clean-shaven.

His smooth appearance revealed the sharp edges of his jawbone and the hard square cut of his chin, even his lips looked fuller. He appeared younger, neat, and courtly without his close-cut beard, and I couldn't help feeling he'd gotten rid of it because of my comment from before the Hymma.

I said I liked it, so naturally, he had gotten rid of it.

It was a slap to the face. He didn't want me liking him—any part of him.

While I preferred his rugged scruff, he was painfully beautiful either way, but in this moment I couldn't stand the sight of him.

"Takoda and I got this. You don't need to come," I said, receiving his message loud and clear. He was in love with a ghost. I couldn't compete with that, and he was asking me not to.

"Who else is going to keep an eye on you, Copeland?" he asked, walking right up to me, his fluid movements like a lazy river, but I knew his calm exterior masked a raging undertow of pain and anger just beneath the surface.

Regardless, his patronizing tone was getting old.

"Not this again."

"I'm sorry if it upsets you," he said, not sounding sorry at all. "But I made a promise to Nepta to protect—"

"—Protect me? Yeah, I get it. You've made it very clear you're only doing this for Nepta." He flinched, and a stray lock of his dark brown hair fell into his face. On instinct, I wanted to push the chocolate curl back from his eyes, but I kept my arms stiff by my sides.

From here on out, I would train my brain and body to see him as nothing more than an associate with vested interests. I could do that—as long as he stopped looking at me like that, like he was reaching out to me while asking me to stay away.

"You will barely even notice I'm here."

Somehow I doubted that very much. "When will I be able to roam freely without you as my irritating shadow?"

"How about we say..." he raised a hand to stroke his smooth

chin as if contemplating a deep thought, "when you can knock me on my ass," he said smugly. "So it might be a while."

I don't know what came over me. Maybe it was the overconfidence from taking Dyani down or the fact that I was so fed up with Rowen's savior complex, but I couldn't take that pompous look on his face for one more second.

I wound back and unleashed my fist as hard as I could, aiming directly at Rowen's infuriating clean-shaven face.

I braced for the pain his sharp jaw would inflict on my hand, but it never came.

Rowen plucked my wrist out of the air with ease and pulled me within an inch of his mouth. "As I said, it might be a while, sweet girl."

Holding my closed fist to his chest, he was near enough that I could smell his rosewood and charcoal scent as it enveloped me wholly. I raised my seething stare up his mountainous frame, trailing upward until our eyes locked. "When I do knock you on your ass, I'll make sure you feel it for weeks," I said, my chest heaving from outright fury.

"Sounds delightful," he said in mock pleasure.

His gaze dipped to my mouth, then connected quickly back to my stare, challenging me with his eyes.

I'd never been prone to violence or aggression. I don't think I ever even raised my voice too loudly. I knew now it was because I had been drugged within an inch of my life, but Rowen was still bringing out sides of myself I'd never felt before. And my body trembled with the mixed emotions.

Being this close to him, cloaked in his gaze, scent, and size, made my blood burn. I told myself it was only because he was beyond infuriating, but I wasn't sure that was entirely true.

"However, in the meantime, you'll carry this," he said as he slipped a sheathed knife into the front of my pants, just enough that the rough hilt rested against the divot of my abdomen.

"Not sure why I need this when I have you," I said sarcastically, shoving him off me.

Rowen released me with a shrug and a wicked grin. "This is far from a relaxing journey. Hopefully you know what you're doing. There won't be time to waste."

"I was hoping it would just sort of come to me once we got there," I confessed, knowing it was far from ideal.

"Wonderful," he replied grimly, then clenched his back teeth, tensing his jaw in all new fascinating ways that were once hidden from me.

Takoda, who'd been patiently waiting for our battle of wills to end, slung his quiver and pack over his shoulder. "If you two are quite done quarreling like younglings, let us leave," he nodded to both of us, looking somewhat entertained. "Now."

―――― ·（ ·⦅ · ● · ⦆ ·）· ――――

We hiked up the verdant slopes of the Sillarial Peaks, the crisp air mingling with the fragrance of the forest. I inhaled deeply, savoring the returned strength my body so desperately missed.

I would never take for granted the simple act of walking without losing my breath ever again.

We traveled through nature's beauty in silence, the stress of the trial weighing heavily on our every step. For all we knew, this could be the last time any of us saw the village ever again.

Now and then, Takoda would fill the tense quiet, explaining the different medicinal uses of varying plants, blossoms, and roots we passed along the way.

It amazed me how the very land itself could cure and heal the people who lived upon it. How herbs could be used to treat colds, aching joints, and upset stomachs. They could even be concocted into more potent remedies for illnesses such as fevers, diseases, and from the sounds of it, certain mental health concerns.

Occasionally Takoda would quickly collect a plant, thanking it before carefully tucking it away in his cloth satchel.

His knowledge of the land and all its bounteous gifts was astounding. The kindness I saw in his eyes extended to every living thing, even the plants. He handled all he touched with such reverence and respect.

We hiked on, every step bringing us closer to the ever-present stars, and I could almost feel them twinkling against my skin. However, the longer we walked the more the landscape gradually desaturated from the bright hues of life to the stone-cold colors of death. It was as though we had walked through all the seasons in the matter of a morning.

The dark, sickened forest was identical to the one I had first spoken to Rowen in. When I'd asked him what happened, he told me *its life was stolen*. What he meant was, it could no longer survive without me, without the power I held somewhere within my flesh and blood.

Hopefully, finding a noxlily would unlock a piece of my abilities and make the others believe; if not, we would all die trying. There was no returning empty-handed.

The sun crested over its zenith as we entered a clearing of dried bristles and long-dead flora.

"Do you feel anything?" Takoda asked me with a gaze full of hope while Rowen created a wide berth around us, his falcon eyes keeping watch over the barren land.

Here? This couldn't be the right place. The valley from my dreams had brought my senses to life, awakened me as if the earth's roots traveled through the soles of my feet and intertwined with my veins.

But just like Maddock in the hospital, there was no life here, none at all.

I knelt to the ground. "I have no idea what I'm supposed to do. What if this is all wrong? I'm too small, just one person, I can't do this alone."

"Feel the push and pull, Keira. It's running through your veins; you just have to find it."

I side-eyed him skeptically.

"We are all connected," Takoda said, his onyx eyes deep pools of wisdom. "You, me, the smallest stone to the grandest mountain, the nearest seed to the most distant star; our very bodies made of sand and stardust. It is because of this that we are one with everything and everything is one with us. Much like how you are the Alcreon Light—a gateway between darkness and light. In a sense, we are all a gateway to something greater than ourselves. You are far from alone."

His words washed over and comforted me. It was a beautiful belief, one that didn't seem that hard to accept and I nodded, absorbing his every word.

There was no time to waste. Not when a darkness was settling over the woods in a slow petrification of death. We were fighting the clock blindly, not knowing how long before everything froze forever—if it wasn't already too late—or how long until Erovos found me.

I knew the power was within me. I'd felt it after the Hymma, and I wasn't the only one. Rowen had felt it too. Merely touching him had rushed the light in me to the surface. I wondered if he even knew the effect he had on me? The impact he had before I even knew he was real.

I stole a peek at Rowen out of the corner of my eye. He was giving us space just as he promised, his shoulders tense and his hand never leaving the eye of his holstered ax. He was on guard, wary and watchful of what lay hidden in the stale wind.

I looked away and squeezed my eyes closed, trying to concentrate. Attempting to think of anything but Rowen, I thought of my parents, but a quick whip to the heart stopped me. Recalling anything from back home was off limits.

My mind slowly wandered back to Rowen, to the first time he had touched me, that lightning I felt, to this morning with his hands on me, and all the stirring little touches in-between. I thought of when I had first learned I was an astral traveler. That Luneth was real, my dreams were real, Rowen was real.

A slight tug pulled at my fingertips, building in pressure. My hands became alive, buzzing, and a beautiful glow began emanating from my fingertips, peaking out like timid bits of moonlight behind heavy storm clouds.

I sensed Takoda beside me, looking on with ecstatic wonder.

I touched my hands to the barren soil, sinking my fingertips into the blighted dirt. I waited for hundreds of silver roses to bloom and unfurl their petals, but nothing happened, and my hands flickered out like a broken bulb.

"You did it, star-touched," Takoda said with unadulterated pride.

"Then why isn't anything happening?" I asked disappointedly. I'd harnessed the Alcreon Light and it had done nothing. Had the drugs broken the Light? Was *I* broken?

Takoda scooped up a handful of dull soil and dropped it into a vial before placing it in his pack. "You may yet have sparked life. Time will tell."

Unsatisfied, I tried again but Rowen sprinted over to us, his eyes wide with terror. "Forest laiths are headed this way," he said, ax drawn.

Takoda immediately shot up from the ground, stringing his bow and arrow with fluid dexterity. "They never roam this far from the Weir."

Rowen moved to me as I stood and pulled the knife from my pants. He inspected my grip with satisfaction. "Good girl. If anything should happen, cut them once and make it count," he said as he brought his hands to either side of my neck and pressed on my hammering pulse. "Slice here," he instructed, never taking his eyes off me, and I nodded within his grasp. "And here," he said again, his hands lowering to my ribcage, his thumbs pushing into the soft flesh between my ribs and up into my lungs. "And here," he said finally, his touch sweeping against my inner thigh.

"G...got it," I replied through a constricted throat, though if I never saw one of those creatures again it would be too soon.

Takoda's eyes narrowed. "They must have sensed you, Keira, or were informed of your location. It would be best if we left now."

We moved in unison, eager to return to the safety of the village, when a small pack of laiths emerged from the shadows, blocking our path. The white figures were slightly hunched, panting, and baring several rows of razor-sharp teeth.

My heart caught in my throat. They were even more terrifying than I remembered.

Their flat faces peered towards us with starved fascination, and their verdant hair hung long over their sunken-in cheeks and elongated bodies—even their antlers tipped towards us with claiming aim.

But it was their slow blinking gaze that frightened me most, red upon red upon red, their eyes held no white whatsoever.

I had never wanted to be close enough to know such a thing about them.

Rowen said their eyesight wasn't the strongest during the day, but their carnivorous eyes seemed locked on us now, and thick ropes of drool dripped from their salivating mouths and blood-stained chins. Their claws flexed open, ready to strike and take down their prey.

With piercing shrieks and lethal instinct, the beasts charged toward us. Rowen grabbed my arm and I lurched forward with him as the three of us took off running deeper into the Sillarial Peaks.

I kicked up the ground behind me as I sprinted for my life, driving my feet as hard as they could possibly go. I was faster than Rowen and Takoda, leading the pack, but the laiths were gaining on us, already riding up on our heels.

Their raw-boned bodies were lithe, their strides long, and the gnashing of their teeth grew louder behind me. They would catch us and rip into our flesh if we didn't do something soon. There was no way we could outrun them.

Takoda turned and released an arrow with a backward glance, and I couldn't help but follow its trajectory, watching as the arrowhead pierced a laith right through the eye. The gargled screech echoed throughout the forest and sent ice-cold daggers of dread down my spine.

I shot my head forward and kept running, only to see two more laiths charging straight towards us. They'd had us surrounded long ago.

I skidded to a stop and I looked down at the knife in my palm—there was no question I was going to need it. I'd have to thank Rowen later, if we made it out of this alive.

One lunged at me, fangs pointed at my throat, ready to rip and tear and break. I thought I heard someone scream my name as I braced myself, holding the dagger as Dyani taught me.

Suddenly, the laith lurched forward and dropped to the ground as if it were made of sap and bark, not skin and bone. Landing face first in the dirt, the creature lay dead, Rowen's single-handed ax squarely lodged in its back.

Undeterred by its fallen comrade, another laith launched at me, claws flexed and crimson eyes pulsing with hunger. As it leapt, my body seemed to move on its own accord, and I lunged at its ribcage, thrusting my blade forward as I'd practiced on the training field.

The mass of white collapsed down on me like an avalanche, caving me under its immense weight as the hard ground rose up to meet me.

I expected the laith to lash out, but the body remained lifeless on top of me, seeping the air from my lungs one breath at a time. I tried to push the mammoth beast off, but my arm was bent at an awkward angle, and the laiths were heavier than they looked. I wasn't budging.

The impaled creature reeked of blood, moss, and raw meat, and a warm sticky liquid pooled on me as its life-force drained from the wound by my hand. My stomach churned, and I wanted to vomit.

Trapped, I could do nothing but listen in terror as the fight continued on around me in deathly thuds and mortifying screeches.

Suddenly the tremendous pressure of the dead laith was lifted from my chest, and I held my breath as I waited to see what uncovered me.

To my immense relief, it was Rowen who hefted the creature off me and helped lift me to my feet. "Are you hurt?" he asked, his panicked face scanning my body for injuries.

"I'm alright," I said as I did the same to him.

Satisfied that the blood I was covered in wasn't my own, Rowen glanced at the dead mound beside me. "Well done. Now, aren't you glad you had the blade?"

"Not the time," I panted.

"Later then?" he asked, prying his ax from the neck of a dead laith, and I grimaced at the sickening squelch.

Takoda ran up beside us. "They should never have been here," he said, looking grieved by all the still and bloodied bodies. "It is by no chance this pack happened upon us. We must leave."

Before I could catch my breath and fully process what I'd

just done, two more laiths came charging towards us, their green hair and red eyes the only slash of color in this bracken-grey forest.

With barely a moment's reprieve, the chase for our blood ensued. Our lead, however, wasn't as great, and one barreled right into Rowen, knocking him off his feet. I heard him grunt as they tangled and rolled across the ashen earth.

"Rowen!" I veered to the side and ran to him. Fear ripping at me like its own clawed beast.

The laith was on top of him, viciously snapping at his face. Rowen managed to keep its savage mouth at bay, holding it back by one of its antlers as it ferociously bit at him. The creature reared back its clawed arm, readying to slash Rowen to pieces.

I was too far away. I wouldn't get to him in time.

Just before the deadly blow could land, Rowen swung his blade, gutting the laith's torso wide open. Intestines poured out of the beast's middle in gushing, bloody waves, and I gagged at the gruesome scene.

Rowen, doused in blood, rolled out from under the maimed figure and leaned over it in what looked to be an embrace.

What was he doing? Whispering a warrior's death rite into its ear? We didn't have time for that!

After what felt like several wasted seconds, Rowen finally shot up from the slain laith, panting, when more of the pack emerged from the trees.

How many were there? They just kept coming!

Three flanked mine and Rowen's left as two others zeroed in on Takoda's right.

They were driving a wedge between us, separating us farther and farther apart as we ran. I heard one of Takoda's arrows whizz by, selflessly taking down the beast closest to me and not himself.

"Takoda!" Rowen yelled.

"Go! Keep her safe!" he shouted, disappearing through the trees, the laiths swiping dangerously at his back.

Panic rose in my throat now that we were separated from Takoda, but we could do nothing as we ran for our lives. My legs burned and my lungs squeezed, begging me to stop lest they give out of their own accord. I was a sprinter, not a long-distance runner, there was no way I could keep this up forever. And I soon realized I wouldn't have to as our runway grew shorter before us.

Bracing myself for a hard stop, the ground dropped away into a steep cliff, and I teetered over the ledge before Rowen yanked me back against his hard wall of muscle. There was nowhere else to run, nowhere else to go, we were forced to the edge with no escape.

Two more laiths prowled toward us, joining their pack for the spoils of battle. Their jaws were unhinged, opened, and ready to feast. Our reflections shimmered in their feral eyes, the taste of victory already drooling from their tongues.

My pulse pounded in my ears, deafening me to everything but the countdown of my heartbeat. Our backs were towards the plummet and my heel slipped over the edge as we backed up farther.

The creatures did a slow, stalking dance toward us, and I realized it wasn't the pounding of my heart I was hearing but the massive crashing of water down below.

We were standing at the top of a giant waterfall, and it was only now that I felt the water showering against my skin.

I stole a quick glance at the raging ravine. So far down.

Rowen turned to me, his eyes piercing with panic and adrenaline. "We have to jump," he yelled at me over the roaring of the water.

"We won't make it. It's too high."

The beasts were a talon slash away, almost completely upon

us, but the choices were clear: stand and fight with the odds against us, our bodies already exhausted, or jump.

I looked down at my empty hands. I must have left my blade in the body of the dead laith. Now only one of us had a weapon against the four. The odds were not good.

Rowen was right, we had to jump. It was the only option where we stood a chance, however small it was. Surviving a jump this high was slim to none, but I grabbed Rowen's hand and nodded.

He looked me deep in the eyes as he clasped me back tightly, his free hand grasping his ax.

The laiths closed in, their salivating tongues slithering out of their mouths in anticipation for the spoils of not one body, but two, and all at once they leapt upon us.

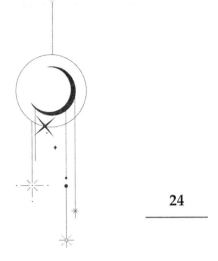

24

I was falling.

Rapidly plunging through a wind tunnel that rushed all around me. The air whistled past so fast I couldn't see or hear anything. All I knew was Rowen's hand holding mine in a vise grip.

My stomach lodged in my throat as I awaited the concrete impact. I tried to angle my body, knowing it would help me slice through the water more easily, giving me a chance. If there even was one at all.

I braced myself for the collision, catching a blur of white in my periphery, but nothing could have prepared me for the frigid waves that crashed into my body as I hit the water. I shattered through the surface, my body fragmenting into a million tiny pieces as I plunged deeper and deeper into the bubbled abyss.

Water burned as it rushed into my eyes, ears, nose, and throat, drowning my senses. All except for one. Touch. I could still feel Rowen's hand in mine, squeezing so tight the bones in my hand ground together.

I kicked and pumped my legs through the water, hoping I was pushing toward the surface and not just deeper into the void. My lungs were on fire, I needed to breathe, but the waterfall relentlessly churned me in its swirling ball of foam.

Rowen kicked alongside me, pulling at my arm as we warred uselessly against the elemental force.

On the verge of convulsions, I finally broke the surface. One sweet breath of air was all I was granted before I was dragged back beneath the undertow.

A powerful surge of the water plowed against Rowen and me and pushed us into the river's current, dragging us mercilessly along her raging whims. I could feel Rowen's grip on me loosening, our fingers slowly slipping from each other's grasps. I tried to hold him tighter, but it was just our fingertips clinging to one another's now.

We fought to hold on, but the current was stronger than us both, and it ripped his hand from mine.

If I thought I was afraid before, I was now absolutely terrified swirling in the liquid darkness all on my own. I somersaulted in the water, head over feet as the waves thrashed and pummeled into me like I was a punching bag, bruising me deep.

With all the strength of a leaf in a tornado, I could do nothing but be carried along by the tumultuous waves that reduced me down to three simple words.

Kick. Fight. Breath.

It was my new life; repeated over and over again on a never-ending loop.

Kick. Fight. Breath.

Kick. Fight. Breath.

Lifetimes passed before the current finally slowed and I was able to retake control of my body. I barely managed a sloppy freestyle as I made my way to the bank, my arms and legs dragging with the weight of iron.

Kicking with my last ounce of energy, I stubbed my foot on something hard.

Ground.

Finally, solid ground.

I grasped and pulled at the mud and watery vines, dragging myself out of the water one handhold at a time. I desperately clawed at the earth as if I were climbing up a mountain, not crawling across a riverbed, but I was terrified of losing my grip and falling back into the violent whirlpools. I managed to make it onto all fours like a near-drowned cat, coughing and choking up all the water from my mouth, nose, and belly.

My exhausted arms caved out from under me, and I collapsed to the rocks. My cheek landed on a sun-baked stone, and its solid warmth was the most exquisite thing I'd ever felt.

Lying half sprawled out of the water, my breathing slowly returned to normal, but I decided to rest a bit longer, giving my numb mind and shot limbs a chance to recover. My body ached from the impact of the fall, not to mention the beating I took from the rampant waves.

Too waterlogged and bruised to move, I hoped Rowen was somewhere nearby. He'd probably made it to the bank before I had. I would go upstream in search of him soon, but right now, it just felt so damn good to be still. Unmoving. Alive.

I don't know how long I lay there, weaving in and out of consciousness with the waves lightly lapping at my legs, when suddenly, my peaceful resting was rudely disturbed. Strong hands grabbed me by the back of my vest and the waistband of my pants and flipped me over like a flapjack.

I kept my eyes shut, avoiding the bright sunlight that threatened to beam into my swollen lids. "I'm fine," I thought I said out loud, but frantic calloused palms were at my cheeks, pushing my wet hair from my face.

"I'm fine." I thought I said again, more loudly this time.

I squinted my eyes open a tiny sliver, only to see a glowing god hovering above me. The setting sun was directly behind him, casting him in a perfect burnished halo of light and fire, and I marveled as he blazed and dripped with liquid gold.

I thought such beings were devoid of feeling, but this beautiful god looked down at me with sheer dread. I wasn't sure why. I was pretty sure I'd told him multiple times I was fine.

Abruptly, my upper body was yanked up by the front of my vest, and the first few rows of my lacing came undone as I was lurched forward into a half-seated position.

Stupid, forceful god. There was no need to manhandle! I was perfectly capable of getting up on my own.

His strong hand was between my breasts, clutching a fistful of my shirt to hold me in place. His other hand swiftly hit me on the back with a fully opened palm, forcibly and right where my lungs were.

Ow!

"Open. Your. Eyes," Rowen said, a clipped command in every word, then he swatted me again.

"Ow! I said I'm fine. I'm fine, I'm fine, I'm fine," I repeated in rapid succession, batting and pushing him off me.

"You're alright," he said as relief washed over his features and his shoulders relaxed. "I thought you... you looked..."

"I'm okay," I said shakily as I struggled to sit up on my own.

Rowen was on his knees beside me, inhaling ragged breaths. His soaked linen shirt molded to his body, clinging to every contour of his sculpted chest. Water dripped from the dark wavy strands of his hair, plastering a few curls to his face and neck, and a single droplet hung from his lips like a golden gemstone.

I tore my eyes away from his mouth only to notice blood seeping through his now see-through shirt. The crimson stain at his side was growing, spreading through the light fabric. And fast. Much too fast.

"You're hurt," I said, reaching for him.

He went to stand but growled out in pain as he sank back

down to a knee. One of his arms hugged tightly around his middle while the other braced himself against the ground. His face was down, and I heard him suck in several quick breaths before shaking his head as if trying to clear his thoughts.

"It's from a laith," he said calmly, though I could see the unease ridged throughout his body.

My eyes shot wide. I remembered him telling me outside of Weir Falls that a forest laith's scratch contained venom. Venom that caused hallucinations before promising a painful death. One must have slashed him when he was tackled to the ground.

"We need to find cover," I urged, worried we were still being hunted. "Then we'll take a look."

He nodded in agreement, took in one more breath through clenched teeth, and stood, but not to his full height. His injury must be bad. Blood was already seeping through his fingers.

I took his free arm and draped it over my shoulders, helping to carry his weight as we walked into the thick of the trees. I was glad he didn't argue with me. He needed to preserve his strength.

My mind raced with what to do. If we headed back to the cliffs, we would surely find a cave for shelter, but who knew how far the raging current had pushed us or how long it would take to get us back there. We didn't have that kind of time. Rowen was getting weaker with each step, slowly leaning on me more and more. He weighed a ton, and I was buckling under his mass.

I would need to treat him soon, but I knew next to nothing about healing. The little I did know about venomous wounds was that you could tourniquet a limb to stifle the blood flow, but it was around his midsection and wouldn't be of much help. There was also the option of sucking the venom out, but his gashes seemed too deep for that to be a viable option.

Rowen wasn't saying much as he battled the poison coursing through his veins. I could tell he was putting all his concentration into his next step, and his next, and just before we both almost collapsed to the ground, I spotted the mouth of a cave.

Practically dragging Rowen with all my strength, I made a beeline for the wide opening and lugged him through it. The cave was shallow but relatively tall, and most importantly, empty.

I eased Rowen to the ground, already feeling his temperature rising through his drenched clothes. I propped him against the rock wall, hoping the upright position would keep him alert longer, but it was clear the poison was quickly taking hold of him.

"Rowen, I need you to tell me what to do while you're still lucid. How do I draw out the venom?" I asked, carefully lifting his shirt to assess the damage. He grunted as the cloth peeled from his wound, and I gently slipped the garment over his head. He was now naked from the waist up, carved with three gruesome slashes along the side of his ribcage. The skin puckered an unhealthy black around the edges.

I winced at the torn flesh, blood still seeping out in a slow and steady rhythm.

"My pocket. Check my pockets," he said between hastened breaths, his taut stomach moving in quick, shallow breaths.

Without asking why, I dove my hand into one of his pockets. His pants were still soaked, making it difficult to search the fabric suctioned to his body, but after a thorough look, my hands found nothing.

I moved to the other side, and my hopes dashed as I came up empty-handed once more. I searched both pockets again just in case I missed something.

"Rowen, there is nothing in your pockets," I said with sickening dread, afraid he was already hallucinating.

"After the laith attacked me, I pulled moss from its body. Keeping it in case I needed to use it on you, in case one of them hurt you, not realizing it had already gotten me." His speech was laboring, and I was worried he wouldn't be able to finish, but he struggled on. "It must have been lost in the river."

"Rowen, I don't understand," I pleaded, trying to make sense of his words.

"The moss," he said, visibly battling the poison coursing through his blood. "The moss that grows from the laith's body is...is the only cure."

My heart plummeted.

So that's what he did when he leaned over the laith—he'd cut off a piece of its mane. I was angry with him in the moment for wasting time, but it turns out he had been thinking of me when he took those precious seconds to tear the moss from the dead laith.

A revolting pain wracked me from the inside as I took in his eyes. His pupils were huge and blown out, only the thinnest ring of green surrounded the fathomless dark holes that were swallowing him up.

Our only hope had been washed from his pockets, lost in the fury of the river. There was nothing I could do. The poison would slowly but surely claim him until his heart stopped beating.

Rowen would die tonight.

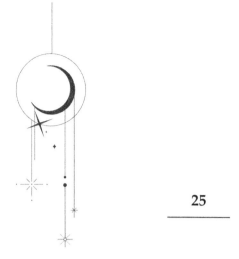

25

"There must be something else," I begged desperately, my mind refusing to accept the reality of the situation.

"When we...when we jumped a laith fell with us. I think...I think I killed it as we fell, but—"

I remembered the flash of white falling beside us. "I'll find it," I said without hesitation, an ember of hope swelling in my chest. Now that I knew his salvation was out there, nothing was going to stop me from finding it.

"Don't you dare leave this cave, it's not safe. Takoda will find you..." he trailed off, then was silent for so long I was afraid I'd lost him.

"You don't get to be a martyr for me, Rowen. You'd never stop reminding me," I said, not believing I could lose him. I understood what I needed to do to keep him alive; the decision was already made.

I reached to his waist and grabbed the blade from his holster. It would do me more good than him at this point. Especially if Rowen was wrong and he hadn't killed the creature.

I choked at the thought of a laith roaming the area very much alive, agitated, and hungry, but I swallowed down the fear.

"I'll be back. I need you to fight it for as long as you can. Do you understand?"

He shook his head no, still trying to convince me to stay as his eyes fluttered and his head slumped back to the wall.

"Rowen?" I called as I shook him with panicked urgency.

When I received no reply, I dashed out of the cave without a second thought.

As much as I wanted to, I couldn't stay with him. His only chance of survival was out in the forest, hidden within the dense brush—a needle in a haystack.

If Rowen had truly killed the creature, its lifeless body would have been carried farther along the river; if not, it would most likely come up from behind me before I even knew it was there.

Trying to see everywhere all at once, I made my way downstream, praying I was making the right decision. I scrambled through the branches and bushes like a madwoman, frantically scanning both sides of the bank for the forest laith, dead or alive.

Ominous grey storm clouds roiled through the sky, their bulging bellies of water and lightning promising a brutal storm. In affirmation, an earsplitting boom cracked like a whip, and a bright white light pierced the darkening sky in half. Pellet-like rain began descending upon me, crashing and stinging against my skin with every drop.

I needed to hurry.

By now, Rowen could be lost in the throes of a hallucination, bleeding out, succumbing to an unbreakable fever, or—and my mind jerked at the possibility—he was already dead.

I pushed the useless fears aside and persisted on. I had to keep a clear head if I was to have any chance at saving Rowen, but my search was proving to be in vain. His salvation was nowhere in sight.

I wildly scanned the banks for the laith, worried I had chosen the wrong direction or that the current had already carried the body miles and miles away from me. Or worse yet, I was the one being hunted through the foggy sheets of rain.

I'd been desperately searching the rough terrain for what felt like hours with my heart in my throat and my nerves unraveling by the second. The worsening weather grew to mirror my spirit, and as my despair multiplied, so did the storm's fury.

The straight river took an abrupt bend to the left, causing the raging water to crash against jutting grey rocks.

Wanting to stay near the shoreline, I walked across the stones, but they were slipperier than I anticipated, and I fell, jamming my elbow against the ground with a crack. I screamed in a howl of pain.

Fighting back tears of rage and desperation, I climbed back onto shaky legs, but just as I went to take another step, a massive torrent of water shot from the stone like a geyser. The force was so powerful it almost picked me up and sucked me back down with it.

I fell back onto my palms and scrambled backward, breathing in the jagged bits of air that were almost stolen from me.

I was on the verge of falling to pieces, of screaming and crying and cursing until my voice gave out: I had failed Rowen; the forest laith was nowhere to be found. My heart, lungs, and limbs cramped; and the water coming at me from all angles obscured my vision. Even if I turned back empty-handed, the chances of finding the cave in this weather were slim to none. I wouldn't even make it back to be with Rowen in his final moments.

Lost, defeated, and exhausted, I was unsure if I should keep searching forward or double back the way I'd come. Either option seemed bleak. I could barely see as it was, and the more tears that wrung from my eyes, the more the sky pounded.

But I couldn't give up, not until my body forced me to.

With a dying hope, I squinted up through tears and rain and almost choked on a breath of relief as I spotted an unmoving pelt of white in the distance. I dashed to the lifeless creature, making sure to clear a wide berth around the gaping hole that had nearly sucked me down into its watery dungeon.

The laith's matted body was crumpled, dead, and face up against the rocks. I dropped to my knees beside it, and with Rowen's ax, I quickly hacked at the moss growing from the beast's fur.

Revulsion rose in my throat at having to touch and cut away at the dead spirit, but I fought back the burning bile. Stinging bullets of rain fell into my eyes, making it hard to see and even harder to keep my hands steady as I cut the moss with one hand and stored it in the fist of the other.

Another blast erupted from the geyser like thunder, shooting and spraying river water toward the heavens before plummeting back down to earth.

I closed my eyes, wiping the rainwater from my brow with the back of my arm, and when I looked back to finish the job, what I saw stopped my blood.

Two breaths of warm puffy steam exhaled from the creature's glossy snout.

———— ·(·⟨ ·● ·⟩ ·)· ————

I froze, still holding a lock of fern-like hair in my hand.

I couldn't leave now. There was no way I had enough moss.

More carefully now, I slowly cut a few more clumps of greenery from its mane, making sure not to stir the beast. Its massive white chest rose and fell with gurgled hisses, and it twitched and spasmed as rain barraged down upon its flat face.

A stray lock fell from my hands and tumbled down upon the

forest laith's neck. It grunted loudly and convulsed in its sleep, nearly stalling my heart mid-beat.

I needed just a bit more.

But before I could fully saw off another section of thatched tresses, ever-red eyes snapped open, locking on me with a keen inhale.

The laith launched to its haunches and swiped at me like a giant feral cat. I jumped back, narrowly missing being gutted open.

One of the beast's arms hung by a bloody sinew from its shoulder, dangling like a piece of deadwood by its side. It didn't even seem fazed by its injury as its predatory sense of smell kicked in and renewed the hunt for my flesh.

A scream tore from my mouth as it lunged at me again with its good arm, and the moss fell from my fingertips. With trembling hands, I firmly gripped Rowen's blade. But having never practiced with this type of weapon, the weight felt clumsy and bulky in my grasp. I knew I didn't have the skillset to wield it the way Rowen did. It was next to worthless in my hands.

I quickly glanced behind my shoulder into the dense forest, searching for a means of help. Any help. And as impractical as it was, I hoped to see Rowen emerging from the trees, healthy, whole, and ready to fight.

Another jet of water erupted from behind me and an idea struck.

It was a long shot, but it was all I had.

I spun on my heel and ran full speed toward the chasm in the ground. The wounded forest laith charged after me, its worthless arm not slowing it down in the least.

I had tried my hand at long jump throughout my track career, and while my marks were decent, they weren't enough to land me in a division-level spot, but I hoped they were enough to land me on the opposite side of that bursting water hole.

Charging my runway, I came to the last step of earth before the ground plummeted down into a watery prison. I planted my dominant foot on the pit's edge, swung my lead knee and opposite arm upward, and jumped forward.

I propelled myself across the chasm, the forest laith leaping right behind me. The swipe at my back let me know I was mere inches from being shredded apart, and I barely cleared the jump as I fell on the other side in a slippery mess.

Just as I thought I had timed it wrong and that the beast would crash down upon me, a violent pillar of water shot from the deep hole like a cannon blast. Nature's hydrous claws caught the beast mid-jump, and in a flurry of white, green, and blue, the laith was dragged down into the abyss of churning water.

I clambered up from the wet ground and darted towards the fallen moss, scooping it up before searching my way back to the cave. I didn't even look behind me as I sprinted through the unrelenting rain, praying Rowen was still alive. I had no idea how long I'd actually been away from him—adrenaline had a way of skewing your sense of time. But I was grateful for that adrenaline; it was fighting off the impending shock I knew would catch up with me eventually.

Especially the trauma of taking the life of two creatures today. I'd never killed or harmed anything in my whole life, and even though it was in self-defense, knowing it was them or me, I still felt changed for ending the existence of another creature.

I hated it and hoped I never had to do it again. But I couldn't dwell on that now, I had to find my way back.

I don't know how, but as I ran through the fog, rain, trees, and pitfalls, my feet knew exactly where to land to bring me safely back to Rowen. And thankfully, he was just as I left him, slumped against the cave wall, unconscious, and breathing in convulsive shallow gasps.

I dropped the ax and raced to his side.

Fingers trembling, I took the slimy bundle of smashed green moss and pulled the lichen into long, thin strands.

I knew everything had an antithesis, a counteraction, a cure —fascinating how sometimes the very thing that weakened you was also the very antidote that healed and strengthened you.

I placed the first bit of moss onto his opened bloody flesh, begging it to work.

Rowen inhaled sharply as my fingers gently prodded and adjusted the dressing onto the uppermost gash, and his eyes shot open from the pain.

As soon as the moss touched his mutilated wound, tiny tendrils of vines reached out and clasped onto Rowen's torn skin like a symbiont latching onto its host. It was creating its own sealed bandage, stopping the bleeding and mending the mangled flesh with a webbed netting. I only had a moment to marvel before I went to work on the next slice of his skin.

His whole body was tensed and flexed beneath my touch, and his bulging chest and flat stomach glistened with a sheen of sweat. A fever had set in.

"It was dead?" he confirmed in a pained rasp, tilting his head back to reveal the throbbing pulse at his neck.

"Nearly."

His eyes shot to me, searching my body with concern. "Are you h—"

I shushed him before he could continue. "Save your strength. I'm fine."

"The moss will help with the wounds and absorb the venom, but it won't stop the hallucinations from running their course," he said through clenched teeth, the burst of lucidity most likely brought on by the awakened pain.

I sealed the last of his gashes with the binding moss, pained that his ordeal was far from over. He was dangerously hot, and I knew a high fever could be just as fatal as any blade to the heart.

What would Takoda do? I tried to remember what he had taught me earlier today, hoping with my whole being that he was alright. I flipped through the Rolodex of memories trying to recall if he had said anything about fevers. Strange how that already seemed like a lifetime ago.

I looked down at the remaining bit of moss in my hand.

Takoda's words flashed through my mind. *Everything is connected.*

"Rowen, eat this," I said as I handed him a web of wet moss. "It will go directly into your system, helping heal you from the inside out." I spoke with such conviction there was no way it could be anything but true. It had to be.

Without hesitation, Rowen slowly reached and took the greenery between his broad fingers. He ripped off a piece with his teeth and began chewing.

"See, aren't you glad I came along, Copeland?" he asked through a pained smile after swallowing the last bit of moss.

It seemed to be working!

"Of course, but only for the joy of rubbing it in that *I* saved *you*." I smiled at him and handed him another section of moss.

"I've never had a problem with you saving me," he said evenly, and though he was slightly more coherent, his dilated eyes ensnared mine. "I didn't know I still had a soul until the moment I saw you, Keira. This isn't your first time saving me."

His words heated my skin and seared my blood, but I had no way of knowing if it was him or the fever talking.

Seeming to remember where we were, his eyes darted around the cavern. "Where's my blade?"

"Near the entrance."

"Grab it. I don't know what I'll do. What I'll see. You may need to use it..." he swallowed thickly, fighting to stay awake, fighting to warn me of what could happen, "...on me."

"You won't hurt me."

"I wish that were true, but I see myself hurting you every day, and I hate mys..." The words barely escaped his lips as what little energy he had left vanished. Exhaustion overcame him, and he slumped back, closing his eyes.

I knew Rowen would never hurt me, but that didn't stop me from trying to decode his cryptic last words.

As he slept, my eyes roved over his bare skin, truly taking in the lean cuts of his abs and molded chest, noticing his two necklaces—one of earthy gems, the other pure metal.

It was strange seeing this strong and lethal man so vulnerable. So still. He was more fragile than he looked, and I cringed every time my gaze passed over a scar. They were all over him, scattered like markers on a map of torture.

There was an especially nasty-looking one on his left pec, fully healed but puckered and raised.

These must have been the wounds Takoda had healed, slowly bringing Rowen back to life after he found him dying in the woods.

The thought of someone inflicting these injuries on him made my blood boil, and my fists curled in rage.

As for his current ailments, I had done everything within my power to help him. Now all I could do was wait. Wait for the remedy to silently work its way through his body and heal him.

I touched my hand to his forehead. He was still so hot, and I bit at my lip, feeling helpless. At least it appeared he was sleeping soundly, though I had no way of knowing if horrible images haunted his dreams.

The sun had completely set while the storm continued to rage, battering the trees and cave walls like a tempestuous lullaby. The air grew cold, and I looked to Rowen, unconscious and barely breathing. We wouldn't make it through the night with our wet clothes and hair and no blankets or warmth.

I would need to start a fire.

Luckily Quiya and Nyvari had taught me how back in the village. Had they not, we would be so screwed right now. I silently thanked the sisters again for their quiet patience and calm tutelage. It had taken me over an hour to finally catch a flame with them, hopefully I'd be faster now that our lives depended on it.

I collected the fallen branches, twigs, and dried tree needles that had made their way into the cave, saved from the downpour outside. I also found a rock similar to the flintstone the sisters had shown me.

I scraped the blade of Rowen's ax over and over against the flint. The life-saving act was taking longer than expected and I cursed several times, but once the spark caught the tinder and I fed the flames with my breath, it blossomed into a meager fire. I was so proud of myself that I let out a victory squeal. I glanced to Rowen, expecting to see him looking at me with an impressed expression on his face, but he remained still and sleeping.

Tending to the fire, it flourished steadily, but I still shivered as a cold draft swept through the cave. I would never warm up with my damp clothes and hair clinging to my body.

I stood up, shimmied out of my wet leggings, and placed them on a rock near the fire to dry. I contemplated taking off Rowen's pants but decided against it, they were nearly dry anyway. Plus, I didn't want to jar him awake in case it brought on a hallucination. Luckily, it seemed like he hadn't suffered from one yet. Maybe he wouldn't altogether.

I could only hope.

Attempting to keep from going mad with worry, I sat and stared at the leaping flames in my underwear and vest, my knees pulled up under my chin and my hands wrapped around my shins. Letting my thoughts wander, I couldn't help but think how much my life had changed in a matter of weeks. If someone would have told me I'd be tending a fire for a wounded half-naked man in a cave, I would have handed them my parents' business card, imploring them to seek psychological evaluation.

I thought about my parents and how they must have reacted to my unaccounted-for body. Was I considered a missing person, or had my parents gone through the trouble of arranging a funeral? Either way, I'm sure they were disappointed at the loss of their key subject and the derailing of their groundbreaking case study.

The memories hurt more than I cared to admit and I was still in disbelief that they were real. I couldn't fully comprehend it, like shadowed memories from a dream.

It seemed that no matter where I was, I couldn't get a grasp on reality.

My thoughts wandered to Natalie. How had she been able to drug me for so long without me ever finding out? I felt so stupid for letting her into my life. Especially when I knew to keep people at arm's length. But I had allowed her to sneak in and take root in my heart. I wanted to believe someone could love me for who I was. Astral traveling and all.

I couldn't help but wonder if Natalie had found a new room-mate. Now that my mother was no longer paying her, had she moved out? An unpaid intern could only survive so long without a salary.

I berated myself for even caring one iota about her welfare, but it was hard to erase five years of memories with the snap of my fingers. I knew she cared about me, even if it was in her own twisted way.

Would I ever see any of them again? Did I even want to? I was making a home for myself here, fighting for myself, and fighting for others who needed me.

I knew a darkness was coming, but I still preferred facing that than returning to a life where I'd felt empty and mostly alone with no purpose.

Suddenly, Rowen jerked violently and I dashed over to him. His eyes rapidly shifted beneath his translucent lids and he stirred again.

"Fou?" he asked in his delirium. "Fou, is that you?"

Fou? Who was Fou? Was that the name of his past love? The woman he sought and called out to in the darkness? Hoping and praying each night she would reach back and curl up in his embrace?

It was a name I knew I wasn't meant to hear.

"Fou!" he called again as his veins strained in sinuous columns along his neck.

I moved closer to him to rest my hand on his shoulder, but as soon as I touched his skin, his black eyes flashed open.

He grasped my arm with reflexes I didn't think were possible. His other hand grabbed my hip and he pulled me down on top of him, guiding me to straddle his lap. His eyes were open but unseeing, and his skin was on fire. Was the moss even working? Had I given him enough?

I quickly scolded myself for not being more concerned about sitting directly on top of a wounded man who most assuredly thought I was someone else.

"I was wondering if I'd ever see you again." His voice was deep, ragged, and as far away as his eyes.

Coming to my senses, I tried to push off his chest, but he pressed me back down against him, locking me in place. His hands were at my waist and his fingers created divots in my flesh where they dug into my hips. I was painfully aware of how little separated me from Rowen's hard body between my legs. I hadn't had a chance to put my pants back on since taking them off to dry by the fire, so his touch burned directly through the fabric of my underwear.

More than anything I wanted to melt and burn right along

with him. But this wasn't right: I was pretty sure he was hallucinating I was his deceased lover.

Nothing could be more wrong.

He would hate me in the morning if anything happened. He would hate himself.

I had to get away.

I tried to push off him with more force, but I didn't budge, and he pressed me down harder against his firm thighs.

Rowen cinched his large hand around my wrist and asked, "Where do you think you're going?"

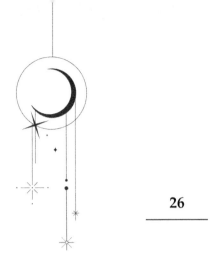

26

Rowen jerked me violently towards him, stealing a quick inhale from my mouth.

"I asked you a question," he said, slanting his head toward me as he brought his lips closer to my face.

Oh no. This couldn't be happening. He was going to kiss me. I had wanted this for so long but not like this. Never like this.

Just when I thought his lips were about to press against mine, he lifted me off him and stood us on our feet in one swift motion. The way he was holding me was almost like we were lovers, but the way he gripped me was too tight and his face twisted into outright revulsion.

My eyes widened in terror, but before I could speak, he whirled me around and slammed me against the cave wall. The force knocked the wind out of me and I struggled to pull air into my lungs. Before I could even get my next breath in, his hand was at my throat, pushing against my windpipe.

Had I got it all wrong? Did he think I was the one who killed the woman he loved? The one who murdered his other half before beating and torturing him within an inch of his life, leaving him to bleed out and die alone in the woods?

If so, I understood the unfettered hatred in his eyes, however misplaced it was upon me.

The look wasn't burning like the rest of him though. No, it was ice cold and terrifying. I tried to struggle free but he raised my wrist and slammed it above my head on the sharp rocks. He held it there, pressing harder and harder into me, and I winced at all the rough-digging edges.

How had I misread the situation so thoroughly? I was sure I sensed a moment of desire in him, but I now saw that desire was only to kill. To kill whomever he thought I was in his delirium.

"How I imagined doing this to you," he whispered almost seductively against my neck, and my skin prickled. "Always wondering if I would have the strength to go through with killing you." He pulled back with a growl, staring at me but not seeing *me*.

"Rowen, if you can hear me, it's me, Keira," I barely managed to gasp out as blood rushed to my head and made me dizzy.

A disgusted laugh rattled through his chest. "I will never believe another word that comes out of your mouth."

The pressure at my throat intensified. His towering body leaned into me, trapping me between his wall of muscle and the rocks that stabbed into my back. His gaze hazed over, and his lips pulled back into a feral growl.

"Rowen, I am trying to save your life. Let me. If you don't, we could both die in here."

He pulled me forward, offering a brief reprieve, only to slam me against the rocks once more. Stars bounced across my vision as he pushed his body against mine, his chest and acute hatred smothering me.

Rowen could have easily killed me by now, but he was toying with me, drawing out his retaliation in a slow, torturous dance.

He was stiff to the point of breaking, but would he break me first? Only to snap out of it in the morning to see what he'd done. Mourning my lifeless body crumpled on the cave floor?

"Rowen, you need to listen to me. You are hallucinating from the venom in your wound. The wound I just mended," I gasped out, my eyes pleading him to remember. He had warned me the hallucinations would happen, but I could never have predicted they would turn this violent—this deadly.

I thrashed beneath him. "Please, Rowen," I begged, hoping to get through to him. After everything, I was going to die here at the hands of the one sworn to protect me at all costs.

Rowen's grip grew tighter around my throat, strangling me, his face indented with murderous determination. The time for talking had ended. He meant to kill me now.

He leaned in, bringing his lips to my ear as if he wanted whomever he thought I was to intimately hear this last curse. Was this what he had been so carefully hiding behind that indomitable mask? This vendetta. This deep-seated kernel of revenge that had grown and twisted into a noxious thorn bush.

I did the only thing I could think of. I had always wanted to do it, and now right before I died, would be the only chance I'd ever get. So I'd take it, even if it was the last thing I ever did.

I slowly turned my head as much as I could against his tightening hold and kissed him featherlight upon the cheek.

As the glisten from my kiss evaporated on his face, his body wavered, and his hands loosened around my throat. Whatever hallucinogenic spell he was under broke, and his eyes snapped to mine. "Keira?" he breathed out my name as if it were a sacred prayer.

Overcome with relief, I gulped in all the glorious air I could.

Cradling my neck, he slowly tilted my gaze until I was staring directly into the pools of his evergreen eyes.

He was seeing me now.

His thumbs lightly grazed along the curve of my jaw. "Keira," he groaned again, his voice husky and low, and his eyes drank in my face as if it were the first time he'd allowed himself a drop of water.

Before I knew what was happening, he crashed into me, his lips on mine. I gave out a small cry of surprise as his mouth claimed mine hard and fast enough to bruise. His hands were in my hair, then at my waist, roving all over my body like he couldn't hold me close enough. My entire being responded to his in a way I'd never felt before—he called to my every fiber, igniting the canvas of my existence to life. And I crashed right back into him.

My fingers threaded through his hair, my mouth opening to his as his tongue pushed between my lips, and I tasted him for the first time in a burst of ginger, musk, and minted moss. Rowen groaned at my returned fervor, his tongue tangling against mine, beckoning me to push back. Which I did, gladly. I drove my kiss just as hard as he delivered his, the both of us searching and devouring.

His kisses were urgent and starved, all tongue and teeth and roaming limbs. I burned everywhere as he consumed me, our bodies melting into an all-engulfing fire—neither of us a care in the world for what would emerge from the ashes.

Rowen firmly traced up my body, following the outline of my hips and ribs until his fingers grazed the sides of my breasts.

But his weren't the only roaming hands.

I caressed my fingertips down his strong chest, along his two necklaces, and my touch hitched at the scar right above his pounding heart. My strokes explored down, tracing the outlines of his sculpted abdominal muscles, and I grazed past the moss bandages flush against him like a second skin. Rowen shuddered as my touch left tiny trails of shimmering iridescence on his body.

"Please," he groaned desperately against my skin, clutching

me as if I were a dream on the cusp of fading. "Tell me this is real."

"It is," I managed to breathe out.

"Thank fuck," he said before possessing my mouth yet again. He pulled me harder and tighter against him, his hands finding never-ending ways to entangle me. His calloused touch brushed past my hip bones and overtop my underwear, my thighs inching open for more. Suddenly, he was between my legs, palming and rocking me with the heel of his hand. My moan echoed throughout the cave as his hungry mouth dove to my neck.

I let my head fall to the side, further exposing the length of my throat to him as his lips trailed down my sensitive skin, claiming me with swift flicks of his tongue and teeth.

My legs turned to mush beneath me as he touched me through my panties, touched me everywhere. His broad fingers explored me over the thin fabric, slowly tracing and discovering the shape of my clit as our lips thundered together again, our kiss deepening.

Where just moments ago his touch was preventing me from breathing, he was now the only thing keeping the air in my lungs, and I couldn't get enough.

I didn't know a kiss could feel like this, like I was coming undone. The tendrils of my aura extended and intertwined with Rowen's until I couldn't tell where one of us ended and the other began.

Rowen wrapped his arms around me and effortlessly lifted me up by the backs of my bare thighs. He hoisted me on his waist, and I locked my legs around him, threading my arms behind his neck.

I was lost to all time and space and reality as I kissed the man once hidden in the mist of my dreams. Weaving my hands through his soft, thick hair, he was as real as anything, strong and solid beneath me, and I wanted him.

I rocked my hips against the outline of his hard cock, and a deep groan spilled from his mouth, filling me with a breath that went deeper than oxygen ever could. I went to undo the lacing of my vest only to remember Rowen had loosened it earlier today.

Good. I was already halfway there.

Rowen suddenly went still. "Keira," he whispered against my kiss.

Why was he stopping? I wasn't done with him, not by a long shot. I refused to break my mouth from his, wanting more. Needing more.

He smiled against my lips, then pulled back fractionally, and my whole body leaned forward to find him.

"My bandage. Your leg." His eyes flared with heat but his body froze. Two warring emotions.

Despite everything within me, I pulled back an inch and looked down to where my thigh rubbed against his injured side. The moss had pulled from one of his gashes, covering the inside of my leg in his blood.

Undeterred by his torn bandage, he didn't release me, he just continued to hold me up with his forearms. I made no move to withdraw myself either and I settled my hands on the mounds of his muscled shoulders.

I met Rowen's smoldering stare and held it, our chests heaving from the need and desire we just ripped from each other. The lingering effects of the venom must have been wearing off because even though his pupils were still huge, they weren't as blown out and crazed as before.

My hair was a mess from where his hands ran through my waves, and my lips felt puffy and swollen, but the way he was looking at me shifted something fundamental within my core. It frightened me, yet I wanted more.

"You're so beautiful," he said, lightly placing kisses along my jawline, cheekbones, and forehead. Each plant of his mouth sent electrical shocks through me like a live wire exposed to rainwater. "Every part of you."

"So are you," I unabashedly admitted. "I've always thought so, even when I hadn't been able to fully see you beyond the mist. I knew."

He smiled, the luminance of happiness etched into every line and curve of his face. I had never seen him this happy, this incandescent. It was magnificent to behold and I wanted to spend however long I could making him look that way, but in an instant, it was quickly shadowed over with anger, or was it regret?

My body went rigid in confusion.

Did he already regret what we'd just done? What he'd said? Did he remember almost killing me?

My breath caught in my throat as his complete demeanor changed. This couldn't be the same Rowen who'd kissed me like his life depended on it. Like I was what tethered his very soul to his body.

It was a devastating look that scared me and chilled my roaring fire into a single aching ember. He seemed to be raging war within himself, and he looked as torn as I imagined a person could be.

Still, he didn't let me go, our bodies clinging to each other in the belly of our cave. It reminded me of a mutual zugzwang in chess, where the only move, was not to move.

He appeared uneager to set me down as if I might disappear and break the connection in half, separating us permanently, something he both wanted desperately and yet not at all.

"I better fix your bandage," I finally said; eventually one of us would have to move, acknowledging the stalemate. I couldn't take the look on his face for one more second. Was I the one causing that look of regret mixed with something else I couldn't quite place? If so, I couldn't bear to be the one that made him look as if his whole world was crumbling beneath his feet.

He gently slid me down off his body, making sure I was perfectly placed on my own two feet. His hands lingered on the bare sliver of flesh between my vest and underwear, embossing his fingerprints into my flushed and needy skin.

He dug his fingers into my hips and tugged me flush against his body. He dipped his head to run his nose along the curve of my jaw. "Keira. I'm so sorry, but I can't have you." His tone was strangled with torment, and his words hit me like a gut punch. Those weren't the words I wanted to hear from the lips I'd just tasted.

His hands fell away from me completely, leaving an ache where his touch had been. He looked at me through darkened eyes, then twisted his torso and fixed his bandage, realigning the moss to secure it in place.

"I shouldn't have done that. Kissed you. It won't happen again," he said, taking a step away from me, punching me again while I was already down. I was not good with receiving rejection; I was normally the one doling it out. But I had never been in a situation like this—where someone was still so obviously in love with a ghost.

"I understand. You still love her." It was the hardest thing I'd ever said, and the words tasted like ash in my mouth. Maybe saying it out loud would help me get over him. I couldn't compete with a lost love, and I had to—no—*needed* to accept that. The sooner the better.

His eyes narrowed and his nostrils flared. "You understand nothing."

He might as well have slapped me across the face with how much those words stung.

"Then help me understand. I've been trying to understand you for weeks." My temper was taking over. For all I knew about him, he may as well still be the cloak-and-dagger figure hidden within the shadows of my darkness.

Now that I was awake, I felt further away from him than ever —this beautiful man who had stolen a piece of my soul on the edge of darkness. But it seemed he held no piece of me, nor did he want to.

I had warned myself that he was dangerous, but I just couldn't resist.

"Understand that I need to keep you alive. I almost failed at that today, more than once. Do you think I could live with myself if anything happened to you?" His voice was strained and the muscles in his jaw and temples hammered.

"And what about me? Keeping you alive. Protecting you!" I made a broad sweeping gesture at his bandaged body, the cave, and the burning fire. "I still managed to do it without being a cold, insensitive asshole."

He cringed at that last part. Good. He knew it wasn't a compliment.

"Thank you for saving me. I'd say I owe you my soul but it's already yours. It's my heart I can't give," he said with near pleading in his eyes.

It cut me in two. One half knowing somehow he was mine, just not in the way I wanted, the other half trying to understand the unfathomable pain of losing someone you love.

The flaring shadows of the fire bounced off the cave walls and onto his skin, making him appear like a lenticular picture. From one flicker of light to the next, with strobe-like precision, he flipped between two images. One moment he was the man who wanted to kiss, burn, and claim me, the next he was the stranger who kept me at a distance.

"I understand you feel some sort of misplaced obligation to keep me safe, but let me just relieve you of that right here and now," I said, my timbre rising. "I don't need saving."

His voice remained infuriatingly calm. "I'm not letting you out of my sight."

"You don't get to make those kinds of decisions," I snapped harshly.

"Like hell I don't," he said, closing the distance between us and grabbing me by the shoulders. He towered over me and held me within his clutches like a beautiful monster, unsure of whether he wanted to kill or claim me.

Without warning, Rowen swayed on his feet, and caught himself with a bracing hand against the cave wall.

Wow. I was a piece of work. Wanting something from a man who—making it out of this cave alive was still very much a touch-and-go scenario at this point.

I put my hands on his bare corded arms. "You're still burning up. You need to rest." I helped lower him to the ground then grabbed his bloodied shirt and rolled it into a pillow to place under his head, giving him some comfort against the hard, unforgiving ground.

I crouched beside him and cupped his beautiful fevered face in my hand. "You and I, we are okay, alright?" I said softly. "Just focus on getting better." His eyes were exhausted, painted with dark purple smudges, and a whirlpool of agony swirled in his gaze.

A chill crept over me, either from the defeated look on his face or the cold draft, I didn't know, but I shivered just the same.

"You're cold." Rowen gently took hold of my hand. "Lay with me?" he asked.

I nodded inherently as if he'd asked me this question a thousand times across a thousand different worlds, and my response was always the same.

He pulled me down into his all-encompassing embrace and cupped me within the curve of his body. He curled one arm under me until my head rested on the nook of his shoulder, and his other arm wrapped around my ribcage, landing a palm on my stomach as he pulled me closer. The fact that I fit so perfectly along his body was equal parts pleasure and pain.

I didn't know how it was possible, but this felt just as intimate as our kiss. Maybe even more so.

"I can never love anyone again," he said into my hair. "She made sure of that. But if this is the only way I can have you for one night, I will selfishly take it."

I wasn't sure if it was him or the fever talking, if he would even remember any of this come morning. But if he could be selfish for a night, then so could I.

I nuzzled deeper into him, and just as he'd always been there for me, I would not let him face this night alone.

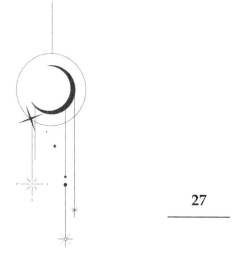

27

Sleep hadn't come easy on the cold, hard ground of the drafty cave. The storm persisted all night and the man I'd been entangled in was fighting for his life.

Not once did he let go or loosen his hold on me, as if the only way to make it through the night was to fuse our bodies together and draw from each other's strength.

The helpless worrying of whether Rowen would survive had felt endless, while lying peacefully in his arms flashed by in an instant. But when I woke he was no longer holding me, and I twisted up, rising on my elbows to look for him.

He was seated beside me with his elbows on his knees, the distance reinstated between us.

"How do you feel?" I asked tentatively.

"Better," he said, idly fidgeting with his ax. The pallor of his skin was almost back to its healthy bronzed glow, but the look on his face was withdrawn...aching. And while immense relief swept over me that the moss had worked, a tiny fissure cracked in my already broken heart and I brought my fist to my chest, trying to ease yet another invisible break.

"I can't thank you enough for all you did for me last night," he said quietly, and I paused. "Without you I would have died, most likely very slowly and painfully."

"What kind of friend would I be if I let you die?" I replied, telling myself that was all Rowen and I could be. Friends.

His breath trickled over my lips, burning me with the kiss he said should never have happened.

Seeming to remember his own words, Rowen further retreated behind his mask of stone, shutting me out. I painfully extricated myself from his indifferent stare and stood. I wouldn't press him about last night. He would tell me when he was ready.

"I'm going to go wash up by the river," I said, grabbing my dry pants by the fire that was nothing more than faint embers, just like the flames of my soul.

Rowen sat forward with a grunt. "Then we will make our way back home."

Home. I liked the sound of that.

Rowen shifted, examining the moss bandages that had saved his life. His whole stomach flexed, revealing each and every block of abs, his muscles moving in the most hypnotizing ways.

Friends, I reminded myself again. *Friends. Friends. Friends.*

I quickly made my way to the river and cared to my morning needs. I splashed the cool running water on my face and shoulders and scooped in a handful to rinse my mouth. Before sliding into my pants, I washed the caked blood from my thigh. Rowen's red life force was a reminder we had made it through the night, but not unscathed, not untouched.

The water-swollen ground imprinted with the weight of my footfalls, and the soaked trees dripped with the overnight rain. But it wasn't a cleansing or a promise of new growth. No amount of rain would bring the dead parts of the forest back to life.

My purpose glared me in the face, and the wind stirred around me in a gentle yet urgent nudge. I needed to get back and focus on learning how to harness the Alcreon Light. The power stifled within me was Luneth's only hope.

I was almost back to our hollow cavern when I heard voices echoing from inside. Without thinking, only reacting, I sprinted towards the dark opening.

Inside, Rowen stood next to Takoda, Demil, and two other warriors I'd seen training but had yet to meet. One of them being the petite woman who trained with Dyani.

I ran to Takoda and threw my arms around his lean body. "You're alive!"

"I made it back to the village and gathered volunteers to help trace your steps. We made it to the waterfall's edge. There didn't appear to be a struggle so we assumed you jumped. We've been scanning every cave along the river line for hours," Takoda said, releasing me from his hug. His calm aura set me at ease and I was relieved we wouldn't be making the journey back without him.

"It's good to see you, my friend," Rowen said as they clasped each other's arm just above the wrist and embraced.

Takoda gestured to the moss bandages at Rowen's side. "I am glad to see you've made it through the night."

"A thanks owed to Copeland," Rowen said clinically, but the slight tick in his throat betrayed our moment of passion.

"Then my gratitude is to you, star-touched," Takoda responded with a slight bow and a hand to his heart.

Demil scanned the cave through narrow eyes as if trying to discern what could have transpired here in the night. His gaze raked over me, snagging on my slackened lacing and wild hair. I tried to keep my face passive, not revealing a single secret. "Couldn't let him die thinking he was saving me now, could I?"

Takoda's mouth pulled into an amused smile. "Indeed. Come, let us leave this place."

I didn't need to be told twice. I was ready to leave this cave, along with a piece of my heart inside it.

After hours of walking on foot and being fed rations by our rescue party, I realized just how far the raging river had carried Rowen and me. I shuddered remembering tumbling through those endless violent waves. They seemed an impossible thing to have survived. But Rowen and I had survived, that, and much more.

Just when I thought we should be coming up on the Wyn village, a frigid draft wafted over me and settled into my bones, causing my hairs to stand on end. Something felt terribly wrong. I looked to Rowen, Takoda, and the other two warriors, but none of them seemed to notice or be affected by the icy wind that had me stopped cold.

"Copeland?" Rowen asked, sensing my abrupt change.

"Do you feel that?" I whispered.

My entire party stopped dead in their tracks, and stood still as statues. After a moment they shifted their eyes to one another skeptically.

Takoda was in front of me, his onyx eyes all I could see. "Feel what, star-touched?"

"It's…" I looked around trying to pinpoint the source of the chill. "It's coming from there." I pointed to a long lightning-shaped crevice etched into the side of the bluff. The crack was pitch black, all sharp and jagged angles zigzagging back and forth like an impatient scribble of ink.

Icy pinpricks hooked onto my skin and tugged at me like fishing wire, pulling me to enter the slight opening.

I took a step toward it.

Takoda's hand landed on my shoulder, stopping me. "We mustn't tarry here." His concerned gaze darted all around.

"But..."

"Whatever is calling to you has succumbed to a fate far worse than death. Do not seek this out. There is nothing that can be done."

"Whatever it is, it needs my help."

If I was the only one who could feel it, maybe it was asking the Alcreon Light for help. I wasn't sure what I could do, but I couldn't just leave without trying.

"You can't seriously mean to go in there?" Demil asked incredulously, his face all hard planes of disbelief.

"I do."

"We've been searching for you all night and morning, wondering if you were alive." Demil's voice was clipped and assertive. "I'm not letting you go in there now that we've found you."

"I don't think that is up to you." I couldn't believe I had to say that out loud. Who did he think he was? I was trying to keep calm but my composure was slipping. "Whatever is in there needs my help."

Rowen's hand was on my elbow with a gentle squeeze. "Let's get back to the village, rest, and discuss this later with a clear head."

I shot him the most injurious glare I could conjure. Some friend he was turning out to be.

I gazed at the other faces around me. They all seemed to be in agreement, I was outnumbered five to one.

"Fine."

If whatever was calling out to me was dangerous, I didn't want to subject the others to more horror and uncertainty. This was something I would have to do on my own. I could feel it.

Tonight, when the village was asleep I would make my way back. There was nothing to discuss.

The setting sun finished warming our cheeks as its glow descended. We had been walking all day, and thankfully there were no other sightings of forest laiths to speak of. Their abnormal appearance on the bluffs still a mystery.

We weren't even fully to the village before Sabra and Ven came bounding toward us. The majestic white beast charged, her tail wagging excitedly behind her, and she tackled me to the ground with her furry weight. She covered my face and arms in her wet licks and kisses, and Ven, not far behind, threw his spindly arms around me in a tight squeeze.

"When we heard you were missing, I wanted to send Sabra. She can sniff out anything, but it rained so hard there was no trace of your scent." Ven's innocent and pure heart beamed through his umber eyes.

Rowen had said in the cave that we'd be going home, and coming up on the village, seeing the earthy domes and my small greeting party, it truly felt like a place I could call home. The gaping hole in my heart from where my parents and Natalie had blasted through it filled marginally, relieving the ache just a bit.

"Come. It's been a long few days for us all. You must eat and get some rest. And Rowen, I would like to take a look at your injury before you retire," Takoda said, his long form motioning for Rowen to follow. "And Keira, Nepta will want to see you come first light."

"Of course," I nodded innocently. I should be back by then.

"Goodnight, Copeland," Rowen said, shifting his gaze to me. "I will see you tomorrow."

"I'll be here," I replied sweetly. I should be back by then. "Goodnight."

I turned on my heel and made my way to Rowen's dome

without further conversation from anyone, playing it off like I was exhausted. But I wouldn't be getting any rest. At least not tonight.

Inside Rowen's home, I changed into the fresh pair of leggings and forest-green top neatly laid out for me. Someone was really on top of their game with my wardrobe. I would make it my mission to seek them out and personally thank them.

There was also a fresh spread of flatbreads, cheeses, and fruit that I dug into hungrily, washing it down with a mug of sweetened ale.

It wasn't quite dark enough for me to start my mission yet, but I knew if I sat down, even for a moment, I would plummet into my fatigue and not rise for days, so I began perusing Rowen's room more intently than ever.

Since commandeering his home, I'd opted to give him as much privacy as I could, but now I was too curious. I wanted to know who Fou was. Maybe there was a clue as to who Rowen called out to in the dark—the name he uttered when he thought no one was listening.

I continued to snack on the platter as I searched the room for a picture, token, or mention of who Fou might be. Then I remembered my first night here, all the journals that had been stacked at his desk. Most of them were gone now, but a few still remained and I leafed through them, skimming over paged star charts, maps, and ancient moon patterns.

I bit into a dried forest berry as I stopped on a page detailing the locations and terrains of surrounding providences and sovereignties. I'd heard mention of a few of them in passing, but the Wyn people didn't seem to have any foreign relations to speak of. There was little need of it as they made and grew everything they required.

I scoured the rest of his room. Any drawer, nook, and cranny,

I searched, but I was unable to find a single detail that led to his old life. The only thing that indicated he even had a past at all was the metaled necklace he wore. I kicked myself for not examining it more closely when I had the chance.

Whatever the necklace meant to him, he wore it close to his heart, along with the beaded necklace made in Wyn fashion—his past and present, I now realized.

No closer to solving any of Rowen's secrets and near time to leave, I walked to his weapon rack and examined the deadly silver pieces. I wasn't naive enough to go without some form of protection, and I decided on the largest blade to keep me company.

After having used a weapon, and coming in way too close contact with my enemy, I wanted the lengthiest and biggest weapon I could find. The longer the reach, the better. I strapped the hefty blade to my leg with one of Rowen's spare thigh sheaths, and adjusted the strap to fit my leg.

I'd never carried a weapon like this before, and I had to admit, I looked like a badass.

I let the thought fill me with confidence because I knew if I didn't leave right now, I never would.

Now that it was dark enough, I slowly rotated the round door and squeezed myself out of Rowen's dome. A villager walked by and I pressed myself flat against the outside wall, holding my breath. I didn't want to be seen. I knew if I was spotted it wouldn't take long for word to spread. My presence here was still somewhat of an exhibition.

I carefully traversed the village, taking refuge in the darkest of shadows, watching, waiting, ensuring no stray villager saw me in the night. I was almost at the outskirts of town, barely breathing as I carefully maneuvered my way through the wooden domes.

Just a few more steps and I would be in the clear.

I turned back one last time to ensure no one had seen me. All was silent and empty, and I smiled, pleased with myself that I hadn't been caught. I flipped around for the final step into the dark forest, but I plowed into something with a solid thud, banging my nose against molded granite.

Momentarily stunned, my eyes focused on the dark figure barring my path. "I'm curious. Was that you trying to be sneaky, Copeland?" Rowen asked with unexpected delight. "If so, it was quite adorable."

Damn.

"Don't try to stop me, Rowen. I'm going." I said, trying to side-step the mountainous shadow he cast me in.

"I see that," he said, casually moving to block me. "I just hope the rest of your strategy is a bit more thought-out than your attempt at being stealth."

"I thought I did pretty good," I said aggravated, rubbing my tender nose. "How did you spot me anyway? I didn't even see you."

"I've known all along you meant to go back by yourself. And you're a fool if you think I'm going to let you go alone."

"You're not coming," I said defiantly. "You're injured and... and not invited."

He flashed his bright smile through the darkness. "And just how do you mean to stop me?" he asked casually, then moved so fast my eyes couldn't follow. His hand suddenly clutched my hip, and I gasped when he tugged me towards him. He removed the weapon from my thigh and proceeded to waggle it in front of me. "With this?"

I tried snatching it from him. "Hey! Give that back!"

"It's much too heavy for your slight frame. It must be very uncomfortable, and your journey's only just begun." He tsked, feigning concern.

It irked me to no end that he was right: the weapon had

started to pull on my leg uncomfortably. I wouldn't let him know that though.

"Here, try this." He pulled a much thinner blade from his holster, arcing it gracefully through the air. It flashed in the moonlight like a shooting star and I instantly wanted it in my hand. He chuckled at my pining interest and extended it out to me, tucking my old blade in with his.

I attentively curled my fingers over the smooth crystal hilt that thrummed at my touch. It was beautiful and light and felt amazingly balanced in my hand. Without a word, I sheathed the new blade.

It fit like a glove.

"You're still not coming," I said, knowing it was childish of me, but I was still bitter about him not defending me when I had initially wanted to go.

"Don't look at me like that. It was better to wait until tonight anyway. Demil has a hard head, and it wasn't worth the argument. And while I would prefer it if you didn't go, I know I can't stop you."

Pride aside, I needed to see what was in that crevice, it might hold the answer to tapping into my full potential. But I had no idea if the icy tug calling to me was dangerous or not. I didn't want Rowen getting hurt again on my account.

Trying to get one up on him, I asked, "What about your injury?"

"Takoda gave me a clean bill of health, thanks to your excellent mending." He did look alert if not a little tired, but overall healthy and clean in a new loose shirt and trousers. His roguish beauty was faintly lit by the glow of distant luminorbs, and though I missed his beard, he was still the most mesmerizing human I had ever seen. "In a few days the moss will have fully dissolved, and the scars shouldn't be too bad."

"What about your rest and recovery? You look exhausted," I said, grasping at straws.

"What about you having no idea where you're going?"

Checkmate.

"Alright, you win." I walked off without allowing him to gloat, then stopped in my tracks, realizing he hadn't moved. Rolling my eyes, I exaggeratedly swept my arm in front of me, "After you," I said, because he was right. It was too dark to find the crevice on my own.

He chuckled again with dark satisfaction and sauntered ahead of me. "It's actually this way," he said, uncovering a small luminorb to light our path.

Ass.

Walking alongside one another, we wended between the sentineled trees, their silhouettes dark and jagged against the canvas of night. The sky was crisp and clear due to last night's rainfall, accentuating every twinkling star, comet, and spiraling galaxy across the blue-black velvet of space. By all accounts, it was a perfect night, but as we ventured further into the woods and the lightning-shaped crack loomed up ahead, my skin prickled. It almost hurt how on-end my hairs stood.

Did I still want to do this?

The feeling of pain and anguish brushed along my senses and curved around my body. It was too late to turn back now, and nothing deserved to feel such emptiness.

"Wait here," I said to Rowen.

"Absolutely not."

"Whatever is in there, I don't think it will show itself to me if you come. I'll call you if I need you. I promise."

His smooth jaw set. "No."

"Have I not proven I can handle myself?" I asked, gesturing to his moss-healed side.

Rowen sighed none too happily and handed me the lumi-norb. "I'll be right here."

I nodded once and turned back to the serration in the mountainside.

The forced perspective from where we stood made the split seem like a narrow fissure, but the closer I walked towards it, the wider the chasm grew. The cool breath of the crevice pulled me along by a million invisible strings as it opened just for me.

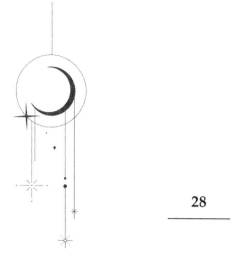

28

I lifted the orb as I walked through the passageway, zigzagging my way forward. The cold feeling intensified with every step, sucking all the warmth and light out of my pores.

Just when I didn't want to take another step, a small den was revealed by the light at my hand. At first glance, it appeared empty, but a bone-chilling moan echoed through the opening. It froze the base of my spine, and I knew I wasn't alone.

I raised the orb higher, squinting to get a better view of what could make such a noise, when I saw the hunched-over figure of a man.

He was dressed in tatters of what appeared to have once been fine clothing. His face was slightly turned from me, revealing only his profile.

He was stooped over, pronouncing the skeletal ridge of his spine. And through the thin fabric hanging from his gaunt form, his sharp shoulder blades jutted out like folded bat wings.

"It's raining," he said in a voice with absolutely no emotion or inflection.

It stopped my blood cold.

He must be confused, it had rained yesterday, but today

there wasn't a cloud in the sky. I strained my ears, waiting to hear something beyond the lightning split. Maybe it had started raining again. But there was nothing, just a hollow silence deafening in its emptiness.

"What...what happened to you?" I asked, trying to hide the terror in my shaky voice.

"It's raining, " he said again in that dreadful lifeless pitch.

"It...It's not raining. Why don't we get you out of here."

It seemed he didn't hear me or couldn't register what I was saying because his body began to sway and convulse. Rocking back and forth he muttered the only words he seemed to remember. "It's raining. It's raining. It's rain—"

"Come with me," I interrupted, hoping to break his cyclical rainstorm. I wanted out of here, badly. And even though I didn't particularly want to get any closer to him, I took another tentative step towards the suffering man. "I can help you out of here."

"It's pouring," he said, which was progress considering it was a different word, albeit still along the same vein. Who was this man, and where was he from? How did he come to be here, and why was I the only one who could sense him?

He slowly began turning his face, so stiffly and incrementally it reminded me of a broken animatronic moving on rusted cogs, his eyes just as lifeless. "He bumped his head and couldn't get up in the morning."

My heart stopped. He was reciting a nursery rhyme from Earth. He was from Earth! Could this crevice be some sort of rift between our worlds? Was he an astral traveler like me?

Excitement quickly turned to dread as his neck twisted to face me, and I flinched back in horror, unable to stifle the sickened gasp that escaped my throat.

The top right side of his head was covered in blood with bits of raw flesh peeling and dangling from his skull. The wound looked as if his head had hit asphalt and then was shredded to ribbons as it skidded against the gravel. Even though his face was hollow and sunken in, there was no mistaking him. I had seen this man before.

It was Maddock Mosa. The comatose patient who had lain a wall away from me in the hospital. His once handsome features and modern clothes were now glaringly obvious.

Somehow, after his head trauma, his consciousness had become stranded here in Luneth, separated from his body. His mind so far gone he could only recall embedded phrases from an old children's rhyme. One that was disturbingly similar to his own tragic story.

"Maddock, do you remember who you are? Did you feel me in the hospital?" I asked, feeling a sliver of hope. Was that what connected us? Was that what drew me to him?

"I feel nothing," he agonized, his wails bouncing off the cave walls. If only his family knew the horrors he was living through.

Suddenly, I wanted very badly to leave this cave, but I couldn't go without Maddock. His situation felt too close to home. It could have just as easily been me in his shoes, lost and stranded from myself.

But I had found my way back, and maybe I could help him find his way back too. Even though his mind might never recover, it had to be better than this. "I want to help you, Maddock, but first let's get you out of here."

He wasn't looking at me anymore, and I was thankful I couldn't see the chunks of loose skin around his temple. "I've felt nothing for so long," he said as he rocked back and forth.

I reached out to touch his shoulder, but my grip never truly found purchase and went straight through his bony frame as if he were made of spun webbing.

His head snapped to mine, the dangling flesh whipping around with the turn of his stare. His eyes widened and locked onto me, and for a hopeful second, I thought he remembered who he was.

Maddock slowly stood, shoulders slumped with his head drawn down, gazing at me through the tops of his faded eyes. "But I feel *you*," he said, tilting his head to the side, his lip curling with starved desire. "I'd very much like to feel more *through* you if that's alright. Just one little touch. I'll give you your body back in one piece. I promise."

The blood drained from my face. His astral self, soul, or whatever it was, long deprived of human flesh, sensed my body could give him what he long desired—a host through which to touch, taste, and feel.

I fled, but before I reached the first bend, he was on me.

I dropped the orb to the ground, my body stiffening and bowing back as Maddock crashed through me like a phantom ship.

"Ohhh," he moaned, his wraith-like being absorbing into me. "You feel so good. Just a little more."

My blood turned to ice.

When I tried launching him off me, he dove into my mind with ferocious ghostly lashings. Mentally, I pushed back, but Maddock thrust himself against me violently, ripping and twisting at my mind as he forced his way through, shredding my consciousness to bits as he burrowed deeper.

The dark cave vanished, and a foreign memory flashed before my eyes.

Cate, my perfect-bodied girlfriend, blonde and beautiful with her left hand extended out, and me, slipping an exorbitant band of diamonds around her finger. She smiled. It wasn't love, but it looked good.

The memory faded, and I reeled at the intrusion. I blinked back to my body, grasping at who I was. It took me a moment to gather my bearings and understand the severity of the situation.

Maddock was invading my body memory by memory. Soon this vessel would be his.

What would happen to me if he succeeded? Would I be forced to live a cohabitated existence in one body, always fighting for control, or would he push me down so deep I faded into nothing but a faint echo?

Another memory sieged my brain.

Huddling up with my parents who hated each other, smiling fraudulently yet another year in a row for the charity photo-op. Keeping up with so many charades, I was losing count.

Wantonly and savagely, he lacerated my memories, making room for his own, not a care in the world for the irreparable pain and damage he inflicted on me.

I tried to shove him out again, but he was ravenous and plowed back into me with a jarring force. A muffled cry escaped my lips, and tears streamed down my face. Even if I could move my arms to grab the weapon at my side, it was useless against these phantom attacks.

I couldn't even scream out to Rowen in my paralysis.

Takoda had been right. *A fate worse than death.*

I felt him go further into my mind, my head exploding with more unwanted memories.

Dodging another priceless vase to the head as Cate discovered I hadn't truly quit my not-so-secret door of revolving women.

Disgusted, I threw up a wall around my thoughts, imagining the toughest, most impenetrable steel.

I could feel him just on the other side, banging at the wall like a deranged madman. "Let me in. I need you!" he wailed, clawing at me as if I were the last life vest on a sinking ship. And maybe I was, but I could never let him have me.

Black-tar anger fueled through me like gasoline. The Mercer deal had gone wrong, horribly, horribly wrong. All the bargains, lies, and false promises I made to preserve my own legacy. Meaningless.

Sitting astride my motorcycle, I started the ignition. Despite the weather forecast and grey storm clouds, I plowed my way forward.

Too far.

He was in too far. Already occupying a small part of me, his memories were mine. I fought to hold him at bay, but more and more memories from that rain-fevered night leaked through the cracks. My barricade against him was breaking.

I pushed harder and harder against the throttle, ignoring the pellets of rain in my eyes and the dangers of a slick road.

I already knew how this story ended, and some part of me was aware that if this memory played out fully before my eyes, he would own this body.

I slowed my breathing, calmed my thoughts, and set my intention.

Get him out. *Now.*

I could barely see. My headlight flooded with the hammering rain, obscuring my vision with a million droplets of water.

An oscillating pressure built beneath my skin. A push. A pull. A subtle glint of rippling light coursed through my veins like streaks of shimmering lightning.

I lost traction. My tires hydroplaning over the thin wet surface, my center of balance wavering.

The fluctuation intensified, cresting into a swell of polished pewter. It grew larger and larger, sucking me in like the tide and overcoming me.

I let off the accelerator, fighting against the inevitable. Careening dangerously, I could do nothing to stop my fall.

Completely out of control, I was overtaken by a molten mercury wave of surging power. It built and filled and flowed until it was all of me. All of me against...

Fear.

Pain.

Darkness.

...

...

A tidal wave of light shot from my body in the brightest flash of gibbous iridescence, swallowing the dark in a seismic blast of liquid diamonds.

It was all silver. I was all silver.

The very same silver of my changed eyes, of the once forgotten rose, of the moon and stars and galaxies.

Of me.

The haunted form of Maddock Mosa launched from me, flying flaccidly through the air before landing in a crumpled mess at the foot of the cave.

I knew there was no saving him.

So I turned and ran, and I didn't look back.

I had no idea where I was running, it didn't matter. I just kept plunging into the darkness, blinded by my pulse. This mindless adrenaline rush was the only thing keeping me from falling apart. I was already barely hanging on by a thread.

Too much had happened too quickly. I hadn't processed or dealt with any of it, and now it was all crashing down on me with the weight of the sky. It was too much. I'd been pushed to my limit, and like a collapsing star, I was falling in on myself.

Hanging branches whipped at my face and arms, mushing me to run harder, farther, and faster, so I picked up my speed.

Some small part of me knew what I was doing was dangerous, running blindly into the pitch-black forest with no direction or knowledge of the terrain. But I was in a state of decline, running solely for survival. If I stopped now, I knew I would crumble.

Painful images flashed across my vision.

My mom concocting her mind-numbing narcotic. And Natalie in the kitchen, quickly peering over her shoulder, making sure I wasn't around to see her adding the drug to my food.

The men at Prism who continued to touch and grope and lick even as I begged them to stop.

The kiss with Rowen that should have never happened.

Forest laiths hunting my scent. Maddock violating my mind. The silver power leaping from my body.

And Erovos with his blighted tree that somehow called my name.

My foot caught on an upturned root and my body lurched forward. All the speed I had accumulated worked against me as I crashed to the ground, hard, taking a few violent tumbles before I lay still in the leaves and bramble.

I was vaguely aware I may have twisted my ankle, but I was too consumed with the violent shudders raking through my body. All the pain and heartache I'd been outrunning had finally caught up with me.

It hurt. Everywhere. The pain found me in every in-between space that held this body together. If this was what it was to feel, I didn't want it, any part of it. There were too many cracks to hold myself together, a broken dam of my emotions drowning me.

Rowen was suddenly beside me, swiftly gathering me up in his powerful arms and holding me close. I forgot he was even here, I must have run right past him. It's not like he could have caught me if he wanted to, but I didn't even remember him calling after me.

Maybe he hadn't. Perhaps he knew I needed to run, to forget, to remember. To *feel*. So he simply let me go.

He was on the ground, cradling me against his body, gently rocking me back and forth. It was in that moment the floodgates fully burst and I sobbed into Rowen's chest. I was feeling every single suppressed emotion, betrayal, and wound from my past. Everything that had been pushed down, smothered, or ignored, fought to be felt. And I did, I felt it all.

And it was excruciating.

It was ugly and messy and loud. Not to mention wet: I completely soaked Rowen's shirt through to his warm skin.

For however long I was lost in my sobs, Rowen held me and stroked my hair without uttering a single word. He didn't have to.

I cried and cried until my voice was hoarse and there were no more tears left to spill.

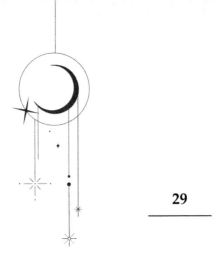

29

I woke three days later.

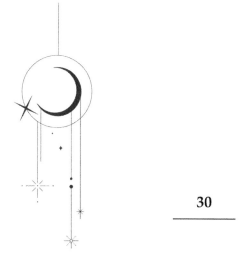

30

"Three days?" I asked aghast, repeating Takoda's words back to him. My voice raspy from lack of use.

I could barely believe I'd been out for so long. That blast from the crevice had nearly taken everything out of me.

The last thing I remembered was crying in Rowen's arms. Only now, vaguely recalling the slow walk back to the village, one arm strung around Rowen as he helped me limp back home.

Sitting up, I saw I wasn't wearing the last thing I put on.

I glanced to Takoda, his silver hair down in its full glory. "One of the women helped change you into something more comfortable, and I've been monitoring your condition. With a few scratches and a twisted ankle, your injuries were easily tended to," he said, gesturing to the vine-filled hydroponic tube he held in his hands, indicating the leaves and roots he'd used in his healing poultice.

"Drink this," he said, handing me a cup of deep-berry liquid. "It is filled with all the sustenance you will need to regain your strength."

I took several replenishing sips, and the cramping in my stomach sighed with relief. "It's delicious, thank you."

Already feeling better, I removed myself from the depression of the bedroll and tested the weight of my wrapped ankle. Feeling no pain, I asked, "How does it work, your healing?"

Takoda pondered my question, sliding the glass vial through the empty slot in his wooden terrarium, adding it to the line of other propagated plants. "We are all born with heightened gifts, though some forget this as they grow. The energy from this earth is ready to give, if you know how to ask. Wounds of the flesh and living medicines speak to me; bones, however, are another matter. There are times a body can be too broken to mend."

Relieved I hadn't broken anything, I gulped down the rest of the nutrient-infused drink.

"Is she awake yet?" Demil's voice carried from outside the dome.

"No, not yet," Rowen said, sounding beyond exhausted. My eyes shot to Takoda, but he was too engrossed in situating his supplies to notice. Even though he was acting oblivious, it seemed he wasn't above a bit of eavesdropping himself.

"Hmm," Demil hummed before asking, "What happened that night in the cave?"

"Not now, Demil. I'm not in the mood."

"I don't mean to pry, but it appears you have been enjoying the fruits of your labor a little too much."

"I said, not now," Rowen growled.

"She is the bearer of the Alcreon Light, and now a charge under all our protection. If you've become too clouded, there is no shame in stepping down as her guardian."

"I wonder who would be the first to volunteer to take my place." Rowen's reply dripped with sarcasm.

I didn't hear Demil's response. I was too busy barreling towards the door, ready to let them know I was indeed awake and perfectly capable of joining their lovely conversation. But as I was about to reach the handle, Rowen entered the room with Demil on his heels. He stopped in his tracks. "You're awake," he said, studying me with dark circles under his eyes.

He hadn't shaved in a few days; the rugged stubble I loved so much had grown back across his tight jaw. His face was etched with worry, and his dark hair was tousled from continually running his hands through it. Where I had gotten nothing but sleep, it looked like Rowen hadn't slept at all.

Rowen's tired eyes wandered to the frayed hem of my shirt, short across my exposed thighs. My mind instantly shot back to our kiss in the cave, when his hands had run up and down nearly every inch of me.

I wondered if his mind went there too, to the touch of my skin beneath his fingertips, to my bare legs wrapped around his body, or the way he held on to me as if he were afraid I would slip through his fingers.

His gaze shot back to mine. "What happened in that crevice?" he demanded darkly, supplying no other greeting. The shadows cast upon Rowen's exhausted features deepened. "You were completely out of it, murmuring over and over again that he was *inside you*." I'd never seen his expression so easily readable; he looked as if he was ready to tear down the world with his bare hands. "What happened in there, Copeland?" He braced himself for the worse, even Takoda and Demil completely stilled.

I sat back down on the bed and told them everything.

I told them of the lifeless body next to mine in the hospital. How I'd pushed my consciousness outside of myself and reached into Maddock's vacant mind. How there had been nothing there. Nothing at all.

How the cold pressing chill calling to me had been the connection I'd forged with Maddock Mosa. And how he had savagely tried to overtake me. How he'd almost succeeded had it not been for the powerful force of the Alcreon Light shooting him out of my body.

Takoda stood wide-eyed, and Rowen ran his hand down his mouth. "Thank the Spirits you're alright, Keira. You've no idea how I've tortured myself. Playing out every single scenario of what could have happened to you in there. Sitting beside you for days, unable to ask you what happened."

"I really thought I could've helped," I said, devastated yet relieved to have made it out. "I was so sure there was something I could have done."

I realized now how stupid that was, how careless I had been with myself and the enormous power I held within my veins. It wasn't mine, it didn't belong to me. It was entrusted to me to wield and protect, and I had put it in enormous jeopardy.

I saw Rowen's green eyes replaying the description of Maddock forcing his way into my body—my mind—looking like he was about to be sick. "I knew I should have gone in there with you."

"There was nothing you could have done. I should have listened. I should never have gone."

"There is a clarity and a new sense of purpose I feel in you," Takoda replied, always finding the good in any situation, never accusatory or chastising in any way.

My eyes slid to Rowen, "I want to say thank you. I know I didn't want you to come but I'm glad you were there for...for after." When I had cried and screamed my soul out, dowsing him in my snot and tears.

"You ran right by me as if the Dark Spirit himself were chasing you. I called and called after you, but it was like you were in a trance, so I just ran with you." His eyes danced across me as if the memory replayed itself upon the screen of my face.

"I'm surprised you were able to keep up," I said playfully,

bumping my shoulder into his. The air in here was too heavy, too serious.

Despite everything that happened, I felt good. All the tears I had shed had been cleansing, renewing, and I felt like an aquatic phoenix slowly emerging from her pearlescent flames.

"I couldn't," he replied with a wry smile, glancing down at my wrapped ankle. "If I could have, I would have tackled you down before you got hurt."

"This? This is nothing. I've been hurt much worse missing the timing on a hurdle," I said, grinning back. "Plus Takoda sorta knows what he's doing when it comes to healing."

"It was an honor." Takoda's smile consumed his whole face; he couldn't be disingenuous if he tried. "And there is one more thing."

"What?" I asked, remembering I'd failed the one test set out for me. I would probably be kicked out of the village tonight.

"A noxlily bulb has taken root from your light-touched soil," Takoda said, beaming, and I stared at him astounded.

"It worked?"

"It has yet to fully sprout, but the Summit now knows you bear the Alcreon Light. There is much to celebrate."

"So I'm allowed to stay?" I asked, hope cinching around strangled words. I was more afraid of the answer than I wanted to admit.

"You are allowed to stay, star-touched," he laughed whole-heartedly.

Demil cleared his throat—I had forgotten he was even in here. "Is anyone going to tell her about tonight?"

"Why?" I asked, perplexed but immensely relieved I was able to witness another night in this village. "What's tonight?"

Without explanation, I was escorted from the dome by two women I had yet to meet. Pia and Xala.

They led me to an enchanted bathing suite dripping with vines and soft glowing flowers. But instead of leaving me to get to it, the women entered the room right behind me. I insisted several times that I was perfectly capable of using the facilities on my own, but they were adamant about joining me, standing firm that their required presence was a direct order from Nepta —a gift.

Skeptical as I was, I let them guide me into the bubbling white stone bath, which they filled with different colored bath milks and mineral salts, adding purple petals that floated like lily pads.

The scented water swirled like a midnight nectar fit to pollinate the heavens, and I couldn't help but feel they were preparing me like a piece of meat for a holiday dinner. It even seemed like they were trying to fatten me up with the plates of food settled around the tub's edge.

I tried to relax, but I was a ball of nerves. I'd managed to tap into my newfound ability, and though it had been beautiful and powerful, it had also been frightening, unhinged, and...unpredictable. I'd summoned it in a moment of sheer terror and adrenaline, but I didn't want such a sacred power to be elicited by fear.

Although that wasn't the only thing that made me spark.

The Light had shown its shy radiance with the lightest of Rowen's touches—but I didn't want that either. However much I tried to deny it, there was nowhere I could push Rowen where he wouldn't be felt. I couldn't have something so massive and important, be contingent on such unreliable and untrustworthy emotions.

I didn't want to think of what I could become if I grew enslaved to those feelings, but I knew all too well the imprisonment of indifference. To be trapped by emotions or against them were merely two corners of the same cage.

I thought back to the crevice and how the power filled me like a veined well flowing inside me, but I had lacked any control over it as it wildly shot out of my body.

In the midst of wondering how I could become the source, pump, and spigot for my abilities, Pia and Xala ushered me out of the tub.

They guided me, dripping wet, into a small anteroom lit by petite stained-glass windows dotting the walls and ceiling. The violet, honey-yellow, and aquamarine glass illuminated the room in hazy beams of light as though viewing the sky from beneath a petaled garden.

Xala indicated for me to lay on the marble slab in the sweet-scented room, and in the half-light, I could make out Pia preparing some kind of hand-sized stone.

This was all seeming like an extravagant spa day, and I wanted to politely decline, but my muscles ached from the fatigue of the last few days, and a rub-down didn't sound half bad.

Giving in, I laid down on the marble pallet, waiting for Pia to begin the stone massage. She lifted my arm and began rubbing the stone back and forth across my skin in an elliptical motion, and I immediately yanked my hand back in pain. It felt like sandpaper!

She and Xala giggled at my response, and I noticed she held a rough-hewn pumice stone in her hand.

Gift? Being rubbed raw by a pumice stone hardly felt like a gift. Now I *knew* Nepta was out to get me.

"It's good for the skin," Pia explained.

"By removing it?"

She chuckled again. "Yes, it will renew your skin, leaving it smooth and beautiful. Try to relax. This is a room of well-being."

Not wanting to insult her or her culture, I nodded for her to continue.

I winced the entire time as Pia removed the top layer of my skin from toe to chest. But she was right. I had never felt softer.

Then she rubbed the lactic acid and knots from my body in a heavenly deep tissue massage. Blocked energy flowed through me, reviving my limbs and sore body. Next, both women bathed my body and washed my hair with fragrant berry- and almond-scented lathers.

This was all quite over the top and had me worrying they were gussying me up for some intense Alcreon Light ceremony. I really hoped that wasn't the case.

Finally cleaned to their specifications, they wrapped me in a linen robe and sat me at the wooden vanity.

Together they tamed my hair into smooth curls that fell long down my back, loosely twisting and braiding small sections away from my face. Xala added a bit of charcoal to my eyes, further winging out the ends and darkening my lashes. She also placed a dab of rose paste on my cheeks and lips, bringing out the pink undertones of my pale skin.

Pia carried out a billowing garment slung across her arms.

"Okay, what's going on? Do either of you know what's happening tonight?" I asked, hoping one of them would fill me in because this was getting weird.

"It's a most marvelous event that hasn't happened in many years. It was thought to have disappeared forever," Xala said solemnly before excitement crept back into her voice. "It has been over a thousand moons since it was last seen. Some say it is you who brings its return."

So that explained everyone's enthusiasm. A rare event was to take place tonight. And because of me?

I doubted it, but the more questions I asked, the more the

two women refused to tell me, all the while assuring me I would absolutely love it.

"But what about the—"

Before I could get the question out, a garment engulfed my head and muffled the rest of my thought. The lightweight dress tumbled down my body in a thin layer of sheer white fabric. The material was just translucent enough that it highlighted the silhouette of my bare legs beneath, and the cinched bodice gave my runner's body a pleasing curve. The neckline ran low across my chest, lifting and accentuating the hollow cleavage between my breasts. Long, see-through sleeves draped off my shoulders and fastened delicately at my wrists with crystal-tipped ties. Tan strappy sandals were slipped over my feet and laced up my ankles like pointe shoes.

"One more finishing touch," Xala said with a pleased grin as she placed a shimmering head chain upon my hair. Pieced into three sections, one strand of the headpiece lined directly down my middle part, while the other two bowed lightly around the crown of my head. A hanging tear-dropped moon crystal rested at the center of my brow, bringing out the mirrored silver of my eyes.

I had never looked more beautiful, yet something was missing. Even though I hadn't owned it for very long, my thigh ached for the weight of the crystal blade Rowen had given me.

Seeming to have read my mind, Pia turned, and in her arms she held my elegant yet deadly weapon. "Looking for this?"

I smiled broadly as I took it from her delicate hands.

Both ladies helped me lift my dress around my hips as I fastened and secured the blade in its accompanying thigh sheath.

Perfectly in place, I nodded, and they let the dress tumble down to my feet in billowing blooms of fabric, completely concealing the weapon. It would be difficult to get to in a pinch, but at least I could feel its reassuring presence resting against my skin.

Now I felt complete.

I thanked Pia and Xala over and over, especially when I found out they were the ones who had been laying clothes and food out for me all this time.

Feeling closer to them after everything we just went through, bath and all, I threw my arms around them in a hug of immense gratitude.

"Go to the shore," Xala instructed. "The village awaits you."

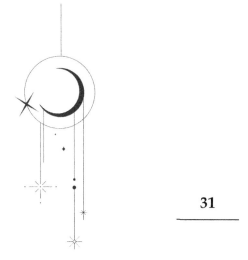

31

I walked to the beach along the flagstone path that could have easily been mistaken for trailing pools of moonlight. My feet gently padded across each stone as if I were a water pixie skipping across a pond.

The waft of the breeze tousled my hair and the flowing bits of my dress, and I wished Pia and Xala were with me. But the girls needed to get ready themselves and promised to join the festivities soon.

I made my way to the large group of villagers gathered where ocean, shore, and forest converged. By now, the sun was only a blazoning scarlet line between sea and sky—a trail of lit gunpowder on the horizon, coating the stars in drops of molten sunset.

The scenery was a beautiful reminder of the Light inside me, yet as I looked at the ethereal Wyn people, I felt like such an unworthy vessel for their praise and protection. With their silver-sleek hair glinting in the fiery starlight, they were the bright points of a living, breathing constellation, each one of them a star I couldn't let down.

They were dressed in their handwoven garments, varying in

all shades from warm to cool sand. Some carried wooden flutes, drums, or other rhythmic instruments, while others held flowers, fronds, or what looked like carved wooden hoops and Cyr wheels for dancing.

The anticipation of what was to come was killing me, but everyone seemed content to simply stare at the last few rays of the sun before they seeped into space. Which was marvelous, but it happened every night.

I got scrubbed raw for this?

My nerves were taking over, and I began to wring my hands in anxiety.

Suddenly, Driskell's voice rang through the crowd. "The Alcreon Light has returned to us!" he shouted, and seemingly all at once, the entire village turned their warm faces to me. They began cheering and singing while tossing tiny dried petals around me like confetti. Driskell made no mention of the false prophecy or the fact that I'd been missing for over twenty years. Like a true politician, he only stuck to the positive points, but I didn't mind. The joy around me was contagious.

I was lost in the celebratory sea of faces when Rowen drew my gaze like my own personal beacon. He walked toward me with a deliberate, magnetized gait that echoed across the sand and pulled my steps in his direction. He looked much better than he did earlier today. He must have finally been able to get some rest.

He wore stone-grey pants and a low-opened shirt that provided a peek at his two necklaces. His dark wavy hair fell around the nape of his neck in a perfectly coiffed halo, a few loose strands falling into his evergreen eyes. And to my delight, the scruff remained.

He stopped in front of me as the crowd melted away. "Copeland, you look..." He swallowed, accentuating the divots in his temples.

"Clean?" I offered.

He threw his head back and laughed a rare laugh. "Yes, that's exactly what I was going to say." His hand raised towards my face, and my heart picked up speed as he gently tugged a stray petal from my hair. His fingers seemed to linger as my brown curls slowly cascaded over his knuckles, and our eyes locked. I sipped in the tiniest breath of air, immersed in his gaze dancing with the reflection of the stars.

Back in the bathing suite, when I gazed into the mirror, I'd never looked more beautiful. But it wasn't until this moment, where Rowen stared at me as if galaxies were colliding before his very eyes, that I truly felt beautiful. Every part of me. Even the ugly parts. The parts that were raw and scarred and the parts that were still healing or coming into their own.

Every part of me was staring back at Rowen, but looking at him left an excruciating ache deep down in my stomach. I knew he was beyond emotionally unavailable, but that wouldn't stop me from admiring him while I had the chance. This look in his eye might never come again.

"You look..." I paused, grasping for the words.

"Rested?"

It was my turn to laugh. "Exactly."

With the last traces of the sun vanishing, the only light beamed from the stars. Not a single fire or luminorb in sight for tonight's festivities. Even the village lights were extinguished behind us.

Sheeted entirely in night, everyone on the beach talked excitedly with their faces turned toward the ever-battered shore. I glanced out to the open sea before turning back to Rowen. "Are you going to tell me what's going on?" I asked impatiently.

"Shhh," he murmured as he placed his hands on my chin and directed my gaze back to the ocean. "Look."

Slowly, just beyond the horizon, curtains of rippling light

rolled through the sky like millions of phosphorescent galloping horses. Vast waves of color water-painted the night in vibrant hues of violet, fuchsia, cerulean, and pale green.

The celestial lights danced and swept across the sky, illuminating everything in an auroral display of undulating swirls. The spectacle had me breathless. It was so magical that I wanted to cry and laugh all at once. I could already feel tears welling in my lower lash line, threatening to spill over at the sight.

I couldn't look away as Rowen's breath danced across my cheek. "These are the lights of Celenova."

It was the most miraculous thing I had ever seen. It reminded me of the Aurora Borealis back on Earth, only instead of remaining in place, it soared through the air like a giant cloud of monarch butterflies. It mirrored across the sea, reflecting its other-worldly image back at itself like a Rorschach inkblot.

The ethereal waves were almost upon the beach, and I heard Takoda yell, "The Alcreon Light has returned," followed by a quick vocalization pattern that the entire village echoed back as one. Then, as if on cue, the Wyn villagers erupted into song and dance.

Drums, flutes, chimes, and joyous voices erupted in a festive allegro. The upbeat melody filled the space between the lights and the dancing bodies gracefully flowed through it all.

Celenova was a grand conductor, orchestrating a performance of light, sound, and movement.

The first wave of light passed over my body, alighting my skin in a kaleidoscopic map of shapes, colors, and patterns— ever-shifting and ever-changing. I lifted my hand in front of me and watched as the colorful ripples played across my skin, marveling at the light leaping and pirouetting around my fingers.

With my mouth parted in an unbelieving smile and my eyes wide with wonder, I turned to Rowen to see if he was witnessing this too. But he was already looking at me, eyes alight as if I was his own personal meteor shower.

As I took him in, I could see why.

The way the light moved upon his face and body was hypnotizing. I tried to capture this perfect photo of him in my mind. But before I could fully commit it to memory, the lights and colors shifted across his features, creating a different yet equally marvelous image. I tried to memorize the new changes, but they quickly evolved again, and I soon realized that capturing such a thing was like trying to catch the very light itself. Impossible.

I leaned in closer to Rowen so he could hear me through the loud music and singing. "It's breathtaking."

He said something back to me, but I couldn't make it out over the new song that exploded through the air.

"What?"

Rowen placed his hand on the small of my back, releasing a swarm of colorful butterflies throughout my stomach. He led me to a small, secluded cove, isolating us in our own swirling paint palette.

"I was worried you wouldn't wake in time to see them," he said, for what I assumed was the second time.

"How did you know they were coming?" I asked curiously.

"Nepta. She could feel the rumbling over the ocean days away. About the same day your noxlily sprouted."

Hearing Nepta's name, I scanned for her wizened face amongst the crowd. It wasn't hard to spot her with her long quartz headdress and tall double-mooned cane. She looked ethereal, ascendent, and godlike as she weaved her free arm through Celenova, manipulating the light into giant waves that soared and crashed into a group of children squealing with delight.

"I wonder where they've been?"

"Some say Celenova are the lost tears of the Elder Spirits."

Remembering Xala's words, I said, "Celenova hasn't appeared in over a century. My disappearance couldn't have been the cause."

"Perhaps it is your reappearance that calls them back," he said like it made all the sense in the world.

I looked out at the seemingly endless waves of Celenova, my gaze following its glowing path as it washed across the ocean and beach, then up and over the trees and mountains, dousing everything in a heavenly fire. I couldn't fathom how something so incredible could possibly have anything to do with me.

With no end to the lights in sight, I asked, "Why me?"

A pinch appeared between Rowen's eyebrows. "When I first came to be with the Wyn people, my waking thoughts felt like a nightmare. All I wanted was to close my eyes forever, but sleep was no sanctuary, it brought along demons all its own. Unable to rest, I took to walking the forest at night. Oftentimes I would walk until I crashed from exhaustion. Even though they offered me a home and a bed, I started to build small encampments around the village, never knowing where the night might take me. And I came to know this land like a perfectly balanced blade in my hand."

My body stilled as he spoke, as if I was dealing with a wild animal that would flee at the first sign of movement.

"One night, after many sleepless years, a summoning-demon appeared near the village, dangerously near. It was mid-hunt when it came across my scent, and viewing me as a threat to its prey, the horned beast attacked me. I thought it was my lucky night. Finally, an avenging reaper come to kill me. And believe me, I wanted to die. But in the last second, one thought led me to raise my blade in defense. Takoda had worked so hard to keep me alive. Letting myself be killed would be a poor way to thank him.

"I fought the demon and almost got my wish. I may have

won the battle in the long hard end, but I was left with my fair share of fresh wounds. Running into a summoning-demon is a rare occurrence, one you would never want to repeat, but a few days later, another one appeared. This one nearly scorched me to death before I slayed it.

"Only something with immense power could conjure such devils that lay in wait for their target, especially two in a row. Whatever they were looking for was near my new home, and as I came to see it, too close to a kind and accepting people. I took it upon myself to protect the Wyn from every demon and summoning that hunted too near. And hunt they did.

"It was one of the quieter nights when I first heard you call out in the woods. At first, I thought you were a ghost come to haunt me. I tried to ignore you, thinking I'd finally gone mad, but you called out again. And I realized it was a voice not meant to torment me, but a voice just as tortured as my own screams in the night."

He let out a breath, and I realized my hands were shaking.

"I found you then, but I could barely see you. A cloud of black smoke surrounded you. I strained my eyes to see you through the gaps in the darkness; you seemed so small compared to the creatures I had come to expect. You were hardly wearing anything at all, not even shoes on your feet. You looked so fragile, so breakable. I tried to go to you but found no matter what I did, I couldn't get close to you, touch you, or even speak to you. It was as if the smoke was keeping you caged."

Hearing Rowen describe my nightmares from an outside perspective was startling, but everything he said rang true with all I had felt.

"You couldn't see me, didn't even know I was there, and I contemplated leaving you. For all I could do, I might as well have been an ocean away. But then you fell to the ground, and the darkness bore down on you even harder. I stayed, betting it would finish you off right then and there. There was no way you could survive, but you fought your way back to your feet, and you kept going through what I could only imagine was your own personal hell. Alone in impenetrable darkness. The world invisible to you.

"But you didn't give up, curl in a ball, and submit to your fate. You got up, and kept fighting your way through the darkness with only your strength of will, as if you knew to move was to survive. In that moment I realized I couldn't leave you, even if you had no idea I was there. So I stayed with you all night, would stay with you however long you needed me, but once the sun began to rise, you disappeared."

His bleak eyes met mine through the rainbowed light, and even through his stubble, I saw his jaw twitch.

"I had no idea if I dreamt you or if you would ever return, but that didn't stop me from trying to find you again. It was by complete chance that I'd found you in the first place; there was no way lightning would strike twice. But then you appeared to me again, and I almost collapsed in relief.

"Some nights you were nowhere to be seen. On the nights I did find you, I noticed you were the one attracting the demons, and I briefly wondered if I was one of them too. I knew I couldn't leave you or help you out of your darkness, but I could keep at bay the shadows and teeth that lay in wait for you, even if I might be one of them myself. And I did. I killed anything that came even close to you in a malicious manner."

I was sure I had completely stopped breathing. The fighting shadows I'd seen had been Rowen saving me from the creatures of the night. All that talk I had spewed about not needing any help from him had been completely wrong. He'd told me I was being hunted, but not that I came close to being slaughtered multiple times.

"One night a summoning scaib found you—a wisp-wraith of

a creature with a stinging telson. The scaib was crawling all around your orb of darkness, testing it, probing it, trying to find a way in, until it started to somehow get through. I could tell by the look on your face, you could feel it too.

"Its curved tail wriggled in excitement, and I knew I had only one chance to kill it before it struck you. The scaib was too preoccupied with you to even sense me standing there, targeting its exposed belly. My aim rang true, and it attacked me, nearly severing my arm, but at least it was away from you."

It felt like my feet washed out from underneath me. I remembered that night. The sticky hot breath on my neck and the misty fingers stroking my skin. The screech that seemed to rip through my eardrums before the creature slithered off me.

Now I knew. It had been Rowen who saved me.

"Weeks passed, and the darkness slowly started to lift around you. The first time I saw you clearly, I couldn't look away. Your eyes were so beautiful, yet terrified, caged, and drowning, but also determined. I could see in your face that no matter what was thrown at you, you would keep getting back up. You wouldn't let anything defeat you.

"I kept thinking to myself, how much more of this can she take? Why are the demons of the night drawn to her? I didn't know what you were, but despite the monsters I had kept at bay, I knew things much more sinister would hunt you down." Rowen looked haunted, like he was going to be sick. "And when they came for you, I would be by your side, even though you had no idea I existed.

"Until the night you broke from the dark cloud and looked up, directly at me. I swear I almost ran right to you, but you looked so afraid of me that I didn't dare move to scare you further. We were entirely alone, yet somehow I heard someone shout your name. You looked back as if contemplating leaving, and I immediately hated whoever called out to you so freely, hated that they had liberty to talk and touch you in a way I couldn't."

I remembered that night, when I'd almost succumbed to the drug planted within my bloodstream. But I had beaten the substance fighting to suppress me, and the first thing I saw when I lifted my eyes was Rowen. I had no idea he had been there the entire time, watching me, protecting me. It explained why I had been so inextricably drawn to him from the moment I first laid eyes on him. Some part of me must have always known he was there—the hand I always imagined reaching out to me.

"Even as you broke from the confines of your blight, I knew no matter what came at you, you would stand and keep going, keep fighting. And that is why, Copeland. That is why it is you. Never question why the Light chose you again." He swallowed hard, accentuating the severe line of his mouth. I wanted to trace my tongue along the seam of his lips, to ease the tension and thank him for everything he had done for me.

When my astral traveling began again, it was utterly haunting. I had never felt so empty and alone. But I hadn't been alone, had I? Rowen had always been there.

Even though he couldn't speak or reach out to me, he'd never left my side. He was my eyes when I couldn't see and my arms when I couldn't fight. I had no idea the battles he raged just beyond my periphery.

It was a selfless act.

He watched me intently, the suspense for what I was about to say written across his face. "You were always there," I said, thinking at first it was a question but then realizing it was the answer. For the past few months, Rowen had been my rock, my lighthouse, my silver thread guiding me back to myself. Who knew how many times I would have been lost in the darkness had it not been for his mooring presence. "I'm sorry for all I've put you through. I didn't mean to bring you more pain."

A flash of violet swept across Rowen's face, and an exhale escaped the crescent shape of his lower lip. "You have to know I would die, and fight, and burn, over and over again if it meant keeping you safe." His eyes were like emerald whirlpools, sucking me in and drenching me completely. There was no more denying it. All the things Rowen had done for me just out of sight, in the wings of the stage, made me love him even more.

The realization took my breath away and rocked me to my core.

I love Rowen.

I always had, and I always would.

I felt pure elation, a golden light growing and expanding within my chest. It was a physical sensation unlike anything I'd ever felt, but suddenly it twisted and convulsed, bruising me from the inside out.

He didn't love me back. Or if he did, he was fighting it.

The feeling was a double-edged sword lodged in my heart, but I could live with the tender, hurting flesh. I'd lived through worse—I knew what it was to feel nothing at all.

I questioned whether it would be better to be numb to this heartbreak but to feel Rowen in any capacity was better than to not feel him at all.

The loud bang of a drum jolted me back to our conversation, so intimate on the hem of such a public celebration. For a moment, it felt like we were the only two people on the beach, the sounds and cheers merely existing in the next dimension over.

Rowen seemed to remember the celebration as well. "I've kept you too long." He smiled, a broken yet beautiful smile and the dagger in my heart thrust even deeper.

We made our way back to the jubilant festivities with the weight of his confession. Though the demons and summonings hadn't been able to reach me within the village, Erovos was still out there patiently waiting for me.

Despite the flashing joyous faces and the flow of limbs, I knew the danger wasn't gone. We all knew that, but Celenova had given us room to let go, to breathe, if only for a night.

"Keira. There is something else I need to tell you."

I tilted my head, waiting for him to continue, still in disbelief at how drawn to him I was.

For a split second, I could see him second-guess himself, which was odd. He was always so self-assured and decisive. "You should dance," he said, changing the subject as we approached the ring of dancers.

"Is that you asking me to dance?" I asked sarcastically, already knowing his answer.

"Not tonight."

"What were you going to say?"

"I'll tell you after." His words told me to go, but his eyes pleaded with me to stay.

With no preamble or warning, hands grabbed my waist from behind and wrenched me away from Rowen. I was whirled around into the strong embrace of Demil, who threw us into the circle of dancing bodies.

"Bold of you," I said to him. "I was in the middle of a conversation." Even though I knew once Rowen made up his mind he stuck to it. Whatever else he wanted to say, he would tell me later.

"You look much too beautiful not to be shown off tonight," he smiled arrogantly, the lights of Celenova reflecting in all new ways against his cool skin, and I gave in to his charm.

We picked up speed in our dancing as he led and spun me effortlessly through the tangle of dancers. Our feet kicked up sand as we jumped and skipped to the beat, laughing and shouting as we went. Demil knew what he was doing on the dance floor. His grasp on me was firm yet pliable, making it easy to steer and direct me through the crowd.

I let my head fall back to stare at the swirling iridescent sky, and knowing Demil wouldn't let me fall, I lost myself in the spinning lights.

The song came to an end, offering a small respite, and I flicked off my shoes, feeling the sand between my toes.

I glanced around the celebration, searching for other familiar faces, when my sights landed on Ven, dressed in his best yet still somehow looking a ragamuffin. He was leaping around his majestic white wolf, who jumped playfully at the light, trying to catch it between her gleaning incisors.

My gaze continued to roam until it fell on Xala and Pia enjoying a refreshing beverage as they laughed and talked with a large group of men. Their eyes caught mine, and feeling drunk on the night, I slightly lifted my dress and curtseyed. They laughed from across the way, receiving my message of gratitude.

They both had changed into long flowing dresses of mint julep and blue clay. Pia's hair was tied up in elegant knots, whereas Xala's flowed like silk straight to her hips. They were stunning, and the eyes of the men around them glistened with desire for the next dance.

Before I could make my way to mingle with my newfound friends, Demil yanked me back into the cacophony of dancing.

In this dance, the partners were passed off down the line, and I found myself dancing with half the village. Meeting new faces while putting names to familiar ones.

Through the whirling bodies, I could make out Quiya and Nyvari, the sisters who had taken me under their wing and taught me so much about the Wyn people. They had their fingers laced through one another's, their arms flowing between them like two flower children at a festival.

I even saw the members of the Summit enjoying themselves.

Driskell and Alvar raised their goblets to me in a silent toast of gratitude, and I danced briefly with Takoda before I wound up back in Demil's arms.

The lights were only now beginning to taper off slowly, and I was perfectly happy, exhausted, and content in the moment.

The only thing that could make Celenova even better would be one dance with Rowen. I would have to find him soon and convince him that spinning me around was in his best interest. He couldn't brood forever. His feelings had to extend to more than a guardian role. He just hadn't admitted it to himself yet.

I smiled at the thought of dancing with Rowen, of spinning in his arms, but I was suddenly pulled out of the joy of the moment when a blood-curdling scream sliced through the night like a hot wire.

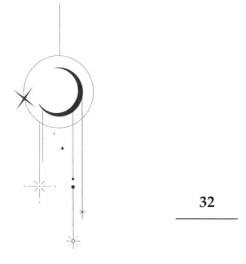

32

The celebration came to a screeching halt, and it took my mind a moment to comprehend the horrific scene unfolding before me. The enchanting village I had come to know and love with every broken yet healing piece of myself, was caught in a brilliant blaze of red and orange chaos.

My home was on fire.

The breathless beat between laughter and terror was nearly seamless yet wholly nightmarish. Mass hysteria erupted around me in screaming wails and shoving bodies. People desperately searched for their loved ones amidst the rapidly growing flames.

Demil grabbed me by the shoulders, jerking my frozen stare of disbelief toward his enraged face. "Stay here, on the shore, and don't move," he demanded, then released his bruising grip on me. He disappeared into the sea of panicked bodies with only a backward glance.

Was he crazy? I couldn't stay here and do nothing; with the number of times I'd been stomped on and shoulder-checked, I ran the risk of falling and being trampled.

Moving with, rather than against the barrier of pushing

bodies, I searched for Rowen, hoping to catch a glimpse of him in the unfurling mayhem. Several villagers were throwing baskets of water onto the fire, trying to quell the raging crimson beast from destroying their homes and livelihoods.

It was a paltry method for how massive the flames had become, especially for such a skilled and sophisticated village. They were unprepared and ill-equipped for this; they must have never had to deal with a fire of this magnitude.

Despite the turmoil, some semblance of order began forming as children were shepherded away from the fire. Men and women who weren't fighting the flames gathered and stacked baskets of dried food, herbs, and medicine just on the outskirts of the village.

Several crates of precious commodities had already been reduced to char and dust. When the flames finally decided to settle, what would be left?

I gathered up my dress and sprinted into the horror, searching for a way to help. This was my home too, and I'd be damned if I stood by and watched it all turn to ash.

I spotted a basket of grains dangerously close to catching aflame. I heaved it up by its handles, and ran.

The villagers' stash of collected bins was too far away from me, not to mention through a ring of fire. It wasn't the safest route to repeatedly run back and forth from, especially with loaded arms, so I started a new cache of salvaged goods on my side of the flames.

I charged back into the inferno, scanning for more undamaged necessities that could be pulled from the wreckage.

A devastating crash of wood erupted right beside me as one of the domes collapsed in a plume of smoke, another falling right on its heels. They crumbled like paper to a match, utterly destroyed and completely unsalvageable.

The fire was wild and rampant, and villagers ran past me with bleeding wounds, burnt arms, and stunned expressions.

I raced to help an older villager bleeding profusely from a head wound when I heard a muffled scream coming from inside one of the domes. If someone was caught within the burning pyres of canopied wood, smoke inhalation could kill them faster than the fire.

I ushered the wounded man to the beach, then whirled to a nearby house, throwing open the door as sweltering heat rushed at my face and dried my eyes. "Is anyone in here?" I called out, only for a cloud of smoke to choke down my nose and throat. I didn't think anyone was in here, but it was hard to tell.

Daring to move on to the next home, I pushed at the wooden entrance, but it was barricaded shut by something heavy on the other side.

I was about to head to the next home when I heard another scream from just beyond the obstructed door. With newfound urgency, I plowed my shoulder into the doorway until it slowly gave way, inch by agonizing inch.

Finally, I managed to slip through the narrow opening. Covering my mouth and nose with the crook of my arm, I desperately searched while weaving between the burning debris and red-hot flames. I spotted a young girl huddled beneath a desk, mouth open in a wail.

Somehow, she'd become separated from the other children on the beach. She must have come back here looking for her family, only to find her house empty and crashing down all around her.

I snatched her from her hiding place and hoisted her up on my hip. Squeezing us both out through the small space, I ran with her to where I had stashed the basket. Setting her down, I gently wiped her silver hair from her smoke- and tear-stained face as she clutched at my dress.

"Everything's going to be alright now," I said as calmly as possible, inspecting her for any cuts or burns. Other than being shaken, she appeared fine. "I'll be right back, okay?"

She shook her head and gripped my skirt even tighter.

"I have to see if anyone else needs my help. While I go look, could you watch this for me?" I asked, indicating to the basket, hoping it would keep her distracted and away from the flames.

Hesitantly, she nodded with her big, wide eyes, and her tiny hands loosened from my dress. "You're very brave. I'll come back and get you when it's safe. Don't go anywhere, alright."

It wasn't lost on me that I'd told her to do exactly what Demil had asked of me. I just hoped she was more obedient than I was.

I stood and turned to make my way back into the blaze when I caught sight of Rowen through smoke and fire.

He was covered in ash and soot and sweat, and his soaked-through shirt clung to his taut muscles and broad back. His hair was unruly, the ends drenched and sticking to his face. I knew he was looking for me, but his searching gaze hadn't landed on me yet. Despite being evidently wracked with grief over the ruin of his village, he looked to be in one piece.

Relief wended through me like a long-awaited summer storm, and I wished this feeling could rain down from the sky and douse the pillaging flames and smothering smoke. But there wasn't even a cloud in the sky to wish upon.

I made my way towards him, eager to show that I was alright, when a looming figure stepped casually in front of me, blocking Rowen from my view.

I had never seen him before, but I immediately knew he didn't belong here. This man, with his black breeches, red tunic, and crimson hair, looked like the male embodiment of the flames destroying everything around us. Even the jeweled sword at his back beamed with shimmering rubies.

"There you are," he sneered, his eyes burning into me from the deep recesses of his shadowed brow.

He stood between me and the entire village, whose people were too preoccupied to notice this man so out of place. So wrong.

Then it hit me like a blistering wall of hot air—these flames weren't natural. This was arson, and he'd been the one to light the match.

"You did this," I hissed at him in disgust, wanting to rip the hair out from his head. "Why? What have these people ever done to you?"

"They harbored you," he said as his hand swept over the macabre show from hell. "So I guess you could say this is all for you." His eyes gleamed with satisfaction and the timbre of his voice betrayed nothing but dead serious conviction.

The air thickened, closing us off from the village in an arena of smoke and faded firelight.

I stepped back in horror, my eyes flashing to the little girl I had just promised everything would be alright to. A promise broken in a matter of seconds. The man from the seventh ring of Hell followed my glance, and even though he noted her presence, his sole focus thankfully rested on me and me alone.

Knowing I had only a few precious seconds to act before he came at me, I debated spending that time reaching for my concealed blade or grabbing the girl and running. Weighing my inexperience against the fact he was still somewhat of a distance away, potentially leaving us room to get lost in the smoke, I chose the girl.

But within a few steps, I was suddenly knocked off course, and pain flared in my cheek as I scrambled to right myself. Somehow the man was standing right next to me, as if he'd been there the entire time.

He looked at me, smiling with eyes that both fed and

absorbed the heat of the flames, and it took me a moment to realize he'd struck me on the side of the head.

How had he moved toward me so fast?

He grabbed for me, and I shot out my hand, straight-arming him away when a surge of power rolled through me with a single ripple of my cells. Light shot out of my palm in a spotlight of silver, hitting the red man right in the gut. The force was so strong it propelled him back by his middle, pulling him out of view until even his fingertips were swallowed by the smoke.

I darted for the girl again, and just as I was about to reach for her, I was flung off my feet by the back of my hair.

I hit the ground flat on my back, knocking my head against the unforgiving surface. My skull exploded, the pain making my eyes lose focus.

How had he made it through the smoke so quickly?

Infuriated, I kicked my foot out, landing my heel right against the tender skin of his shin.

"You little bitch," he howled in agony and punched me in the jaw. Stars erupted in my already blurred vision, and I tasted the copper tang of blood on my tongue. Dazed, I struggled to glance up from the ground, hoping not to see any sign of the girl, but I found her peering at me from over the basket, her eyes were wide with palpable fear. I wished she'd run from here. I didn't want her to witness this.

This man, whoever he was, knew me, knew what I was, and his sick determination wasn't faltering in the slightest as he grabbed for me again. He was at least twice my size, so I had no hope of beating him in a fight. Unless...unless I could shock him again. Harder. Like I'd done to Maddock back in the crevice.

I tried to summon that building pressure in my hands, imagined it flowing within me like a subterranean well, but nothing came.

I searched for it, begged for it to come, pleaded even. Still nothing.

I needed to think of something, but I couldn't concentrate past the ringing in my ears which most likely signified a concussion.

"Trying to shock me again?" he said with a snarl. "That was a very nifty trick. You might be more valuable than I was led to believe."

"Keep your hands off me, you sick bastard," I spat at him while kicking out, aiming between his legs. I hit him in the thigh, and he cried out as his leg went dead. I kicked him again, but he caught me around the ankle and dragged me across the forest floor.

I clawed at the dirt and grass, trying to find purchase as he pulled me along. When that failed, I swiveled onto my back, shrieking and kicking my legs furiously for him to release me, but he was too strong, his vice like metal. Another of my kicks hit him in the stomach, and he grunted, wrenching my leg at an unnatural angle. I screamed out as the pain in my head pierced through me all over again.

"You're lucky she wants you alive, or I would slit your throat right here," he said as if he was doing me a favor.

She?

I knew absolutely nothing about this veiled enemy, and I didn't want to stick around to find out. We had all been so focused on Erovos, we never stopped to think someone else might get to me first.

I scrambled for my blade but something was wrong, I was moving too slow. It must have been the multiple hits I took to the head.

It was definitely a concussion.

The man's eyes narrowed into firm slits of deep concentration, and he began muttering words in a language I didn't understand. The very air in front of him started to ripple and tear apart, revealing a dark sliver of whirling midnight.

My words and reaction time seemed sluggish. I couldn't move or think fast enough. It felt like I was in one of those nightmares where you try to move, run, crawl, anything, but it feels as though you are wading through tar. No matter what you do, your fate is inevitable, and even though you wake just before horror strikes, you know how it ends.

Unfortunately, there would be no waking up from this.

"Whaass...that?" I slurred incoherently as terror settled in my bones. I couldn't distinguish what I was seeing, it looked as if he was opening a rift in space itself. Was that how he had moved so fast? Through tunnels of darkness?

"The Dark Spirit has taught my queen a great many things. Even how to manipulate the energy of others to use as your own," he said, just as the little girl collapsed to the ground without a sound. And the black hole grew wider.

The scream that lacerated my throat consumed me.

I wailed and cried and thrashed, but the red man grabbed my hands, stopping me from fumbling through the layers of my dress to get to the concealed weapon at my thigh. He slammed my wrists together and held them both within his large grasp.

I looked back at the burning village and the small girl crumpled on the ground. Tears fell from my eyes, stinging the cuts on my face, and I desperately hoped for one last way of escape, one last way to save the town and people I loved.

Thrashing to escape, the sky above me roared with thunder, and a streak of lightning flashed overhead, clearing the smoke.

Rowen's face snapped directly to me as the beam engulfed me in its spotlight, and his eyes locked with mine from across the field. I barely had a moment to note the look of utter shock and horror on his face as I was violently thrust into the dark sliver of the unknown.

Rowen's name echoed from my lips, and then all went silent.

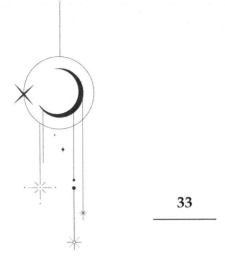

33

My eyelids fought to open, but they felt thick and weighted with the remnants of a deep unnatural sleep. Overhead, morning light glinted and bobbed through the wind-blown trees, casting flickers of light against the weakened shutters of my lids.

When I rolled to my side, my head roared with the pain of being severed in two, and a wave of nausea lurched through me. Crimson, black, and orange memories flickered through my mind in a revolving wheel of hell.

The village! The innocent people who were punished for no other reason than knowing me.

Guilt and remorse clutched at my gut, twisting with a steel-clawed fist. All that flamed destruction and death had been nothing but a grand distraction—a distraction to steal me out from underneath Nepta's nose.

The raging fire would most likely be out by now, absorbed and captured by the dawning sun, but still, I cringed to think of the wreckage revealed by the light of day. And the bodies of those who hadn't made it out unscathed.

I'd taken a pretty hard hit to the head myself, and a sour fog threatened to pull me back under. Battling to stay conscious, I recited one by one all the people I hoped made it out of the fire safely: Rowen, Takoda, Ven, Sabra, Quiya, Nyvari, Pia, Xala, Nepta...

If I had learned the little girl's name, hers would be repeated as well, but I had to suffice with the image of her trusting little face, hoping that whatever the red man had done to her, he hadn't killed her.

I kept repeating their names...on and on the list went, doubling back over itself until it became a calming mantra.

The strength of their names fueled me with enough energy to concentrate my breathing. I had willed myself to other locations before, whether knowingly or not, so I knew I could do it again, but as I reached out to leave, my body stayed firmly rooted to the ground.

I tried everything, searching for any thread or reaching out to any outstretched hand. There was nothing. I imagined myself in Rowen's bed—knowing how well that worked for me in the past. But still nothing.

Feeling desperate, I tried bringing myself back to my old room, Harlan's room. Hell, I even tried Natalie's room.

My head wound might be worse than I feared, and the ringing in my ears held my vibration in place like a note plucked from the string of a harp.

I opened my eyes and tried to right myself, but my arms didn't appear to be working.

"You're awake," came a voice that made my skin crawl. Long hands reached out to steady me, but I flinched back, remembering his violent flames.

"Don't touch me," I snarled, but it was weak and set my head blazing once again. He let me go, and through my weighted lids, I bore my seething gaze into him, wishing he'd catch fire and burn, and crash into dust.

My glare of unadulterated loathing seemed completely lost

on the red man. He merely glanced at my face and let out a bothered exhale. "My queen will be very displeased with me for the ugly albeit necessary marks I left upon your face."

I reached up to inspect the damage radiating around my lip and cheek only to find my hands had been bound, palm upon palm as if in devout prayer. I struggled at the bindings wrapped around my wrists like coiled pythons; the harder I fought against the rope, the tighter it squeezed, cutting off my circulation.

"Need to keep those hands of yours in a safe place now, don't we?" he said, rubbing the phantom lash I whipped upon his stomach. If only it had been more.

My eyes followed the slackened line from my joined hands to the belt around my captor's slender middle.

He had tied me to him! Any movement I made, however subtle, would be felt by this masochistic man. Whoever he was, he had gone to great lengths to ensure I wouldn't be going anywhere. But why, who was I to him?

Despite my curiosities, I knew I needed to focus my slipping mind and put as much distance between me and this man as possible. But, remembering I wore no shoes, it wasn't likely I'd get very far.

The red-haired man grabbed a tin from the satchel at his side and moved closer to me. I tried to squirm away but knew it was futile. My head throbbed to the point of splitting open, I was injured, bound, barefoot, and had absolutely no idea where I was.

"You put up quite a fight last night, so I had to get a little rough with you," he said like he was relaying daily weather patterns, not casually remarking on beating me senseless and kidnapping me. "My queen will not appreciate you in this state. She usually prefers a blank canvas when she orders any punishments upon her enemies." His outward demeanor appeared neutral and aloof as if this was a perfectly normal conversation for a Tuesday, or whatever the hell day it was! But like old achy bones before a storm, I knew something much worse lay just beyond my horizon.

Matching his tone, plain and diplomatic, as if it *were* any old weekday, I asked, "Enemies? I have no qualms with her. How can I when I don't even know her."

"You may not know her, but believe me, Queen Aliphoura most assuredly knows of you. She has eyes and ears everywhere. Nothing slides past her gaze unnoticed."

"What need does she have with me?"

The red man grabbed hold of my shoulders and twisted me to face him. "It appears you have something she wants," he said as the jarring motion sent a shockwave of pain from my head to my tailbone.

So Aliphoura wanted the abilities of the Alcreon Light? Well, she could get in line. They barely even appeared for me. "Tell her I said good luck," I jeered, taking in his freckled face. The light spots dabbled across his narrow nose would be charming on anyone else, but not on this face, this face with its permanent scowl and soulless gaze. His dark, hooded eyes held a powerful fury just waiting to explode—a short fuse on a stick of dynamite.

"If anyone from the village is hurt, I swear to God I'll kill you," I said, sealing every word with a licking flame of promise.

He seemed unbothered as he scooped a gelatinous glob from the tin and brought his hand to my face. I jerked my chin away, repulsed.

"Don't fight me. I'll clean you up one way or the other," he said, sinking his fingers deep into my jaw and aggressively wrenching me to face him. I stilled in his tight grip and winced as his other hand worked the substance into the cut on my cheek.

Red's blunt fingertips moved to my torn mouth, slowly

rubbing and tugging at my trembling lower lip. I wanted to bite and snap at his fingers, but I couldn't deny the balm's soothing effect on my split skin. I almost leaned into his touch, begging for more, hoping whatever medicinal substance he used would seep in and clear my pounding headache.

Squatting in front of me on his heels, he dropped his hands and stared at me expectantly, breathing tightly through thin nostrils.

I shifted under his stare and realized the cool, hard crystal of my blade still rested against my thigh. Its reassuring weight was a blessing in more ways than one. He hadn't searched me, hadn't trailed his hands along the skin of my unconscious body. I almost let out a sigh of relief, but Red eyed me warily.

"If you're waiting for a thank you, you won't be getting one anytime soon," I said, trying to account for any minute changes he may have noted in my expression.

I needed to get the drop on him somehow to help my escape.

Feeling my full bladder, an idea struck me. "Untie me. And... and I'll need some privacy." Despite my ragged, vulnerable, and abused state, I spoke with all the dignity I could muster. I was covered in mud and grass strains from being violently dragged across the ground, the sleeve of my top had been torn off my shoulder, my head chain had been ripped from my head, along with several chunks of hair, and my skirt was torn all the way to my hip, revealing the lily-white flesh of my entire leg.

Thankfully not the leg that concealed my hidden blade, but still, my bareness had me nervous. And while I knew he would like to deliver me mostly untarnished, he could inflict injuries that were harder to see.

"Anything you need to do, you will do in front of me," he said, dashing my hopes. I shuddered in disgust thinking of him watching me, even though he spoke in the most disinterested tone. He hadn't glanced once at my exposed skin, and it eased me in part, knowing I was safe from him in that aspect at least. It created more room in my mind for clarity and careful planning.

"That will be a no then," I said through gritted teeth.

He nodded with indifference, then returned the tin to his satchel and stood, the entire length of his body towering over me. Even though he wasn't as wide as Rowen, he was taller, maybe by half a head, and his muscled reach was long, would be even longer if the ruby sword strapped across his back was in his hand.

Escaping him would be a challenge. He had managed to destroy a village, fight, kidnap, and subdue me, all without drawing his weapon. I would hate to see what he could accomplish with the sharp steel in his hand.

He gathered his satchel and straightened his red tunic with military precision. Everything about his strict appearance indicated that of a well-trained soldier, even down to his tightly cropped ginger hair and mission-driven focus. "This is as far as my abilities were able to take us. We walk the rest of the way."

"I'm not walking anywhere with you," I hissed.

He waited a moment, but when I refused to stand, he curled his long, slender fingers under the knot at my wrists and yanked me to my feet. The message was clear enough; he fully intended for me to walk with nothing to protect my feet, and who knew for how long.

I jerked against the rope, refusing to comply. "I'm barefoot."

He released the sword between his shoulder blades and pulled me closer, ensuring I understood every meaning behind his lowered voice and pointed weapon. "I just cleaned up your pretty little face. I'd hate to have to mar it again before we make our destination. I would suggest making this as easy on yourself as possible, so keep your mouth shut and do as I say when I say it. My queen expects us by nightfall, and any delays from you will not go unpunished."

His words sent warning flares all along my skin to fight, beat, and curse him. But my main goal at present was to keep him calm, ease him into a false sense of comfort. Now was not the time to fight.

So I'd be obedient.

For now.

The vengeful feline in me would bide her time, crouching low in the brush, hiding, studying, waiting for the right moment to strike.

Without another word, he turned from me and began deliberately walking towards the sunrise. I knew if I didn't comply, he would likely drag me the rest of the way by my wrists.

So with panic welling in my gut and hope resting on my thigh, I took my first bound step.

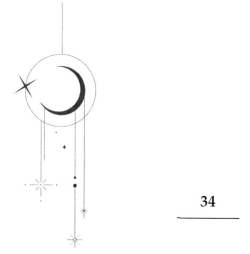

34

The red man kept my leash taut as I walked behind him, preventing me from reaching for my knife, so I did what I could —I divided my mind in half.

I became a river of two flowing channels, one half preoccupied with keeping him talking, while the other formulated a plan of escape. He said his strange power was depleted, so I was at least safe from his dark traveling tunnels. Yet no matter how many times I played out the scenario in my head, succeeding always came down to one single variable—that I was faster than him.

"You would do your queen's bidding," I asked, trying my luck at distracting him, "even if it means burning an innocent village to the ground and harming those who live there?" I waited with my heart in my throat, unsure if he would answer with his words or with his violence.

The moment hung in the air, heavy and suspended on an invisible hook, the mere weight of a feather enough to tip the scale.

Red didn't even turn around or slow his relentless steps as he answered, "I would do whatever it is that my queen asks of me, even if she asked me to fall on my own blade. I would do it. I would do it for her."

Great. A fanatic willing to sacrifice himself for someone else's gain. His blind loyalty absolute.

"You would take your own life for her?" I further prodded, needing to keep him talking. I still had no idea what Aliphoura intended to do with me or how she would take what she wanted. Maybe I could glean more about this mystery queen from the person closest to her.

"I would take much more than that," he said, barely twisting his face to look back at me over a well-muscled shoulder. "My queen found me and brought me up from nothing. She saw the depths of my fealty and promoted me up the ranks until I was right by her side. There is no detail she would spare me. I'm her most trusted and valued soldier, her favored." His head cocked at an odd angle, and his chin raised with an air of pride. "She entrusted me with delivering you to her. I thought it would be more difficult from what I've heard, but it only took burning one village to the ground to find you."

Beyond the horror of what he was telling me, I realized he was a sycophant in love. Obsessed even. Indoctrinated and brainwashed.

I had to get away, and soon.

I meant to make my move when we stopped for water, but he was ruthless, mushing me along mercilessly without even the briefest reprieve. We had been walking for hours now, but he showed no signs of stopping anytime soon.

No matter the terrain, he made me walk it, over dirt, sharp rocks, sticks, and burs, even across hot stones from the afternoon sun. Each and every step was a painful wince, but the fear of stopping outweighed the pain of trudging on, and I cursed myself for removing my shoes on the beach.

We climbed over boulders and fallen trees, scratching up my body and feet more and more.

One of my most valuable weapons was being destroyed with every step, and there wasn't a thing I could do about it. So I kept going, trying to pretend like I didn't have feet at all.

Being a runner, I had a slightly higher endurance than most, but my shredded soles could only take so much.

My bound hands weren't helping the situation either. Without my arms to help for balance, I'd fallen several times, scrambling back up as quickly as possible. When I didn't walk fast enough to his liking, he would violently tug at the rope, yanking me to quicken my pace.

Walking the outer rim of a geologic uplift, I noted how the expansive scenery succumbed to a stagnant death below. The healthy green woods slowly morphed into a sickly grey land-scape before entirely succumbing to the sleek black silence of a frozen forest.

Where the land was eerily calm in its petrified shock, the vast lakes and rivers raged savagely, veining off into webs of tired waterways and weary streams. Without an adequate host for the Alcreon Light, and with people brutally taking from the land, the balance was tipping, churning all into chaos.

Monolithic grey mountains towered above us like long-forgotten titans, impassively gazing down upon us mere mortals and the destruction we wrought. A flock of purple birds soared through the cold breeze of the valley, their membranous bodies shining iridescently with each labored stroke of their wings.

My heart ached at the sight.

"This place has turned useless," he said after a while, indicating to the lifeless forest. "No longer providing for Aliphoura and her people. She moved us to a place where this death couldn't touch us."

My feet were raw, pulverized messes, and stains of blood

dried around the edges of my feet and toes. I stole a quick look backward, only to see my bloodied steps echoing behind me like footprints in the sand.

It may have been a trick of the light, but I could have sworn each stamped sole shimmered with a pearlescent gleam upon the earth.

Countless times I'd contemplated making my escape as the landscape gradually morphed, but it could be detrimental to rush this. The slightest tug or jerk from the rope would alert him to look back, which he frequently did as it was. I couldn't risk him seeing me grab for my weapon. Plus, his hand never loosened or relaxed from his rather large sword.

I would have to wait until we stopped for a drink, when it would be the easiest to reach for my blade. But escaping the queen's favored was only half the battle; the other half was making it back to the Wyn village in one piece, which was a long shot considering I had no idea where we were or how far we traveled from the sliver of darkness he pulled me through.

Finally, after more than half a day's journey, we stopped by a creek crawling across a drying bed with desperate watery arms. This was the moment I had been waiting for, but now that it was here, my legs almost collapsed from underneath me.

The red man roughly wrapped one hand around the back of my neck and forced me down to my knees in front of the water.

It was now or never.

"Drink," he commanded with annoyed detachment. The very fact that I even needed to stop and take care of my basic needs seemed to agitate him.

I leaned over the stream, making a show of how I was struggling to bend and scoop water into my tightly bound wrists. Despite my trembling nerves, my hands had a steady calm about them, ready and accepting of what they were about to do.

While I was down, I took in several replenishing gulps of

water and slowly brought one leg out from under me. The movement wasn't lost on Red, I just hoped he took it as me adjusting to better hold myself up while I drank.

Thanks to the ripped slit in my dress, I could spread my knees farther apart, granting me access to the weapon strapped at my thigh.

I crouched further over myself, concealing my middle as if to reach for more water. I'd only have one chance at this and one chance only. It would have to be as I'd seen Rowen and Dyani do it—in one swift motion.

With my bound hands, I reached through the slit of my dress. All ten fingers wrapped around the smooth crystal hilt, zinging at the contact.

Wielding all the force I could muster, I swung the blade out from under me, unfolding the torque of my body as I hurled to my feet. My knife whistled as it arced up in a semi-elliptical fashion, flashing with an almost imperceptible trail of light.

I easily severed the rope binding me to my red-headed captor, but I knew that wouldn't be enough. Following through, my stroke tore through the air like a violent strip of lightning, and I slashed the red man diagonally across the face from chin to temple.

Howling in agony, he dropped his weapon and clutched his torn face.

I didn't stick around to find out what he did next. I was already gone, flowing skirts in hand. I heard his fury chasing after me, screaming and cursing my very existence through the destroyed forest.

This was it, the moment of truth. Could I outrun him?

Despite Aliphoura's wishes to keep me unharmed, he'd most likely kill me if he got his hands on me again. He was practically screeching all the ways he would torture me—his threats whipping at my back like snapping icicles.

I pushed harder, ignoring my pounding feet as they further ripped, tore, and bled. The drag from my dress and my bound wrists slowed me down considerably. And the headache that never left reverberated through my skull with each stride.

I had a lot working against me, but my few advantages gave me hope. So I ran, and ran, and never looked back. I didn't even slow down as his enraged bellowing grew fainter and fainter behind me until eventually dying out altogether.

My legs burned with lactic acid, begging me to stop, but I kept running.

It wasn't until I buckled from complete and utter exhaustion that I let my body lay still and unmoving on the black forest floor.

I knew I couldn't continue to lie out in the open, sprawled in the mud and panting with the taste of blood in my lungs. I lifted my chin, noticing a dense tangle of roots, large enough that I might be able to fit inside.

Inching myself forward by my elbows, I squirmed under the thick brush until I was completely covered within the den of twisted mangroves. The space was much larger than I anticipated, and from the inside, it encased me in a woven cage of branches.

I rolled up into a seated position and examined the bindings at my wrists. The redhead knew what he was doing, this was a very skilled knot, tight and unforgiving.

With my dagger still tightly clasped within my white-knuckled grasp, I carefully flipped the blade over until the tip pointed directly at me. Using only my fingertips, I slowly began to saw away at the thick rope that bit into my skin. Severing thread after painstaking thread was slow work, but with the snapping and falling of each small strand, I celebrated a silent victory.

Finally free of the bonds, I tossed them aside and rubbed my tender and swollen wrists. I listened intently for any indication that the red man was near, but all I heard was the chirping and clicking of the unknown creatures around me, either settling in for the day or awakening with the night, but no sign of my hunter in tow.

The stale, heavy air was worse here than any of the other stunted forests, and it sent a terrified shiver through my being. I could only imagine what dark shadows these woods concealed. There could be more tracker demons or summonings out there looking for me, even encountering a run-of-the-mill starved beast was a likely scenario.

I tried again to still my mind to take me home, to take me anywhere but here, but reaching up and feeling the huge knot at the base of my skull, I knew with a sickening dread that I was well and truly stuck.

My next realization hit me with an even sharper stone-cold clarity—I wouldn't survive out here long. I considered whether it would be best to hunker down, wait for Sabra to hopefully find my scent and track me down, or keep moving.

I heard Rowen's voice in my ear as though he were sitting right beside me, *to move is to survive.*

It was decided. I'd give my feet and head the night to rest, then at first light, I would try to find my way back. I knew as much to follow the sunset, but that was about it.

Surviving this would be a miracle, but I knew in my bones Rowen was searching for me. Especially after his confession at Celenova.

My heart twisted painfully at the memory.

He would come. I just needed to hold out until then.

· (C · ● · ⊃ ·) ·

After finding an area to finally relieve myself, I sat with my back against the tangle of branches, the sounds of the forest closing in around me. Curious animals and insects crept closer to inspect me as if they were inherently drawn to me like flowers towards the sun.

My body may as well be a flashing neon sign attracting anything within a hundred feet.

I quaked uncontrollably with my knees drawn to my chest. I desperately clutched my blade in front of me with a bone-white grip when a twig snapped to my right.

Jumping, I clasped one hand over my mouth, masking my frightened breathing. If it was the red man, I had the chance of him passing me by unnoticed. If it was a beast, it already knew I was here.

Another branch snapped from a different direction, and I startled again. Then another snap. And another until I was completely surrounded. My hope that the creatures were merely curious, and not hungry, was thrown right out the window when deep carnal growls and yips filled the night around me. It sounded like an entire pack celebrating an easy catch, because whatever they were, I had absolutely no chance of fending them all off.

My only chance would be to kill them one by one as they tried to enter through the small opening of my hideout, but how long could I keep that up before I was overrun?

Operating on nothing but sheer terror and adrenaline, I raised my weapon and braced myself. An eruption of broken twigs crashed behind me and a slicing pain lanced across my bare shoulder. To keep from screaming and attracting any more attention, I bit down on my lower lip so hard that blood welled on my tongue.

More and more scratching talons broke their way inside, pawing and swiping at me through my wooden enclosure.

Snarling lupine snouts bit their way through from above, snapping and gnashing their fanged teeth.

My breath battered against my ribs as I drove my blade into the chaos of attacking creatures. A piercing whine echoed through the night as a wounded beast backed away, but as soon as one retreated, another filled its place.

One had already found the opening of my hideout.

A giant bundle of dark fur made its way into my sanctuary, trapping me in a shrinking cage of wood, claws, and fangs.

There was no clever way to escape. Not this time. I was going to be eaten alive. A rogue claw from above swiped and grazed my newly healed cheek.

The black beast who had found the opening was already halfway through, and I reared my blade, ready to drive it down upon its jugular when something stayed my hand.

I couldn't do it.

Why couldn't I do it?

The massive beast was completely in my shelter now, rising to its full height as my sanctuary tore down around me, and I had to tilt my chin back to take in its whole form.

I would at least have her look me in the eyes before I was killed by her.

Her? How did I know it was a her?

She was the most magnificent creature I'd ever seen, and I dropped the knife to the ground.

She was a great fox-like creature covered in luxurious midnight fur. A small mane streamed down her regal head and surrounded her neck. She had narrow legs, pointed ears, and purple eyes with a delicate heart-shaped nose.

What really had me in awe was her long fluffy tail, flowing and hovering around her like fanning peacock feathers. Her proud chest and the tufts of fur at her feet were wispy white, a stark contrast against the rest of her ebony body. The very tip of her tail was tinted a pale purple as though dipped in ink by an artist's hand. Her keen slender face regarded me with regal impassivity, and her slanted fox-like eyes spoke with an ancient understanding known only to her and the land itself.

Transfixed, I realized the animals were no longer mauling their way inside. The being's powerful presence ordered every other creature to remain at bay, and now all was utter stillness.

Slowly and tentatively, I extended my hand to her beautiful face. She closed the distance between us, bringing her narrow snout to the palm of my hand, and her warm breath puffed at my skin. I gave her satiny fur a few stokes before she lay down at my feet.

Fully relaxed, she gave me several knowing blinks, then rested her head on her forepaws and closed her eyes. For whatever reason, she had chosen to protect and guard me throughout the night. Without her, I doubt I would have lived to see the dawn.

I shivered. Not just from the knowledge of my narrow survival but from the biting cold of the night. I could only feel it now that my fight-or-flight adrenaline had cooled.

My breath clouded in the air in front of me, and my fingers were losing feeling, but there was no way I could start a fire. It would be a shining beacon leading the red man right to me.

Seeming to have read my thoughts, my savior raised her velvety tail and gently swatted my back, urging me closer to her.

I lay down beside her, bringing my body close to the warmth of her belly.

The steady rhythm of her breathing was deep and wild, like the very thrum of the beginning of time. Her canny tail swept around and encased me in her deep fur like a downy blanket.

I rested my head against her. "Thank you," I said, knowing she was saving my life. Her eyes remained closed; only the slightest twitch of her ear indicated she'd heard me all.

Nepta mentioned the spirits still roamed the land as animals, trees, or other various forms of life.

I closed my eyes, somehow knowing the truth—this magnificent creature was brought to me from the land itself, knowing full well who and what I was, but more importantly, why I was.

And just like that, I slept safe and curled in the presence of an Elder Spirit.

———— ·(·(·●·)·)· ————

The next morning my giant fox-like guardian had vanished. Having fulfilled her purpose in keeping me alive throughout the night, she wisped away like the morning mist of a pond.

My feet and shoulder throbbed. The chill of the night had numbed my injuries, but now in the thawing morning, they were stiff and tender. I would have to find a creek to clean my wounds in and fashion some sort of shoes from the fabric of my dress.

Luckily the beasts who sliced me open didn't appear to be poisonous or diseased. If they were, it might still be a few hours before symptoms showed, but I couldn't stay here forever. I needed to keep going, keep making my way back to Rowen.

To move is to survive.

Before I left my safe haven, I grabbed my knife and listened to the sounds of the forest. Dead silence, not even the scuffle of a leaf stirring. The spirit had done a thorough job in clearing the area.

Slowly, I began crawling my way out on all fours when an intense and brutal force knocked me in the face.

My whole body went limp from the blow, and I fell to my stomach with a thud. A strong hand grabbed me by the hair and lifted me until I was face to face with the enraged eyes of the red man. I held his wrists, trying to stop the pulling at my scalp, but my world was spinning, and I could barely see straight.

The caked blood that dripped down his face like a ghastly sash was my only reality. He hadn't cleaned it or applied any of the salve he'd used on me. He must have been searching for me all night.

"You're a dead bitch." He continued to hold me up by my hair. My scalp screamed as he pressed his nose into the side of my face, and I could feel his lips across my skin. "I can't wait to slowly carve out every last inch of you before you die. In the end, my queen will demand that of me, and I will take great pleasure in doing so, carrying it on for days as I repay you for the lovely token you left upon me. And it will be this face that gladly watches as you take your final begging breath."

I got one last look at his enraged and maimed face before he slammed me back against a tree, and hitting my head in the same spot as the knot, I saw no more.

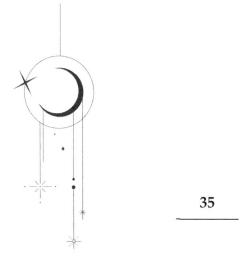

35

The alarm on my phone began rousing me from the darkest sleep I'd ever known.

It was so quiet I barely noticed it at first, but the grating noise persisted, growing louder by the second.

Wait. If I had my phone, that meant...

It had been a dream—all of it.

How many times had this very sound pulled me from Luneth, a world that could never have possibly been real.

The glaring truth was too much. I wasn't ready to face it, wasn't ready to open my eyes. I couldn't accept the last few weeks had been nothing but a dream spanning the length of a single night. A lie.

I blindly reached for my alarm to silence the chime pounding in my skull. I begged and pleaded for the dark silence to return, if only for a little while longer. I didn't want to wake to a world without Rowen, without Luneth. Not yet.

I had convinced myself so thoroughly that it was real. That every moment, conversation, and touch was the most alive I'd ever felt. I'd brought myself up too high, and now the fall back down would surely break me.

I would go to my parents and tell them everything. It was time. I couldn't live like this any longer, with absolutely no control over my mind or thoughts. Any drug they wanted to give me, I would gladly take, any treatment they wanted me to try, I would willingly participate in.

My alarm was blaring now, and I kept searching for my phone, desperate to shut off the horrid sound, but I couldn't feel it anywhere. The vibration of my phone was so strong it was shaking my entire bed, filling my head to the point of bursting.

Fed up, I finally opened my eyes, but not to the four walls of my room.

It wasn't the sound of my alarm I'd been hearing but a cavern filled with hundreds of people surrounding me, jeering and shouting at me to wake.

Panicking, I took quick assessment of my body and noticed I still wore my ripped Celanova dress.

I had never left!

But where was I?

I could tell I was underground by the weight pressing all around me. Surprisingly, the air wasn't stale but cool and fresh, most likely circulated from the surface.

I scanned the subterranean amphitheater. Masses of unknown faces muddled together as they watched me like I was some odd rarity on display for their viewing pleasure.

It seemed the raucous crowd hadn't done anything but jibe and gawk at me. But where was the red man? With the unbound fury I saw in his gaze before he knocked me out, I was surprised I even woke at all.

"Ah, there is our sweet little star coming to," said a melodic female voice that immediately silenced the crowd. The sound was beautiful yet unforgiving and reminded me of a black widow, mesmerizing as she spun her thread into beguiling designs, only to realize too late it was you she wound in her fatal web.

Searching for the source of the hauntingly lovely sound, I managed to push and steady myself up on my arms. My vision and head spun, and if I'd had anything in my stomach, it would be well on its way to covering the cold, hard ground.

Lifting my eyes, my gaze followed the stark-white trees growing throughout the massive underground chamber like branches of spilled milk. Their trunks reached and extended up in membranous wooden columns. Lining the walls and ceiling of the black basalt cave were twinkling crystals that mimicked the starry night.

It was enchanting and dazzling. And it was a prison.

"Welcome to my Crystal Crypts," came the lustrous voice once again.

I followed the sound of that lilting alto until my eyes landed upon the most breathtaking woman I'd ever seen. Raised on a dais, she sat upon a seat of thinly twisted trees, woven and manipulated into an intimidating chair that reached to the cavern's ceiling.

Realization came slowly that I was in the throne room of a queen.

"I was wondering when you would wake. It would be a shame for you to miss your own welcoming party," said the woman who could be none other than Aliphoura. She was devastating to look at, the pure embodiment of elegance, composure, and beauty. Silky raven hair framed her heart-shaped face and fell to her waist in thick, luscious waves, a stark contrast against her pale white complexion. A crown of what looked like carved bone and smoked diamonds sat atop her burnished mane. The bodice of her tight emerald dress clung to her body like a shimmering glove; the corset followed the hourglass shape of her torso before falling around the base of her throne in regal swells of billowing silk.

Standing next to her up on the dais was the red man.

The hideous wound I gave him bisected and marred his grimacing face. He seethed and twitched with the pent-up aggression of a trained beast waiting for its command to taste blood. My blood.

He would be wanting to exact his revenge, cash in on his deadly promise to me, and I knew it was only a matter of time before Aliphoura released him from his leash.

"An invitation would have sufficed," I ground out, still folded on the floor in front of her, and a wave of murmured shock flared behind my back. I'd almost forgotten the audience of loyal subjects here to witness whatever horrors she had planned for me.

Despite my impending predicament and the dozen or so soldiers lining the crowds with staffed rapiers, Aliphoura's subjects did appear to be in the middle of a party. They were all clad in thin drapes of fabric that swooped and gathered around their pale sun-deprived bodies. Many of them were lounging across each other, feeding one another from the large banquet tables piled high with delicacies, or drinking the light pink liquid that dripped from crystal fountains.

Her lovely red lips smiled, reminding me of one of Mother Nature's crueler jokes—the more beautiful something was, the deadlier it could be. "I couldn't run the risk of you declining. And it was so very sweet of Caeryn to come and fetch you for me." Her elbow was propped on a branched armrest, her chin resting delicately over elongated fingertips. "You've been laying at my feet for a day now, sweetling. You did keep us waiting." She pouted her lips, and following her cue, the crowd responded with booing as if suddenly remembering to agree.

Abhorred, I pulled myself up to my shredded feet. I had lain here for hours while a party commenced around my unconscious body. My eyes darted to Caeryn; he must have carried my limp body the rest of the way here and dumped me right at his queen's feet.

Aliphoura saw where my gaze pinpointed its hatred, "Ah yes, it sounds like you two had quite the adventure together. The mark on his face will forever provide a distinct reminder never to disappoint the one who saved him. Saved us all. Isn't that right, dear?"

Not even the slightest tick surfaced across his face. "Yes, my queen." He had learned to submit and soldier through her treatment. The others in the room were no better, looking nervous at best, only a few looked downright terrified.

"Stop this madness," a voice rang through the cavern. "You are no real savior."

Aliphoura's eyes snapped furiously to the crowd. "Who said that?" she demanded, but when no one confessed, she merely shrugged her shoulders. "It appears the offering hour is upon us then." She reached out a slender arm, pointing to someone in the crowd.

The multitude of voices gasped in horror as a young woman draped in silk clutched at her neck, scrambling to breathe. She collapsed to the floor in a flourish of cloth and golden hair, and as her twitching slowed to the stillness of death, Aliphoura's veins darkened across her alabaster skin like injected ink before dissipating into her flesh. "Do I not provide for you all? A sacrifice made by one of you each day is what gives me the power to keep us thriving, keep us living. You would do well to remember that."

Horrified and revolted, I realized the people of the crypts were surviving off the life force of the sacrificed.

"You've lied to these people, led them here under false pretenses," I snarled with all the resentment I could throw at her through a fogged mind. "You will never truly have their loyalty."

Her eyes, like wells of melted gold, turned to me. "I don't ask for their loyalty. I demand it."

"Then you have their fear."

"I have their obedience," Aliphoura said, ever the portrait of poise, and my jaw hitched. Looking at their frozen faces, I knew she was right. "You pity them. But I wouldn't if I were you, because in the end, I'll have what I want from you as well."

"Are you going to tell me what that is, or are you going to keep me guessing all night?"

Her eyes momentarily slipped away as she stroked the green silk of her dress. She quickly waved it away. "I may eventually have use for you, but in the meantime, we might as well entertain ourselves, shall we?" Turning to Caeryn, she said, "You mentioned something about a spark earlier. I have never heard of such a thing, and I must admit it intrigues me. This weakling claims she is the Synodic Prophecy. I think I should like for her to prove it." She addressed her audience. "Wouldn't we all like to see it?"

The crowd roared in agreement, apparently too terrified to do anything else.

She was toying with me, a cat playing with her catch, and I knew no matter what I said, her game would only end when she wanted it to.

"You can do what you like with me. Just let these people go."

Brushing my comment aside, she leaned forward in her chair. "The spark, Caeryn, tell me. How did you make it happen again?" Her eyes gleamed with excitement.

"I hit her, my queen," he said, not even batting an eyelash. "She struggled and tried to fight back, that's when a silver beam shot from her hand, and the skin upon her flesh glowed like the stars."

"It sounds absolutely fascinating. Show me," she said with a flick of her slender wrist.

And there it was, the releasing command of her hound.

Caeryn's vindicated smile and charging gait had my legs begging to run, but I was completely surrounded, not only by Aliphoura's play crowd too terrorized to act out, but by her armed sentinels as well. I'd be lucky to make it more than a few steps.

If I could just give her a taste of what she wanted, maybe that would appease her enough for the night, and I could spend whatever time I'd earned figuring a way out of here.

I wanted to be afraid, but something much greater consumed me. There was no room for fear, only survival.

I extended out my hand and implored for my power to come. I needed to light a spark before Caeryn got to me, the smallest bit of glowing silver could grant me precious hours. But not even an ember sparked from my fingertips, my head still swimming from the trauma of last night.

Caeryn lunged, and though his fist came flying at me, I didn't cower. I was too preoccupied fighting for the glow that would emanate at any moment. I didn't even try to dodge him, believing up until the last second that I could save myself. Which made the swift punch to the stomach that much worse. I doubled over in pain, clutching my middle, wheezing.

Please come, please light.

I kept trying but my body remained as it was, pale and unglowing. Aside from Caeryn's little blast, I'd only really seen it in the crevice with Maddock, pushing him out of me like a cosmic blast through the night.

I knew the power I could wield, as trapped as it was behind my concussion.

Another of Caeryn's fists came at me, this one landing on my cheek. It was too much, and I fell to the ground, my lip split open again. I was vaguely aware of the crowd cheering and hollering as though we were battling in a colosseum.

Caeryn hovered over me, and just like I knew he would, he kicked me while I was down. The point of his boot connected with my ribs, and I felt something inside me crack as I screamed out in imploding pain.

He walked over my crumpled body. I was too tired, starved, and broken to fight back in any meaningful way, but still, I tried. I kept imploring my gift to make itself known, but it was as dormant as a dead star.

Rowen. I had never told him I loved him. I let his face fill my mind as Caeryn grabbed my hair in his hands. I wouldn't survive another blow.

"Enough!" Aliphoura yelled through the clamoring crowd and noise. "It seems our little star has forgotten how to shine. Let's give her the night to remember, shall we?"

Much to Caeryn's disappointment, he shoved me to the ground.

"We will simply have to try again tomorrow. And the next day, and the next, until our sweet little bird remembers how to fly."

Caeryn vowed he would torture me for days, and here it was, the start of his fulfilling promise.

Aliphoura gracefully rose from her throne and sauntered towards my suffering body. I could only raise my head to her, my teeth bared and breathing heavy.

She bent down in front of me and ran a soft hand across my cheek, gentle and lovingly. "I ended up being led to quite a pathetic creature. Although I can't say I'm entirely shocked, I'm not an easy act to follow."

I spit a wad of blood on her exquisite dress as a royal fuck you.

Her chest heaved a disappointed sigh before she snapped to no one specifically, "Take her to the crypts."

—— ·⟨ ⟨ ● ⟩ ⟩· ——

Somehow I was still fighting and squirming as arms lifted me from the ground and carried me through narrow tunnel after narrow tunnel. It darkened considerably outside the throne room, but a twinkling of mica minerals always remained, lighting the way.

It wasn't long before skulls began lining the tunneled earth, and I saw firsthand how the Crystal Crypts earned their name. This place was built on the bones of the dead.

Dread muddied my senses, and it felt like I was perceiving my life through a foggy television screen. The nondescript characters in this particular horror dumped me in a small damp chamber, leaving me alone and injured with nothing but an empty bucket.

Crouched over in pain, I explored every inch of my cell, studying it, looking for weak points or possible exits, but the only way in or out was through the heavy metal door slotted perfectly within the stone. I was trapped deep in the belly of the earth, imprisoned by the same hard glistening rock of the throne room.

Shivering from the cold condensation leaking through the walls, I found the driest bit of ground I could and rested, with thoughts of clawing my way to the sun.

After who knew how long, my cell door began to creep open.

The guards would never open the door so gently.

Had someone from the Wyn found me? Was it Rowen? But how? If Sabra caught a trail of my scent, it likely vanished the moment I was brought below ground and buried alive.

I had lost hope of ever being discovered down here, but I still found myself holding my breath. I yearned to see the face that once haunted my dreams but now ignited them to a point where I couldn't picture my life without him—and I didn't want to.

As they quietly entered my room, the figure turning to face me wasn't Rowen at all but a woman with warm brown skin and braided jet-black hair. Her kind citrine eyes were a beacon of sunlight and lost humanity in this empty darkness. Gold freckles swept across the bridge of her nose and planes of her cheeks, and a single strip of golden specks fell from her bottom lip to the tip of her chin.

"My name is Rayal," she said with a smooth voice of sun-soaked sand. "Her Highness has asked me to bring you food. The guards outside let me enter."

She knelt down and lowered a gleaming silver tray of fresh fruit, creamy dips, and puffed pastries right before me.

The spread was lavish and ostentatious and looked like it had been snagged right off one of the throne room tables. I didn't think Aliphoura was in the business of treating her prisoners to the same delicacies as her court. Whoever this woman was, she had snuck in under false pretenses.

"Thank you," I said, trying my best to chew an airy tart through my aching jaw. "I'm sure it's at a great risk that you're here."

"And you, who are you to find yourself in the false queen's wrath, more so than the rest of us?" Rayal asked, dropping the act she'd been sent here by an altruistic monarch.

Not sure how much to reveal to this mysterious yet welcoming stranger, I said cautiously, "Someone with something she wants."

"If you are who I think, and I believe you are, what you have can never be taken. Changed and altered, yes, but never taken."

"How do you know who I am?" I asked, afraid and comforted all at once.

Her lids closed intently as if listening to a far-off symphony, hearing only beauty in such a hopeless place. "I can hear your blood. It is singing," she said, her eyes opening gently to meet mine. "The power that runs through your veins is in your blood. It's been passed to you, making you who you are, and that can never be ripped from you." Her fingers absentmindedly stroked the gold choker around her throat.

"What do you know of my blood?"

"That it's very old and hums of stardust, yet it's young and budding, like ancient imprints flowing within a newly sprouted blossom. The moment you entered the throne room, I could feel it."

"How did you come to be here?" I asked through the searing pain in my side.

"Many people from my village fled here, believing Queen Aliphoura would save us from our dying lands. But she possesses no power of life, only death, and we are as trapped here as the stones. Her dark power is said to come from Erovos himself.

"We are nothing but tributes living in comfort until we are sacrificed for the lavish survival of others, often beaten if we step out of line. We may have all we could want, but it is at a great and unnatural price. One of us is sacrificed each day, and once inside there is no escape."

"How does she do it? Can she be stopped?"

"Energy can be redistributed but never plucked from thin air. Everything has a cost, and unless given freely, the energy must be stolen, sucked from an alternate life source and fed elsewhere. Aliphoura siphoned her land dry to maintain power and control, and now that the earth is used beyond repair, she must resort to her people.

"By the day her masses grow as more are tricked into following her, providing her the numbers she needs to sustain her daily offering hour. But to do such a thing is greatly taxing; she is only able to do it once a sun."

As I listened in horror, three aggressive knocks pounded on the prison door, jarring us both to the reality that we were not alone and far from safe. "Hurry up in there," one of the guards shouted.

Rayal's hand flew to her necklace in startled panic, and this time I noticed the choker she stroked with such reverence was engraved with a line sweeping over and under two circles. While she wore the billowing fabrics of the Crystal Crypts, she held this unique piece of herself close and protectively. It must be a totem of her life from before.

Her voice lowered in a hushed whisper, and she took my hand, laying her palm flat on mine, "I wish there were more I could do to help, but like you, I am a prisoner here. If you should survive and ever find yourself where sun casts upon sun and your shadow greets mine, know that you are amongst friends."

She stood and released me with a pained regret that swallowed her lovely features. And without another word or glance, she slipped back through the prison door, leaving more questions upon my yearning tongue.

‹ ⟨ ⟨ · ● · ⟩ ⟩ ›

I wasn't sure if it was my third, fourth, or hundredth time being dumped back in the glittering black prison. Deceived by the fact that, through my continued abuse, I oftentimes lost sense of whether I floated in the vastness of space or was trapped in a small, stifling cage.

Either way, it was cold, wet, and endless.

I made a point never to take in the faces that transported me between the cell and Aliphoura's throne room. It seemed every few hours I was brought back to her feet, each interaction unfolding as the one before.

Aliphoura demanded her pretty bird spark, and when I couldn't comply, Caeryn's fury was unleashed upon me. Whenever he laid his hands on me, he gladly bruised, cracked, and broke my bones until he was commanded to stop.

Despite the pain and fog, I fought to clear my mind. I hoped Caeryn would stay away from my head long enough for it to heal, so I at least had a chance of escaping. I tried telling them through labored speech that blows to the head were counterintuitive, and if they kept at this rate, the only thing they would eventually see from me would be a corpse, but they never listened.

I eventually became grateful for my muddied mind, which progressively worsened. I'd come to know it helped the next round of torture not hurt so badly.

I tried screaming at her crowd, begging them to see reason, but they were all too frightened of the repercussions. Aliphoura kept a tyrannical rule over her subjects—even the ones who wanted to leave couldn't.

It was for more than sport that Aliphoura was keeping me alive. She said I would eventually become of use to her, but after multiple beatings, I was still no closer to figuring out why.

"I am beginning to question if what I heard about you is true," she said after a particularly nasty beating where my eye was already swelling shut. "And I have to confess, I don't know whether to be relieved or disappointed."

I learned to no longer rise to the bait of her questions. Her answers were always more cryptic than informative, and who knew if anything she said rang with a lick of truth.

I did know, in no uncertain terms, that once she got the reaction she wanted out of me, she would discard me with a simple command.

Knowing I needed to stay sharp, I attempted counting the number of days since the fire. There was no sun, moon, or even regularly scheduled meals to help convey any real sense of time. Only the screaming from the daily offering hour let me know I'd been here four days.

All the food upon the silver platter had long gone, and I'd been drinking the dripping cave water to sustain me. Rayal hadn't returned either. It was most likely too risky, or she'd been caught and punished for helping me. But talking with her solidified my need for escape. I'd take her and anyone else with me who wanted to leave.

Several times I thought I saw Rowen entering my cell, but it was always just my broken imaginings and splintered dreams. There was no way he would find me here. He'd tried and failed several times to find these crypts as it was.

I attempted to sleep, rest, heal, and plot my escape, but every action was listless and fitful, and I could do nothing but exist in perpetual torment. When I managed sleep, all I could see was Caeryn's menacing brown eyes lashing out at me, my power nowhere in sight.

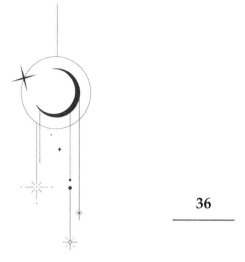

36

I lay in a small broken heap after yet another merciless beating, not even stirring from where the helmeted guards dumped me on the prison floor. I no longer needed to worry about staying warm and dry in my dripping wet cell. That time had long passed.

And much like the dreams I used to have before Rowen appeared, I found myself in yet another waking nightmare.

Dark.

Endless.

And isolating.

Rowen had seen my suffering then, when I had been fighting off the worst of my mother's concocted drug, and he prided me on how I always managed to get back up, to somehow keep rising. I kept replaying his words from the night of Celenova in my mind, *I knew no matter what came at you, you would stand and keep going, keep fighting.*

But I couldn't keep fighting, not anymore. My body had been broken so many times that the only thing left to break was my spirit, and it was fading by the second. The Wyn people and Rowen had no way of finding me down here.

Crumpled on the cold, hard ground, I didn't even shiver. I knew I should be more alarmed by how little I felt. This total detachment couldn't be a good sign. I was pretty sure my leg and arm were broken, along with several ribs and fingers, and who knew what else. My lip felt huge, and one of my eyes wasn't opening properly. Not to mention my head injury that hadn't healed since the day of the fire.

Even if I was found, I was too far gone for Takoda's healing. Aliphoura's sick game of cat and mouse was just prolonging the inevitable—I would die here.

My hope was the Alcreon Light would find a new host. Someone worthy. I'd held out as long as I could. I was on death's doorstep. I could taste it on my tongue like dried petals and dust, it wasn't so bad.

I began to write a farewell letter in my head, one that nobody would ever read or even know existed, but at least somewhere floating between two worlds, my words would exist.

I may die a captive in a cell, but I refused to die a captive of my mind.

I brought my theoretical pen to paper, ready to let go of all the hurt and betrayal in my life, not only from my parents, teachers, friends, and Natalie, but also from myself. I sealed the letter and sent it off deep within the infinity of myself. I closed my eyes for one final dream, when suddenly, my prison door began to creak open.

It was always a guessing game as to who it would be. Was it the guards sent to deliver me for my next beating? Caeryn come to finish the job? Or was it Aliphoura herself, finally deciding to get her hands dirty?

I didn't shift to look. Whoever they were, they were already too late.

Calloused hands touched my shoulder, and I didn't even flinch.

"Keira," an agonized voice whispered through the swallowing dark.

I knew this voice. Through any darkness, through any light, I knew it because I had come to love this voice.

Rowen.

Of course I would conjure him here in my last moments.

"Keira," he repeated with a choked sob, and if I wasn't already broken, the sound would have surely cut me to the ground. His gentle hands roamed and checked my beaten body, but the contact was nothing more than a dull throb. I couldn't really feel anything anymore. "What have they done to you?" he asked, sickened and repulsed.

Rowen slowly rolled me into his arms and carefully lifted my upper body until the side of my head rested against his strong chest. I could hear his heartbeat through his shirt, and despite the sped-up hammering, it was powerful, comforting, and steadying, and I latched onto its thumping.

This was the sound I chose to fade away into.

I must have blacked out for a moment because I was abruptly shaken awake. "Don't you dare close your eyes again, Keira. Look at me!" he demanded.

I opened them wearily, wanting to obey, but my ability to focus had gone. I wished I could see him clearly, but once again, he had been reduced to a foggy image.

His hand looped around to the back of my head, searching through my knotted hair until his fingertips gently examined the painful protrusion at the back of my skull.

I winced.

Why was I imagining Rowen only to have him poke and prod at my every injury? I didn't want to waste what little time I had left focusing on all that hurt.

Needing to feel one last good thing, I tried to reach for him, to caress his face and run my fingers through the dark scruff on his jaw, but my limp arm hung pathetically by my side, refusing to comply.

I whimpered in frustration. You'd think in a hallucination things would go a little more my way.

"Don't try to move," he said, his voice wracked with anguish. "I'm so sorry, this is all my fault."

I struggled to speak, to tell him it was alright, that it wasn't his fault—but my battered body wasn't executing any of my commands.

Out of my fuzzy periphery, I saw he was holding something glowing in his hand, but I couldn't quite make out what it was. My vision was narrowing.

I could sense Rowen fussing over my leg with it, but I felt nothing. "Your noxlily bloomed, Keira. It was Takoda's idea to heal you with your own light. Do you hear me? We are going to walk out of here together."

I wanted to ask him how he knew where to find me, but my eyes felt as heavy as velvet stage curtains. To let the grand drapes shut even for a little while would feel so nice, so welcoming.

"Stay with me," Rowen pleaded with a desperate fury, "stay with me, Keira. If you fall asleep now, you will slip away from me forever, and I'm not going to let that happen. Do you understand me? You aren't leaving me."

I ignored him and closed my eyes soundly, searching for the soothing beat of his heart. It was better than listening to his wracked voice that sounded as if his very soul was being ripped from his body.

"You have accepted this as peace and I cannot allow it," he said, sweeping my matted hair off to the side. "I'm going to heal your head injury next. It will cause the pain in the rest of your body to worsen, and for that I am sorry, but I need you to feel. To fight."

More pain? How was that possible?

I wanted to tell him that I was uninterested in this plan of his, that I'd rather sleep, but my lids and mouth wouldn't open.

"I need you to stay with me. I should have told you from the first moment you came out of the darkness that I love you. I love you, Keira." The voice sounded just like Rowen's, though I knew he wasn't really here saying the words I'd always hoped to hear. But I smiled anyway.

My head lolled to the side and my entire body went limp in Rowen's arms. I had the vague feeling that he was violently shaking me, demanding I open my eyes for him.

I would love nothing more than to make Rowen happy and do as he ordered, but the silence had claimed me now.

Suddenly, with a whip of lightning, two things happened simultaneously. One: my mind rushed to the surface, swimming into clarity as the deathly pall around my consciousness cleared.

And two: pain.

Vicious, blinding pain like an archipelago of volcanoes erupting over my entire body, savagely detonating all at once.

My eyes shot open as my whole body bucked and arched off the filthy ground. I didn't want this white-hot searing pain, not when I had just accepted the black stillness. I was furious at Rowen for making me feel this. It was like receiving every injury all over again.

My head wound had been dulling the pain, nearly all of it, and now I was fully aware of every damaged and broken piece of me.

I went to look down at my body, but Rowen caught hold of my chin and forced my gaze back to his tortured eyes. He seemed to be hurting just as much as I was. "Don't you dare look."

I couldn't nod, only stare on as Rowen plucked a petal from my flower and pressed it to my worthless arm. It absorbed into my skin, and I heard the jagged crunch of my bones snapping back into alignment before I felt it. And when I did, I wailed out in excruciating pain, expecting the walls to tremble with my cries, but Rowen planted his lips over mine and swallowed my scream.

"Shhhh, I must ask you to be brave once more and try not to scream," he whispered, his tone strangled as he rested his forehead against mine.

I now realized what Rowen had intended by making me completely lucid as he healed me. A body that felt kept you fighting.

Drawing himself back over me, he respectfully slipped aside the rags that hung from my body, better exposing my marred skin for healing. He worked the noxlily petals into my middle, and I felt my ribs crack back into place one by one. I tried not to scream, but I couldn't help the sounds that escaped my throat. They were foreign and disturbing, and I knew they would haunt my dreams forever. I'd never been in such pain before, but Rowen plunged down and kissed me again, consuming my earth-shattering agony.

He continued his work, healing one broken piece of me at a time, his lips only leaving mine to find the next bit of abused skin and bone to mend. Each of my screams, moans, and pitiful whimpers fed into his mouth, and he swallowed every one.

He inhaled every destroyed part of me as it left my body, almost as if he was drawing and sucking out the pain one kiss at a time. I knew it was his kind and gentle way of absorbing my cries to keep us from being found out.

Who knew how long he had been muffling my screaming, and despite his best attempts, anyone could have heard us by now. Caeryn was probably already on his way here, most likely with reinforcements. I could endure the pain if I had to, I'd done it once I could do it again, but to think of Caeryn hurting Rowen, that...that would destroy me.

But no one came the entire time Rowen painstakingly healed and kissed the pain away.

Slowly I became whole again as sinews of flesh mended together and bones set back into their rightful place. Rowen settled what was left of my dress back over my body, and searched for me within my eyes.

The last of the pain lingered heavily in my mouth, a reminder of how close I'd come to death. And if it weren't for the dried bloodstains, the tattered clothes, and my filthy body, I would have thought it all a dream.

I still didn't quite believe it wasn't.

I desperately needed to touch Rowen to assure myself that he was real, that it was all real. I lifted my blood- and grime-covered fingertips to his face. "You're really here with me." My voice was weak and hoarse, and I didn't recognize it, but they were the first coherent words I'd spoken since Rowen appeared.

Relief washed over him like a flash flood.

He carefully took my chin in his hand and tilted my face up to his. He bowed his head toward mine and placed a featherlight kiss upon my lips. I didn't blink, my eyes wide open and staring as he took my mouth. I couldn't look away as I drank in his beautiful face kissing mine. It was tender, soft, and light, yet it contained every kiss, glance, and touch we'd missed since that first day in the forest.

He may have healed my body from the brink of death, but it was this kiss that truly healed my soul.

Still holding me, he pulled away from my lips and met my gaze. "Where else would I be?"

———— ·(·❪·●·❫·)· ————

The pain was gone. All of it.

I moved my arm and leg, rolled my shoulder, and took in a

deep breath, bracing myself to hurt. It was all I'd known for the past few days, but there wasn't a single trace of lingering pain. It was as if my many tortures had never really happened.

A flash of cinder and crashing beams flashed through my memory. "The village? There was a little girl, I tried—"

"Everyone is alright," Rowen assured me, holding me tight and calming my panic. "Ninette is weak but recovering with Takoda's help, as is everyone."

Relieved no one had been irreparably hurt, my mind rushed to the present, and I waded through fractured memories. Had Rowen really told me he loved me? Or had I only imagined it in my delirium? The kiss must have been real, I still felt it like fire upon my lips.

"How did you get in here?" I asked, his presence propelling my sanity to the surface. We were deep underground, who knew where, trapped within an endless maze of tunnels and chambers. It was a miracle he had even found me at all.

"I will tell you everything once we are safe from this place, I swear it to you." Rowen stood, unraveling the length of his intimidating body as he reached for me. He was dressed from head to toe in all black, a color I'd never seen him in. I knew it was to blend in with the darkest of shadows, but I couldn't help thinking he looked like a dark angel who'd just scoured the pits of Hell to find me.

I took his hand, eager to leave the room I'd thought would become my grave. He helped lift me to my feet and pocketed the stem of the flower that had just saved my life. "You need to get yourself out of here. Take yourself back to your home, far from here where you can't be found."

"I'm not leaving you, especially to cower in a world where I don't belong."

"I don't deserve your loyalty. Even if I spent lifetimes trying to earn it. I'm the reason you almost died in this evil place."

"Rowen, stop. This isn't up for discussion. We are both getting out of here together like you promised. You told me to go back home, but you are my home, and I'm not leaving here without you."

His clenched jaw dipped in acquiescence as if he knew the feeling and understood I wouldn't back down from this.

Taking me with him, he slowly opened the heavy plated door and peeked his head into the hallway. Verifying no one was roaming the narrow passageways, Rowen pulled me through the threshold and guided me over the bodies of three dead sentinels.

I hadn't heard so much as a scuffle, and apparently neither had they as Rowen crept up on them like a silent demon. Only the rows of silent skulls bore witness to the guards' impending doom, their empty eye sockets watching and their mute mouths smiling.

There was so much racing through my mind as we fled through the tunnels. How had Rowen found the Crystal Crypts? How had he known I would be here?

I needed so many answers, but it would have to wait. Right now I needed to help guide us from this labyrinth of death. However, after a few minutes of creeping along tight passageways, it appeared Rowen knew exactly where he was headed. He must have memorized the paths on his way in.

Always uphill, Rowen led me through corridor after corridor. Some tunnels looked to have been dug then never visited again, while others were adorned with carved white doorways, long runners, massive hanging portraits, and flamed wall sconces. The more decorated hallways seemed to be the residential area of the crypts, and if it weren't for the occasional blood-curdling scream or trickles of falling earth, you could almost imagine you were in an opulent resort.

One of the doors opened unexpectedly, and Rowen slammed

me against the nearest wall, shielding my pale glowing skin from the spotlight of darkness. His hastened breath and rough stubble stroked across my temple as two people hesitated mere feet from where we stood. "It is said the queen has already performed the daily offering hour," an unfamiliar voice whispered to his companion. "We live to see another day."

"Thank the Spirits," the other replied as their footsteps echoed away.

"We can't leave them here," I whispered to Rowen.

"I know. And we *will* come back for them. When we are stronger. Right now my only goal is to get you out of here safely."

I nodded. He was right. Now that we knew where Aliphoura's lair was, we could devise a proper plan for freeing the people held captive here.

Rowen's fingers loosened around my forearms, and we continued our silent underground journey until we came to a dead end. My heart plummeted. After all this, we were still trapped.

Rowen indicated for me to look closer, and I saw the near-invisible slits of a hidden door. He pressed his broad fingertips against the wall, prompting no sound whatsoever as the door gently pivoted open.

I couldn't see beyond the doorway. It was pitch black, but the fresh waft of air was a drug calling to me, and my skin craved the taste of the sun.

Rowen and I took each other's hands and walked towards freedom.

But where I had expected there to be solid ground, there was nothing. I grappled for purchase, but there was none, only a bottomless pit through which we fell as we were dragged back down to the belly of the crypts and swallowed whole.

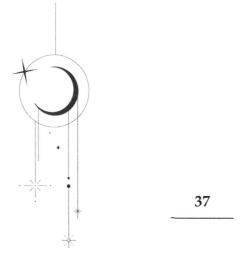

37

Rowen and I landed in a hard heap, bones smarting from the impact of a stone-cold floor.

"No," I heard Rowen growl before I could make out where we'd fallen.

A delighted chuckle echoed around me like an intimate whisper upon my skin. The sound, as lovely as it was terrifying, skirted up my spine and locked each of my vertebrae in place.

Realization sank in that I was back in the queen's throne room, back where each and every one of my horrible tortures had been doled out. Only this time, there was no roaring audience, just her legion of red-dressed soldiers standing in militant watch.

"You're looking well, little star. And I see you have a visitor, but it appeared you two were on your way out without a proper farewell. I know you would never intentionally be so ill-mannered, so I took the liberty of guiding you back with a dark doorway of my own. Now, I'd love for us all to get to know one another a little better, but should you decline, I'll regrettably be forced to subdue you," Aliphoura cooed, threatening us with the charm of a hostess, all while poised upon her towering throne of bone-white bark.

Unsheathing an arsenal of weapons from his body, Rowen glared with such raging violence that his eyes almost appeared calm. He placed my crystal blade in my hand with a centering squeeze. How he found it, I had no idea.

His trusted ax in one hand, Rowen finished arming himself with a long curved blade that arced back over his forearm like an assault shield. He moved in front of me, planting his feet as he settled into a defensive position. "Touch her again, and it will be the last thing you ever do," he growled.

"Very well. Restrain them!" Aliphoura commanded her small army. "I want them alive and uninjured. For now."

Blood screaming, I mirrored Rowen's stance. We were trapped with our backs against the wall, vastly outnumbered by the guards closing in around us.

Aliphoura had led us to believe we were on the brink of escape, only to drag us back down using the same dark portal as Caeryn, her entire armed guard lying in wait. I wondered whose life had been taken to create it.

Rowen lunged, slicing the first soldier within arm's reach. Then he moved on to the next, and the next...

Swinging his dual blades in a deadly dance of hit, shield, and slash, he left each opponent dead or howling on the ground. Trails of blood shot past my line of sight as he took down Aliphoura's sentinels one at a time.

So far, he'd kept the brainwashed guards from getting too close to me, but it was impossible for him to hold them all back.

Eventually, a guard drew up and reached for me. I twisted away to the right and drove my blade down, slashing open his femoral artery. His flesh cut like butter, but before I could watch him go down, another sentry was on me.

Rowen told me to use my speed to my advantage, to dart and

splice quickly, never letting them get their hands on me, so I darted again. Off the downward momentum of my last strike, I arced my blade up, slicing the new guard from navel to chest.

He fell, adding one more to the growing pool of bodies at our feet.

I was able to get a glimpse of Rowen, his body deadly as he cut down the field of soldiers like stalks of wheat. He was vicious, ruthless, and fluid as he delivered the most incapacitating damage in the quickest amount of time.

I turned around just in time to see Caeryn charging toward me, the usual wrath burning in his cleaved gaze.

Rowen was currently swarmed, fending off three other guards blow for blow.

I would have to deal with Caeryn myself.

As was in his nature, he lunged at me. I'd seen it enough to know it was coming, and now that I was healed, I was able to duck from his grabbing reach just in time. Caeryn's marred features snarled, puckering and pulling at the gash I carved across his face. "Someone's got their fight back, I see. Though it won't do you any good."

"Tell that to someone who doesn't wear my mark upon their face," I said, wanting to finish the line I'd carved in him, trace over it again, except this time longer, deeper. Deadlier.

Propelled by my rage, I did what Dyani inadvertently taught me on the training field. I dropped to the ground and swept my leg out behind me, landing a decisive blow to Caeryn's Achilles tendon. His legs popped out from underneath him, and he crashed to the ground in a fury.

I crawled over him savagely, sitting atop him as I reopened his wound with my blade, but he grabbed my wrist and wrested the knife from my hand.

Wrenching me to my feet, he whirled me around with his strong arms and slammed my back against him. He palmed a fistful of my hair, and I cried out as he pulled my head back to rest unnaturally on his shoulder. Then he pressed the edge of his blade into the pulsing vein at my throat.

"Keira!" Rowen screamed desperately, and I could do nothing but watch as he was overpowered by the guards. There were too many of them. It was taking four of them just to hold him as they tried to bind his hands behind his back.

"Well hello, handsome, I heard you were on your way," Aliphoura said, her voice dripping with golden honey. She walked toward Rowen, her personal garrison of three following in her wake. Her hips swayed seductively past her delicate wrists, and the gold gown that clung to her body looked coincidently similar to my Celenova dress. Her crown of bones jutted from her straight dark hair like fingers curling up and cursing the sky. "I wondered how long it would take you to work past my little memory block. I'll admit I was beginning to lose hope. I nearly disposed of the little star, but just like my father, I hate to be wasteful, and I almost put her to good use in the pleasure rooms."

Fury boiled over Rowen as he charged toward Aliphoura. A cage of arms and ropes quickly detained him, leaving him immobile and panting like an animal in a trap.

Just out of his reach, she asked, "Tell me, have you thought of me much, my beloved?"

My beloved?

Her golden eyes traced his body with a look of remembering, and his honed muscles flexed uncomfortably beneath her piercing gaze. The close proximity of her body was enough to pull a growl from his lips.

Ignoring his apparent discomfort, Aliphoura ran her fingers through Rowen's hair, rearranging the dark waves to her liking, and his nostrils flared at her touch.

My heart hammered through my chest. I thought it was me

she wanted. Why the sudden interest in Rowen? Could his presence derail her mission with me so thoroughly?

I struggled and failed to keep up with the perverse and serpentine reasonings of a madwoman.

Silently, I pleaded for Rowen to make eye contact with me, but his defiant stare never left Aliphoura's beautiful face. He was refusing to even look at me.

"He is quite the exceptional lover, don't you think?" she asked, turning to me as she ran her hands down his neck and shoulders. Her words and actions failed to match Rowen's complete rigidity beneath her caressing strokes.

Disgust clenched my stomach. Her touching him so familiarly and possessively made me sick. I wanted to tear and break her hands from him, making a crown of my own with her broken digits.

"Leave her out of this, Fou," Rowen said as he struggled against the arms and restraints that held him.

Fou?

My mind raced to keep up, to piece it all together. But Caeryn's blade sank deeper into the soft flesh of my neck, making it hard to think beyond the sting of his weapon.

Fou.

Shock lodged in my throat like burnt coal as it finally clicked into place.

Fou was Rowen's moniker for Aliphoura. At some point it must have been an endearing nickname, said out of love and devotion, but now the word dripped maliciously from his mouth. I remembered back in the cave when the poison had overtaken his mind. He'd thought I was Fou, and he had wanted to kill me.

All along Rowen's love had been this deranged queen?

I assumed whoever it was had died and that Rowen was

mourning a lost love. Not this sick, very much alive, sadistic woman.

My insides twisted at the jarring realization. It was all coming together: the dark, shadowed looks, the pained remarks of his past, the smiles that were always so quick to evaporate. He had been suffering from her. But had he been enduring the guilt of loving her or the remorse of losing her while she still breathed?

Was that why he would barely touch me?

"Oh," she said, somehow reading the look on my face. "He hasn't fucked you, has he?" Her eyes glinted merrily, and she laughed, the mirthful sound filling the entire cavern like a swarm of malefic pixies. "Pity."

Rowen slammed the back of his head into one of the men holding him in place with a sickening crunch. The soldier screeched, his hands flying to the blood pouring from his broken nose. The binds loosened enough for Rowen to snatch a hand from his shoulder, and sweeping out from underneath it, he hyper-extended the arm until it snapped. Grabbing another's head from behind him, he threw the guard over his shoulder and slammed the body to the ground, breaking his neck.

"Uh, uh," Aliphoura tutted, calm as can be. "So predictable, but another move like that, my beloved, and I'll have Caeryn slit her pretty little throat, dousing your shoes in her blood."

I cried out as Caeryn yanked my head back even further against him; a slow trickle of blood seeping down my neck.

Rowen immediately stilled, and one of the uninjured guards punched him ferociously in the stomach, while another slammed his fists into the back of Rowen's neck. More guards joined to replace the wounded soldiers, and an unfair beating ensued.

"Stop! You'll kill him!" I screamed and pleaded at the top of my lungs as fists, feet, and elbows collided with Rowen's unre-sisting body.

"Enough!" Aliphoura shouted to her guards.

They immediately ceased their barrage but continued to hold him with his arms twisted behind his back. Rowen sagged against them but remained standing. He turned his face to spit out a wad of blood, then looked back to his once love and asked, "Afraid of what I'll do if I get my hands on you?"

"Oh no, my beloved, that is what I am counting on," she said with a wicked grin.

"I'll kill you first," he growled.

"Holding onto grudges? Are you still displeased with me for killing your precious lord?"

Rowen's eyes warred and lashed in a way his restrained body couldn't. "He was like a father to me."

"But he wasn't your father, was he? He was *mine*."

"You've always been rather fond of that word. Haven't you, Fou? Taking what you believe to be yours by any force necessary. Tell me, what will you do when there is nothing left to take?"

Aliphoura's glittering stare darted from me to Rowen. "There will always be something for the taking, always a means of keeping what's mine. You know my father treated you more like his own blood than he ever did me. A son was all he ever dreamed of, and you filled the role perfectly. How could I ever compete with that?"

"It was never a competition. That you couldn't see that, proves you don't deserve his legacy."

"A weakened legacy in need of rebuilding, but never mind all that," she said, intimately tracing her fingers along Rowen's heaving chest, stroking his exposed skin. "Did you ever wonder why you could never utter my name? Or find your way home? Did you ever question why you always felt me near? Always sensed me over your shoulder, listening?" she asked, plucking the stone medallion out from his shirt. "I hated having to curse you with your mother's necklace. I really did, but I knew you were too sentimental to ever remove it."

Rowen's eyes widened in horror.

"I may have eyes and ears everywhere, but none more helpful than the oculus around your neck. Your last treasured possession. I cursed it long ago to keep an eye on you. And I did warn you, darling. If I can't have you, no one can. You used to fight for me the way you fight for her, which leads me to believe she must be very valuable. I think I should like to keep the little star for myself. Perhaps as my chained pet?" She laughed airily, enjoying each and every moment as this nightmare unfolded to her whims.

"No," I barely breathed, finally seeing the trap she'd so carefully woven around us all—the moment she'd been waiting for.

"Let her go," Rowen said breathlessly, his broad chest jackhammering beneath his rising chin. "Take me and let her go."

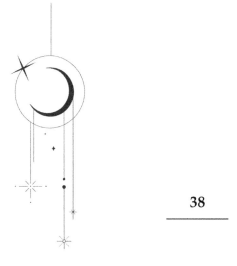

38

An eternity seemed to pass before Aliphoura smiled a grin so wickedly beautiful it could bring empires to their knees. "I heard whisperings the Synodic Son had returned. Naturally, my curiosity got the better of me, and my search to find him began. Imagine to my surprise when I learned she was a woman and that you were the one to find her. I'm not sure I get the fuss, though she did manage to survive Caeryn longer than most." Her voice was unhurried and relaxed as she held our fates within the palm of her hands. "However, if you continue to do as I say, she will remain unharmed. If anything happens to me, she dies. Do I have your compliance?"

Rowen seethed from every pore but agreed with the slightest tick of his jaw, and Aliphoura motioned for her guards to stand down. They roughly released Rowen from their grasp, and he staggered as he fought for his footing.

Aliphoura took another stride towards him, her shadow guards moving with her in lockstep. She pressed her slender body against his, not taking her eyes off me as she did so. She wanted to watch me as she took what I would never have.

"Prove to me in a token of goodwill why I should agree to

such a trade," she said gently, tilting her delicately long neck back to look at him.

Rowen's entire body stiffened, but he didn't resist or push away in the slightest as Fou brought her perfect blood red lips to his unresponsive mouth.

I could see his fists clenching white-knuckled at his sides and the veins bulging out of his rigid neck. Anger flared in me. I wanted blood. Aliphoura's blood. Dripping from my fingers for all the pain and suffering she'd caused.

Aliphoura broke the kiss and looked at Rowen disappointedly. "That's not how I remember it. I know you can do better than that. Do you need more convincing?" She turned to Caeryn holding the knife at my throat, and my entire body stiffened in dread.

Rowen's green eyes finally met mine, and I had never seen such utter anguish as I did in that moment. His beautifully tormented expression broke me into a million pieces—a blown-glass sculpture irrevocably shattered upon the ground.

Fou wrenched Rowen's face back to hers, bringing her lips to his once more.

This time his lips moved in the slightest against hers. Sweat dripped down his face like tears as she flicked his lips with her ripened tongue, prodding him to submit to her further.

Rowen opened his mouth for her in what looked like a silent, desperate cry, and I futilely struggled against Caeryn.

The queen was slow and deliberate as she re-familiarized herself with Rowen's mouth, and my jaw ached from clenching my teeth to the point of cracking. I wanted to rip her throat out.

She continued to kiss and lick and bite at Rowen's mouth, and she placed her palm on the front of his pants, hoping to elicit a response. "I've missed you," she said, her voice like dark chocolate coating a rotten strawberry.

A tortured groan escaped his lips and he swallowed hard.

I wanted to vomit at the unnatural sight of it, I could feel the bile rising, burning at the back of my throat. But Rowen didn't move—he had completely surrendered to Aliphoura as she touched him in whatever way she pleased.

I was disgusted, but couldn't bring myself to look away. It was like a horrific car accident—no matter how gruesome and disturbing, you couldn't tear your eyes from it. I didn't want to see this, but to turn away would be a betrayal. He was doing this for me, subjugating himself to this degradation for me. Surrendering his body to her *for me*.

Even Caeryn shifted uncomfortably by my side.

I felt sick all over again. As much as I didn't want to witness this, at least he was within my sight. I was even more terrified of what she would do to him if she got him alone.

Aliphoura continued to rub and grind herself against Rowen, kissing his jaw, neck, and chest as she ran her fingers through his hair, a euphoric yet determined look on her face. Occasionally she would turn to me as she pressed her lips to Rowen's skin, making sure I witnessed every moment.

I wouldn't shirk from her gaze. Just as Rowen had never left me, I would be with him now, giving him my strength for as long as I could.

The tension in the cavernous crystal chamber was so palpable and dense you could slice it with a hatchet. No one spoke or moved at the intimate display of horror.

I saw Rowen trying to fight it, to look anywhere but at her, to escape to a safe place somewhere inside of himself, but Aliphoura was everywhere. All over him.

She wanted more and looked to me to remind him—to remind him to cooperate. "I hear others are looking for her too, wanting to do far worse to her than me. Perhaps I'll bargain a trade with them instead?"

Her threat snapped something within Rowen, and he finally

broke. He threw his large muscular arms around Aliphoura's slight waist and pulled her close. Crushing her against him, he kissed her with a ferocity that felt like I was intruding on a private moment. If it weren't for the lurid nature of it all, it could almost have appeared beautiful.

"Say she means nothing," Fou panted between kisses.

"She means nothing," Rowen repeated before his mouth was captured once again.

My heart seized. It had to be a lie. Rowen had confessed to loving me not but an hour ago. Though now I wondered, had I heard correctly? Had the pain made me hear things?

But the kiss, after he'd healed me. It wasn't a kiss of comfort or a means of silencing my screams, it was a kiss promising that all he said was true.

He loved me, was doing this for me. Offering her all he had left to give in replacement of me. Himself.

After what felt like forever, Fou finally pulled back from Rowen's vacant expression. Even when he had hidden himself away from me and everyone else, he had never looked this detached, this...this empty.

Witnessing this form of abuse was far worse than any of the torture I'd endured down in this hellhole, but I'd gladly take it all over again if it meant she would just take her depraved hands off him.

"Let her go now, Fou. She doesn't need to see your twisted game play out any further. You have me. I won't fight you. Just let her go," Rowen said, his lips inflamed and swollen.

She searched his deadpan eyes with a starry-eyed expression, and the look took me aback.

It was then I realized she was still in love with him, if she was even capable of such an emotion. She wanted him back, that much was clear. But where I first thought she was just toying with us all for her own amusement, I now saw it was much more than that.

She was never going to let him go. Not again.

Aliphoura's look of hungry possession wasn't lost on Caeryn either. "I thought you told me he was dead," he said.

She'd made Caeryn believe she loved him. But now after years of servitude and blind loyalty, he could finally see the truth written across her face. She didn't love him. She never had.

"I said he was *probably* dead."

"You stabbed him in the heart. How could anyone survive that?"

"I must have narrowly miscalculated."

"Conveniently miscalculated."

My heart lurched. The massive and mottled scar on his chest was from her? I could have never fathomed it was put there by someone he loved.

"Rowen, come to bed. I've let you play in the forest with the elves for far too long. My sheets are in need of your warming."

"You'll let her go?" His voice was rough and his emerald eyes pleading.

"Rowen. No. Don't!" I wailed against Caeryn's arms.

"Yes, on my word," Aliphoura said. "But you are to never leave me again. Ruling by my side and keeping me satisfied as you were always meant to do."

Rowen snatched her by the throat, snarling and exposing the peaks of canines. "Then lead the way, my queen."

She smiled with satisfaction, motioning for her personal guard to stand down their quickly drawn blades. Would they follow them into the bedroom, be watchful guarding eyes as Rowen pleasured her with his body, forcing him into the role of an enslaved plaything?

It enraged me how thoroughly Aliphoura was debasing Rowen, using me as the bargaining chip.

Watching the man I love give in to this sick woman's pleasure raised a furious wrath within me I didn't know I was capable of. It surged ravenously through me, destroying everything in its path until I was nothing but my blood and fury and hatred.

Every molecule, every atom, everything I had within me was directed at Aliphoura in pure and unadulterated rage, and my fingertips swelled.

The light was small and barely there, but I could feel it all the same.

I called for it, coaxing it to grow.

There was no denying it anymore—my powers were inextricably linked to my emotions, and my emotions were inextricably linked to Rowen.

I felt the power building within me and I grabbed on, breathing in tandem with the budding silver tendrils. I just needed to buy more time.

"Caeryn, do you hear that? She's taking another man to her bed," I said through the strain in my neck. "She never loved you. All this time she was using you to get to him."

Doubt loosened his grip.

Aliphoura's lioness eyes snapped to mine murderously before smoothing over and landing on Caeryn. "My dear, that simply isn't true. This man betrayed and hurt me deeply and now I demand his debt be repaid with absolute fealty."

"What about my fealty?" he asked.

I had him now. "Think about it, Caeryn, delivering me to her was sure to bring him here. You are nothing but a glorified errand boy. She didn't choose you. She'll never choose you."

He looked to Aliphoura questioningly, demanding answers.

But she would give none. "Guards," she ordered, gesturing to both Caeryn and me. "Kill them both."

"Wait!" I yelled just as Rowen screamed, "No!"

Some cosmic gong rang inside me, sending a single pulse throughout the ether of my body, awakening my senses to a new level of awareness. It was ancient, wild, and it was terrifying.

The flux of energy was taking too much. I couldn't stop it.

Everything has a cost, Rayal had said. And I was paying with my life.

I didn't know if I would survive this, but the thought of freeing Rowen, Rayal, and the other prisoners from the crypts was enough to pacify my dread. Or accept it.

I raised my arm, my skin glowing in blinding rays of incandescent silver. "You wanted a spark?" I shrieked as my hair cracked and whipped around me. "Well, here it is!"

My power was a foreign entity I had almost no control over as it unleashed from my body in a heavenly torrent. I directed my blinding beam right at Fou's lovely face, but at the last possible second, an invisible hand of air gripped my wrist and pushed my arm upward, throwing off my aim. And instead of hitting Aliphoura square between the eyes as intended, my blast rammed into the crystal ceiling.

What I'd just done had left me depleted, empty, and spent. There was nothing left, and I folded down to my knees.

Everything I had to give, I gave. I gave it all.

And I had missed.

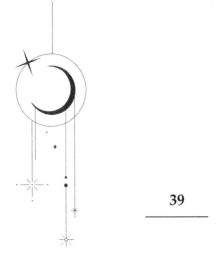

39

The cavern trembled with a quaking roar, rocking us all where we stood.

"What are you waiting for?" Aliphoura shrieked on the heels of the aftershock, displaying her first show of fear. "Get them!"

Her fleet stalked toward me with their weapons raised, clearly shaken but obedient to the core. Now, with orders to kill.

Rowen charged towards me in a stumbling sprint as bits of roof dripped on our heads in veins of glittering sand. Even if he made it to me in time, there was no way to defend ourselves against the armada headed my way. We were exhausted, trapped, and weaponless.

Before either could reach me, a more violent second tremor shook the chamber, splitting the ceiling that hung precariously overhead. Fou's men stopped to cover themselves against the jagged pieces of crystal that rained down upon us like splintered icicles.

My lost aim had invariably sealed all our fates—the Crystal Crypts were caving in, and they would bury us all.

Rowen dove into me, knocking me flat on my back. Using his body as a shield, he lay over me, taking the brunt of the falling crystal blades. I wanted to move, to trade places with him, but my limbs were heavy anchors holding me down.

"I'm so sorry, Keira," he said, looking into my eyes, wincing and grunting as his back and neck were sliced open. Blood dripped down and around his neck, and a vein bulged from his strained forehead. "You have to know. That kiss. What I said. It meant nothing. My soul would be forever tormented if you never knew. You mean everything to me."

The look on his face alone told me he had just uttered his final confession—we weren't making it out alive.

"I know," I said. And I did.

"I missed my chance with you in this world," he said, holding me tight. "I'll find you in the next, and when I do, I swear I'll never let you go."

"In another life," I agreed as his tears crashed and collided with mine; some distant part of my brain knowing Aliphoura was shrieking orders to kill.

"Just look at me, love," Rowen breathed as our fate closed in around us.

I immersed myself in the smoky green of his eyes. It was a waiting game now, with little importance as to whether her loyal guard got to us first or the cave collapsed. We were already dead.

Suddenly, another blast larger than the rest erupted throughout the underground chamber, blowing my hair about Rowen's face and dowsing us in bits of rock and dust. Rowen completely collapsed down on me and threw his arms around my head, burying his nose in my neck as the earthy shrapnel swarmed us in a mushroom cloud of sand and stone.

Disoriented and wondering if I was already dead, I peeked through Rowen's arms. The entire side of the cavern had been blasted open.

Squinting through the raining dirt and crystals was Nepta, leading a pack of Wyn warriors through the threshold of the

Crystal Crypts. Dust whirled around them in a giant plume of black powder and motes of speckled light.

"Kill them. Kill them all," Aliphoura wailed in a retreating shriveling mess, far from the vision of cool perfection she so consciously cultivated.

The relief of the Wyn's presence was short lived. The force from the blast only accelerated the cave collapsing down upon us all, and if Fou's guard didn't stand down, we would have a savage war on our hands; the casualties too precious to fathom.

The continual stream of slicing and impaling crystals didn't deter the sentinels in the slightest, they had their queen's orders, and they would follow them through to the death.

Nepta raised her arm in a sweeping motion, stilling the pointed shards in midair. Slowly and in perfect unison, they all turned like a swarm of murderous hornets, their deadly tips poised right at Aliphoura's men.

Controlling the trajectory of the crystal knives, Nepta brought the sharp edges down upon the soldiers' jugulars. Nepta was truly a terrifying marvel to witness, the way she knew exactly where to point and target the lethal objects based on vibrations and sound alone.

Whatever spikes missed, the Wyn soldiers picked up the slack. One by one, Fou's men fell to the ground, arrows and splintered crystals lodged in their limbs, eyes, and throats.

Dyani's whipping hair caught my eye as she ferociously felled a wake of opponents in her path. Her movements and skill were unrivaled as she moved through the air like a hawk on a tailwind, even contending with Rowen's formidable abilities.

Speaking of, my one-man army was cradled over me, unconsciously pinning me to the floor. I searched for Caeryn and Fou, and my eyes landed on a vengeful red beast and his petrified prey.

Watching Caeryn unleash his wrath on someone other than

myself was a terrifying relief. He strode towards Aliphoura, quickly ending her smaller elite force of soldiers, leaving them crumpled, mangled, and unmoving on the cold stone floor.

Fou's eyes were desperate and pleading, and her face ran with streaks of blood. "Caeryn, my beloved, I didn't mean it," she said as she scrambled at the cave wall she'd been backed into. "This was your final test to prove your love to me. And you've won it. I'm yours. Take me, Caeryn. Take me away—"

Caeryn knelt before his queen and affectionately cupped her face; the soft gesture disarming to witness. He wiped the tears from her eyes with his thumbs, whispering soothing words of comfort. Bringing his lips to hers, he kissed her with the love and devotion only a queen's favored could. Then in one quick, twisting motion, with his lips still on hers, he snapped her neck just as easily as he would the stalk of a rose.

The echoing screams of horror, death, and blood filled the catacombs.

Then all was eerily silent.

The dust finally settled, and I had no idea who remained standing: friend or foe.

Rowen's weight slowly lifted from my chest, and my body tried to chase him as he left me. I didn't want him where I couldn't see or feel him.

Nepta's wise eyes appeared over me. "Good. You're alive," she said with a curt and to-the-point greeting.

Demil shouldered his way toward me and helped me sit up. Surrounding him were Nepta, Dyani, Alvar, Takoda, and several other warriors from the village. They were covered in blood with already bruising eyes, limbs, and lips, looking fierce in their post-victory adrenaline.

"Keira, we've been so worried. Why didn't you stay put on the beach?" Demil asked, keeping me clasped in his hand as he swiped at a nick of blood on my cheek. "Takoda, heal her!"

Struggling to find any energy after my depleting blast, I pushed out of Demil's hold. "I'm fine," I said, desperately searching for any part of Rowen to lay my hands on. "Rowen first."

During the quakes, I'd sustained a few minor cuts and scratches, but Rowen had taken the brunt of the damage. Apart from his lacerations, who knew the internal damage his body had suffered from being beaten into submission. But as Rowen slowly came to with Takoda's masterful healing, my choking dread alleviated.

Fighting through tears of relief, I helped Rowen up as Takoda left to make his rounds, healing anyone in need while bypassing the littered bodies of the dead. Those who hadn't surrendered fought to the death for their queen, and in death they followed her.

Rowen clasped my face in his hands, bringing my forehead to his. "It seems this world isn't done with us yet," he breathed against my lips.

"Good, because I've only just found it," I said through laughing sobs, holding his face as he held mine.

"You're lucky we made it in time," Dyani interjected, wiping the gore from her blade.

Still in disbelief, I turned to Nepta. "How did you find us?"

"We followed your trail," Nepta answered simply.

"What trail?"

"The trail of life. A dark magic tunnel leaves a stain upon the land, and once we found its end, a footpath of life growing from the deadened soil led us here."

"How?" I asked in shock.

"Where are your shoes?" Nepta asked, though her eyes never dipped to my feet.

I grimaced at the memory. "I removed them during Celenova and I...I was forced to walk here barefoot." Rowen flinched beside me as my eyes scanned for Caeryn, but he was nowhere in sight. Neither was Aliphoura's body.

Nepta placed a comforting hand on my cheek. "Thank the Spirits that you did. It was by the bloodied soles of your feet that the forsaken forest was brought back to life, leading us to you both."

"It is true," Rowen said, addressing my look of bewilderment. "It is how I found your blade hidden within the brush. And another much smaller trail, like droplets of greenery, led me here."

"I told you your blood sings to this land," said a voice that had my head spinning around so fast that my vision swam. "It has healed what once was dead." Rayal stood before our huddled group, a hopeful glint shimmering in her arresting eyes.

A dark fear loosened around my heart as the people from the crypts fled to the throne room, searching for any escape from the crumbling caves.

"Rayal, you're alright," I said, not wanting to leave Rowen's side but lifting my hand to hers.

"We must get you back to the village," Nepta interjected. "I cannot protect you here."

I glanced at the droves of prisoners rushing out of the cave Nepta had blasted open. "I can't leave. These people need help."

"They are free now. We must go. I cannot protect you away from the village," Nepta urged. "The cave will hold until everyone has escaped. I will leave the warriors behind to ensure the crypts are emptied. But you cannot stay here. It is you who holds the Alcreon Light. Protect it."

Rayal squeezed my hand. "Go. We will be well now, thanks to you all."

I was skeptical of leaving. There were still so many souls fleeing the crypts, crying in relief as stars twinkled through the false sky that had been their reality for so long.

Rowen's hand landed on my shoulder, offering a warm comfort that flushed and radiated throughout my body. "Keira, I know many of these people. They are strong. They will find their way home."

Nepta waved the point of her cane, stirring the air until a swirling corridor of light emerged from the fabric of space.

"Why does yours look different?" I asked, not quite ready to go through another tunnel I couldn't see an end to, but I also marveled at how she managed to conjure such a thing without breaking a sweat.

"There is a difference between asking and taking the energy that flows around us, a difference between accepting what is given over forcing what is not," Nepta explained as she motioned for me to step through.

I looked back at Rayal, immensely grateful for all she had risked for me. She nodded with a slow, affirmative blink—a quick eclipsing of her sun-bright eyes. "Go."

I finally agreed, and one by one, we walked through the shimmering pool of light.

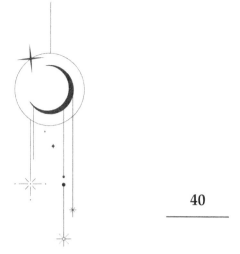

40

Upon returning to the timber-canopied village, a place I thought I would never see again, Nepta turned to me with thoughtful eyes and asked, "Is there anything you need, child?"

The sight of the burnt wreckage charred my soul, and even though it wasn't near the devastation I had pictured in my mind, my throat choked on guilt-ridden ash. I hadn't been able to stay and help the people of the crypts, but there was no reason I couldn't be put to good use here. "The village. I need to help clear up the damage," I said, weary to the bone yet still finding the determination to take a step toward the debris.

"First a bath, then you rest," Rowen interjected firmly, reaching for my arm to stop me. "The village can wait until tomorrow."

"I'm the one responsible for this," I said with what defiance I could muster as I swayed on my feet.

"You will not bear such a weight, child," Nepta demanded. "Not when you are the reason still so much of it stands. You summoned a bolt of lightning that brought rain down upon land and flame."

Utterly perplexed, I looked to Rowen.

"You started a rainstorm, Keira," he said, his green eyes gently caressing my face. "You smothered the fire before it could fully take root. If it weren't for you, there would have been no village to return to at all."

I remembered wishing through my tears there was something I could do, anything at all, and then a large flash of light engulfed me before Caeryn swallowed me with his dark magic powered by Ninette's life-force.

I couldn't believe I had started a storm. Would anything ever feel normal again?

In a trance, I turned from everyone and everything as I made my way to the private bathing suite. I'd received and experienced so much in such a short amount of time, I couldn't process it all. It was too much to take in tonight.

Tomorrow.

Tomorrow I would unravel the strangeness of my abilities. Tonight I needed to wash the horrors of the crypts from my skin, although I doubted the filth of it would ever leave my mind. But whatever horrors I'd faced had been worth it to free the prisoners from Aliphoura's underworld.

Once inside the bathing chamber, I undressed out of the once exquisite Celenova dress, turned to nothing but filthy scraps. I couldn't rip the cloth from my body fast enough, careful not to look too closely at the stains of dried blood.

I climbed up the pebbled staircase and gradually entered the basin of swirling bath water, feeling the cleansing liquid rise up my ankles, thighs, hips, and shoulders. I let the water soak into my sore and weary limbs with a shuddering breath. Rowen may have healed me, but still, a toll had been taken on my body. The memory of the torture was a physical suffering, no easy thing to rid my mind of, and the extinct breaks in my bones left a phantom pain that might never go away.

Not to mention I had almost extracted everything out of

myself to summon that blast. I had no control over the Light inside me, and until I did, I was a massive liability. I'd almost brought the crypts down upon us all.

But now here I was out in the open, something I thought I'd never experience again. I still couldn't believe I'd escaped from the jaws of rock and crystal that had nearly become my tomb, my final resting place.

I lowered myself beneath the bubbling water, ready to be cleansed of the filth from the crypts. But all at once, I was imprisoned within its darkness, lost within the small cage of eternity.

No.

I couldn't...not again. I needed air, freedom, the openness of the sky. I shot my head out of the water and screamed a gargled plea into the midnight air.

Rowen charged through the hanging curtain of vines, ready to destroy. "Keira!"

He came to a swift halt just inside the bathing suite and lowered his weapon. The look of dread on his face slowly transformed into confusion as he saw me visibly unharmed, panting, and trying to catch my breath.

Of course he was here, always protecting and guarding me, even when I didn't know it.

"Keira," he repeated my name breathlessly, the realization that the enemy he rushed in to fight was invisible. How could one battle a tightly clenched fist around the soul?

His attention shifted to the dress on the ground, then snapped back to my wide-eyed expression. He stared for several beats as he took in my drenched appearance and the locks of wet hair dripping around my face and naked shoulders.

"Oh—I'm sorry," he said, clearing his throat. "I had to make sure you were okay. I'll go now." He turned to leave, his eyes about to tear from mine.

"Don't go," I said before his stare disappeared.

When his eyes were on me I felt stronger, safer. Alive.

I needed him. The mere presence of him seeped into my lungs and gave me back my breath.

The need to be closer was mutual, unspoken, and we moved toward each other like mirror images. I waded through the water and huddled against the side of the tub, my fingertips curling over the basin's lip. Rowen stalked toward me with a deliberate gait, meeting me at the tub's edge.

Even though the bath was raised, with me kneeling and him standing, the top of my head came to his chin. He bowed toward me; we were almost eye to eye, and mouth to mouth, brought together like the gravitational pull of two celestial bodies, inherent and unstoppable.

Rowen's pulse was rampant, and his body swelled with muscle and need, and I could tell he was barely containing himself. "I never want to leave you again."

The worry I'd been holding, for fear his feelings had changed above the ground, loosened. "Then don't," I said, my words assuring him as his eyes brightened to the richest shade of the forest. "Stay with me."

He nodded in visible relief, and I reached for a nearby bar of soap, glad he didn't want to leave me just as badly as I didn't want him to go.

"Here. Let me." He took the soap from my grasp and dipped his hands into the water that whirled around me. My body tightened and flushed at the intimacy of his long, tapered fingers joining the water that engulfed my naked body.

He worked the bar between his calloused palms, forming a sudsy lather, and I couldn't take my eyes off him. Watching a man with such deadly capabilities do something so simple was captivating.

"Turn around." His voice was husky and low as he directed

me to move, and I did as he said. Then his hands were on me, grazing the curve of my collarbone and bare back as he gathered my waist-length hair into his hands. He soaped and washed my filthy hair with a reverence that lifted an immeasurable weight from my shoulders.

He finger-combed through my matted rat's nest, gently pulling at my roots and sparking my sensitive hair follicles. Once the knots were mostly untangled, Rowen rubbed my scalp with pressurized strokes that liquified my body into a vat of warm honey. My eyes rolled into the back of my head and I couldn't help the low moan that escaped my lips.

His fingers stilled, then moved to the nape of my neck, guiding my body for a rinse. My neck arched back, exposing the curve of my throat to the cool night breeze. Somehow Rowen picked up on the fact that I didn't want to go under, to be swallowed up in the darkness of water, because he never fully submerged me as he worked the bubbles from my strands.

He slowly brought me back up to face him and our eyes locked as he held the back of my neck. Droplets fell from my hair to my cheeks, seeming to hover and fall in slow motion before crashing against the floating swells of my breasts.

"You must be so tired," he said, his eyes dipping to my mouth.

Yes. Every part of me. Except for the part that was wide awake and aching—for him. "No," I breathed as my eyes zeroed in on his mouth framed perfectly by his dark stubble.

Rowen's hand shifted to cup the side of my face, his fingers lost in my wet tresses. His thumb rested on the edge of my cheekbone, and I tilted my head back, drinking him in and meeting his heady gaze.

With the speed of a lit match, a wildfire blazed in my blood, needing to be stoked. Fed.

His eyes told the same, mirroring my long-tampered fire that was ready to burn and blaze and consume. The shared look stripped us bare until we were nothing more than the twin flames flickering in our eyes.

Rowen's thumb stroked my cheek, and his jaw flexed with a hard swallow before his mouth slightly parted. Like aligning magnets, he sealed the distance between us, colliding our breath and lips into one.

Our mouths moved and tangled against one another in a soul-deep kiss that was purposeful, slow, and vast. His tongue pressed against mine in languid waves that coaxed the winter of my bones into a blossoming spring.

He had never kissed me this way before.

The night he was poisoned, our kiss had been carnal, uncontrolled, and filled with tormented urgency. In the crypts, it had been shrouded in fear and pleading desperation. But now, the way he took his time tasting me and exploring my mouth was deliberate, deep, and held the whisperings of something immeasurable.

"I need you closer," I said against his mouth, pulling at him ardently, the lip of the stone bath still between us.

He didn't need to be told twice.

Quickly shedding his shoes and weapon, Rowen hoisted himself up and over the bath's edge, barely making a splash as he lowered himself into the water. He gathered me into his embrace and wrapped my legs around his narrow hips. He pulled me closer until my bare and needy skin was flush against his clothed body.

The water lapped around our entangled limbs, cushioning us in a midnight ocean, and our kiss deepened to a lower shelf of the sea I didn't know existed.

Rowen's hands roved over my slick wet skin, exploring me thoroughly for the very first time. His broad fingertips outlined the silhouette of my hips and waist, tracing over my ribs until one of his hands palmed my heavy breast. He ran the pad of his thumb over my taut nipple, and a rumble tore through his chest, feeding into my mouth. "Keira, you are perfect. My hands were made to touch you, to feel you."

I couldn't hold him close enough as his hands slid around my neck and back to hold me as he guided me against him, my bareness rubbing on the hard length of him through the material of his drenched pants.

"More," I pleaded, trying to tear at the heavy fabric suctioned to the hard planes and divots of his body.

"Keira, whisper you want this and I'm yours. I've always been yours, but I need to hear you say it." His voice was ragged, and I could barely think straight as his nose traced my jawline. As if I wasn't already coming undone, his mouth dropped to the soft spot between my neck and ear, making it even harder for me to form words.

"I want this. I want you. Always," I panted into the air and let my head fall back, granting him greater access to nibble and suck at my neck.

"You can't imagine how happy it makes me to hear that, Keira. But I shouldn't touch you, not until you know everything —if you would still want me this way after knowing what I've done."

I knew what he was talking about, but I didn't want to rot the moment with her name. I brought my gaze back to his, infusing my words with all the conviction my heart and soul could convey. "It's always been you, Rowen. Can't you see that? Despite the past, it doesn't matter. Nothing you could ever say would change my mind."

The flames in his eyes burned brighter at my words, and his green irises unfurled like the petals of a succulent. "Then I'm all yours, for as long as you'll have me, but tonight you need rest."

"I don't think I'll get any rest tonight. I...I'm still too on edge."

"Then perhaps I could help you...unwind," he said with a mischievous glint, and underneath the water, his fingers traced up my inner thighs. His touch found me, my very center, where all my nerves pulsed between my legs, and an aching moan was my only reply.

He touched me with long glorious strokes, slowly exploring me, and I bowed back, arching my peaked nipples into his clothed chest. I needed this, his hands on me in this way. It helped chase away the darkness.

But I needed more, so much more.

"I want to see you," he rasped deep from the back of his throat, and his broad hands moved to latch onto my waist. "All of you." With ease, he stood and lifted me onto the smooth edge of the swirling pool.

His eyes danced and dined on my naked body displayed just for him. My pale skin glowed in the night, and my dark wet hair wrapped around my body like tendrils of kelp on a selkie.

Rowen's chest thundered with desire. "You are absolutely magnificent, Keira."

My body bloomed under his gaze. "Now it's my turn to look at you."

He ripped his soaking shirt from his body and tossed it without care. I barely had a moment to admire the soaked chiseled planes of his body before he crashed back into me with an unbridled moan, kissing me breathless.

The stars and planets that refused to dim shimmered down on our bare skin, casting the droplets of water on our bodies into jewels of twilight. Comets and galaxies churned around our tangled bodies in whorls of liquid night and rippling diamonds —we were a very part of the starlit sky that reflected into the eddying water.

Between us, Rowen's fingers found me again, swirling deliciously and more acutely on the spot that was sure to detonate me if he kept moving like that. His touch lowered, tracing me tortuously before entering me with a thrust, and I gasped, my body bucking into him.

He gave me a few deep, exquisite pumps before he withdrew his hand and tasted me on his finger. His eyes dilated as if he'd just consumed a drop of ecstasy, and I nearly spiraled out of control right then and there. "How am I to enjoy anything else when I've just had a taste of the heavens," he hummed, slowly sinking back into me with two fingers, and I moaned loudly, throwing my head back.

His hand was controlling my whole universe, it would obey his every command.

It already was.

My head lolled into him until my lips were on his collarbone and my fingertips dug into his muscular shoulders. The slow glow of pressure built deep inside as he worked me thoroughly, but my mind and body seemed stoppered with worry—my release trapped within the fists of my trauma.

"Keira, let go. I have you," Rowen encouraged, slowly stroking my clit with his thumb, and I had no choice but to submit to his command. Trusting him with every piece of me, I let go and began riding his hand with abandon. "That's it. Good girl. Come for me."

The scale of stars and moonlight was tipping, tipping, tipping until it spilled over entirely, bursting and filling me to my every horizon with a pleasure I could have never fathomed. I cried out Rowen's name. Releasing all the tension, strain, and suffering I'd been holding on to, my body quaked and shivered in utter captivation.

Rowen slowed his rhythm and brought me down gently, melting me into a pool of shimmering silver. Completely drained but entirely filled, I sagged forward into Rowen's hard chest, his arms catching and holding me from drowning.

His hand landed on my bare back, slowly caressing me up and down my spine as he held me tight, kissing my ear, temple, and brow. Rowen had just given me the gift of mind-numbing pleasure that healed my soul just as much as it destroyed my demons.

And I wanted to return the favor.

I drowsily fumbled at the front of his sodden pants, my fatigued body desperate to touch him.

He placed his large hand over mine, stopping me.

"Let me touch you," I said, trying to fight my mutinously tired body. I wanted it more than anything, and I could blatantly see that he wanted it just as badly.

"Keira, you're exhausted, your body entirely spent. I want you wide awake and rested when you touch me."

I was fully prepared to argue with him and get my way, but I must have drifted off as he continued to caress me in our never-ending pool of swirling galaxies, because the next thing I knew, he was whispering low and throaty in my ear, "Let's get you to bed." His full lips skimmed the shell of my ear, and no matter how much I wanted to stay in this suspended animation, I knew it was time to go.

Rowen moved me to the side, reluctantly letting go. "I'll be right back. Don't fall asleep again," he warned, and I sleepily agreed, although I couldn't make any promises. It felt like I had been repeatedly hit by a speeding bullet train, and the horrifying reality was that that wasn't too far from the truth.

A sweeping bit of adrenaline coursed through my veins as I watched Rowen rise to his full height. His waterlogged pants hung dangerously low on his hips, revealing the deep creases of his lower abdomen. He turned to walk up and out of the water. His slow descent down the pebbled staircase gave me plenty of time to take in his broad back that tapered into a pert backside.

I hadn't had the time or leisure to fully take in his shirtless body, but I found I immensely enjoyed it.

"I can feel your eyes on me, Keira," he said with a side smirk.

I lowered my chin and mouth into the water, still peering at him with my eyes. He disappeared into the bathing suite's anteroom, returning a few minutes later wearing dry pants and carrying a long piece of fabric.

At the top of the stairs, Rowen held the garment up with outstretched arms, inviting me in. With exhausted limbs, I met him at the tub's entryway, where he wrapped me in a blushing terracotta robe dress. The three-quarter length sleeves ended in frayed strands that fell to my wrists, and a delicate loose threadwork rimmed the entire kaftan.

The lightweight garment hung open on my body, and Rowen's eyes didn't miss an inch of my exposed skin as I turned to face him.

"The things I want to do to you, Keira," he nearly growled like a starved beast against my ear. I thought he was going to rip the robe right back off and devour me, but instead he closed the two sides of the robe and sealed it with the tassel-trimmed tie around my waist.

His self-control was astounding. I definitely couldn't say the same for myself.

I knew there were things he needed to say to me before we went any further. For both our consciences' sake, he wouldn't touch me again until I knew everything.

Appreciation for Rowen wanting to share the details of his past while I was of sound mind swelled through me, but I didn't know if I could wait that long, his dark gaze was already stirring another pooling ache in me. "Then do it."

"You need to sleep."

"I'm not tired," I lied, still trying to get my way. But my heavy legs almost gave out from underneath me and gave away my lie.

"You are. And believe me, it's taking every ounce of my control not to have you crying out my name like that over and over again, but I will see to it that you get your rest, you're going to need it for what I have planned for you."

I gulped. Rowen had just given me a taste of his capabilities, but I knew his large, muscled mass was capable of much, much more.

Before I could further protest, Rowen swept my legs out from under me and carried me away.

———— ·(**C** · ● · **Ɔ**)· ————

I was weightless, floating above the ground on an invisible track that carried me on a wild breath of the forest.

My eyes slanted open, revealing the night sky overhead. The bespeckled stars glimmered like flecks of lambent paint on the broad canvas of night. Normally they looked random and chaotic, but not tonight, tonight they looked *familiar*.

The sky...it was becoming my own.

"What are you smiling about?" Rowen's voice rumbled deep in his chest, vibrating against my cheek, and I remembered he was carrying me.

"I'm home," I said dreamily before sleep blanketed over me again and swaddled me in the calmest rest I'd ever known.

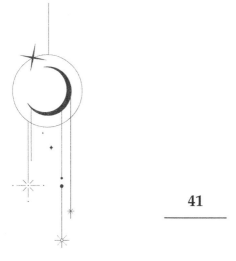

41

I woke to Rowen stretched out beside me on his bed, wearing nothing but the pants from last night.

"Good morning," he smiled at me through my wild curtain of hair. "You hungry?"

Next to him was a large rattan tray containing a colorful spread of ripe berries, leafy greens, grains, and sweet nectars. I was so out of it, I hadn't even noticed him leave my side, much less return with a mound of glorious smelling food. Not having eaten a proper meal in days, I immediately dug in, gorging my stomach well past its shrunken limits.

"Slow down," he murmured gently. "You'll make yourself sick."

"It's too delicious. And I've never had breakfast in bed," I said, scooping yet another forest berry through the sticky-sweet honey before sucking it into my mouth. I savored the dripping juices. Licking my fingers, I eyed Rowen watching me intently with a grin, one hand relaxed behind his head. "What?" I asked skeptically, matching his wry smile.

"Do you know how many mornings I wished I could wake up next to you like this? Never imagining how much I would enjoy watching you. You know, you are quite adorable when you drool on my sheets."

"I don't drool," I said, chucking a berry at his face which he promptly caught between his sparkling teeth. He smiled as he chewed and swallowed, but his mirth slowly paled, sinking into a humorless sigh, and his body shifted into a serious upright position.

In all the nights I slept alone, his bed had felt too big, too empty without him, but now it was overcrowded and not by his commanding body, or the large tray of food between us, but by the story left untold upon his lips. "If you're feeling up to it, I'd like to explain everything now."

I nodded. Last night I had been too tired to care. My weighted and exhausted body had only wanted release, but now I wanted answers.

"I never wanted you to find out about Aliphoura and me in the way you did. I hate that you heard it from her lips, on her terms. That is something I will never be able to take back, never be able to forgive myself for." Rowen's eyes held the burden of immeasurable guilt. "I wanted to tell you the night of Celenova, to find someway around her curse, but we got separated before the fire broke out."

He had wanted to tell me something as the auroral lights danced around us in a celestial serenade, but Demil had snatched me away, taking the moment along with him.

"The memory I told you about in Weir Falls." He looked to me inquisitively and I nodded in recollection, encouraging him to continue. "It's the memory of the day Fou plunged her dagger into my heart," he said, running his fingers over the scar that marred the skin just to the left of his sternum.

"Fou and I grew up together, in what used to be Viltarran. The entire landhold was her birthright, to be inherited upon the passing of her father, Lord Leones. My mother was one of the many maids who lived within the massive walls of Leones' palase, a meagre citydom where all labored for everything they had.

"Becoming with child, my mother feared for her position and the life of her unborn babe should she be discovered. She concealed her swollen belly and gave birth to me in the cellars. She hid me for as long as she could, sometimes in cupboards from sunup to sundown, until I was big enough to start earning my keep, earning my right to breathe and eat scraps of food just as everyone else. My mother made the best of every moment and I was happy. It was more than most had."

My mouth went dry, and my heart pained for how Rowen had been raised in the earliest years of his life. But I knew this was just the tip of the iceberg of the pain he'd experienced throughout his life.

"I started as an errand boy in the kitchens and scullery, working there for years before I ever saw Fou. Not much older than I, she was so clean and beautiful, wearing the finest clothing I'd ever seen. She reminded me of the sky sprites from the stories my mother whispered to me as she put me to bed. Stories of tricky skylings transforming themselves into beautiful maidens to bewitch and beguile anyone in their path. And this captivating little sky sprite was using her magic to convince an entire galley of adults to give her the freshly-baked sweet breads per the demands of her father.

"Walking out with a wicked smile on her face and a basket full of sugared cakes, I moved in front of her. I blocked her path, unsure whether I wanted to follow her to the heavens from which she came, or call her out for her lies. As if she knew my contemplations, she offered me one of her stolen cakes—either for my silence or solidarity, I never knew which, but from that moment on we became inseparable.

"I was always drawn to how she could command a crowd of

fools, use her sky magic to convince anyone of anything if it helped her get what she wanted. I thought I was above all the rest, that I could see through her. Little did I know I was just a fool as anyone.

"After my mother passed unexpectedly, I was no longer allowed in the kitchens. Alone and in mourning, I took whatever work I could find, sleeping anywhere I could. I began earning my keep in the fields and stables, longing for the life of a Viltarran soldier. Bearing no birthing papers, all I could do was watch and learn from the sidelines, practicing their movements over and over again in the shadows, then improving upon them.

"Over the years, Fou always supported and believed in me, even helped me build my own personal training field up in the mountains. It grew to be our sanctuary, where we'd spend most of our days together, but word began to spread that Lord Leones' prized daughter was spending time with the likes of a young man no better than a mutt. Infuriated, he sent his guards to follow us, catch us red-handed and bring us back to him for questioning.

"His soldiers bombarded us in our safe haven. One of them laid a hand on Fou as she scrambled to dress, and I lost my mind, taking out a handful of Viltarran's best men. I was sure I would be put to death or banished, but Leones was impressed with my talent for combat, and my skills weren't to be wasted in his citydom. He put me straight to work training a small battalion of his army, a position that kept me close by his side.

"I never knew my father, could scarcely imagine what having one would feel like, but I looked up to Leones in the way I imagined having a father would be. He was a young ruler, not even to his half-life with a long rule still before him. He gave all that he could to his people, trying his best as the land began to die and wither all around us. But for as long as I could remember, Fou only spoke of what a fool he was, how the citydom suffered from his soft old ways. She always spoke of the future, a future she would command when her father was gone.

"When her father died, it shocked us all. Having left this world so suddenly, Leones never wrote his final rights and all was bequeathed to Aliphoura. As the new ruler of Viltarran she slowly began ordering the most drastic and ridiculous of changes. Raising the courtier's taxes, demoting and banishing those most loyal to her late father, putting unnecessary burdens on local markets and traders. It was absolute madness but I chalked it up to the loss of her father, even when she declared herself Queen over her inherited title of Lady.

"I was loyal and stayed by her side through it all, trusting her vision of our future together. She said we would have it all, but I didn't want it all. I just wanted her.

"When I would voice my opinion or disagree with a new decree, she would placate me in the moment yet still carry out her wishes in a more clandestine manner. We fought more and more, especially when she began to dig and tear up the ground, depleting what precious natural resources we had left, needing to preserve them rather than burn through them faster.

"With no end to her madness in sight, her ideas became more radical and frightening by the second. She began building massive chambers beneath the ground, claiming it was in preparation for the sky that would eventually foul as well. And as slow as a boiling pot of water, she integrated the whole citydom and its people into the crypts just below the ruins of Viltarran. There was nothing left of the home I had loved and lived in with my mother. It had been buried. All of it. Even the people. Except those who went missing. Subjects who objected too loudly mysteriously disappeared, even those who objected quietly were never seen again. She had eyes and ears everywhere, heard every whisper and saw every transgression against her. She was always ten steps ahead of us all.

"The Crystal Crypts became the new world I could never accept. My heart ached for all that was lost, and I would often sneak to the surface by way of my hidden door. By that point, all we did was fight and disagree. I wanted to leave, but how could I? How could I ever leave her? She was my future. My everything. I thought if I stayed, I could change her, help her see the flaw in her ways.

"It was hard to admit for how long I had been deceived, how long I thought I could convince her to change her ways. How wholly love blinded me. I questioned how she was sustaining all her subjects for so long, and it wasn't until I walked to the lower cells and saw all the missing souls lined in the skulls of the dead that I knew just how far Fou had fallen.

"There was no way to fix her or all that she had done, I only realized it too late. All her beautiful talk of the future had been for her, not for her people. Leones' people.

"The day I confronted her, I asked her to take a walk with me to our favorite place on the mountain. It was my final effort for her to see the damage she caused, to remind her of our time in the sun, and convince her there was another way, that we would make it work.

"She took it as a sign that I had never loved or believed in her. That I had been lying all along. And right there in her anger, she confessed to killing her father in my ear. How she had been jealous that he saw me as more of his legacy than her.

"Seething with hatred and anger, I drew my blade on her. It shook in my hand. What was I going to do with it? Kill her?

"She'd been suspicious of me for quite some time and ordered her guards, my friends, to follow us, to lie in wait for her inevitable command. She had poisoned them against me, claiming I had killed her father.

"There were too many of them. She knew my abilities and had carefully outmatched me. She may as well have delivered each and every blow. Every slice I received was as if her own hand cut me open, and with each drop of my blood she betrayed every good memory, every time I told her I loved her, held her, made love to her. She shattered it all and I wanted to snap her neck for it. All of it."

It all made sense now, what happened in the cave, how right before he snapped out of his poisonous hallucination he had wanted to kill me, thinking I was Fou, someone he had once loved.

Rowen took a long breath, exhaling with a finality that this would be the last time he'd let this memory hold power over him. He was going to see this through to the very end.

"She asked me one last time if I would change my mind, to stand by her side. One word and she would take me back. But I looked her in the eyes and denied her with my entire being. It had never been love at all.

"I saw it coming, didn't even try to stop it as she plunged her blade into my heart. And as my flesh clenched around the knife held by her hand, she whispered a damning promise in my ear, worse than if she'd just killed me. 'If you survive this, I will destroy anything you ever hold dear again. Because you couldn't love me, I'll make sure you never love again, and because you turned your back on your people, you will walk the land without your home, alone until you decide to return to my side.'

"As she cursed me, my second in command fell to the ground, sealing her promise in blood. She slowly pulled her dagger from my chest, looking like the small girl I had met in the kitchen, that same wicked smile upon her beautiful face. All it took was a nudge and she pushed me off the side of the cliff."

My own heart hurt, tearing in on itself as if Aliphoura had planted her dagger in my chest. If she wasn't dead, I'd kill her all over again.

"I wandered the forest bleeding for days, ready to die,

accepting the part I played in her sick machinations. I had already given up when Takoda found me. He refused to let my body give out, but something else died in me that day. As I healed, I searched for Viltarran, only to remember I'd been cursed with never returning to the land of my mother. Fou had destroyed me in more ways than one with her dark power, a mastery she'd studied right beneath my nose.

"She locked me in a prison, one I'd have to carry with every step. Not willing to sacrifice anyone for the sake of my heart, I closed it off forever. Until the moment I saw you. Keeping my distance was the only thing I could do to keep myself from admitting I wanted you, but the very confession in itself put you in danger. Any whisper or admission she would hear, and she would come for you.

"If I were a better man, I would have left you right where I found you that first night. I should have turned and never looked back. But I couldn't bring myself to do it. I found that I needed you, felt a little more alive when you were near.

"I was a glutton for punishment, needing to be by you, but never touch you, never tell you how I felt. If Fou ever found out about you, I knew she would kill you, and she almost did. I will never forgive myself for that, Keira. Never. I will carry that guilt with me the rest of my days."

My heart ached for the burden of his guilt. We would both need to find a way to heal from all this pain together.

"I saw how much I was hurting you, and it killed me. I wanted to tell you so many times, tell you everything, take you in my arms and never let you go, but I couldn't risk Fou ever catching wind of such a thing, couldn't risk you opening your heart to me in any way. Even when I tried, I found I couldn't consciously say her name.

"How I hated myself for finding you and potentially placing a death wish upon your head. Placed there by a woman who once had my love, shared my bed. I knew her eyes and ears were everywhere, but I could have never fathomed her curse was placed in the one possession from my old life, my mother's necklace."

The fury in his gaze blazed, and the heat coming off his body was palpable.

"By the spirits, Keira, I tried to deny you. The first time I touched you it nearly knocked me off my feet. I vowed I would never touch you again. But you kept showing up everywhere I went. I would be in the forest, walking, trying to get you out of my mind, when you would appear right before me. It was like you were taunting me, torturing me. It was then I realized it was too late for me to leave. We'd made our mark on each other, and I feared that no matter where I went, you would follow. I learned the truth of that the hard way on my scouting mission to Weir Falls. I never would have gone if I'd known you'd show up."

I remembered back to the Falls, what he'd said to me after I accused him of being the one to show up unwelcomed. *What if I told you, it was you appearing to me, disrupting my life?*

I had point-blank laughed in his face, but now I saw it for what it was.

The truth.

I thought he was the one tormenting me. Not the other way around. How backwards it all really was.

"You were right that day by the creek," I said, finding and meeting his heavy gaze. "I would have never believed it, but you were right." I was drawn to him. From the start. Subconsciously using my astral traveling abilities to be closer to him. It explained why I always appeared where he was: in the forest, in Weir Falls, in his bed.

His lips pulled into the mimic of a smile, but it was still pained and held the anguish of one last confession.

"The night of the fire, I knew she was behind it, I recognized the color of Caeryn's uniform. When he pulled you through that dark tunnel, I knew exactly where he was taking you, just not how to get there. It didn't stop me from trying, and eventually I came upon your bloodied footsteps turned to life and vegetation. You brought me back, Keira. You lead me home. To you."

It was all out in the open now, the memory that plagued him and why he had tried so hard to keep it from me. Dreading any whisper would find its way back to Aliphoura. I remembered the shadow that fell across his face every time he recalled his own personal hell. And now I knew why.

Was that why our hearts knew each other? Because we had both been betrayed by the people we loved, the people we trusted most with our hearts. Me, by my parents and best friend, and him by his childhood friend turned lover—both of us finding refuge in the Wyn village.

"And when she made me kiss her, your life was at stake. I had to make her believe. So I thought of you, imagined tasting your lips, feeling your skin on mine, and when the time came, I would have imagined you beneath me as I fucked her with my soulless body. It's sick and I hate myself for using my feelings for you in such a way, but if I couldn't convince her, she would have never let you go."

Outside a dark cloud lifted, mirroring the clearing of our shrouded souls, and the golden light of day slanted in through the canopied dome, illuminating the map of scars upon Rowen's body. My eyes dropped, and where I expected to bristle at the gruesome defacement above his heart, I only beamed with pride and respect. Rowen had offered his body in every way imaginable and had never let it affect his integrity. He was good through and through. How had I ever doubted it?

I put my hand over his heart, "Rowen, you did what you had to do. We all did. Aliphoura would have eventually found me whether you loved me or not. She said it herself, she was in search of the Alcreon Light. Don't ever hate yourself for anything, because I never could." I held the stare of his emerald gaze, and I opened my mouth for the words I feared I would never get to say, the words Rowen needed to hear for his own redemption, and the words that would answer his long-suffered admission from the crypts.

And so I said to Rowen what I had always felt, always known, and would never forget, "Because I love you too."

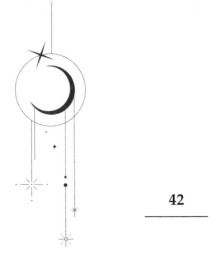

42

The sun set on the outside world, slowly dimming as the room's luminorbs came to life. We hadn't ventured out from Rowen's dome once today. Lost in conversation, the sky continued its circumnavigation around us, the moon pulling the night back overhead on the wings of a silver chariot.

Stretching my legs, I walked around Rowen's room, his sharp eyes following my every move.

I immediately stopped short.

Stacked one on top of the other were the journals I'd noticed my first night here. They had mysteriously gone missing when Rowen offered up his home to me, but now here they sat, a beige tower of rough-hewn bindings and warped pages begging to be leafed through.

"These were here my first night. You moved them," I said, gesturing to the stack of worn books now plopped on his desk for anyone to see. "Scared I was going to take a peek?"

"Can you deny your curiosity wouldn't have gotten the better of you?"

"I would never," I said nonchalantly, knowing full well I had gone on a serious manhunt trying to find them. The glint in his eyes told me he expected as much, but I'd be damned if I was going to admit it.

"Go ahead, take a look. I brought them back for you."

My heart stutter-stepped in my chest. What else could Rowen have kept from me, but was now willing to share? Beyond intrigued, I ran my finger up the rugged spines and selected the volume sitting highest atop the stack. I opened the worked cover, allowing it to naturally fall where the binding creased the deepest. And what I saw before me sucked all the breath from my lungs.

They weren't journals at all, but sketchbooks.

I was looking at a charcoal drawing. Beautiful. Dark. And haunting.

Harsh depressed lines swirled elliptically, drawn overtop each other again and again in aggressive strokes. In the center of the thick black cloud was...was me. Glimpses of my body peeked through the gaps of spiraling darkness. From what I could see of my face, it was angled and defiant, vulnerable and afraid, but still standing strong. Resisting.

Is...is that what I look like?

To view myself through the eyes of another had me feeling raw, found, and utterly seen. Even though it was a drawing of me, it felt too intimate to look at. A moment so frozen it could shatter.

I flashed my eyes to him.

He was preternaturally still, waiting for me to react as if I were a too-wild creature that would dart at the slightest sign of being captured. But he already had me, held something deep within me I thought I had lost long ago.

"Rowen. This is...you are...remarkable," I said, almost choking on the words full of emotion; another revelation of this enigmatic man brought to the surface. This explained why his fingers always looked covered in soot. His charcoal-smeared hands were not just the tools of a warrior, but of an artist.

I lightly traced the movements of the dark graphite, feeling the depth of each stroke. The emotion put into every line seeped through the pad of my finger and the rhythm of the shading vibrated in my pulse as if I were reliving the memory of him sketching it.

Inhaling the earthy scents of parchment and charcoal, I flipped through page after page of impressive renderings. Occasionally there were drawings of the Wyn village, its working people and sweeping landscapes, there were even some of a strange city with crowded buildings, pointed archways, and cobblestone streets, but the reoccurring theme throughout his sketches was me, covered in varying shades of darkness.

At first, they were small, angled snippets of my face and body, fighting the weaning effects of the drug that had been suppressing me for years. Gradually the black cloud faded, revealing an almost unrecognizable woman, wild with her free eyes and bare skin.

"If I had known I was being watched I might have opted to wear more clothing."

"While I certainly didn't mind it, it wasn't what made me seek you out and draw you each night." He stood from the bed and every muscle, large and intricate, shifted as he walked toward me, spellbinding me with yet another work of art—his body. Standing in front of me, he opened his palms. "These hands were responsible for so much horror, bloodshed, and death, that I wanted them to be responsible for something beautiful too, so I began drawing as a way to...cope. But when you appeared to me, you woke up a part of me I'd never known. However long you stayed was all that I truly existed. And if by some cruel twist of fate I never saw you again, at least I would have these to remind me of how I felt. That there was good, somewhere out there, and that she had come to me, if even for a little while."

The sincere vulnerability on his face, so open and clear with no traces of his once concealing mask, broke me in a way that somehow put me back together again, the way I was always meant to be.

Overcome with emotion, I tore my eyes from his face and looked at the sketch on the final page.

Drawn so lightly and timidly, as if to press any harder would be to draw the ink from his own blood, was yet another picture of me. It was a close-up of my face, flickering in the light of the cave the night I saved Rowen's life, the night he kissed me.

This image wasn't drawn in his usual crisp stylings but slightly shifted, as though I'd moved during my picture being taken. It was how he must have seen me as he fought the effects of the poison that coursed through his veins, as he battled his visions of Fou.

It was then I realized the last touch that lingered on him was hers.

I had to remedy that, erase her oily touch from him just as sure as he had erased so many of my traumas.

I looked up into his heated gaze as he slowly removed the book from my hands, placing it face-down on the table. "What do you think?" he asked, his cool breath washing over me as he lightly traced his finger down my arm, causing my skin to erupt into goosebumps.

"They're alright."

It was a lie and he knew it. They were spectacular. I had no idea Rowen possessed such a gift, and it broke my heart that he kept it from me, thinking it would protect me from ever knowing how he felt. To never give me any hope.

But I had hope now, and my mind couldn't stop conjuring all

the ways we could be happy, ignoring the parts of my brain that warned Erovos was still searching for me.

He raised one dark eyebrow, not believing me for a second. "Just alright?" he asked, taking my bait.

"Well, there was a drawing I didn't see."

"Oh?" His hand trailed its way back up my arm in a featherlight stroke that sped up my breathing. "And what would that be of?"

"Me," I said, honing in all my concentration. His touch was sending my mind reeling a million miles away while keeping my body at rapt attention exactly where I stood.

A laugh rattled through him. "I think we've established they are mostly of you." Rowen's touch continued, tracing electrifyingly along the curve of my collarbone, and he watched as my nipples tightened through the kaftan.

"Yes," I said breathlessly, looking at him through my lashes, my chest heaving, "but one where darkness or poisonous hallucinations aren't wrapped around me would be nice."

"Would you like to be wrapped in something else?" His eyes sparkled mischievously. "You do look rather appealing in my sheets. Would that appease you? If I drew you in nothing but them?"

"I would like that," I barely whispered, heat pooling in fervent pulses between my legs.

"On one condition," he said, picking up and twirling a lock of my hair. "That is, if you agree to it." His eyes shot to my face.

I could barely think straight, let alone breathe properly. Rowen intoxicated me with his gaze, his breath, his tantalizing touches. I would agree to anything he asked. "And what would that be?"

"That before I do, I get to thoroughly and utterly explore you, taste you, and exhaust you."

Rowen's words had my entire body throbbing to the point of pain, and I curled my fingertips around his neck to keep steady.

Our gazes never broke, acknowledging the desire we had both been fighting for so long. A mutual agreement that we were done denying the aching flames burning within us.

My hands slid from the tops of his shoulders, down the front of his molded chest, feeling the strength and need pulsing beneath him like a surging tide in his veins, the necklace gone. My own heart pumped faster. "Well then, what are you waiting for?"

Without another word, Rowen swept me up in his arms, and a breathy gasp escaped my lips in surprise.

He carried me to his bed, stopping when his knees hit the cushion. He guided my body through the opening of the draped canopy, and the lightweight fabric brushed against my sensitive skin. Sitting me down in the center of the bed, he prowled the rest of the way through the netting.

He took a beat back on his heels, looking at me. His dark hair fell across his brow and his stubbled face regarded me with tamped carnality. "A fitting place for you, is it not."

"Only when you're in it next to me."

He smiled that wicked smile that exposed the white tips of his canines. "The possibilities of the things I will do to tire you into sleep, only to wake you in a similar fashion, are endless." His words quickened my swirling pulse, and his wild need for me both scared and thrilled me.

He leaned forward and climbed up my body, my eyes tilting up as his lengthy form settled above me. I panted in achy anticipation, needing his touch more than I'd ever needed anything in my life.

Unable to wait a moment longer, I pushed my hips against his, and all at once, his steely control shattered. The invisible leash that had held him back for so long snapped, and with a pained groan of my name, he crashed down onto me, taking my mouth with his, starved and unrelentingly.

I gasped into his hungry mouth, surprised by how much he had been holding back with me before. How utterly he had been depriving himself.

Taking advantage of my parted lips, his tongue dove inside, tasting and pushing against me in a devouring kiss that was surely consuming my very soul. I gave it gladly, knowing I was taking a piece of his as well. We were both giving and giving, but nothing felt taken or lost. We were two auras merging together, creating a third color unknown to any spectrum, wholly me and wholly him, but something *more*.

Nothing existed beyond the encased netting of his bed, our fervid breathing the only sound echoing in the absolute space that held us.

Rowen's broad calloused hand traveled up the length of my leg, slowly opening the slit of the robe with his trailing touch. His fingers roved over my thigh and hip bone, exposing a significant slip of my skin to the cool wafting air. He untied the knot at my waist and peeled back the garment one side at a time, unwrapping my naked body like a priceless wonder.

My chest heaved up and down, revealing the ridges of my ribcage as Rowen traced his fingertips down my arm, pulling the sleeve with him. Gliding the fabric across my skin, he released my arm and kissed my bare shoulder before making his way to free my other arm.

His eyes drank me in as he stripped me, completely baring me beneath his powerful body. He pulled the robe out from under me and tossed it aside.

"I'm aching for you, have been aching for you since I first laid eyes on you," he said, his hand making its way back down my body. He lifted my leg from behind the knee and propped it up before pushing it open, exposing me to him. "Tell me, have you ached for me?"

My body, erupting in quivers, was answer enough, but it wasn't until he touched me wet and wanting, that he growled in mutual need. Feeling my warmth and readiness for him, he slowly sank a finger inside me, and I arched against the bed, whimpering.

His lips kissed up my ribs, one at a time, until he captured my budded pink nipple in his mouth, flicking it with his tongue. It felt like he was everywhere, all over me, branding my skin.

The attention he paid my body was nothing short of worship. It was beautiful, empowering, and I understood why the gods demanded it.

Then he slipped in another finger, and I moaned uncontrollably.

His tongue on my breast matched the rhythm of his fingers inside me, and slowly, coaxingly, he fed the ball of light growing within me. It grew brighter and brighter until it exploded, filling my whole body with star fragments that pulsed and sparked in my every nerve ending.

"So beautiful when you come for me. You're glowing," he said before his mouth found mine again. I was reeling and already spent, but he wasn't done with me yet.

He worked his tongue and lips down the other side of my body, ensuring not to neglect a single part of me. The stubble across his jaw aided in the delicious sensation of his hot breath and searching tongue on my skin, and I couldn't get enough. Then, his mouth was on me, in between my legs, licking and lapping at the taste of me, assisting his already busy hand.

The multiple rhythms had me forgetting my own name. He was working me thoroughly with his fingers and tongue, and I twitched and writhed beneath his worshiping ministrations.

There it was again, that light filling me.

No! Not another one.

This had never happened before. I didn't think I was capable of multiple orgasms, but Rowen was showing me how wrong I was, how much more my body was capable of in his adept hands.

I exploded again, a sea of blinding stars. "Rowen!" I called out, burying my fingers in the thick waves of his hair.

His fingers withdrew from me, but he was still starved, and his lips never left me as he brought me down carefully, only to bring me back up again. "Rowen, I can't," I said, shifting my hips, but Rowen's firm hand landed on my belly and pressed me back down, holding me exactly where he wanted me as he fucked me with his mouth.

I looked down to protest, but seeing his beautiful face between my legs, I came on his tongue once again.

He smiled against me.

"You looked pleased with yourself," I panted as he continued to lick me slowly with the drag of his tongue.

"I can't help that you are so receptive to my touch," he said, giving my sensitive clit one last kiss before drawing up over me.

He had promised to exhaust me, and he was well on his way to doing so, but I needed to touch him before I was completely and utterly spent.

"And what about my touch?" I asked, fingering down the etched mounds of his abs.

His vibrating groan and strained pants told me that I was just as potent to him as he was to me.

Anxious to see what other sounds I could make come out of his mouth, I quickly undid the lacing of his pants and slid them past his slender waist. His intoxicated eyes watched me as I lowered his breeches as much as I could before he helped kick them off the rest of the way.

Then I saw him. All of him. Every glorious inch of him.

He was absolutely marvelous.

Every chiseled plane of his hard body molded perfectly into the next. The pleasant aerodynamics of his physique were sculpted peaks and valleys that flowed seamlessly to his aching cock.

I swallowed in anticipation.

I went to reach for him, to wrap my hand around him, but he hesitated for the briefest of moments, and I stopped cold.

Was he afraid? Afraid that the last woman who touched him like this would spring to his mind? Afraid that he wouldn't be able to feel pleasure without seeing her face?

He grabbed my hand, holding it tenderly in midair. "I wasn't sure this would happen, would barely let myself believe it could. That you would want me, in this way, after I told you everything. I went to Takoda this morning on the small chance you would, and he brewed me a tea that will prevent a child. In case you should ever want to leave, there will be nothing tying you to me."

Relief flooded through me, not just because he wasn't thinking about another woman as I had feared, but because he had been prepared and thoughtful in the important responsibility of protection.

"I told you, nothing you could say would turn me away from you. And I meant it. I want you now and always."

Rowen's forest eyes breathed a sigh of an eternity turned over, and hearing what he needed to hear, he plunged into me with a soul-shattering groan as if it was impossible to go even one more second without being inside me. He stole the air from my lungs as he stretched and filled me, leaving me breathless as I adjusted to him.

He pulled out of me slowly, and I felt every excruciatingly wondrous inch of him. "Lift your hips again for me, Keira," he commanded quietly in my ear. And I did as he said, rising up to take in his cock before sliding back down.

He shuddered uncontrollably, then he dove back into me, pinning my hips to the bed as he ground me into oblivion. And with an ancient understanding that locked into place, our bodies moved as one.

Somehow his body could sense everything mine wanted, but he took it a step further, going beyond in ways I had never imagined. As far as my mind could go, he met me there, then jumped a chasm into a realm I didn't even know existed, didn't even know how good it could feel. And I came once more.

My parted mouth found Rowen's and never left as I rode the blinding waves of my orgasm. Rowen followed soon after, finding his own mind-numbing release with the utterance of my name. I was a glowing comet, leaving trails of stardust in the wake of my beaming light as it engulfed us both.

We collapsed side by side, our chasing breaths ragged and our heaving bodies glistening.

Rowen pulled me close, and I nestled on his shoulder, still coming down from the multiple highs. He tilted my chin up until we locked eyes.

There was a silent moment, a breath of revelation between us before we both laughed in complete satiation, shock, and amazement.

I was ruined. Completely and utterly ruined for anybody else ever again.

It was always him, had only ever been him.

His cock hardened against my hip, and I took his impressive weight in my hand, guiding him into me once more.

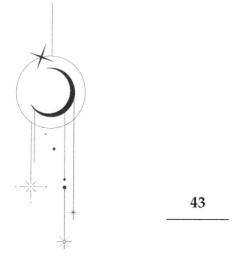

43

I blinked awake to Rowen's sleeping face, his arm draped around the indent of my waist. His chest rose and fell like a calm summer tide gently rolling from shallow seas. The slightest trickle of his breath washed over my lower lip, granting me the smallest taste of his peaceful ocean drifting, and I knew he hadn't slept this well in a very long time.

His full lips were slightly parted, and his long dark lashes rested on his sun-peaked cheekbones. His hair was disheveled from where I'd repeatedly run my fingers through it, and every muscle, down to the crease in his brow, was entirely relaxed.

If I could draw, I would draw this.

I raised my hand to his face and gently trailed the tip of my finger down the bridge of his impossibly straight nose. He didn't stir in the slightest at my touch.

Tendrils of warmth and light snuck through the air and danced across my raised arm. I hadn't properly seen the sun in days and the burnished sliver of dawn called to my vitamin deprived skin.

Rowen looked so wonderfully content that I couldn't bear to

wake him from his sleeping reverie. Plus, I would be back before he even knew I was gone, returning the favor by surprising him with breakfast in bed.

Slowly, I peeled myself from under his heavy arm, careful not to disrupt him as I crept through the hanging canopy. I silently stretched up off the bed, feeling everything Rowen had done to me last night like a map upon my body. Remembering how thoroughly and profoundly he'd handled me sent flushes of heated blood through my veins. Warming me as if I had never known fire.

Spotting the robe he'd stripped me of last night, I tiptoed over to the terracotta-colored garment laying forgotten on the floor. I wrapped it snugly around myself and slipped out the revolving door of Rowen's dome.

I still couldn't believe last night was real, but with every step I took along the path, my body reminded me just how real it was. It was an exquisite sort of reminder. No one had ever touched and claimed me the way Rowen had.

It was hard to fathom how the past few days had been the best and worst of my life.

Basking in the sun, I thought about Rowen's tongue leaving trails of gunpowder along my skin, catching fire and exploding with every kiss, and a radiant smile lifted my lips. I absentmindedly stroked my fingers down my sternum, between my breasts, committing to memory every moment of our night together.

The mere thought of Rowen had my breath speeding up.

I'd wanted a quick walk in the sun, having been deprived of it for several days, but now my pulse sped and my mouth watered for his touch.

I stopped on the trail, noticing I was walking along the village outskirts.

Turning back the way I came, I smiled wider, thinking about

sneaking into the tousled sheets and snuggling up to Rowen while he still slept, waking him with him fisted in my hand. I wanted to be the first thing his green eyes took in as I lured him awake with the pumping of my fist. Breakfast would have to wait.

Picturing his serene face morphing as he slowly realized what I was doing, I turned and took one step back towards him, eager to make my daydreaming a reality. A twig snapped to my right, ripping me from my blissful musings. I gasped aloud and whipped my head to the source of the sound.

A beautifully bronzed body slowly emerged from the forest foliage, pushing aside a thick wall of branches before stepping onto the path in front of me. As the dark, hooded brow slowly lifted, early morning light hit and illuminated the hidden face.

"Demil," I laughed nervously in relief, "you startled me."

I clutched my wildly beating heart, willing it to slow from its panicked state. Man, was I jumpy. But in my defense, why was he lurking just off the trail behind the trees? Had he been watching me long or had he just happened to stumble upon me basking in bliss?

"Keira," he said, his light yellow eyes scanning my body, no doubt taking in my flushed face, wild hair, and deeply swollen lips.

I pulled the robe closer around my body, unable to place the look I saw churning in his gaze.

Uncomfortable with his intensity, I shifted slightly, trying to smooth my wayward hair; it was definitely a little more than your typical bedhead.

"Where is the lucky man?" he asked casually, looking about me and scanning the area. Seeming satisfied that I was alone, he took a step toward me. "I see you've had a busy night."

"Not that I need to dignify that with an answer," I retorted, insulted by his brazen comment, "but yes, very busy. Busy recuperating from nearly being buried alive."

"Don't be angry with me. Can you blame me for being envious of the one who snatched the heart of the Alcreon Light?" he said as his stare swept over my eyes; what made me The Marked.

He took another step closer, crowding my space and raising my irritation to getting-punched-in-the-face levels. "I was hoping it would have been my bed you warmed last night. Have you not seen how I've cared for you?"

My jaw dropped at his forwardness. I knew he sensed some sort of kinship towards me, maybe even felt a bit protective, but *this*? This was too far.

"I need to get back." I tried to step around him, circumnavigate his large column of a body, but he took a solid step to the side, blocking my path.

"Let me by," I demanded.

When he didn't move, I wound my fist back to meet his face.

"Ven needs you," he blurted, his eyes pulsing as he took in my clenched fist.

I dropped my hand in shock. "Is he alright?" I asked, concern overriding all other emotions.

"He's fine, but he's asking for you specifically."

A moment ago he seemed quite intent on aggravating me, but now his unreadable look turned cold and serious.

"Why was that not the first thing you said to me?" I asked, making my frustration apparent. "Instead of wasting my time sizing me up and harassing me."

He shrugged his shoulders. "Curiosity got the best of me. You're right, though, it seems the time to bring up such things has passed." He ran his hand down the back of his head tensely, causing the lean muscles in his arm and obliques to bunch and contract.

Had I made him uncomfortable?

Good. Let him get a taste of his own medicine.

Ready to be far from Demil and his strange energy, I asked, "Where is he?"

"I'll take you to him."

"Fine, but let's get Rowen on the wa—"

I was cut short by a distant yell that echoed from deep within the trees, rustling the birds around us. It was a voice not quite to full maturity, someone young, and it shook me down to my gut.

"Ven!"

Whatever joy I felt moments ago was completely washed away by overwhelming panic. Even Demil's face whitened at the piercing scream. Apparently, Ven's situation had worsened since he'd seen him last, which worried me even more.

I took off running in the direction of the scream, my heart pulsing in my throat. Rowen would have to wait. Hopefully he wouldn't worry, thinking I intentionally left him with nothing more than the cold side of the bed.

I could feel Demil running at my flank. "I swear he was fine when I left him," he called out from behind me.

Too preoccupied to unpack his statement, my mind raced with what could have happened to Ven to make him scream like that. I knew he was quite the intrepid little explorer, but even this seemed much too far from the village for him to travel to in good conscience. He was smarter than that.

I skid to a stop as the land before me turned grey and cold—a clear line of division between life and death. My eyes prepared to scan wildly for Ven but they shot right to him on the other side of the line, and my blood turned to stone.

Wrapped in impossibly thick arms, a purple-faced Ven struggled against a headlock. His face contorted as he tried to pry himself from the unrelenting grip of the mountain that was Graem.

Standing next to him was the smooth, vile face that haunted my every day and every night— Erovos himself—in the flesh. A dark hood of smoke billowed around him, and his skin was stretched tight across the sharp lines of his face.

Fear cast aside, I chased toward Erovos to scratch his face off and tear him apart, but Demil pulled me back with a firm grip on my upper arm.

What was Demil doing? Why wasn't he charging with me to save Ven?

"My long-awaited light, my, how you have evaded me for quite some time. I wouldn't move if I were you. One word from me, and Graem will twist his little head right off his neck." The emanating power from Erovos was oil-slick, choking down my throat and clogging my veins.

Ven squirmed but didn't look afraid, more indignant and frustrated than anything else. He fought uselessly against the colossal man's arm tightening around him, and I willed for him to stop struggling, to remain as still as possible. The foul giant didn't even know his own strength; the slightest tick from him could snap Ven in two.

"Demil! Help me," I pleaded, pulling against his hand cuffed around my arm.

"You said the boy wouldn't be hurt," Demil said with a tight throat.

This couldn't be real. I was in a play. I had to be. All of us actors, rehearsing and running our lines with a false realism that would drop the moment someone shouted 'cut' But no one ever did. The play continued on, and it was a tragedy.

The horror set in, turning me as frozen as the dead forest hovering around Erovos like a billowing cloak of decay. I turned to Demil's square face, his hard gaze revealing a small layer of guilt.

"Demil, what have you done?" I asked through strangled rage. It had been him all along, befriending me to my face, getting close to me, only to report back everything to Erovos.

"It could have been different, you know. If you would have given me a chance. Do you think I like always coming in second? All my life living under the shadow of my sister, Rowen, of everyone. This...this was my chance to be *seen*."

I blanched. This all stemmed from a jealous brother, warrior, lover...it didn't matter. Demil could never measure up.

"You're pathetic. Betraying all your friends, your family, the people that love you."

"No one loves me, not like they love you and my sister. I'm merely a tolerable expenditure to my people, to you."

"What will you be when the dust settles and everyone sees you for who you truly are?" I asked with seething rancor.

"I will be remembered. That is all I ever wanted."

"You'll be hated."

"Demil shall be favored by all my children," Erovos spoke through his thin lips. "And your light shall feed them all."

In a leap of white fur and fangs, Sabra lunged out of the forest bushes, sinking her teeth into the meaty flesh of Graem's forearm.

Graem howled with a force that rocked the trees. With his free hand, he grabbed Sabra by the excess fur around the nape of her neck, and wrenched her from his arm. The white wolf never released her jaw, and the oaf never stopped pulling, and with a fanning spray of Graem's flesh and blood, he slammed Sabra against the nearest tree.

The wolf hit the wide trunk with a heart-wrenching yelp, then fell limp to the ground. My stomach dropped sickeningly as Sabra stayed an unmoving mass of white at the base of a tree.

Ven's tortured scream ripped from his throat in agonizing waves of rage. Tears ran in rivers down his dirt-smeared face. He hadn't seemed truly afraid until that very moment.

My wrath turned to a deadly silver glow, filling my fingertips and veins with a vengeance of ethereal light.

But whatever this ability was, I still had almost no control over it. It was wild and unpredictable. Back in the crypts, when I'd aimed for Aliphoura, I'd missed considerably. I could have hit Rowen, or even worse, brought the whole cave down upon thousands of innocent lives.

I wouldn't risk that with Ven—another innocent. I was backed into a corner, and against every blaring instinct, I lowered my hands.

"Fascinating," Erovos said, taking in my glowing fingertips. "Wise decision to lower that weapon of yours." He huffed a laugh of disbelief. "All this time thinking such a power lay within a man, a Synodic Son. The Elder Spirits were wise to divert our attention with lies and mistranslations—we were never waiting for a returning son, were we? But a returning *sun*. And you, my little vessel, are most certainly a brilliant light. But where are the Spirits now for their precious Synodic Prophecy? Their precious celestial light cast far from its homeland, far from *me*. My, how you must have suffered in a world where your very essence didn't belong, waiting in misery for destiny to return you to the place of your beginning. Rather selfish of them, don't you think? I, on the other hand, have a much greater use for you than hiding you away."

"I will give you nothing," I seethed with unadulterated fury.

"Well then. Graem, finish the boy."

"Wait," I screamed desperately, stopping everyone in their tracks. "What do you want?" I spat at him in disgust, although it wasn't too hard to surmise his desires.

"All I would like is for you to take my hand and quietly leave this place by my side. If you do this, I vow no one will be hurt," Erovos said as if his vow was law.

My eyes darted to a too-still Sabra. But someone already had been hurt.

I wished my eyes could turn into incinerators, searing him to ash for what he'd done. "Deny me, and the boy's neck will be snapped, and I will crumble the entire village to the ground." He said it so nonchalantly you'd think we were conducting a simple business deal, not bartering lives.

I wouldn't let Ven lose his life for me. He was merely a sacrificial pawn in this game of chess, but one forfeiting move by the queen could spare him. Spare them all.

I knew I was playing right into Erovos' carefully crafted strategy, but I had no other choice.

"I'll go with you if you swear to let him go and that you'll leave the village and its people unharmed," I said, refusing to show him the river of fear raging through me.

"You have my word," he replied, his soulless orange eyes never leaving their prize. "Who would have ever thought, a woman? Now it seems so obvious. Of course a light so beautiful would find safety in a vessel as equally beguiling."

Feeling sick, I looked at Demil with scalding eyes. "You betrayed us. You betrayed us all."

Erovos had taken advantage of Demil's jealousy. Exploiting his insecurities of coming in second in almost every aspect of his life. Looking and fighting for his own glory, he would find none here.

Erovos offered me his arm as if he were escorting me to the dance floor.

I wouldn't even get to say goodbye to Rowen, to the people I'd come to love. I couldn't bring myself to regret all that I was sacrificing for that love—it was what brought my dormant heart to life.

I walked the distance between us, between life and death. And with the glowing of my skin, I took the Dark Spirit's hand and dissipated into the mist.

To be continued...

ACKNOWLEDGMENTS

Where to begin? So many incredible and talented people have helped bring Synodic to life. From a story that began as a dream almost fifteen years ago to now writing the acknowledgments is quite surreal, and I can't thank my support systems enough. It really does take a village.

To my coworker turned best friend turned surprise cousin (yes, in that order), Robby Harrington, I don't know what I'd do without you. From creating our first book club—shoutout to the Lit Lemonheads—to interviewing authors together on your podcast, you never once doubted when I said I would one day be a published author too. Love you, hens.

So much gratitude goes out to my incredible beta readers. Taking the time out of your busy lives to read my story meant the world to me. An extra-special thanks to Gizel and Eryn for sharing and supporting Synodic on IG. Really, I would cry every time.

I would especially like to thank my mom and fellow author Eileen Travis; guess the apple doesn't fall far from the tree. All the late-night reading sessions, phone calls, brainstorming bouts, and line-by-line edits turned Synodic into something I am immensely proud of and love with all my heart.

There is no way I could not bring up my two adorable fur babies, Rogue and Quill. Thank you for all your snuggles and snores while I wrote almost every word. You are both my little galaxies.

Thank you to Courtney Schrauben Haik for being the best

critique partner. JJ Otis for sensitivity reading our fierce and no-nonsense leader, Nepta. Mandy Lehman for the beautiful interior art designs. And Lara Koppenhoefer for helping with edits and orchestrating the cutest author interview.

To my mother-in-law Debbie, who practically read the story as I wrote it, always encouraging and asking for the next chapter because she couldn't wait to see what happened. It helped me to know that my story and characters could mean something to someone. And for that, there is not enough thanks I could give.

I am so grateful to all my friends and family who had to hear me talk about my book for years with nothing to show for it. Every time you would ask how it was coming along, my heart would burst.

To my online followers, friends, and Booktok community, every like, comment, and share made me feel not so alone in what could otherwise be an isolating craft. Thank you all for being on this wild and crazy journey with me. You've made it so much fun!

Don't think I forgot you, dear reader. Your support means everything, and I hope you love this story as much as I do.

And finally, thank you to my incredible and supportive husband, Daniel Jackson. Recreating and reenacting scenes from my book and making fools of ourselves online were some of the best, most hilarious times. Thank you for always being my silver tether, my rock, my biggest supporter and believer of my dreams, my twin flame, and the love of my life. I would find you in any world.

ABOUT THE AUTHOR

Kristin Travis has an insatiable need to seek the magical, whether found with her twin flame and pups in their backyard or in far-off jungles of Thailand with rescued elephants. Her travels, love of animals, nature, and space continue to inspire her writing, and she finds she's in no short supply of the extraordinary.

instagram.com/kristin.travis
tiktok.com/@kristin_travis